# TRACKS
## TO FREEDOM

The Auschwitz Resistance - Based on True Events

# MICHAEL REIT

# PART I

CIECHANÓW, POLAND
APRIL 1942

# CHAPTER ONE

It was dark when Joel Kozak pulled the sputtering car into the driveway. He stepped out of the car and hurried to open the door for the man in the back.

"Thank you, *Robert*," the man said as he stepped out. "I know I said you could take the car with you tonight, but it looks like you'll need to fix it first."

Joel nodded. "You're right, Herr Kesler. I'm just glad we made it back. I'll come in early tomorrow."

Kesler shook his head. "Don't bother, I don't need to be anywhere. You can use the morning to work on the car. Do you have an idea what it might be?"

"Probably a broken clutch; it felt a bit heavy. I can take a look now if you want?"

"No, no. Please go home. You don't want to be out on the streets after curfew." Kesler disappeared inside, and Joel sat back in the car. As he turned the key, the engine made a spluttering sound. Joel tried again, but there was only a soft clicking noise. He got out, opened the hood, and the smell of warm oil entered his nostrils. He shined a small flashlight under the hood and cursed—the motor was covered in oil. *Not just*

3

*a broken clutch, then.* Joel closed the hood and locked the car—it was no use trying to fix the engine in the dark.

He stepped into the street, closing the gate behind him. Working as a driver for the Germans meant he enjoyed an amount of freedom few people in Ciechanów did. His driver's permit—secured by Mr. Kesler—allowed him to pass through the German checkpoints unhindered.

The streets were quiet, and Joel checked his watch—almost seven. Even though curfew wouldn't be for an hour, he instinctively checked his jacket for his papers. They were still there, and he let out a deep sigh.

He walked on, and large homes made way for smaller houses packed closer together. The pavement narrowed until it merged into the street. Joel walked through the gates of the city center, the sign above him indicating he was now entering the Jewish Quarter. *Quarter*, Joel shook his head. *They should call it what it is.*

He turned the corner to find the street ahead blocked by a dozen people milling about. They had their backs to him, focused on something on the cobblestones. It didn't take long to see what they were looking at; the bodies of two men lay face down, a dark puddle of blood around their heads—small holes in the back of their necks testament to the execution.

The people crowding around were in various stages of shock. Two women—presumably the men's wives—stood with their hands covering their faces, shaking as they cried. Other people looked on in horror. A man with a determined step exited one of the houses, carrying a set of bedsheets. He put his hand on the shoulders of the two women and gently spoke to them. Through their sobs, they nodded, and he knelt beside the bodies. A lump formed in Joel's throat. *Those poor women.*

"Can you give me a hand?" The man spoke to no one in particular, yet to everybody. When nobody responded, Joel stepped forward. The man looked at him in surprise but quickly handed him the other side of the sheet. Two more men found their courage, wrapped the first man in the sheet, and carried him inside the house.

Two other men stood a little distance from the group. Joel's blood ran cold when he saw the glint of the lightning-strike-shaped *S*'s on their dark green uniforms. A German patrol.

"Well, well, look here." One of them spoke as Joel and the three other men returned. "You'll need to hurry, it's almost curfew." The man looked to be in his early twenties, only a few years older than Joel.

No one responded, keen to finish their gruesome task. Joel knelt and gently lifted the dead man's feet when he felt a presence. He turned and found one of the SS men hovering over him. He met the man's eyes and was dismayed to see a spark of recognition.

"You look familiar," the man said, his brow furrowed as he scanned Joel's face. "But I can't quite place you." His eyes ran over Joel's arms, and his expression changed from one of curiosity to suspicion. "Where's your armband?"

Joel's eyes followed the man's gaze. The other SS trooper joined them. "What's going on, Gerhardt?"

"He's not wearing his Jew armband," Gerhardt said, taking a step closer, forcing Joel to readjust his stance to avoid tumbling onto the dead man on the pavement.

"I'm not a Jew." He reached into his jacket and produced his driver's permit. The German inspected it, his eyes narrowing as he read it aloud. "Robert Kozak, a *Volksdeutsche*." Then, a triumphant smile appeared on his face. "So that's why you look familiar. You work for Kesler!"

"I run errands for Mr. Kesler," Joel said, carefully replacing the permit in his jacket pocket.

The German looked more relaxed, but his partner spoke in annoyance. "What are you doing in the ghetto? Don't you know aiding Jews is forbidden?"

Joel stood up, towering over the Germans. "I'm sorry, I was rushing home and didn't realize I was passing through the ghetto. Before I knew it, I ran into this group, and they needed a hand." He waved his hand at the mourners looking at him wide eyed. "I thought we couldn't just leave these bodies in the street. What would the city come to if we just leave people to rot?"

"I don't care about Jews rotting in the street." The SS man looked at him with a neutral expression. "They should've thought about the consequences before doing whatever they did to get shot."

Joel gritted his teeth. "I understand. I apologize for my mistake."

The trooper was about to say something when Gerhardt spoke up. "Come on, Hansie, let's move on. Mr. Kozak will make his way home and out of the ghetto." He looked at Joel sternly. "We won't see you helping out Jews in here again, will we?"

"Of course not, thank you, sir," Joel said as he turned away from the group. He met the eyes of the man with whom he'd carried the first body inside. An unspoken look of understanding passed between them.

As he walked away, he heard the troopers say. "And be careful in the ghetto. Those Jews might just rob you, or worse."

He crossed through small streets, careful to avoid the main thoroughfares. He couldn't risk running into the SS patrol again, even though he was going a different direction. Five minutes later, he reached a small house, a faint flicker of candlelight making its way through the curtains. He turned the key and opened the door with a creak, the homey scent of lavender hitting his nostrils.

"Joel, is that you?" a familiar voice called from the back.

He hung his coat on the rack. "Yes, *Mama*." Before stepping into the cramped kitchen, he opened a drawer and put his papers inside.

"I was worried; you're home so late," she said, giving him a quick peck on the cheek as he sat down at the kitchen table. She placed a steaming bowl before him.

"I'm fine, Mama, it just took a little longer to get home today." He didn't want to bother his mother with the gruesome details.

She sat opposite him as he almost inhaled his soup. "You know you can tell me when something's wrong, right?"

Joel put down his spoon. "I promise I can take good care of myself." He stood, keen to get to his room. "I'm going to make it an early night. Mr. Kesler's car broke down, so I best be in early tomorrow."

His mother remained seated and smiled. "We are so fortunate you've found a job with Mr. Kesler. I'm not sure how we would survive on normal wages. Especially since it's just you and me." Her smile faded slightly, her eyes suddenly a little distant.

Joel's heart ached, as he hugged his mother. "I promise we'll be fine. Mr. Kesler is very pleased, and there is so much work that he'll need me around for quite a bit longer."

"I know, Joel. I just want you to be careful. Every day I worry you might not come back in the evening. Those Germans are so unpredictable."

He broke their embrace and looked at his mother. "Mr. Kesler is different. We can trust him. He wouldn't have arranged those papers for me otherwise."

She nodded, and Joel kissed her forehead. "Good night, Mama."

He climbed the narrow stairs and headed for his room, where he lay on the bed. He closed his eyes. *Those Jews will rob you, or worse.* He opened his eyes and shook his head, the pillow softly crunching as he did. *If only they knew.*

# CHAPTER TWO

Agnes stood near the bridge. *What's taking her so long? She should've been here fifteen minutes ago.* She tapped her foot, her eyes on the crowded street across the bridge. The sun was out, and it was an uncharacteristically sunny April day for Amsterdam.

The people on the bridge rushed by without notice. A young man caught her eye; late twenties, early thirties, walking purposefully, with a straight back and broad shoulders. He wore a suit—no overcoat was needed today—and carried a doctor's bag. He must've felt her looking at him since he turned her way and smiled. Agnes returned the smile, then averted her eyes. A few seconds later, she looked in his direction again—he was already halfway down the street.

"Sorry I'm late," a familiar voice said, interrupting her thoughts. She turned to find her sister standing beside her. "The tram was stuck, and the driver wouldn't let me get off. I swear I left in time," Yvette said, slightly out of breath.

Agnes looked at her younger sister as she stood panting beside her. Relieved, she hugged her. "I was worried about you, it's not like you to be this late," Agnes said.

Yvette Markx, at nineteen years old, was two years younger but a head taller than Agnes. At first sight, it was hard to believe they were sisters. Agnes had a full head of blond curls, whereas Yvette liked to keep her dark brown hair cropped short. It only became apparent when the girls talked that the pair were siblings: their voices were nearly identical.

"Did you get in touch with Johannes?" Agnes asked as they crossed the bridge.

"He should be at the market now; I handed him our coupons yesterday. He said it wouldn't be a problem."

"Where are we meeting him?"

"The southern entrance. We should still be able to make it," Yvette said as she eyed the church clock farther down the street.

"Yve," Agnes said, using her sister's nickname. "You sure we can trust Johannes?"

Yvette stopped and turned, frowning. "He's done this for other people as well. We can trust him."

*I'm not going to argue with her.* "Great, then let's go find him."

Since the Germans had taken over, they had been imposing new restrictions on the Jewish community. Not being allowed to go to markets made it nearly impossible to get fresh produce. Thankfully, Yvette had come up with the plan to ask some Dutch friends of friends to visit the market for them. She hoped Johannes would come through.

Yvette had picked up her pace and turned into the street leading to the market. As soon as she did, she stopped and sighed. Agnes caught up and understood why. Two trucks on either side blocked the street, and green-uniformed men were busy checking papers. The German *Grüne Polizei*—the Green Police—had set up a checkpoint.

"Great, what do they want to check this time?" Yvette said as she reluctantly joined the small queue.

"They're not really checking anything. You know that," Agnes said as she reached for her papers.

The queue moved quickly, and when the sisters stepped forward, the German policeman gave them a friendly smile as they handed him their papers. Agnes returned the smile, Yvette stared at him blankly.

He opened their papers, and his smile vanished. "This area is closed to Jews." He handed back their papers.

"Why?" Yvette's eyes shot fire.

"No Jews beyond this point." He waved his hand dismissively, indicating for them to move back.

"But we need to meet someone just a little farther up the street." Yvette didn't move, and Agnes' throat felt constricted. *Come on, sis, don't push your luck.*

The policeman cocked his head. "What for? For getting illegal produce from the market?" Yvette blinked hard, and he smiled. "We know you're getting Dutch people to get food from the market for you. Well, not anymore." He pushed Yvette back. "Now get out of here before I decide you're a real nuisance. We have plenty of space in the back of these trucks."

Agnes grabbed her sister's wrist and firmly pulled her away. "Come, Yve, let's go."


"Mom and Dad are going to be furious," Yvette said. "I gave him all our coupons for the rest of the month."

They stood a hundred meters from the checkpoint, where more people were turned away.

"Come, take a breather," Agnes said as she guided Yvette to a small bench. "I'm sure Johannes ran into the checkpoint and will realize what's happening. He's not going to steal our coupons."

"How long do you want to wait?" Yvette looked up at her with tears in her eyes. *She always pretends to be tougher than she really is. She's still my little sister, and she needs me now.*

Agnes smiled. "As long as it takes for him to show up. Did you agree on a time with him?"

"We were supposed to meet around the entrance now," Yvette said as she looked at the clock across the street. "Hopefully, he'll understand we couldn't make it there."

"If not, you'll be able to find him, right?"

Yvette nodded half-heartedly. "Don't you have class?"

"I can wait with you."

"No, you should go. It was hard enough to get into the classes. Papa won't be pleased if he hears you're skipping them. Let's not both disappoint him today."

It had been more than a year since Agnes was banned from nursing school. But the Jewish community in Amsterdam responded swiftly, setting up small underground schools, as Jewish teachers were fired from their jobs as well.

"Come, Agnes, go," Yvette said, interrupting her thoughts. "There's no use in us both sitting around waiting for him. If he doesn't show, I'll find him somehow. Go and enjoy your class. I know how much you look forward to it."

"Are you sure?"

Yvette groaned in frustration and playfully pushed her away. "Argh, yes, go. I don't want you here any longer. I'll see you at dinner, whatever that may be."

Agnes was panting when she arrived at the school—an old office building on the outskirts of town. The back door was locked, as expected. The rules were clear; whoever was late would have to wait for the break to come in. It meant Agnes had to wait for the good part of two hours. Worse, she would miss an exciting lecture. *If I'm going to be told off, might as well make sure I do it properly.* She waited for a few seconds, straining her ears for sounds on the other side of the door before knocking.

Ten seconds later, a muffled voice answered from behind the thick wooden door. "Who is it?"

She recognized her teacher's voice. "It's Agnes, Mr. Klein."

A pause, then the lock clicked. A tall man with horn-rimmed glasses perched on his nose opened the door. Mr. Klein looked flustered and relieved. "Agnes, I was wondering what happened to you." He stepped aside. "You haven't missed a single class, never mind being late."

Agnes entered and let out a deep sigh. "I'm sorry, it was a bit of a mess in the city, and I got stuck on one of the trams." A little white lie she could get away with.

Her teacher closed the door—making sure to lock it—and shook his head. "Well, you didn't miss much yet, so better hurry inside. But Agnes —" He looked at her sternly. "Please don't be late again. I get nervous when students don't show up."

She nodded; Mr. Klein risked so much for their little class of ten. She climbed the broad stairs to the second floor, where she was glad to see the other students sitting around in a circle. She greeted them as Mr. Klein entered, leaving the door to the hallway open. The class resumed, and Agnes caught up quickly. Mr. Klein was an excellent teacher, always able to explain complex material in a way they could all understand. Many of Agnes' friends weren't as fortunate, teaching themselves from old books at home.

Time passed quickly, and when Mr. Klein called for a short break, Agnes was keen to stretch her legs. She found one of her friends, Mario Nacamulli, standing near a window in the hallway.

"Funny how it's so quiet around here," Mario said as she approached. "This area used to be so lively before the war."

"No need for the office workers here anymore," Agnes said. "I'm just glad the owner is letting us use it."

"He's Jewish. Our people are helping each other wherever they can." Mario looked pensive as he stared out the window.

Agnes stood next to him and watched the abandoned square below. Bike racks stood empty; the only sounds were those of a few birds twittering away.

"We need to stick together." She told Mario about the checkpoint earlier that morning.

He looked sympathetic. "I've heard plenty of stories of people approaching strangers to get them something from the market, only to have them run off with their coupons. It sounds like Yvette could trust him, though."

Agnes smiled back, reflecting his optimism. She was about to speak when movement on the square below caught her eye. "Look!"

Mario's ever-present smile vanished. "Oh shit." His face turned a shade paler, and his eyes narrowed.

A dozen men in black uniforms rushed from the road, heading straight for their building. Agnes was dismayed. "How did they find out about us?"

"Someone must've seen us and told the Germans or the police." Mario was already on his way back to the classroom.

They stepped back into the classroom and found Mr. Klein holding a sandwich, in midbite. "What's wrong?"

"Blackshirts are approaching the building." As Mario spoke, there were heavy thuds on the door one floor below. Voices shouted for them to open up, and for a moment, nobody in the room moved. The other students turned to Mr. Klein, fear in their eyes. He calmly stood, adjusted his glasses, and said, "Stay here. I'll handle this."

"Are you sure you don't need help?" Mario said. Agnes froze to the spot.

"That won't be necessary. Just stay quiet. I'm sure I can reason with them." He left the room, closing the door behind him.

"I don't think words will help," she said to Mario. The men in the black uniforms were part of the Dutch Nazi Party, the *NSB*. Similar to the Brownshirts in Germany, they brought violence wherever they showed up.

He shook his head and looked around the classroom. "We need to find something to defend ourselves with." The rest of the students looked scared, a few pleading to let Mr. Klein handle it.

Mario was adamant and searched the cabinets in the room. "If Mr. Klein's plan fails, we can't just let them come in here and give us a beating." He focused his attention on the other two young men in the class. "You're with me, right?"

They reluctantly joined him as the noise downstairs increased. Mr. Klein had reached the door. He was playing dumb, asking the men their business.

"It doesn't sound like they're convinced," Agnes said as she stood by the stairs, ignoring Mr. Klein's advice to keep the door to the classroom shut.

Mario appeared next to her, holding an envelope opener. "Look, Agnes. There are at least ten of them, maybe more. Only three of us, four with Mr. Klein, but I don't know what they'll do to him downstairs. If it comes to fighting, you must take the back door with the other girls, okay?"

She shook her head. "I want to fight."

"No."

There was a tremendous crash downstairs, and Mr. Klein appeared at the foot of the stairs. He looked panicked, his face red as he rushed up the stairs. "They broke down the front door! Get away from the stairs!" His voice sounded unnatural as he used the railing to propel himself up. He had barely reached the top when the first of the Blackshirts followed.

Mario grabbed Mr. Klein's hand and called for the other men to join him at the top of the stairs. "Come on. This is the best place to stop them." The other students were armed with pieces of wood, and it dawned on Agnes that they'd probably smashed a chair to create their weapons. "Agnes, get out of here, and take the other girls!" Mario said. She could see him tightening his grip on the letter opener.

The young Blackshirt paused halfway up the stairs, sizing up the men waiting at the top, hatred spewing from his eyes. *He doesn't even know us.*

Within seconds, the stairway was filled with black uniforms. Agnes counted at least eight on the stairs, with the same number downstairs. "Just come with us now; there's no need to fight," one of them shouted. "You don't stand a chance, anyway, Jew boys." The man's voice boomed through the building, the words landing viciously.

"He's right," Agnes said to Mario. "Come with us. Maybe we can lose them in the streets."

Mario shook his head, focused on the men on the stairs. "I'm so tired of these thugs. It's time to fight back."

"This is not the time," Agnes said. *He's going to get himself killed.*

He turned to her, and as she looked into his eyes, she saw a determination that she knew no words of hers would weaken.

"Take the other girls, Agnes, and run. We'll hold them off as long as we can. Don't worry about me. This isn't my first fight. Now go!" *He's willing to do whatever to get us out.* Mario turned his face back to the Blackshirts, who were now moving up the stairs, one step at a time. They had fallen into something resembling a battle formation.

Agnes turned to find the girls shaking and crying and realized Mario was right: there was no sense in all of them being beaten, arrested, or worse. She swallowed hard as she stepped away. "Follow me," she said to the girls, taking quick steps toward the back entrance.

She opened a window and guided the first girl onto the fire escape stairs. She quickly climbed down; they were only on the second floor, after all. When the second girl climbed out, there were screams from the other side of the hallway. Agnes turned to see Mario and Mr. Klein lashing out viciously at the first Blackshirts. The third and fourth girl hurried out. Another roar as one of the Blackshirts tumbled down the stairs. *Maybe they can hold them off, after all?*

The last girl climbed through the window, pausing to see how the men were doing. At that moment, Mr. Klein fell backward onto the floor. Mario and the others tried to close ranks, but they were too late. Two Blackshirts broke through and were now at the top of the stairs. Mario's small legion was surrounded. They tried as best they could, but soon more Blackshirts poured upstairs, and Agnes reluctantly climbed outside. She looked back, where two Blackshirts descended on Mario like rabid hyenas. He tumbled to the ground, and their eyes met. The last thing she heard was him roaring. "Run!"

# CHAPTER THREE

S amson Tarski was exhausted as he carried his small toolbox. His legs protested as he placed one foot before another, moving almost mechanically among the group of workers entering the city. *Only another kilometer left.*

The day had been like any other, and he'd almost gotten used to the grueling work of sorting scrap metal in the yard outside Kraków. As one of the largest men in the detail, Samson was always picked to push the heavy metal carts from one side of the depot to the other and help load the trucks.

"Keep moving, you dogs! I want to be home in time for dinner!" Jerzy—an especially vicious Volksdeutsche—boomed from the front of the column. Samson detested the Poles who had discovered some distant bloodline making them *part German*, and thus qualifying as Volksdeutsche. It meant slighter better treatment by the Nazi occupiers, resulting in larger food rations and jobs overseeing people like Samson.

The work detail trotted through the city and soon crossed the Vistula River. The walls of the ghetto loomed, and the front of the column entered through Lwowska Street. The Jewish Police, wearing long jackets and hats, were especially vigilant at the gate that evening. They picked out people walking by, interrogating them and then—

depending on the answers—let the men pass or directed them to wait near the wall. The latter was not a good omen. Samson was still a ways from the gate when he felt the gaze of one of the policemen on him. He looked back, trying to appear as composed as possible, but there was no doubt: the officer was focused on him. *What does he want?*

He was still a good fifty meters away when the uniformed man started making his way toward him. Samson gripped his toolbox tighter.

Set up to keep order in the ghetto, the men wearing the badges of the *Ordnungspolizei*—Jewish Police—had taken to the task with a zeal that required little German involvement in making the ghetto a frightening place. They were keen to impress the Gestapo and SS, favoring them over their own people in the Jewish council. Samson kept his head down as he approached the gate, praying he had mistaken the man's gaze.

A strong hand gripped him by the shoulder. "Come with me." Samson was hauled to the side, the other men of the work detail averting their eyes.

"Is something wrong, officer?" Samson said, biting his tongue as he emphasized the last word.

"Shut up unless I tell you to speak." The man spoke in a thick Krakówian accent. "You missed a day's work yesterday."

The suggestion was as ludicrous as it was untrue. Samson had been at the yard for seven days in a row. He was scheduled to have a day off tomorrow, although that was hardly a certainty. He opened his mouth, then remembered he hadn't been given permission yet.

"You know the penalty for missing scheduled work? I'll have to write you up and report you to the council." As he spoke, a smile appeared on his face. He then looked as if he suddenly remembered something. "And to the Gestapo, of course. They'll be very interested in speaking with you."

Samson could no longer hold his tongue. "What are you talking about? I haven't missed a day's work in over a week."

In a flash, the policeman smashed his baton into Samson's groin. He winced and stifled a groan as he bent forward, dropping his toolbox with a clang. A wave of nausea rose but he managed to suppress it just in

17

time. Some of the men passing by looked up in shock, then—realizing what was happening—quickly looked the other way.

"Are you calling me a liar?" the policeman barked at him, using the tip of his baton to lift Samson's head. "If I tell you you've been missing work, that's what's happened, you hear me?"

Samson looked up at him, his vision clouded. He controlled the anger building up inside. Slowly, he straightened his back and looked at the man opposite him. He was half his size, but the unexpected blow had knocked the wind out of Samson. His vision cleared and he looked the man in the eye. The policeman faced him challengingly, and Samson realized he couldn't win this argument.

"What will happen when you write me up, sir?"

"You'll need to report to the council, if you're lucky. More likely, the Gestapo will come and have a word. You can forget about this job in the future, that's for sure." The man looked gleeful as he took out a small notepad. "Now, name."

Those last two words confirmed what Samson suspected; the man had no idea who he was. He was just randomly picked. He'd heard about this happening before, although he'd never seen it happen. Samson looked around and suddenly realized it was an organized effort by the Jewish Police. All around him, men were stopped and interrogated in the same way. They all had been selected; they were strong, healthy-looking men like himself. *Selected for what, though?*

"Have you lost your tongue?" The officer poked him in the ribs with his baton. "Your name, Jew."

Something in Samson snapped. Had this man completely forgotten his background? He looked the man up and down, a foul taste appearing in his mouth. The officer wore an armband: white with the abbreviation "OD" reserved for the Jewish Police. A little to the side, however, on his right breast pocket, he wore the same insignia Samson had. A yellow Star of David. He was no less Jewish than Samson, yet only one of them had sold his soul to the Nazi devil, betraying their own people.

The officer's patience had run out, for Samson saw him raise his baton again. Before he could bring it down, Samson reached for the man's arm, grabbing his wrist. The officer's eyes registered surprise, and then Samson squeezed with all his might. The policeman let out a shriek, dropping the baton. Without another thought, Samson snatched it midair with his free hand. He pulled back his arm and—surprising himself—smashed it into the man's face with all the force his tired arm could muster. The man's eyes rolled back into his sockets as his legs gave out, and he fell down on the cold pavement with a dull thud.

Samson looked at the man on the ground and dropped the baton. It had become eerily quiet around him. The monotonous drone of hundreds of feet passing in the background had ceased. The procession had come to a standstill. All eyes were fixed on him. Their expressions ranged from dismay to fascination—he had done what many of them had only dreamed about, but had thought better of at the last minute. *Oh shit. What have I done?*

Samson didn't get a chance to ponder his actions; the next thing he heard were heavy footsteps approaching. As he raised his hands and slowly turned around, all he comprehended was a ferocious blow to the side of his head and the sky turning black.

# CHAPTER FOUR

Joel took the small bag from the lady behind the counter.

"Don't forget to give my best to your mother," she said with a smile.

He waved as he opened the door. "I will, Mrs. Polak, but she'll ask when you're coming around again."

"Tell her soon," the woman said as she turned to the next customer.

Joel stepped into the street, gently closing the rickety door behind him. Mrs. Polak's ingenuity never failed to impress him. She somehow found ways to stock her little store in the ghetto with a good selection of vegetables. The Germans had severely rationed food supplies in Poland. In response, a thriving black market involving nearby farmers and entrepreneurial citizens like Mrs. Polak had sprung up. Joel was happy she was an old friend of his mother's, and he always smuggled small pieces of chocolate from his boss' home for her.

"Got everything you need?" Joel's best friend Piotr Bartnik waited outside. They had been friends for as long as he could remember, having met each other at their very first football training. They were barely able to kick a ball, but they had instantly bonded. From there, life only improved as they attended the same schools and even insisted on doing their bar mitzvahs together. Their second year in engineering school had been cut short two and a half years ago when the Nazis invaded Poland.

Joel raised the bag. "Mama will be pleased. This should last us for the rest of the week."

"I'm sure you'll be able to track down some more food on your travels later this week. Your mother will be able to cook up a feast." Piotr winked as they walked down the street. "Do you know where Kesler is sending you this week?"

Piotr always searched for ways to keep in contact with nearby cities —and ghettos—now travel was restricted. His family was spread out around the region, and Joel often passed along messages—sometimes more.

"I'm afraid I won't know until I report to Kesler tomorrow. But it's been a while since I've been in Mława. I suspect I might be heading there sometime this week. Don't you have an uncle there?"

Piotr nodded. "Yeah, but I don't want anything to do with him. He works for the police these days."

"That's new, isn't it?" Joel was surprised. It was the first time his friend wasn't interested in keeping in touch with his family. But, then again, he wondered how he'd feel if someone in his family joined the Ordnungspolizei. Even though they weren't all bad, he'd seen too many cases of the power going to their heads.

"Yeah, my mother said he didn't have much choice, but I'd rather not take any chances. You never know what will happen. He might sympathize with the Nazis these days." Piotr rubbed his cheek. "Say, speaking of Nazis, did you notice things are changing here as well?"

"What do you mean?"

"More SS on the streets in the past weeks. And then all these reports of people getting arrested, interrogated, and sometimes killed?"

Joel couldn't escape the image of the two bodies in the street. "Things aren't getting any better. It's also getting more crowded."

"They're moving people in from the countryside. Can you imagine?"

Joel was grateful he was still able to share a home with his mother. They had no family left in the area, and no strangers were assigned to live in their home. Not yet, anyway.

"The new SS troopers are behaving like animals." Piotr's face was flushed. "And most of them are just boys, barely older than eighteen. I'm telling you, Joel, they're sending the worst of the worst to Ciechanów."

They turned a corner and almost bumped into two men coming the other way. Joel mumbled an apology, moving to the side so they could both be on their way. But, as he looked up, he knew it wouldn't be easy to walk on.

"Are you blind? Watch where you're going, Jew pig!" The man, wearing the uniform of the *Waffen-SS*, spat on the ground, barely missing Joel's shoes.

The other man brushed his uniform as if removing dirt. His mouth twisted in a condescending snarl. "And take off your bloody cap when encountering a German in the ghetto."

Piotr quickly took off his cap and inclined his head a little. Joel looked at the SS troopers; young, brash, and abusive. He decided he wasn't just going to take it.

"Apologies, gentlemen, I didn't mean to bump into you. But I must correct you on one count, and that is that I am no Jew. I'm merely going through here to collect someone for work." He pointed at Piotr, who shot him a look. "I'm a Volksdeutsche."

For a moment, the troopers were unsure how to respond. Then, the one with the snarl slowly nodded, his mouth twisting into an ugly grin. "Well, you might not be Jewish filth like that one, but you're still Polish. That's only marginally better. Don't mistake yourself for being one of us. You're only working for us because we need you." Joel stood in silence while the man continued. "Take off your cap."

Slowly, Joel inclined his head, and as he reached for his cap, he caught Piotr's look of astonishment. He winked at him, then took off his cap and doffed it outrageously. He looked both troopers in the eye as he replaced his cap and, mustering up all his courage, walked away from them. He turned back and signaled for Piotr to follow him.

"Not so fast." The trooper's voice was ice cold. "We're going to need to see some papers."

Joel turned back, considering his options. If these SS men had his name, they could harass him at will. They could even report him to

Kesler, although he didn't think his boss would be too concerned. Then it hit him. It might not matter what Kesler thinks. If the SS considered him trouble, they might come for him directly. He could lose his job. He looked at Piotr, who raised an eyebrow. *He knows me well.*

The troopers took a few steps toward them, and Joel made a decision. He turned and sprinted down the street, heading for the intersection only a hundred meters away. He didn't look back as he heard the two men giving chase. The wind hit his face, and he realized SS troopers were armed. They could shoot him in the middle of the ghetto, and nobody would question it. *Shit, what am I doing?*

He was almost at the intersection. But where next? *Didn't really think this through.*

People moved out of the way as Joel neared the intersection. He glanced back over his shoulder. The SS men were catching up with him. He reached the intersection and raced around the corner. Then he slowed down a little, waiting for the soldiers. When they turned the corner, he caught their eyes, and one of them smiled.

Joel ran on but slowed his pace a little, allowing the men to catch up with him. Then, when they were within touching distance, he suddenly stopped and dropped to his knees, shielding his head with his arms.

Caught off guard, the SS men tumbled over him and onto the sidewalk. With the element of surprise now on his side, he sprinted back to the intersection. As he reached it, he saw the troopers getting up, rubbing their elbows and knees. Turning the corner, he bolted down the street—lungs burning—into a small alley. He scaled a low wall and waited on the other side, his ears alert.

After five minutes, he was convinced he had lost them and emerged from the other side of the alley.

The following morning, Joel reported for work early. He'd slept poorly, reliving the chase. Ciechanów was a small city, and its ghetto was even smaller. The chances of running into the troopers again were significant. *I'll have to watch my back.*

Kesler appeared from the house. "Robert, I don't need to go

anywhere today. But I do need you to pick up some people from the fields near Mława."

"No problem, Herr Kesler." He kept his face composed but felt a tingle of excitement upon hearing today's destination. "Where am I taking them?"

"The Mława ghetto. Two families are due a couple of days' break. Just report to Alfred and tell him I asked you to take care of it. He should have a truck ready for you."

Joel walked the distance to the garage, where he found Alfred repairing one of the bigger trucks. He handed him the keys, and Joel pulled a small truck out of the driveway a few minutes later. Even though he had no formal training driving trucks, he'd picked it up soon enough.

He headed north but, before leaving the city, stopped on the border of the ghetto. He pretended something was wrong with the engine and circled his truck. Keeping his eyes on his surroundings, he casually loosened the tarp at the back. Confident there were no curious eyes around, he whistled sharply and pulled up outside a small house. Almost instantly, the door opened, and a scruffy-looking man of about fifty hurried out and climbed into the back of the truck.

"Get to the front and stay close to those crates," Joel whispered as he fastened the tarp. "If I must stop for a checkpoint, hide inside the largest crate and stay quiet. I don't even want to hear you breathing."

Silence. *Good.*

Joel climbed back behind the wheel and left Ciechanów. The drive to the Mława fields would take less than an hour, and he spent most of the time thinking about the man in the back. Alter was a friend of his mother's, and wanted by the Gestapo, accused of stealing tools from the toolbox of his work detail's foreman. The penalty for this offense was death. He wiped his clammy hands on his pants. It wasn't the first time Joel smuggled something out of the ghetto—he often transported food, messages, and even medical supplies—but it was the first time carrying a fugitive.

Driving through the countryside, Joel relaxed a little. He felt contentment in his bones, joyful about his small act of resistance. Perhaps he could avoid the SS troopers in the next few days, and then they would forget about him. He saw the sign for the Mława farming zone and turned off the main road. He bumped along the gravel road for another ten minutes—apologizing to Alter a few times as he hit potholes—until the farmhouse and two barracks came into view.

Up ahead, people worked the fields, preparing to harvest the rising grain in the next few weeks. Joel parked next to the house, and as he shut down his engine, a large man appeared. Pavel, the owner of the farm.

"Robert, you must be here to pick up the workers. They're waiting in the barracks; let me get them. Do you want something to drink, maybe eat while you're waiting?"

"That would be great."

"Just go inside and find Maja. She'll have something for you."

Joel went inside, where Maja handed him a bowl of oats. "They're from our fields," she said proudly. Joel wolfed them down and thanked her. The farmers had to supply the Germans with a set quota, but they could still feed themselves relatively well compared to those living in the cities and ghettos.

He stepped outside just in time to find Pavel and the two families emerging from the barracks. He met them at the truck and informed them he would take them to the Mława ghetto. "You'll be staying there for two days of rest." He opened the tarp and peeked inside. Alter had followed his instructions, and the truck appeared to be empty. The people climbed in silently. Joel closed the tarp and shook Pavel's hand, thanking him for the food. "I'll have them back to you in a few days."

The drive into Mława was uneventful, and he soon reached the ghetto gates. After a cursory glance in the back of the truck, the Jewish police waved him on. They didn't care much about people coming into the ghetto—they were more concerned about the other direction.

Instead of stopping in the middle of the ghetto, which was customary, Joel found a quiet street and parked the truck. He opened the tarp and told the people they were free to go and that someone would pick them up in front of the Jewish council in two days. They quickly left.

Joel waited another minute, making sure there was no one around, then climbed into the back of the truck. He found Alter in a large crate, looking very uncomfortable. "Okay, time to get out of here for you as well. You have a family you can go to?"

He nodded. "I'll go and find them now. Thank you for this, Joel. I won't forget it."

Before letting Alter leave, Joel checked the surroundings again, gesturing for the older man to climb out of the truck. Alter disappeared around the corner within seconds, and Joel breathed a sigh of relief. *Now he is no longer my concern.* He'd need to make one more stop before returning to Ciechanów.

After parking his truck on the small main square, Joel mounted the steps in front of a nondescript building. He opened the door and entered the offices of Mława's Jewish council. A young man behind a desk looked up with little interest, but his demeanor changed when he saw Joel wasn't wearing a Star of David. He stood up, almost springing to attention. "Good morning, sir, how may I help you?"

Joel waved his hand, indicating for him to sit down. "I brought some people into the ghetto just now. They work in the fields. Can I hand the papers to you?"

The man nodded. "Certainly, sir. Where did you say they came from?"

Joel mentioned the farm's name and recognition appeared on the man's face as he scanned the papers. "I'll hand this to the administration."

"Great, thank you." Joel turned back to the door just as someone rushed in from outside. A man wearing the uniform of the Jewish police entered, looking flustered, a little annoyed even. He stopped when he saw Joel.

"Is that your truck outside?" Joel nodded, and the man continued. "You came in from Ciechanów?"

Joel raised an eyebrow. "I picked up people from the farm outside town, which I just reported to your colleague here." He pointed at the young man behind the desk still holding the papers.

"I'm sure you did," the man said. "I think the commander will want a quick word with you."

Joel was about to ask why when the door opened, and two men

26

walked in, escorting another man. Joel's blood ran cold as he did a double take. *How did they catch him this quickly?* To his credit, Alter pretended not to recognize him as he was roughly pushed inside.

"Follow me, please," the police officer said, taking the papers from the clerk before heading toward the stairs in the back of the room. Upstairs, they entered a spacious office, where a man wearing regular clothes sat behind a large desk. Apart from a small filing cabinet in the corner, the room was sparsely furnished.

The man waved at a chair opposite. "Please, sit." The police officer placed the papers on the desk, and then stood a little too close behind Joel. The commander of the Jewish council was a small, stout man. His white mustache curled up at the sides of his mouth, his eyes peered through small glasses. "I'm sorry for the bother, but I just wanted to ask you a few things about the transport from the farm just now."

"Sure." Joel shifted in his seat.

He scanned the papers absentmindedly. "We're happy to have them with us for a few days, but it does seem a little bit of a ..." He paused, twirling his mustache. "Coincidence for us to also pick up a man wanted by the Gestapo in Ciechanów right after your arrival." Even though the commander spoke politely, there was no mistaking the true meaning of his words. "You wouldn't know anything about that, would you?"

"Unless he somehow climbed aboard my truck at the farm, I only know of the two families I picked up. I checked their papers and only had ten people in my truck." Joel felt his neck burn.

The commander looked up, and Joel did his best to hold his gaze. Finally, after a few seconds, the commander nodded. "Very well. It must've been a coincidence, then. I wouldn't know why a Volksdeutsche like yourself would take such a risk, after all."

Joel wasn't sure how to take the commander's words. *Does he believe that?* He stood and turned to leave. As he did, the policeman behind him didn't move, still looking at him with suspicion. Joel decided to ignore him and turned back to the commander. "Did you have any other questions for me? I should get back to Ciechanów."

The commander waved him away. "No, that will be all."

Joel had moved to the door when another man rushed into the

office. "Sorry to disturb you, commander, but I just wanted to ask what we should ... Oh, hello, Joel. What are you doing here?"

Joel's heart sank as he looked into the face of the one man in Mława who knew him: Piotr's uncle. He wore the same uniform as the police officer now standing behind him.

"You know this man?" the commander asked, surprise evident in his voice.

"Sure, he's been friends with my nephew for as long as he's lived. Aren't you supposed to stay in Ciechanów?"

Now the other policeman's eyebrows shot up. "Why would he need to stay in Ciechanów? He's a driver for the Germans."

Piotr's uncle looked confused, and Joel closed his eyes. "Why would they hire a Jew to do their driving?"

The room went silent. The commander leafed through the papers, then calmly spoke. "So your name isn't Robert Kozak?"

Joel shook his head. There was no sense in denying it.

"And you did bring in Alter Jaffe this morning." The commander stood behind his desk. "You must have a good reason for doing so, with the Gestapo looking for him."

Joel thought he saw a flash of sympathy in the man's eyes. "I've known this man all my life, he helps other people, and there's no reason for him to steal those tools. He's got a shed full of them. Moving to Mława is his only chance at survival."

"So you believe he's innocent."

The commander looked thoughtful while the policemen stood by. Joel glanced at their faces and saw Piotr's uncle looking apologetic. The demeanor of the other man had changed as well. He no longer looked annoyed, but focused on the commander, who paced between his desk and the filing cabinet.

"I'm afraid there's only one thing I can do," the commander said as he stopped pacing. "I need to report you to the Gestapo, and we'll have to take Alter back to Ciechanów."

Joel dropped his head and swallowed hard.

"But, that would mean death for both of you," the commander continued. "And even though I believe in justice, I can't send two of my people to their deaths like this."

Joel raised his head, his mouth open in disbelief.

"Here's what's going to happen, *Robert*," the commander said. "We're going to find a spot for Alter in Mława, and you're going back to Ciechanów. If you ever speak a word of what happened in this office today, we'll find a way for you to disappear. Do I make myself clear?"

"Crystal clear, sir."

Joel turned into the driveway of Kesler's an hour later. He was still shaking as he drove past his boss' house. Everything was quiet, with the house locked up. *They must be out; the weather is nice, after all.* As he neared the garage, he was surprised to find the doors shut. That was odd; Alfred normally kept the door open while working. He climbed out of the truck and unlocked the garage, pulling open the heavy door.

He parked the truck neatly beside the other trucks. As he fumbled with the lock, the crunch of footsteps on the gravel grew louder. *Must be Alfred, after all.*

As he turned to greet his colleague, his heart skipped a beat. Three Gestapo men stood a few meters away, pistols aimed at his chest. "Why don't you come with us, *Joel* Kozak?"

# CHAPTER FIVE

Agnes helped her mother clear the plates from the table while Yvette joined their father in the living room. The atmosphere in the house had been tense for the past few days, and Agnes was keen to get her sister and mother talking again.

"Mama, you know she tried her best. But you can't blame her forever; she feels bad enough as it is."

Her mother shook her head. "I know, Agnes. But your sister just seems to attract trouble these days. I don't know what it is with her. You were never like this. Can't you talk some sense into her?"

Agnes put some glasses on the kitchen counter and tutted. Yvette wasn't acting out at all, she was trying to help. "You know she looks up to Papa. She wants to help people, just like him."

"But taking these big risks with our coupons is not the way to do it. We're going to be hungry for the next few days." Her mother raised her voice in frustration, and Agnes' father stepped into the kitchen.

"Come on now, we'll make it work. I can talk to the people in the organization about getting some more food coupons. They've always said if we need anything, we only need to ask."

"Perhaps now would be a good time to do so," her mother said.

Agnes smiled at her father. She adored him; he always knew how to calm their mother down. Or his patients, for that matter. Even though he lost his practice, he still aided whoever needed medical help. People would visit their home, and he would look after them.

With the help of the resistance—the organization—he somehow managed to find the scarce medication. What they located wasn't perfect, but it was better than nothing. Agnes was proud of him.

She walked into the living room, where Yvette sat reading a book on the couch. "Say, want to join me upstairs? I need to study a bit, and it's too crowded here." She nudged her sister toward the stairs.

"Sure, I don't want to face mom anyway."

"It's not your fault, Yvette," Agnes said as they mounted the stairs and entered their shared bedroom. "You tried something, and it didn't work out. Perhaps Johannes will show up later this week."

Yvette looked doubtful as she sat on her bed. "I don't know about that. It feels like he's made off with our food coupons. I shouldn't have fallen for that. And now mom is upset."

"Just talk to her in the morning and promise it won't happen again. Mama will forgive you. Did you hear what Papa said? He's going to fix this." She grabbed one of her books and sat on the bed next to Yvette.

"What about you, though? You're pretending everything's okay, but how are you feeling? Have you heard from Mario or the others?"

"Nothing." Yvette was right. She had tried to forget about what had happened a few days ago. But she couldn't shake the image of Mario from her mind. When she joined the other girls at the bottom of the stairs, they ran and didn't look back. Agnes had made it home safely, but she had no way to contact the other girls. Those were the rules of the school. They would only meet each other there. *Exactly because of this.* If Mario and the other men were caught and—she choked up a little— interrogated, they wouldn't be able to tell the police anything about the other students.

"I don't know Mario or any other people in your class, but I'm sure he's going to be all right," Yvette said. "The Blackshirts might be thugs, but I haven't heard of them ever killing someone."

"I'm not sure the alternative is much better," Agnes said.

The street was dark, the reflection of the moon in the canal in front of their home the only source of light.

"Close the curtains, Agnes," Yvette said. "You don't want a patrol knocking on our door."

Agnes wished her mother had heard Yvette. She sat next to Yvette and wrapped her arms around her. She would never let anything come between them. They sat for a moment, and Agnes felt a calm wash over her—as long as she had her sister, she would be all right.

There were hurried footsteps in the hallway, and a second later they heard their father. "Close the door girls, and stay in your room."

Yvette got up and softly closed the door. They were used to this a few nights a week. "I hope Papa can patch up whoever is here. I wish we could help; I feel useless sitting up here hiding."

"It's for our own good, so we don't recognize anyone, and they don't see our faces," Agnes said, even though she too would love to put some of her training into practice.

They were quiet as they listened for the usual sounds of people shuffling through their home. They always came through the back door, and their father would attend to them in the basement. They heard the familiar pattern—three knocks in quick succession, a pause, and then two more—on the back door, and Agnes breathed a little easier. The first seconds were always the most stressful ones.

Agnes had just picked up her book to begin reading again, when there was a loud crash from the kitchen. The plates she'd put there earlier, perhaps? *But, no, it was too loud.*

Yvette looked up in alarm. More noise; this time there was no mistaking chairs tumbling over. Heavy boots stomped through the living room. Yvette moved closer to Agnes. "What's going on?"

Her sister's question was answered moments later.

"*Aufmachen! Schnell, schnell!*—Open up! Quickly, quickly!"

A shiver ran down Agnes' spine. *Oh no. They're at the basement door.* She heard her father speaking in German. He couldn't find the key; they never used the basement. The Germans weren't buying it and were now trying to force the door open. Her father pleaded for them to stop, but he was cut off abruptly as the door gave way with a crash. Agnes imagined the old wooden door exploding in hundreds of splinters.

The sound of boots stomping down the unbalanced steps faded.

They would find her father's makeshift practice. What would they do next? Papa would be arrested. But what about Mama? And them?

"What should we do?" Yvette whispered, her eyes shooting back and forth between Agnes and the door.

Agnes considered their chances. Could they make a run for it? *No, don't be silly. Where would we go?*

"We stay here, and we stay quiet. Like Papa told us to." When their father warned them something like this might happen, Agnes had always considered the possibility remote. Who would betray a doctor? She had been too optimistic.

Muffled voices emerged from the basement; soon, the heavy boots thudded back into the hallway. Finally, the front door opened, followed by softer footsteps and her father's voice. "Where are you taking us? Can we bring some clothes?" He was met with silence before being escorted outside.

"Please let me take my medication, it's in the bathroom upstairs, I need it," begged Agnes' mother.

"You won't need medication where you're going."

Outside, a truck stopped, the driver not bothering to shut off the engine as it roared in the silence of the night. Agnes dared breathe a little easier with the drone of the engine providing cover, but she kept her ears trained on the events in the hallway. *Are they leaving?*

The same man who'd spoken those horrible words to her mother a moment ago now spoke the words that chilled Agnes' blood: "Go check upstairs; there's supposed to be two daughters."

As the footsteps rushed up the stairs and the light in the hallway switched on, Agnes grabbed her sister's hand. Yvette's eyes were moist, she was biting her upper lip to control herself. Agnes' heart broke. What was going to happen to them and their parents?

"Remember what Papa told us?" she whispered.

Yvette nodded, swallowing hard. "Don't tell them anything."

"That's right. We stick together." Agnes stroked her sister's hair as the footsteps neared. The door swung open—the light from the hallway streaming in—and the silhouette of a large man carrying a pistol filled the doorway. Agnes closed her eyes and squeezed her sister's hand tighter.

She first noticed the smell—pungent, like she was in a forest of rotting trees. The air was heavy, the room dark, a single flickering bulb the sole illumination. Agnes was pushed onto a chair facing a small table, struggling to keep her balance since her hands were tied firmly behind her back. A man bound her legs against the cold iron of the chair, the nylon rope biting into her shins. When he finished he quickly left, the door slamming shut, and Agnes was left on her own.

She scanned the room as she tried to rub her wrists together—her fingertips tingled. The light bulb emitted a buzzing sound, and she could feel a headache growing, her temples throbbing.

*How long have I been here?* She couldn't remember much beyond being hauled off into a truck—one different from her parents'—with Yvette. She'd hardly recognized the dark Amsterdam streets from the back of the truck. The Grüne Polizei officers hadn't spoken a word, but kept their eyes trained on the two sisters.

The truck had brought them to the headquarters of the *Sicherheitsdienst* on Euterpe Street. Agnes had heard the stories of what happened in the basement. And now, she found herself in one of those very rooms.

The door opened, and a man with surprisingly delicate features walked in. Agnes was surprised to see him wearing a neat suit, perfectly pressed shirt, and polished shoes. He wasn't at all what she'd expected.

The man stood opposite her, opening a folder and flicking through some of the pages inside. He tutted, nodded—more to himself than Agnes—and took out a sheet. He placed it on the small table in front of her, close enough for her to read its contents.

"Shall we save ourselves some trouble?" He spoke with the accent of the Dutch upper class. *Surely only Germans worked at the Sicherheitsdienst?* "Your sister has already told us everything. That's her confession right there."

Agnes leaned forward as she focused on the neatly typed lines on the single sheet of paper. There were no more than three paragraphs, and she quickly read through them. What she read sounded so absurd and far from the truth that she couldn't suppress a chuckle.

"Something funny?"

She would've pushed the sheet of paper back to him if she could. Instead, she looked up and spat at him, but he was too far away. A few drops of spittle landed on his shoes.

"That's an unfortunate response." The man took the sheet and replaced it in the folder. He took out a cigarette and lit it, blowing smoke in her direction. She held her breath, not letting him be satisfied by seeing her recoil. *I'm going to be strong.*

The man took another drag as he took a few steps from Agnes, suddenly interested in something on the opposite wall. He turned back to her and pointed at a spot. "These cells are normally used to keep people in isolation. You must've heard what happens here, no?" Agnes glared at him, and he continued, unperturbed. "This mark was left by a woman about your age who banged her head repeatedly into the wall after spending seven nights down here. Can you see the small dents? Probably not, from where you're sitting. Safe to say, things didn't end well for her. We found her the next morning. She'd split her skull open."

Agnes' mouth twitched involuntarily, and he smiled as he took another drag. He blew the smoke against the wall and then dropped the cigarette butt on the damp floor. It hissed softly. He took a step back to Agnes. "Quite a distasteful story, wouldn't you agree? I'm only telling you because I want to warn you. This basement makes people do crazy things."

Her heart beat faster, and sweat flowed down her forehead. As it slowly trickled, she reached to wipe it, only to find her hands still tied. The itch was almost unbearable. She shifted in her seat, which only caused the rope around her ankles to tighten.

"So, Agnes Markx. Why don't you spare yourself such an undignified ending and admit to what your parents have done? We know they were part of a network robbing food coupon depots and assisting the active resistance. Just admit to it, and you can leave." He placed another sheet of paper in front of her. "You don't have to pay for their mistakes. We know you weren't involved."

*There is no way Yvette admitted to this.* She shook her head. "No."

The man's collected composure changed as he frowned at her.

"Well, this is a shame. I was hoping you'd see sense, but if this is your attitude, I fear I can't do anything for you."

Agnes squeezed her eyes harder, hoping it would make him leave sooner. He hovered in front of her for a while, then headed for the door. She opened her eyes as soon as she heard him step into the hallway.

On the table was a piece of chocolate. It was agonizingly close, but there was no way she could reach it. As the door latched, she turned to see him peering through the small window. His eyes went between the chocolate and her, and smiled before disappearing.

Agnes awoke with a start as the door opened. Two men wearing green uniforms entered and unbound her. The piece of chocolate was still on the table, and she snatched it, quickly stuffing it into her mouth. The bitter taste invigorated her, but the relief was only temporary as she crashed into the table and onto the cold floor. The circulation to her feet had been so restricted that she had lost her balance.

The men lifted her upright and escorted her from the cell.

"Where is my sister?"

The men didn't respond, guiding her up the stairs and opening the door to the blinding sunlight. Agnes closed her eyes as they took her down a small set of steps. She heard the rumble of an idle engine, and as she opened her eyes, she found herself facing the back of a truck. Its tarp was raised, and the men lifted her up.

Agnes sat down on the wooden plank on the side of the truck and worried about her sister and parents. Had they confessed, after all? Had they sold her out? Had the interrogators tricked them? A sharp pain shot through her head, and she closed her eyes and waited for it to pass.

The door to the basement creaked open again, and as Agnes opened her eyes, she felt weak with relief to see her sister struggling through. When Yvette saw Agnes, her cracked lips broke into a faint smile. After Yvette was loaded onto the truck, the sisters fell into each other's arms. Agnes could no longer contain her emotions and cried, holding her sister tight.

"Did you tell them anything?" Yvette whispered.

Agnes shook her head. "Did you?"

"Of course not."

The two men who took them from their cells climbed aboard and closed the tailgate. Then, the truck started moving, and Agnes held onto her sister's hand. The drive took only ten minutes, and as they stepped off the truck, Agnes was surprised to find herself at Amsterdam's central train station.

"Where are we going?" she asked one of the men as they joined a stream of people carrying suitcases and backpacks.

He looked at her with pity. "Nobody told you?" She shook her head, confused. "You'll find out soon enough." His words sounded ominous.

They entered the station and were directed to a long train where people were swarming around the carriage entrances. Walking past some of the compartments, Agnes noted they were overcrowded as people pushed and jostled for space.

The man stopped at the next door. "This is you. Get in."

"Can you please tell us where we're going? And why are all these people carrying so much luggage? We have none."

"You're going east. And don't worry about your luggage. There will be clothes for you where you're going. Everything's been taken care of."

# CHAPTER SIX

A glimmer of sunlight shone through the bars above his head as Samson woke up. His back was stiff, and his head was hurting; a continuous throbbing that had made it hard to fall asleep. That and the cold, dirty, overcrowded surroundings. He looked at the men around him; at least a dozen crammed into a space fit for two, maybe three. They'd all found their places on the floor, with the strongest of them, two large, muscular young men, claiming the bunks. They seemed only marginally more comfortable. There were no blankets; their only advantage was not having to sleep on the floor.

Most of the others were already awake. Some chatted quietly, but most kept to themselves. Finally, Samson got up and stretched his legs, relieving his aching muscles.

"Samson?"

He struggled to recognize the man standing next to him. His face was swollen, with his left eye completely shut. His arms had dark bruises around the wrists, and his clothes were torn and caked with blood. Samson's confusion must've shown, for the man stuck out a shaking hand. "Feliks, from the scrapyard."

Samson was shocked. This man looked nothing like the powerhouse he remembered.

Feliks smiled, then winced as his lips cracked a little more. "It must've been a week?" He scratched his head and looked up at the barred window. "I'm starting to lose track of time in here."

"Two weeks. We reported back to the ghetto, and everything was fine."

Feliks only seemed mildly surprised. "Well, everything did seem fine until I came home. There, I found two men waiting for me. They said I had missed days of work the week prior, and they came to take me away."

*Him too, then.* "Jewish police?"

Feliks shook his head. "No, they spoke German but wore no uniforms and weren't armed, or at least not from what I could see. I told them it must be a misunderstanding, for I had worked almost two weeks in a row. They insisted they had the correct information. I thought I could clear up the confusion at their office, and I went with them." He held up his hands. "What other choice did I have?"

"And then they took you here?"

"No, not directly. I was taken somewhere I'd never been, outside the ghetto. They took me into a room and made me wait for hours. When someone finally came, they told me there had been a misunderstanding, and I felt relieved. But then they said someone had come in and identified me as part of the ghetto resistance."

"Who?" Samson was alarmed. He looked around the cell but was relieved to see most of the other men looked healthy enough, or at least were without any bruises.

"I don't know; they wouldn't say. I denied it, of course. I'm not part of any resistance. I just want to work and keep my family safe. Keep my head down, you know." He paused for a moment, his eyes distant. Then he looked back at Samson. "That was when I was taken here, to the jail, and they kept me isolated from the other prisoners. I was in a dark cell where I could only stand or sit, and they only took me out for interrogations. That's when the Gestapo got involved, and well, that's what my life has been like for the past weeks. They transferred me to this cell last night when it was dark, and you were all asleep."

Samson shuddered. *If that's what they're capable of doing to a healthy, strong man in two weeks ...* "What made them move you here? Did you confess to anything?"

He shook his head resolutely. "There was nothing to confess to. They threatened my family, Samson. They said they would pick them up and throw them in a cell to die alongside me if I didn't tell them what they wanted to hear." His eyes glistened, and he looked away. "Or maybe I did tell them something of interest. I was delirious most of the time." His eyes focused on Samson. "But I never mentioned your name, not ever."

"I know you didn't," Samson said in a soothing tone. "I think I was in the wrong place at the wrong time."

Feliks looked confused. "How so?"

Samson told him the story of what happened at the ghetto gate. As he shared how he'd hit the Jewish police officer, Feliks' eyes went wide, and he continued. "I've seen what they've been doing to weaker people in the ghetto. They're common scum in a uniform, enriching themselves from the misery of those they're meant to protect." Samson shook his head in disgust. "No, I don't regret hitting him, but I do fear the consequences." *Especially after what you just told me.*

"At least they won't be able to go after any of your family, right?"

Samson hadn't thought of that before, but now that Feliks mentioned it, it was a relief. His parents had died ten years ago, when he was only thirteen years old. His aunt had taken him in, but she had passed away months after the German occupation, now almost three years ago.

"So you think they're rounding up whomever they can?" Feliks asked.

Samson smiled. How deceiving looks could be: despite his large frame and bulging arms, Feliks was an intellectual and practiced law before the occupation. "Not sure it's completely random," Samson said, looking at the men in the cell. "They seemed particularly interested in strong, young men."

"Might also be why they moved me here, then," Feliks said, following Samson's gaze. They were quiet for a moment until Feliks spoke. "It would explain why they haven't interrogated or tortured you for hitting that police officer."

"Could be." Samson wasn't convinced. He wanted to believe Feliks, but anytime a guard walked past, his body tensed. "I'm hoping they don't care too much about Jews fighting among themselves, even if one is a police officer."

"Judging by the bruises on your face, I think they got their revenge before dropping you off here."

Samson laughed out loud. It was rich, coming from Feliks, who looked far worse off. The big man joined in, wincing as he grabbed his chest.

The rest of the morning crawled by. Guards passed in the hallway but ignored their cell. Samson's stomach grumbled, but he'd already learned there was no schedule for food. They'd receive something whenever the guards felt like it and no more than twice a day. He spent most of the morning trying to nap. He was glad Feliks had joined the cell: at least he had someone he could talk to about the outside.

It was well past noon when there was activity in the hallway. It was different than usual. More voices, more urgency. The energy in the cell changed as every man felt something was different. They turned their eyes toward the door, and Feliks sat next to Samson. "Sounds like a bit of excitement outside, huh?"

Hurried footsteps echoed through the hallway, stopping abruptly in front of their door. Keys jingled, and the door swung open with a loud thud. Samson looked into the barrel of not one, but two automatic weapons wielded by SS troopers. "On your feet, hands on the back of your head, now!" One of the men shouted.

They did not need to be told twice. Within seconds, they all stood as instructed. Samson glanced at Feliks, who simply nodded. *Stay calm.*

The SS troopers marched them through the narrow hallway, which Samson didn't remember coming in through. They were led up a flight of stairs, urged on by more impatient troopers lining the steps. When they reached the ground floor, they were ordered outside. More armed SS men awaited them, as did half a dozen trucks. Groups similar to Samson's streamed in from different sides, all headed in the same direction.

"In here, keep going, come on, come on!" The SS man leading their party stood at one of the trucks. Inside sat another group of prisoners, their eyes trained on the floor. The first of Samson's group climbed aboard, and the rest soon began to follow.

Then, the man in front of Samson stopped and turned to the trooper. "Where are we going?" He was tall, and Samson had seen him in his work detail before.

"Get in the truck," the trooper said dismissively, waving his hand as he looked beyond the man, where another group approached.

The man stood his ground and asked again. "When you tell us where we're going."

This time, the trooper paused. His eyes narrowed as he sized up the man and then—without warning—bashed the butt of his gun into the side of the man's head. Samson took a step back, bumping into the man behind him, as the man in front collapsed to the ground.

The trooper turned to Samson. "Do you also want to know where you're going?"

Samson quickly climbed aboard and found a spot. As the last of their group boarded, two SS soldiers dragged the unconscious body of the man who'd spoken back into the building. Then two troopers climbed aboard, and the truck started moving.

It was only a short ride to Kraków's Główny train station. They were told to wait as two trucks parked alongside them. SS troopers jumped out, guns drawn, before forming a corridor into the station.

Samson climbed out of the truck, stunned to see almost sixty troopers lining the way into the station. They stood still as statues, only their eyes shifting, missing nothing. More trucks pulled up, and soon the SS were herding them into the station. Samson waited for Feliks to disembark, and together they joined the procession.

"Where do you think we're going?" Samson said in a low voice, keeping his eyes on the soldiers marking their path. Behind them, commuters looked on with interest.

"We'll find out soon enough. I suppose they'll need us to work somewhere outside the city." Feliks eyed the people on the other side of the cordon. "They must wonder what all these Jews are doing outside the ghetto. Look at their faces. Do you think any of them would help us if they could?"

"They would probably help put us on the trains."

They shuffled into the station and were guided to a side platform in the train yard away from the regular trains. A large steam locomotive stood waiting, impatiently puffing regular clouds of smoke.

"Are those ...," Samson started as he saw the cars lined behind the locomotive.

"Cattle cars." Feliks spoke the words without emotion. "I guess they didn't have any spare *human* compartments for us."

The energy of the group changed when they noticed their method of transport. Even though they were by now used to being treated as second-rate—or even third-rate—citizens, this latest humiliation classified them even beyond that. Samson shook his head but then remembered what had happened to the man at the jail. He wasn't about to make the same mistake.

The SS picked up on the change in energy and became impatient. "Hurry, hurry, get in the train cars!" They pushed and shoved those who didn't move quickly enough, prodding them with rifles.

Samson approached the car he was supposed to board, the trooper gesturing at him to climb aboard.

*"Halt! Halt!"*

The mass of men on the platform turned as one to see a young man racing across the tracks, away from their train. Three SS men gave chase, shouting for him to stop. He ignored them, not looking back as he made for the fence separating the station and the busy street. Samson felt his pulse quicken as he rooted for the young man. Judging from the faces of those around him, they felt the same way.

The young man was only twenty meters away from the fence when it became clear the troopers wouldn't catch up. They stopped in the middle of the yard and raised their rifles. *Oh no.* Samson wanted to look away, but, like the others around him, was too fascinated by the macabre spectacle playing out. The man kept running, unaware of the impending danger. He was now only ten meters away. *Come on. Come on.*

Three shots echoed in the yard, and Samson flinched. The man had reached the fence but froze in place upon hearing the shots. They had missed, but his hesitation proved fatal. Three more shots in quick succession, and as he turned to climb the fence, his head exploded as the troopers fired off another salvo for good measure.

Samson turned away in disgust, and the group waiting to board went deathly quiet. The gentle humming of the locomotive's engine was the only sound interrupting the silence. They stood silently, frozen in place, as they questioned whether the horror they'd just witnessed was real. Then, a voice cut through the silence.

"Enough of this nonsense. All aboard now. We're running late."

# CHAPTER SEVEN

Joel clenched his teeth as the leather tore into his bare back. He refused to make a sound, not giving his torturer the satisfaction.

"Stop making it hard on yourself!" the man shouted, inches from his ear. "I'm not going to stop until you admit it." He stepped away, picked up a bottle of water, and took a sip before he sighed contently. It gave Joel some reprieve, even though his back was on fire. He'd lost count of the number of strokes he'd been given since being hauled from his cell. His hands were tied in front of him, while his legs were secured to the rear of a chair. Sweat was dripping from his face.

*Snap!* The whip came down again, this time tearing strips of flesh from his back. Joel could no longer contain his agony and screamed out in pain.

His torturer seemed satisfied. "Ha! Finally. Not many men hold out this long." His face was next to Joel's again, his foul breath making him gag. "Tell me where Kesler keeps the radio. Which stations did he listen to? Did you listen to the radio as well? I know you did. Just tell me, and we can end this."

Joel spat blood on the floor, shaking his head, and braced himself for another lashing when the door on the far side of the room opened. A Gestapo man wearing civilian clothes walked in, his shoes clacking. He held the door for two uniformed men of the Jewish police dragging a woman in tattered clothes. She slowly raised her head, and Joel was shocked to see the face of Maria, Kesler's housekeeper. Her face battered, bruised, and her mouth gagged. Yet, despite the black rings surrounding her eyes, she looked at him with defiance.

"Ah, yes, there she is," the interrogator said. "Why don't you put her over there." He pointed at a chair opposite Joel. "He'll have a good view of everything this way."

They strapped Maria onto the chair, much in the same position as Joel. As they secured her, the interrogator knelt next to Joel and spoke in a soft, almost soothing voice. "You know, you can stop what is about to happen to her. It doesn't have to be this way."

Joel met his eyes and was surprised to see something there. The man had worked on Joel with fierce determination for over three days, never showing any emotion other than joy at inflicting pain. Now, he saw something else, something new—there was desperation in the German's eyes. Joel suppressed a smile and averted his eyes, focusing on Maria instead.

She looked back at him and shook her head, mumbling something incomprehensible through the rag in her mouth. Her eyes shot between Joel and the interrogator with urgency, and Joel thought he understood what she was saying. He blinked hard and nodded.

The policemen finished securing Maria and left. The Gestapo man remained in a corner, silently observing the proceedings. Joel felt his torturer move beside him, picking up the whip as he approached Maria. He stood behind her and looked at Joel. "Last chance to tell me about the radio." He cracked the whip in the air, and Maria flinched but then looked at Joel and shook her head again. As she did, the man brought the whip down on her back, tearing pieces of fabric from her shirt. Maria roared in pain, muffled by the piece of cloth in her mouth. Joel looked away, but the torturer quickly crossed to him, slapping him in the face with tremendous force. "Don't look away! For every time you do, I'll lash her again. She won't survive twenty lashes; I promise you that."

Joel forced himself to look at Maria. Her face had gone deathly pale. Another lash, and Joel kept his eyes firmly on hers. He felt her pain, and as the man brought the whip down for the third time, Joel's determination wavered. Maria's shirt had split in half, the fabric sticking to the sides of her sweaty, blood-soaked back.

"Tell me about Kesler!" the interrogator yelled at no one in particular. Maria hung her head, attempting to find some respite from the lashings, but her torturer had already seen it. He lashed out again, blood splattering in the air as her body convulsed.

Joel could no longer watch, and he opened his mouth to speak, but Maria looked at him with terror-stricken eyes and managed to shake her head. Her eyes rolled into the back of their sockets as she passed out.

"You see?" said the man with the whip. "I told you she wouldn't last long. Only you can make this stop, Kozak." He stepped away from Maria, leaving her limp body on the chair, as he moved back to the table next to Joel.

A thousand thoughts went through Joel's head as the man started whistling while sorting through his torture tools. After a minute, he appeared next to him again, this time holding a small blowtorch. He tested it near the side of Joel's head, the heat scorching the hair around his ear. "This will do nicely, I think."

"That's enough for now, Wolfgang." Joel turned his head to the man in the corner of the room. His voice was clear and authoritative as he stepped from the shadows. His shoes clacked softly on the hard concrete floor as he stood between Maria and Joel. "Why don't you take a break? I'll call for you when I need you again."

The interrogator put down the blowtorch and left without another word.

The Gestapo man knelt next to Joel. "It takes a certain kind of man to see that amount of pain inflicted on a woman and stay silent." He spoke evenly, without judgment. "You know the pain she's going through. He's done it to you for days, hasn't he?" Joel just looked at him. *What does he want?* "Do you know how many men I've seen come through here and admit to their crimes after less than half an hour with Wolfgang?"

The man stood and lifted Maria's head. "And this one, she's not given us anything, either. And you see her state. He took a handkerchief and gently wiped blood dripping from her nose. "You see, I detest violence. If it were up to me, we'd have better ways to get you to talk. But well, there's little use trying to reason with animals and savages." He pointed at Maria, then at Joel. "But you know what I think?"

Joel met his eyes but didn't speak. *Where is he going with this?*

"I don't think you have anything interesting to tell me about Kesler. If you did, you would have by now. But I can see it in your eyes. You're loyal. You won't betray the man who hired you, who provides you with a lifeline not afforded to most in the ghetto. And it's the same for her. She won't betray him, for she knows that when she does, her life is over." He smiled. "We already know the most interesting thing about you. You're not a Volksdeutsche, but Kesler provided you with the forged papers. Perhaps for some people, that would be enough to lock you up, or kill you, even. But I think you've suffered enough in here and learned your lesson."

*This must be a trap.*

The man appeared to read his mind, flicked his hand in a dismissive gesture. "Oh, you think you're getting away easy? Don't kid yourself, Jew. When you leave this building, the life you knew is gone. You will not have a comfortable job with Kesler anymore. Instead, you'll need to forage to survive, just like the rest of your people. And you'll know what happens when you step out of line again." He waved his hand in a semi-circle around the room. "Perhaps this experience will be a good reminder and a warning to share with your people."

The man looked at Joel, who still kept his jaws firmly shut. "Do we understand each other?"

Joel realized the man was somehow, and for some perverse reason, handing him a lifeline. He didn't understand why, but for the first time in three days, he opened his mouth and spoke in a voice he hardly recognized. "We do."

# CHAPTER EIGHT

S amson marched out of his block alongside the other prisoners, all garbed in the same camp uniforms. As they made their way toward the roll call area, prisoners from the adjoining blocks joined them on the main thoroughfare. All with their shaved heads and zebra-striped uniforms. The only differences between the men marching for this Sunday's roll call were their varied states of health. Some who'd been in the camp longer looked like walking skeletons. They were days from collapsing on the way to their grueling jobs in the mines and quarries surrounding the camp. Newer arrivals still had some flesh on their bones. The rigors of the unrelenting camp life hadn't consumed them in quite the same manner. Yet. No matter their state, however, none of the men held any illusions about their chances of survival. Death was present around every corner in Auschwitz.

Samson arrived a week ago. The journey had taken the good part of five hours, the train making plenty of stops along the way. It was an unnecessarily long time for a distance of fewer than 70 kilometers as the crow flies. Samson suspected this had been intentional, ensuring the men arrived at the camp exhausted, thirsty, and hungry.

Upon arrival, they were met by SS troopers and dogs. Carrying nothing but the clothes on their backs, they were loaded onto trucks and dropped off in the camp, where they spent the rest of the afternoon and evening going through the administrative motions. Samson was assigned to Block 4, after he had been disinfected and traded his clothes for the camp uniform. Finally, the hair on his head was removed by another prisoner wielding blunt scissors and an even blunter razor. Entering the block, it immediately became clear there was little concern for the comfort of its inhabitants, and he jostled to secure a spot in the middle of a three-level bunk bed. He shared his space with Feliks and one other man and had struggled to sleep the first nights. It wasn't until the third night that he, exhausted from working in the nearby quarry, fell into a fitful sleep.

He entered the dusty, sandy yard and lined up in a neat row of ten alongside his fellow blockmates, Feliks to his right. He was about to be subjected for the first time to Auschwitz's macabre Sunday *morning sport* rituals.

As the last men arrived, a hush fell over the yard. Samson scanned the area, spotting remarkably few guards. *They're not expecting any trouble.* There was movement at the front, and a man wearing a prisoner uniform confidently marched toward them. He was no ordinary prisoner. He wore the green triangle of a criminal prisoner and fulfilled the position of *Kapo*, a prisoner supervisor, and his name was Vacek. Samson had been warned about him, and here he stood, meters away from him.

"All right, scum," he shouted. "Caps off." As he called the command, the men took their flat caps from their heads and slapped them against their thighs with fury, collectively simulating the sound of a whip. At least, that was the idea. Of course, for that to work, all men needed to time their move perfectly. A snarl formed on Vacek's face.

"Caps on!" The men slapped their caps back on their heads, waiting for the command to take them off again. "Caps off!" The effort was better but nowhere near the perfection the Kapo was looking for.

Samson did his best to time his movements with the majority. He was relieved to see his section did not attract the ire of Vacek, for the Kapo made his way to the other side of the yard. "Caps off!" Samson brought his cap down with force, keeping an eye on the man storming down the yard.

They stood with their caps on their thighs as Vacek burst through the ranks and grabbed an older man. The man pleaded for another chance, but Vacek hauled him toward the wall at the front.

The sequence was repeated for twenty minutes, and by the time they perfected the drill, twenty-five unfortunate men stood facing the wall. Samson was panting but kept his eyes straight ahead, concentrating only on Vacek's instructions.

It appeared the Kapo was satisfied, for he ceased his commands. "Very well, scum. It took a while this week, but at least we've filtered out the weak links." He turned to the men near the wall. "We have no use for weaklings in our camp. You've earned your Sunday morning sport. Turn around!"

The men turned as if possessed. Someone next to Samson sighed, and when Samson looked at him, he shook his head almost imperceptibly.

Four other Kapos joined Vacek, and spread out around the chosen men. Vacek tapped his truncheon softly on his leg, then started barking commands at the men. "Lie down! Get up! On your knees!" The men hit the dirt as quickly as they could, then jumped up, trying to keep up with the barrage of commands. "Give me five! Crawl! Jump!"

The first rays of sunlight streamed into the yard as the sun made its way above the surrounding blocks. Vacek had chosen his spot well: the rays shone mercilessly on the men at the front.

They valiantly tried to keep up, but they weren't the strongest in the yard to begin with, and soon started to falter. As they did, Vacek or one of his cronies beat them savagely with their truncheons. He alternated his commands with insults as he struck blows to the men's bodies first but was soon bashing in their heads. One by one, the men fell to the ground, their broken bodies unable to get up after receiving the final blow to the head.

Samson felt nauseous as he stood meters from the gruesome spectacle. He looked around to see if his fellow prisoners shared his horror, but most focused their eyes on their feet. This wasn't their first Sunday sport. In less than fifteen minutes, twenty-five men had lost their lives. Samson heard Feliks mumble something, and he looked to see his friend's face had gone pale.

All was quiet in the yard when an SS officer descended the steps of one of the blocks. Samson hadn't realized the man had stood there all the time, a detached spectator. As he did, Samson heard hurried footsteps to his right. He was astonished to see a prisoner making his way forward, heading straight for the SS man. *Is he mad?*

"Sir, sir. Can I have a word, please?" The man was slight of frame and wore tiny spectacles. He walked with the air of someone who used to be in a position of power.

The SS man stopped and looked at him with an amused expression.

"I wanted to let you know that that prisoner over there"—he pointed at Vacek—"just murdered those men in cold blood. This is an outrage! We are here to work."

The man's words echoed across the yard, and Samson didn't think the silence could be any louder. He held his breath as the SS man's face twisted into a nasty grin.

"Kapo?" He spoke in the direction of Vacek, who rushed to stand beside him. "Did you hear what this Jew just said?"

"Sure did, sir." Vacek reminded Samson of a puppy eager to please, and felt his stomach turn.

"Can you make sure you take care of this appropriately?"

"Absolutely, sir." Vacek raced back to the group of bodies and picked up his truncheon. He returned with enthusiasm, and without another word, hit the man with the spectacles square in the face. His glasses flew from his nose as he fell to the ground, crying in pain. This further encouraged Vacek, who savagely beat him until he no longer moved. Satisfied with his efforts, he saluted the SS man. "Done, sir."

"Very well." He dismissed Vacek with a wave of the hand, and the Kapo dragged the man's lifeless body to his earlier casualties. The SS officer turned to the rest of the group and without any emotion, said, "Now, are there any more complaints?"

Samson woke up the next morning, the horrors of the day prior still fresh in his memory. After roll call, he'd spent most of the previous day outside, trying to stay clear of the yard, where other prisoners were removing the bodies of the day's *sport*.

The block was awake early, and men prepared for a day's hard labor in the quarries, mines, or fields surrounding the camp. But not before roll call, which could have the men on their feet for anything between half an hour and two hours, if the Kapos or SS found anything they didn't like.

Samson climbed down from his bunk and wasn't surprised to find no water came from the tap in the block. His throat was parched but he wouldn't get a chance to quench his thirst until after roll call. He sighed and headed back to his bunk, where Feliks sat with his feet dangling over the side.

"No water?"

Samson shook his head. "Of course not." He looked at Feliks and was pleased to see his friend's face was healing well. Even though he had lost quite a bit of weight, Feliks had taken to work in the mines much better than the SS jail interrogations. Samson worked in the quarry, and the work was much like what he'd done in Kraków, only dustier.

An SS officer walked in, a rarity. They preferred to have the block supervisors take care of any issues. The man held up both his hands, silencing the room.

"Listen up; I have a job with good, fair pay. Much better than what you're making in the mines or fields. It's more pleasant, too. I need strong men to assist me."

Samson looked around: some of the men looked thoughtful. Feliks tugged at his sleeve, and spoke in a low voice. "We should take the job. We can work together, and look out for each other. It doesn't sound too bad."

"I don't trust him," Samson whispered.

Feliks frowned. "How much worse can it be?" He jumped down from the bunk. "Come on, Samson, let's do it. We'll be in it together." He didn't wait for a reply as he raised his hand and said loudly, "We'll take the job," pointing at himself and Samson.

The SS man quickly appraised them, and then waved them over. "Very well. Anyone else?"

Two others joined, and they were told to bring their belongings. As they left the block, the German was already giving them orders. "You won't have to join regular roll calls for this job. In fact, I'll take you to your new workplace right away." He looked back at them with a grin. "And you won't have to go very far. The job is right here in the camp."

The German had a spring in his step, as if in a hurry. As they walked past the other blocks, they headed toward the camp administration buildings, including the SS hospital, and turned left into a yard cordoned off by a wall. Samson had never been in this area, and judging from the surprised faces of the other men, neither had they. They were led to a building partly submerged under a layer of dirt and grass, a red-brick chimney protruding from the far side of the building. The SS officer led them down a few steps to a closed wooden door.

Samson looked to Feliks, who had lost his cockiness as the German opened the door. An intense heat met them as if a fire was raging inside, and Samson took a step back. The German appeared unfazed and stepped into the darkness without hesitation, urging them on. "We don't have all day—time to get to work."

As his eyes adjusted to the semidarkness, Samson saw there were indeed fires in the room. To his left, he looked into two cast-iron ovens where white-hot coals fueled a raging inferno of yellow and red flames. Two men wearing the same uniform as Samson ran to add more coal to the fire. Another two appeared from the back, pushing a small cart toward the ovens. Samson thought his eyes were deceiving him and had to double-check the cargo. Haphazardly piled on top were seven corpses.

As the cart reached the first oven, the prisoners tilted the cart sideways, and the corpses tumbled forward. The men ran to the other side and pushed the bodies into the oven before rapidly shutting the small door. Samson stood frozen. The gruesome spectacle was executed so quickly that he wasn't sure what he witnessed was real.

"Ha! You've arrived just in time!" A voice boomed from the far side of the room. Samson and the other new arrivals turned to find a young SS trooper carrying a whip. "Come with me. I have work for you, *Juden-schweinen*—Jewish pigs!" Samson looked back to see the man who'd recruited them was already on his way out of the building, closing the door behind him. As he neared the whip-wielding SS man, Samson noticed it was no ordinary trooper but an officer. *What is an SS officer doing in an underground crematorium?* There was no time to contemplate his thoughts, for the man cracked his whip in the air and said, "Come on then, you're needed in the other room!"

As the SS officer led them through the oven room, the smell of death hit Samson's nostrils. He looked to his left, where prisoners were busy unloading another cart filled with bodies into the other oven. He wrinkled his nose and the SS man caught it. "If you've got a problem with that smell, you're in for a tough time, you piece of filth!"

They went through another open doorway, and Samson gasped as he almost tripped over the body of a woman sprawled on the floor. Her cheeks had a blue hue, and her eyes bulged from their sockets, frozen in terror. The SS officer stepped over her without as much as flinching. The room was filled with corpses strewn haphazardly on the floor.

"Enough standing around! Start stripping those corpses!" The SS officer yelled.

Unsure what to do, Samson knelt next to the corpse of a woman a little farther into the room. As he lifted her feet to take off her shoes, he felt her body was still lukewarm, and he let go. He looked at her face, but the lifeless eyes staring back at him confirmed she was no longer among the living. He carefully undid the shoelaces and slid off her shoes. She wore stockings, and Samson felt awkward undoing them. As he struggled to slide the garment down her legs, he pulled too hard and ripped it. In the quiet room of death, the sound appeared to echo against the walls. Before Samson realized it, the SS officer stood next to him and smacked him on the side of the head.

"What do you think you're doing, you idiot? Be careful with those; they need to be worn again!" He knelt beside Samson, breathing hard. "Here, let me show you how it's done." The man showed remarkable nimbleness in unrolling the stockings: this wasn't the first time he'd done this. As he finished, he said, "Now, do better next time. I don't want to see you ripping valuable items meant for the Reich again, or you can join them."

Samson spent the rest of the day stripping corpses. After handing out more punishment to the other newcomers for small infractions or mistakes in undressing the corpses, the SS officer appeared satisfied and alternated between the oven room and theirs. It gave Samson and the others brief moments of respite.

Feliks sat next to Samson as he started stripping a young man wearing a neat suit. His face was pale as a sheet. "This was not what I expected."

"Well, at least we're no longer shoveling dirt in the mines and quarries," Samson said, frowning as he undid the man's tie. He looked to Feliks, who looked like he was about to throw up. "I'm sorry, I didn't mean it like that. You couldn't know it was going to be this bad."

"I shouldn't have been so careless in raising my—no, our—hands. I should've waited to see what the other men did," Feliks said, taking deep breaths.

"Look, we just need to work hard and show that SS man we can take whatever job he gives us. Maybe things will get better," Samson said with an optimism he wasn't sure he felt. "What is this place, anyway? Where did all these bodies come from?"

Feliks was about to answer when a big man wearing a prisoner's uniform approached from the other side of the room. "Hey, you two. Stop talking so much and work faster. Stark is going to come back any minute now, and if he sees you sitting around talking, he will throw a fit." His eyebrows moving at the rhythm of his speech.

Samson and Feliks looked at the man, then at each other, and Feliks quickly moved to the other side of the room.


It took them well into the evening to strip the corpses. Then they were ordered to sort through the various suitcases and bags. Anything of value was to be sorted and reported to *Untersturmführer* Stark. By the end of the day, Samson was exhausted, his lungs filled with smoke and ash drifting in from the other room. The smell of death lingered in his nose and mouth. When Stark finally told them it was time to leave, Samson was surprised to find it was dark outside, the camp quiet. The other prisoners had returned from their work details and had already gone through evening roll call.

They followed Stark across the camp's main road and passed the empty gallows. They looked incredibly eerie in the faint moonlight. They walked to the far side of the camp, and Samson was alarmed when Stark stopped in front of Block 11—the penal block. Most of the men and women who went into Block 11 never came out.

Without a word, Stark opened the door, and the group of seven prisoners, led by the large man who'd spoken to Samson and Feliks earlier, silently entered. They descended the stairs and into the basement. There, Stark handed them over to an SS guard, who led them farther down. He opened a cell door and ushered them in.

The room was spacious enough for their party and even had a small window. The guard shut the door and left them in the darkness, the only light in the cell coming from the weak moon outside. Exhausted, Samson forgot about the day's worries and lay down on the cold ground. *What fresh new hell have I arrived in now?*

# CHAPTER NINE

Agnes and Yvette stepped out of the barracks and into the dewy morning air. It was still early, but they wanted to ensure they could wash up before the rest of the camp awoke. They hurried along the main road, where the night's rain had turned the sand into a muddy mess that tugged at their feet with every step.

Despite that, they kept going and arrived at the bathhouse to find it practically deserted, bar a few other early risers. The sisters stood next to each other at one of the large washing basins.

"Is today your first day at the hospital?" Yvette asked, shivering as she splashed her face with cold water.

Agnes nodded. "Yes, it took me a while to get through to the administration, but once I talked to one of the doctors there, they were happy to have me. He said the camp administration can be slow, but they want everybody to have a job."

"I guess idle hands are the devil's work," Yvette said as she patted her face dry. "It's a good thing they still need people working in the fields. I prefer being outside anyway. However, it will be hard to walk through the fields after last night's rain."

They stepped outside, feeling refreshed, and Agnes looked at the sky. "I think it might clear up later." She pointed at some blue skies farther ahead. "Shall we get something to eat?" Yvette said, not waiting for an answer as she turned toward the communal canteen.

Agnes was happy to eat; she had been awake early and had waited for her sister to rise. She'd spent the first two weeks in Westerbork trying to find something to do. There weren't too many jobs, and as a result, many people spent their time chatting and playing cards in the barracks or, when the weather permitted, on the steps outside. Despite what they told her, the camp administration didn't care too much about what the people did. In the end, she went to the hospital and approached one of the nurses. She had sent her to the camp's head physician, Dr. Brunner, who had been happy to add her to his staff.

They entered the canteen and picked up a plate of toast, a smattering of margarine, and some weak tea. It wasn't much, but Agnes had always been a light eater, and it hadn't taken her long to adjust to the meager offerings of the camp. They sat down and ate in silence as more people entered. Finally, others joined their table. Some were new arrivals, complaining about the conditions in the camp. They felt the barracks were too crowded, the food was inadequate, and they were bored. Agnes rolled her eyes at Yvette, and they quickly got up.

"These people don't seem to understand we're basically in prison here, do they?" Yvette said as they walked out. It had stopped raining, and a weak sun was battling through the clouds. "All things considered, I think it's not too bad. Apart from the fences and not being allowed to leave, I'll take this over an actual prison."

Agnes nodded, and her mind went back to how they got here. "Where do you think they've taken Papa and Mama?" The fate of her parents was always on her mind. She had hoped to find them in the camp but had given up on that after their first day.

"From what I've heard, it's likely they were taken to a camp in the south instead. Some people in the administration told me people suspected of being part of the resistance are taken to Vught."

Agnes wasn't going to find any answers in Westerbork. Not without some connection to the administration in The Hague, but that was unlikely. Who was going to help her? "You know what people are concerned about these days?" She didn't wait for a response as she pointed at a car outside the camp commander's house, about 100 meters away. "All these German army cars were showing up at Schol's home."

Jacques Schol was the Dutch commander of Westerbork. He'd run the camp since it was converted into a refugee camp for German and Austrian Jews in 1939. He addressed them at roll call once a week, and from everything Agnes could see, he had their best interests at heart. It was rumored he'd tried to evacuate the camp's inhabitants when the Nazis invaded the Netherlands in May 1940. When they were stranded in the north of the Netherlands, he resumed his duties as if nothing had happened.

"You think something is about to happen? What are people saying?"

Yvette waved her hand. "You know, people talk, but nobody knows for sure. Some say the Germans will clear the camp and send us east, whatever that means. Others say they're going to take over the camp."

*What possible interest could the Germans have in this small camp in the middle of nowhere?*

Agnes arrived at the hospital ten minutes early. The sun had broken through the clouds, and the good weather lifted her spirits. With a slight flutter in her stomach, she opened the door.

It was quiet in the small reception area. The counter was unattended, and Agnes looked up and down the hallway. The doors to the wards were open, the silence only broken by the occasional cough. She leaned on the counter and considered how qualified she was—her most recent training, in Mr. Klein's covert classroom, had been theoretical.

She sometimes questioned her actions that day, feeling like a coward for running from the Blackshirts. She also wished she knew what had happened to Mario and Mr. Klein, as their faces faded a little more every day.

"Can I help you?"

Agnes glanced up to find a woman in her thirties looking at her from behind the counter. She had striking green eyes under a bundle of frizzy black hair and a friendly smile. Clearly anxious, Agnes struggled to find her words. "I'm here to start work today."

The woman's smile didn't fade. "Okay, dear, calm down. Are you a nurse?"

Agnes nodded.

"Do you have a work slip?"

"Of course." Agnes reached into her pockets and produced a small piece of paper. "Sorry, I'm a little nervous."

"Don't worry about it." The woman quickly scanned her paper. "Agnes, welcome to the hospital. I'm Marion. Let's get you started. You'll need a uniform, of course."

Marion took her to the nurses' room, where she handed Agnes her new uniform before showing her around. "I've been told the hospital might expand next month. It's interesting because we have plenty of beds, so I don't really see the need."

Agnes frowned and remembered Yvette's words earlier that morning. *If they're expecting more people, it makes sense.*

"Most people here suffer from small illnesses, so your job is mostly to monitor them and make sure they receive their medication on time," Marion continued as they walked down the long hallway. "How much experience do you have?"

Agnes hesitated. "Mostly theoretical training. I started my nursing degree, but then the Germans, well, you know." She shifted on her feet.

"I see." Marion looked sympathetic. "Well, you're here now, and we can certainly use your help. What would you feel comfortable doing? Or at least to start with?" Her eyes sparkled, and Agnes instantly felt better.

"I can do all the things you just mentioned, and I'd be happy to learn more if you're willing to teach me."

"I'd love to, but one thing at a time. Let's get you acquainted with the patients." Marion stopped in front of an open doorway. Agnes looked inside and saw eight of the ten beds were occupied. "This is a senior ward," Marion said softly and with a smile. "They're the sweetest people. I think this would be a great place to start." Marion stepped into the room. "Good morning, everybody, I hope you've all slept well. Let me introduce you to Agnes, your new nurse."

Agnes followed, and as she looked at the friendly faces, she knew she was going to be just fine.

# CHAPTER TEN

J oel and the twenty other men slowly ascended the hill on their way back to Ciechanów. Reaching the top, they could see the church steeple rise up. It would only be another fifteen minutes before they'd return to the ghetto. Even though Joel was tired, he was glad the day was almost over. Looking around his work detail, he knew he was lucky to be employed, even if the city—well, the Germans—took half his already insultingly low wages. *It's still better than starving in the streets.*

It had been two weeks since his trip to the Gestapo basement. The last thing he remembered was being lifted off the ground by strong hands. He returned to his senses the next day in his own bed.

It took a week before he walked without pain as the bruises on his body slowly healed. He became restless by the second week and asked his mother to reach out for possible jobs. Without his knowledge, she had gone to the Jewish council and had somehow convinced them to give him a job.

Three days later, he joined a group working the fields outside the city. Even though the cuts on his back were still healing, he ignored the pain as he knew working was the only way to survive. Jews in the surrounding areas were forced to move into the Ciechanów ghetto, and as space, food, and drink became scarce, the corpses in the streets in the morning became more numerous.

Joel looked to their overseer, a surprisingly easygoing Volksdeutsche named Andrzej. Originally from Warsaw, he had moved to Ciechanów a few years ago, looking to escape the big city. From Joel's interactions with him, he knew the man didn't support the Nazi doctrine and had no problems with Jews. His sole motivation for working this job was to support his young family. As a result, he was fair to the men in the work detail, giving them ample rest and never once hitting anyone. In return, they gave him little trouble and spent their time working to meet the Germans' quotas. A light tap on his shoulder shook Joel from his thoughts. A man a few years younger looked at him with anticipation.

Joel raised his brow. "Can I help you?"

"Didn't you used to work for the Germans?" The man spoke in an even tone, keeping his voice down.

"I think you're mistaking me for someone else. Jews can't work for Germans." He turned away, hoping it would end the conversation.

The man wasn't so easily discouraged. "Sure, technically. But I know you were a driver for Kesler. I worked in his garden." Joel slowed down, and that was all the man needed to continue. "He arranged false papers for you as well?"

Joel stopped and looked the man up and down—about the same height as him, standing in a relaxed stance. He met Joel's gaze with confidence, and he detected not a hint of deception. *He's telling the truth.*

"If you worked for Kesler, what are you doing here?" Joel asked.

The man raised an eyebrow in surprise. "I assumed you knew. Kesler was removed from his position two weeks ago." The man looked troubled. "Is that not the reason you're here?"

"Hey! Keep up, guys, no straggling. We all want to get home!" Andrzej's voice boomed from the front. The rest of the group had marched on, and they hurried to catch up. As they rejoined the others, Joel processed the news of Kesler. It made sense that he'd been removed. The suspicion of owning a radio, in addition to employing Jews and falsifying their papers, was enough to have a man transferred. Despite their many faults, the Nazis did not take well to corruption among their own.

"Do you know where they took him?"

The man shook his head. "No, I just showed up one day and was told to leave by the man running the garden squad. He said it was no longer safe for me. In the end, that man probably saved me from what happened to you." His eyes focused on some of the bruises on Joel's face.

"So, what do you want from me?"

They walked into the outskirts of Ciechanów, passing a large medieval castle. "Look, I know you were involved in smuggling people and goods in and out of the city. Most of us working for Kesler did our part."

"A bit of resistance, you mean."

"Well, I think that's too big a word for what we did, but we did take some tools for our use, if you know what I mean." The man waved his hand. "Small acts."

Joel wasn't surprised people knew about his activities. He'd helped many people during his time at Kesler's. "Still doesn't explain why we're talking."

"Have you heard of Hashomer Hatzair?"

"Who hasn't?" Hashomer Hatzair was a Zionist organization with cells across the country and Eastern Europe. Joel knew of their presence in the bigger cities, where they organized acts of resistance. The man looked at him with an odd expression. "Are you suggesting there's a branch in Ciechanów?"

The man nodded. "We're small, but we're here. We want to do something, fight back."

Their work detail slowed down as they reached the ghetto perimeter. There was no wall like in other cities, but the invisible separator was clear enough from the conditions on both sides. As Joel and the other men crossed, Andrzej spoke up. "I'll pick you up from here tomorrow morning at six. Please don't be late, gentlemen. I don't like dealing with the administration. Have a good night." With that, the men of the work detail went their separate ways, and only Joel and the other man remained.

"We're recruiting, Joel, and we thought a man with your background would be interested in joining."

"What's your plan?" Joel was intrigued but unconvinced any organization in Ciechanów would have the capacity to organize anything.

"Join our meeting tomorrow night, and you'll find out. Most of us will be there. We all look forward to you joining." He gave him an address and offered his hand. "My name is Moshe."


Joel joined the group the following evening; he instinctively trusted Moshe.

He crossed through a dimly lit hallway into the back room of a poorly maintained house in the middle of the ghetto. Moshe along with three other men and four women greeted him. They were all around the same age as Joel: early twenties.

"We have a new face joining us today." Moshe nodded at Joel. "Joel and I used to work for a German named Kesler. Joel helped many of our people inside and outside Ciechanów. He even saved some from the Gestapo by smuggling them away from the city."

Joel felt the eyes of the group on him, and he tried to meet them all. They looked back at him with admiration, but more importantly, with determination. "Moshe told me you have big plans. Tell me about that."

The room went quiet as they looked at each other. Eventually, one of the women spoke up. "We want to stage an uprising, but it needs more support."

"Support from whom?"

"The people in the ghetto."

Joel looked at her. "What do you mean? Don't you have a plan yet?"

"We do. We want to reach out to the *Armia Krajowa*—the Home Army—in Warsaw and coordinate our attack on the SS garrison here in Ciechanów. We have the numbers in the ghetto to overwhelm them. We just need to convince people to join."

Joel glanced at Moshe before returning to the woman. "And how do you plan to do that? Do you know anyone in the Warsaw Home Army? Do you know if they're even interested in helping us?"

Silence lingered until Moshe spoke up. "It's still early days, Joel. We haven't established contact with the Home Army yet."

"What about the nearby ghettos? Mława?" Joel asked.

More silence.

Joel stood up and controlled his frustration. Then, calmly, he asked, "Do you have any weapons?"

"We have some knives, and we're siphoning gasoline from SS cars for Molotovs," the woman said.

*Well, that's something, at least.* "Okay, but we'll need guns."

The people in the small circle nodded. "We think the Home Army will help us with that."

Joel leaned against a table. "Okay, I'm not sure how you want to do this, but from what I've learned while working with Kesler and talking to people in different ghettos, you need to show them you can do something smaller before you try to undertake something like this. The Home Army in Warsaw won't back us without us accomplishing something first. I'm sure it's hard enough to get weapons for themselves, let alone hand them out."

Even though Joel had expected their plans to be more developed, he saw that the group of partisans in front of him had the right intentions. They just needed some direction.

"So, what do you suggest?" Moshe asked.

"Let me think about it. I think the most important thing is to try and find more support for our cause, even if it isn't an uprising right from the start." He waved his hand at the group. "We can talk all we want, but we'll need more people to join us if we want to make a difference. We can't do this between the nine of us."

"We have a few more members; they just couldn't make it tonight," the woman said.

Joel nodded. "That's great. I suggest we all sound out our friends and family. Perhaps ask them if they would be willing to contribute in some way. Even if it's just being a lookout when you're stealing gasoline from a German car or if they're willing to help smuggle goods from their work details. Every little bit helps."

"That sounds like a good plan, Joel. We should also keep our eyes and ears open for news around what the Germans are planning," Moshe said. As he got up, the rest did, too.

Joel nodded. "That's a great idea."

With that, the meeting was over, and they left the house in turns, waiting a few minutes in between to not attract attention. Joel and Moshe were the last to leave, and as Joel reached for the door, Moshe stopped him.

"Thank you for coming, Joel. I think we all needed an experienced voice of the resistance to get us focused."

As Joel walked home in the growing dusk, Moshe's words rang in his ears. Yet, he didn't consider himself experienced at all.

# CHAPTER ELEVEN

S amson woke to banging sounds in the hallway and lifted his head from the floor. His cellmates were also roused, and they looked at each other groggily. Through the small window, the sky was still dark.

He stretched his legs and listened to the voices in the hallway. All his senses were on alert when he recognized the raspy voice of the camp commander, Rudolf Höss. "Okay, out with you," he yelled at the prisoners as they were taken from their cells. In a few instances, he allowed the prisoners to stay, and Höss and the guards moved on. They were now only a few doors away, and Samson met Feliks' eyes. His friend looked frightened. *What is Höss doing here?*

He'd occasionally spotted the commander at roll call, looking on disinterestedly. The guards wielded their batons with a little more enthusiasm when Höss was present. Whatever brought the commander to the basement of Block 11?

Höss and his escorts reached their cell door, and everybody held their breath. Of all the cells that were opened, only two of ten men had been told to stay in their cells. The other men had been taken away, some kicking and screaming, others shuffling away in silence. Samson didn't know their fate, but he knew whoever was unfortunate enough to end up in this basement had a bleak future. His hands were trembling as he waited for the sound of the key entering the lock.

After a few seconds, Höss mumbled something. To Samson's relief, the commander walked on. Only when, a few seconds later, the door to the cell next to them opened did Samson dare exhale. He didn't yet dare move, seated with his back to the cold wall and legs pulled up to his chest.

The selection continued for another five minutes, and when Höss walked past their cell, Samson feared he might change his mind. But again, the commander continued, barking orders at the guards. "I want it done immediately; take them out to the yard now." His voice trailed off as they mounted the stairs.

The men around Samson sat a while longer; all worried Höss might return. The tall man from the crematorium stood first. They'd spent the past two days in the cell, and he'd introduced himself as Fischl. He'd worked in the crematorium for over a month, making him the senior man in their small squad. He exuded an air of calm, and Samson had found it easy to like him. A religious man, he sang hymns and recited passages from the *Tanakh*. His favorite book was the *Torah*, and Samson soon found it didn't matter if the rest joined in. Fischl was determined to practice his faith.

"Those men won't be coming back," Fischl said as he moved toward the small window. It was impossible to look into the yard as the lower part was bricked up. This allowed for fresh air and daylight to filter into the cell, but the men were unable to see anything beyond the sky. They would soon find out it was a blessing. "We're lucky the commander and his men passed us by. I know you're all strong men, you've proved as much by surviving more than a day in the crematorium, but it's about to get much worse."

*What could be worse than stripping and burning corpses in the underground hell of the crematorium?* The door to the yard opened with a bang and Samson's eyes went to the small window above Fischl's head.

Heavy thuds of military boots stomping echoed across the yard. As they reached the center of the yard, the footsteps stopped. After a pause, reluctant footsteps followed. The men taken from the cells were now outside, on Rudolf Höss' orders. It didn't take long for the men to realize what was happening, as one of them unleashed a bone-chilling howl.

"No, no! Please don't take me to the wall, please, I beg of you! I will do anything!" The man pleaded, struggling against the men escorting him. Then followed the sickening crunch of a bone breaking. One of the SS men must've used his truncheon or rifle to force him on. The man was crying, but it didn't matter. They soon heard him on the far side of the yard.

A salvo of gunfire ended the wails abruptly, and Samson looked away from the window. His hands were shaking violently as he closed his eyes.

For fifteen minutes, the scene in the yard was repeated. Some men went to their deaths silently, a few managed a cry of defiance, but most went reluctantly: sobbing and pleading until the last moment. *Will I be picked tomorrow?*

It had only been a few hours since the executions when the door to their cell opened. Samson had tried catching some sleep—there was nothing else to do but talk and sleep, and he hadn't felt like talking to anyone.

"All right, Jewish pigs," said the familiar voice of Hans Stark. "I hope you enjoyed your rest because we've got work to do." He banged his truncheon against the metal door. "Get a move on; you've got ten minutes to clean up." Behind him, two guards stood and escorted them upstairs to a washing room Samson had never seen before. His days had been spent in a filthy uniform, the only break in the monotony when a guard would bring them their daily rations of watery soup.

Samson lurched straight to the taps and drank eagerly, as did the other men. They spent only a minute or two under the ice-cold showers before changing into clean new uniforms.

Feliks stood next to him as they dressed. "Why are they giving us these?"

"I don't know, but I'll take it. Anything is better than staying in that basement any longer. And at least they won't kill us in new uniforms, right?" Samson could still hear the wails, then the dull thuds as the bodies of the freshly-executed men hit the cold stones of the yard between Blocks 10 and 11.

"I guess you're right," Feliks said as he pulled his striped shirt over his head. His friend looked halfway decent with new clothes and the cold shower.

Samson's group of seven marched out of the front door of Block 11 precisely fifteen minutes later. The sky was overcast, and the first sunlight pierced the darkness in the distance. It was quiet in the camp; the other prisoners wouldn't report for roll call for another hour.

They returned to the crematorium, where a guard quickly closed the gate behind them. In the yard stood more stern-faced guards. That was unusual. Samson and the other men followed Stark to the crematorium door for another day of stripping corpses and sorting valuables. Stark then turned, not opening the door. He looked at each of them, meeting their eyes as he spoke.

"You're not to speak of anything you see here today. You will only do as you're told, and you will do this without protest. If you even think of speaking about what you see today, I'll have you shot. Your life is worth nothing to me."

Samson met the German's eyes and—not for the first time—felt mortally afraid. This wasn't an empty threat, and he nodded with the other men. He glanced at Fischl, who looked stoic as he stood at the front.

Stark checked his watch, and then eyed the guard at the gate. The SS officer looked impatient, and the guard opened the gate a little, peering out. A faint rumble of engines could be heard in the distance. Stark looked relieved at the sound, and signaled for the guard to open the gate. The trucks made their way into the yard, and just as Samson was getting ready to start unloading whatever these trucks brought, he stopped dead in his tracks. The drivers shut down the engines, and a low hum of voices came from the trucks. A few guards approached the trucks and undid the tarps, revealing dozens of people crowded in the backs.

The guards opened the tailgates and told the people to disembark, shouting at them to hurry. As they did what they were told, Samson noticed these people weren't wearing the camp uniform. Listening to their confused chatter, he realized they were Polish civilians, most likely from the area around the camp.

When the trucks were empty, they pulled out of the yard, the guard at the gate making sure it was properly locked and secured. The people in the yard milled about awkwardly. The armed SS guards surrounding them stood by without a trace of emotion on their faces.

Stark directed Samson and the rest of his crew to a corner next to the crematorium building. "Don't get caught between these people. Wait for my instructions."

For a few minutes, nothing happened, and the people in the yard spoke quietly in Polish and Yiddish. Samson turned to Feliks. "How many do you think there are?"

"Two hundred fifty, maybe three hundred?" he said. "What are they doing here?"

Samson looked around the yard and focused his eyes on Stark, who talked with two other SS officers in hushed tones. "I don't know, but I've never seen Stark this nervous." He'd barely spoken the last words when Stark raised a hand, springing the guards into action. As one, they moved toward the group, truncheons raised, some waving rifles.

"Time to get undressed! Take off your clothes, put them on the ground!" As they neared, the people moved inward: scared, confused, suspicious. A ball of dread formed in Samson's stomach.

"Come on! Hurry up! Are you deaf?" The SS men raised their truncheons as they reached the first people. "Get undressed!"

The people in the yard slowly took off their coats or undid the first buttons of their shirts, but they looked around suspiciously. Samson caught the eye of a man dressed in an expensive-looking suit, stood proudly—back straight, shoulders arched backward. Behind his large glasses his eyes shone with determination as he held Samson's gaze. Then he bent down and started undoing the laces of his freshly polished shoes. He moved gracefully, like someone who had all the time in the world.

The SS did not. They started hitting people indiscriminately—women helping their children undress, elderly people struggling to take off their shoes on their own; it didn't matter to the men in uniform. Samson felt sick as people were beaten bloody. "Hurry up! We told you to hurry!" More people were struck, some landing on the hard cobblestones of the yard, not getting up. There were cries all around, and the yard was noisy. Samson looked to Stark, who looked furious. Next to him stood a man Samson didn't recognize, with a higher rank than Stark. He did nothing to contain his fury, snarling at Stark.

Within minutes, the scene in the yard had changed from one where people reluctantly undressed to one where people now tore the shirts from their backs in order to avoid the guards' vicious blows. After five minutes, 300 people tried to hide their nakedness with nothing more than their hands. Samson looked to Feliks, who seemed distraught, clasping his hands in a failed effort to hide his fear.

"Everybody inside, now!" Stark, accompanied by two troopers, stood by the door leading into the building. He looked slightly less annoyed now that the people hurried to get inside, desperate to escape the chilly May morning.

As soon as everyone had entered, one of the troopers closed the door. It was deathly quiet in the yard. Piles of clothes, shoes, and suitcases littered the ground.

Stark turned to Samson's group. "Collect those belongings and put them over there." He pointed to a corner next to the crematorium. "I want the yard clean within half an hour."

Samson didn't remember much of the next thirty minutes as he and his companions raced around, picking up anything in their way, amassing it into two big piles. When Stark blew his whistle, Samson snapped out of his daze. He turned to the SS man with his sweat-drenched shirt sticking to his back. Stark pointed at two large pieces of tarp, and they dutifully covered the suitcases and clothes underneath. They then returned to their places near the wall. Samson could hear the voices of the people inside the crematorium. They pleaded to be let out for water.

The gate opened, and the gruesome spectacle of people undressing before being herded into the crematorium was repeated. When the last of the unfortunates were inside, Samson's group wasn't required to clear the yard.

Stark bolted the door to the crematorium shut and disappeared atop the building's dirt-covered roof. Samson looked to Feliks, who had regained a bit of color in his face. He didn't dare whisper anything in the presence of the guards. They looked relaxed as they crowded around in small groups, smoking cigarettes.

A few minutes later, it started. People cried and sobbed as they pounded on the door. A few coughs could be heard at first, but they were soon drowned out by insistent banging on the door as the cries intensified. Within a few minutes, it became quiet, the silence only interrupted by an occasional rattle or faint knock on the door. Samson stood frozen, his neck prickling as he processed what had just happened.

Stark appeared to return from the top of the building, a gas mask dangling around his neck. He carried a tin—like one customarily used for foodstuffs—with a warning sign that read *Careful: Poison!*

The SS officer stepped down and approached Samson's group. With a careless flick of the wrist, he said, "Start sorting these belongings. I want it all organized before the end of the day. Banknotes, jewelry, watches on one side, clothing and shoes on the other."

Samson went about his grim task in a stupor. Together with his squad, they worked all day, methodically clearing the yard under the watchful eye of the SS. He didn't even notice the sun setting when they were ordered to clear out. Stark had long since disappeared, and they were escorted to Block 11 by two guards. To Samson's surprise, they weren't led to their old cell in the basement, but one with slightly more comfortable accommodations. There was a bunk for each of them, and food was waiting as they entered. The trooper shut the door, and Samson sat on his bunk, staring at the food. As the men around him dug into their portions, he took a bite and then hungrily shoved forkfuls into his mouth. He finished his food within minutes, then lay down on his bunk, closed his eyes, and fell asleep within seconds.

# CHAPTER TWELVE

Samson sat next to Feliks on his friend's bunk. They were still in the cell they were brought to after the gassing in the crematorium four nights ago. The first day after the terrible proceedings at the crematorium, Samson was convinced the SS would come for them next. Witnessing what had happened would necessitate that they would never speak about it to anyone. Anytime there was movement in the hallway, Samson expected the door to open and them to be led out to the yard.

When the door opened midway through the day, he'd closed his eyes and resigned himself to his fate. When he opened his eyes, he'd been surprised and relieved to find two guards bringing them a large pan of soup and stale bread instead. The men wolfed it down, and when night fell, Samson believed they might not be killed that day.

"Are you okay? You look a bit pale," Samson said as he patted Feliks' shoulder. It felt bonier than usual. His friend had lost quite a bit of weight in the past week.

"Mostly feeling stiff and bored. Even though I didn't think I would say this the day after they brought us here, I wouldn't mind returning to our old block, perhaps even joining the old work crew," Feliks responded. "What about you?"

Even though the work was grueling—and they would have to carry the dead bodies of those who didn't make it through the day back to the camp—they weren't witnesses to mass murder. "I doubt we'll ever be allowed back."

Fischl overheard them. "You have to stay strong. The best we can hope for is that they don't make us join those going into that chamber of death."

They were silent for a moment as the macabre words sank in. Fischl sat on the opposite bunk and studied his hands while he talked. "You know, I was a man of faith in my previous life. I spent my days doing the Lord's work. I can recite any scripture. And I think that's why he sent me to Auschwitz. I'm here to help anyone unfortunate enough to find themselves here."

Samson looked at him with astonishment and respect.

"Will you pray with me?" Fischl asked as he sat on the floor. Samson wasn't particularly pious, but the large man's energy compelled him to sit beside him. Feliks and the others joined, and soon Fischl hummed softly, swaying back and forth as he recited familiar texts from the Torah. Samson found a sense of peace he hadn't experienced since arriving. Fischl finished with a hymn and ended their prayer with an amen that sent shivers down Samson's spine.

The rest of the day, the men chatted, napped, and looked out the window as they fought boredom. They were surprised when a guard carrying another kettle of soup and hunks of bread entered in the early evening.

"Do you think something is about to happen?" Feliks said as he dipped his bread in the watery soup.

"You mean because this is the first time we're getting dinner? I don't think it's a coincidence," Fischl said, looking pensive. "Whatever it is, better make sure we eat while we can."

They did not need to be reminded of that as they inhaled their soup. Samson looked at his fellow witnesses of death. None older than thirty, and they were in reasonable shape. He'd spoken with most of them, and even though they all spoke of the scenes in the crematorium yard with the same horror, their responses were different. Out of the seven, two had withdrawn into their shells. They spoke only when spoken to, and then with as few words as possible. The other two pretended the killings hadn't affected them that much, speaking openly about it and theorizing what would happen next. Samson felt Feliks, Fischl and himself were somewhere in between. They accepted their lives would forever be different, but they tried to support each other and didn't speculate much. And when they did, they kept their voices down.

They finished their dinner and withdrew to their bunks. Sleep wouldn't come to Samson as the men snored around him. He thought of that fateful evening in Kraków, and wondered how different his life would've been had he not struck that policeman. He shook his head. It wouldn't have made a difference. He had already been picked for Auschwitz. As he fell into a fitful sleep, a small smile crept onto his face. *At least I didn't go willingly.*

Samson woke abruptly to the sound of the cell door slamming open. "Wake up, pigs. Time to get to work!" Stark's deep voice boomed through their cell.

Still wearing his camp uniform—the nights in the cell were cold and even though they slept in bunks, they had no blankets—Samson jumped to attention. Stark was already in the hallway, and they rushed after him.

It was still dark when they exited Block 11, and Samson had an unnerving sense of déjà vu as they ran across the camp, through the open gate, and into the crematorium yard. Rubbing the sleep from his eyes, Samson noticed a large contingent of guards spread out near the walls. This time, something was different. They didn't carry their truncheons or rifles.

Stark directed Samson's group to the same spot they'd stood a little under a week ago. For ten minutes, everything was quiet, the atmosphere tense. Then, the rumble of the trucks in the distance, and Samson sighed. He searched for Stark and the other officers, but they were nowhere to be seen. That was odd.

The trucks parked outside the closed gate, and Samson frowned. *Aren't they bringing them inside?* The engines switched off, and the gate opened. It took about half a minute for the first people to walk through the gate—unsure of where they were going, carrying suitcases and duffel bags, some even carrying toolboxes. Some wore suits, others wore the overalls of workmen. Women carried children on their hips, some with their husbands by their sides. They were ushered toward their places in the yard by polite guards, some even ruffling the children's hair. Finally, the last of the procession entered the yard, and the guards shut the gate somewhat impatiently.

The yard hummed with people speaking in Yiddish and Polish. This time, though, they seemed slightly more at ease, even though Samson spotted plenty of men eyeing the guards.

Samson felt powerless as he observed them. *What if I speak up? What if I tell these people they're about to be sent to their deaths?* He looked at the faces of the people crowding around and realized it wouldn't make a difference. The result would be the same. They would all die, including Samson and the six men standing near him.

A sudden hush descended over the crowd, and the eyes of the two-hundred-plus people focused on the man standing atop the crematorium. There, the man who'd observed the previous week's killing stood alongside two other senior SS officers. *Where's Stark?*

"Good morning, ladies and gentlemen," the man started. Samson's eyebrows shot up, and he glanced at Feliks. "My name is Aumeier, and I welcome you to our camp. You have come here to work for the good of our nation. Your contributions will be just as important as those of our soldiers on the front." He drawled his words, and Samson suspected he wasn't completely sober.

The people in the yard shuffled around uncomfortably. Aumeier picked up on the unease, his voice more soothing as he continued. "I know you're not all here by choice, but that is, unfortunately, the nature of war. We all must play our part, but I assure you that whoever works hard will find our camp a fair place." He looked around the yard and pointed at a man. "You, sir, what is your trade?"

"Tailor, sir."

"Excellent, we need plenty of those. I assume you know your way with both men's and women's clothes?" When the man nodded in the affirmative, Aumeier beamed. "Report to me right after your shower, please." He looked pleased with himself. "Everybody will take a disinfecting shower before entering the camp. This is standard procedure, and once you've done so, there will be a hot meal and all the tea and coffee you can drink waiting for you. We need you to be strong and ready for the day ahead!"

Aumeier's words had the intended effect as the crowd looked more at ease. Some were even whispering to each other, hope on their faces. They hadn't expected to be welcomed by such a well-spoken, polite German officer. Samson felt sick as they calmly started undressing, husbands helping their wives down the steps into the crematorium.

"Please remember where you left your clothes and bags, so you can proceed to breakfast as quickly as possible," Aumeier added for good measure.

For fifteen minutes, Samson had to keep his face neutral as people calmly walked through the crematorium door. Some spoke of the jobs they hoped to take, others were more interested in the meal promised after their shower. As the last of the condemned entered, an SS trooper bolted the door shut. At the signal of Aumeier, still standing atop the roof, the trucks outside fired up their engines.

A trooper wearing a gas mask handed Aumeier one and waited for him to put it on before returning with two tins of death. Aumeier then calmly walked to a chute atop the roof, opened it up and dispensed the greenish-blue crystals of death. He repeated this at two other chutes, and minutes later, the horrifying sounds of the dying commenced from below.

Samson closed his eyes and tried to block out the sound. Outside the gates, the trucks' drivers revved their engines. They had been left outside the gates on purpose. They would block out the sound of the dying for any early risers.

It felt like the execution of the people in the crematorium took longer than the first time. When everything went quiet in the crematorium, Samson struggled to breathe himself. He put his hands on his hips and took deep breaths. He felt a hand on his shoulder—Fischl. "Don't show weakness; they'll get rid of you just as they did with those poor souls." Samson nodded and tried to control his breathing.

At that moment, Aumeier stepped down from the roof and into the yard. From behind the building, Stark appeared and headed toward Samson's group. Samson braced himself. Before Stark could say anything, they heard Aumeier shout across the yard.

"Stark, did you pay attention? This is how it's done." He laughed, and some of the guards joined in.

The Untersturmführer looked annoyed but acknowledged his superior with a quick salute. He was curt as he approached Samson's squad. "Sort the belongings. Same as the last time."

# CHAPTER THIRTEEN

Joel opened his eyes and looked to the window. It was pitch black outside, and he groggily checked the watch on his bedside cabinet. A little past two. He buried his face back in his pillow.

"Open the door! Now!"

Joel sat up straight in his bed. The voices came from across the street. He was instantly awake, swung his legs out of bed, and moved to the window. He peeked through a crack in the curtains and saw four men standing at the front door of the house opposite.

"Hurry up, or we'll break it down!" The commands were barked in German, and Joel flinched as he realized the men weren't wearing uniforms—Gestapo. He remained crouched near his window and didn't dare open the curtains any farther. The windows of the nearby houses remained dark as Joel's neighbors prayed they would be left alone. Or better, that the men would leave.

The group's leader ordered the others to force the door open. They started pounding on the wooden door, the sound reverberating through the courtyard. The sturdy door held, and one ran off while the others lit cigarettes. They chatted casually for a few minutes until the man rushed back around the corner, carrying a sledgehammer. It took just four blows to smash the lock from the door.

As they disappeared inside, Joel prayed whomever they came for wasn't at home. He also knew the chances of that were slim. There was nowhere to hide in the ghetto.

The lights went on in the downstairs area, and voices echoed through the open upstairs windows. A few seconds later, all the lights in the house were on, and Joel heard the panicked voices of women. Mr. Tannenbaum was led outside in his pajamas—the man had lived in the house for as long as Joel knew, and he looked utterly confused. One of the Gestapo men remained with him while the others returned inside. Soon, four more men Joel didn't recognize were forced to their knees on the street, guarded by a single German wielding a handgun. They didn't move as they knelt with their hands behind their heads.

Inside the house, the panicked cries had changed into outright wailing and heart-wrenching pleas from the women to join their men. This went on for a few minutes until another Gestapo agent came out.

"The truck should be here any minute, Jens. Are they any trouble?" He looked at the man closest to him, muscular and in his midforties, menacingly.

Jens shook his head and shrugged his shoulders. "They know their place. If they try anything, I'll take care of them right here." He waved the gun at the men, and two cowered as the barrel pointed directly at them. This amused the Gestapo agent, who took a step closer and cocked the gun. "Not so tough now, are we? Should've thought about that before robbing a German store." He held the gun inches from the face of the man, who had closed his eyes. Joel held his breath—it wouldn't be the first execution in the street. A loud click echoed in the stillness of the night as the Gestapo man uncocked the gun's hammer. He spat in the man's face as he turned back to his colleague. "Pathetic."

The man collapsed on the ground with relief. Joel rubbed the scar tissue on the small of his back—it had been less than two months since his visit to the Gestapo basement.

The rumble of a sputtering engine announced the truck's arrival, and soon it pulled up in front of the house. The men were quickly loaded into the back, two Gestapo men joining them. Seconds later, the truck disappeared down the street.

The upstairs lights were switched off in the house, and the windows closed. Joel no longer heard the women's cries, although he hadn't seen the other two Gestapo men leave. *They must still be in the house.* He sat by his window a bit longer waiting for them to come out.

After five minutes, there was a piercing cry from the house, which was quickly muffled. Joel sat up and listened carefully. The soft, muffled crying continued, despite the closed windows. He then realized what was going on, and felt sick. He stood and considered heading over, but stopped himself at his bedroom door. *What am I going to do against two armed Gestapo men?* I'd be shot, in the best case. He sat on his bed, feeling powerless.

Twenty minutes later, he heard the creaking of the door of the house opposite. He looked outside to see the Gestapo men exiting the house. One of them seemed especially pleased, adjusting his belt as they disappeared into the dark street.

Joel spent the rest of the night tossing and turning. When the first morning light shone through his curtains, he got up and quickly dressed. His mother stood in the kitchen wearing her bathrobe—waiting for the water to boil.

"You're up early. You don't have to leave for work for another hour, no?"

"I couldn't sleep any longer, Mama." He sat down at the table, then immediately stood again. He was too restless. "Did you hear what happened at Mr. Tannenbaum's home last night?"

His mother gave him a blank stare, and he told her what he'd witnessed. She listened attentively, her soft eyes showing concern. When he got to the final part of the night, she held her hands before her mouth as she shook her head. "Those poor women. I don't know them, but I do know this is not the first time this has happened."

Joel looked up. "What do you mean?"

"There are rumors about certain Germans going around the ghetto and breaking into houses in the middle of the night. It sounds much like what you described, except from what I've heard, the men aren't always arrested." Her eyes glistened, and she turned away to take the kettle off the stove. "This sounds even worse, Joel, if that's possible. Those poor women are left to fend for themselves while their men are in some Gestapo prison."

"Aren't the Germans forbidden to have any sexual relations with Jews?"

His mother turned around, pouring watery tea into two large mugs. "Well, Joel, the rules don't apply if nobody knows, right? Besides, I'm sure they look away when it's not consensual." She spoke harshly: "They treat us as subhumans, so we shouldn't be surprised that they use us for their carnal pleasures when they feel like it." She set the tea down in front of him, and they were quiet for a moment.

Joel considered his mother's words. Typically a soft-spoken woman, she preferred to let people be and not judge too harshly. Most importantly, she wanted to be left alone. But listening to her this morning, he realized even his sweet mother was on the verge of breaking, and it could go either way. Joel shook his head and took a sip of tea, burning his mouth as he did. He thought of Moshe's words. *People are too afraid to stand up.* Their efforts at recruiting new members had been disappointing, and some of the original members had left. They feared the Gestapo were onto them.

He balled his hands into fists. If this wasn't enough to convince his fellow ghetto inhabitants to rise against the terror, he didn't know what would be.

# CHAPTER FOURTEEN

Agnes smiled as she left her favorite ward. When Marion introduced her to the elderly community in the hospital—now almost two months ago—she felt both nervous and excited. Marion assured her they were the sweetest people, but Agnes hadn't taken anything for granted. As she headed for the nurses' room, she couldn't imagine doing anything else with her life other than taking care of those people. Sure, she also helped out in the other wards—the children's ward her second favorite—but she walked to work every morning with a spring in her step, looking forward to seeing the people who'd become something akin to surrogate grandparents.

She remembered that she needed to drop off some charts and made a turn for the reception area, where they kept most of the patient files. As she did, she almost bumped into a tall man coming the other way, his head down as he focused on a book.

"Whoa! Watch where you're going," Agnes said, jumping out of the way just in time.

"I'm so sorry," he said as he took a step back. "I was so caught up in my own world." He held up the book, and then he looked at her with dark brown eyes that seemed oddly familiar.

"It's all right, you're lucky I'm not carrying anything sharp today,"

Agnes said with a smile. "I usually carry all kinds of tools around this place."

She caught his gaze, and he appeared unsure of himself. "Again, I'm sorry. It's been a long day," he stammered.

Agnes looked him over. Apart from the eyes, she thought she recognized something in the way he carried himself. *His posture?* She racked her brain, but drew a blank. She realized she was staring awkwardly. "I'm fine, really, thank you. It wasn't that bad. We just missed each other!" Surprising herself, she held out her hand. "I'm Agnes; I started a few weeks ago."

He shook her hand reluctantly. "Jacob."

"I don't mean to be rude, but what's that accent? You're not Dutch, but you speak my language," she said.

"I'm from Berlin, but I've been in Westerbork for almost four years now." He smiled as he regained a bit of confidence. "It's an easy language to pick up, especially if you already speak German."

"Maybe you can tell the other Germans," Agnes said, grinning. "They seem to feel a little different." She looked at Jacob, who was fumbling with his books. "So, what are you doing in the hospital? I haven't seen you before."

"Ah, well, my father works in the hospital. You may know him. Hermann Kagan."

"I know Herr Kagan!" *That's why he looks so familiar.* "Are you a pharmacist as well?"

He shook his head. "I've always helped in our pharmacy in Berlin, but I'm not qualified. Yet, anyway."

"Not yet?"

"Ever since we weren't allowed to go to school anymore, my father has been teaching me the basics. We had our first practical lesson in the hospital this evening. I was on my way back to the barracks."

*A lesson?* "That's great! Does he teach a class or something?" She spoke the words before she could stop herself.

"No, it's just me."

Agnes couldn't contain her excitement. "Do you think there might be room for one more? I was in my second year of nursing school when the Germans invaded. I still attended an underground class, but after arriving in Westerbork, I've really missed attending lessons. I would love to join." She was relieved to see Jacob smiling.

"I'll ask my father tonight. I would love some company."

She shared with him her love of working in the hospital, and he focused his attention on every word. Then she looked at the clock. "Oh my, I really need to get going. They must be wondering why I'm taking so much time doing my rounds. Hopefully, I'll see you in class soon?"

Agnes dropped off the charts with Marion. "Did I hear you talking to Herr Kagan's son down the hall?"

"Yes, I didn't know he had a son my age. Did you know he's teaching him basic medicine?"

Marion smiled. "Of course, Jacob is a great guy. He's in the builders' team, so he's often around to fix things. Was this your first time meeting him?"

"Yes, but I asked if I could join the class," Agnes said, a little bashful. "Do you think that was too forward of me? Should I have asked Herr Kagan instead?"

To her relief, Marion waved her hand dismissively. "I think it's a great idea. You're both interested in helping people. I'm sure Hermann will love having you in the class." She paused for a moment, then grinned. "As will Jacob, surely."

She spent the following evening in Hermann Kagan's office, which had been transformed into a makeshift classroom. He had been thrilled to hear of her interest and sought her out as soon as she started work in the morning.

After they finished the class, she walked out of the hospital with Jacob. He'd surprised her with his quick wit—he picked things up very rapidly. Most of the material they'd covered that evening she already knew, but she enjoyed seeing Jacob and his father interact. It reminded her of her own father, and his dedication. Even though Hermann Kagan was no doctor, she had seen enough of the experienced pharmacist to recognize he felt the same about his patients in Westerbork. Him being the first assistant to Dr. Brunner—the head physician—was no coincidence.

"Your father is an excellent teacher."

"He loves talking about his work," Jacob said with a smile. "And my mother is a teacher, so I'm sure she gives him a few pointers here and there."

"I think there's more to it," Agnes said as they walked away from the hospital. "I could tell by the way he explained everything that he knows that he enjoyed his time with us. Especially you."

Jacob nodded, and they walked along the camp's main road. "Back in Berlin, we all assumed I would take over the pharmacy, the way he did from his father. I knew that one day all of that would be mine if I worked hard enough. That future now looks very far away."

Jacob looked downcast, and Agnes felt his pain. "Don't give up on your dream. This war won't last forever." He looked up, and there was a sparkle of hope in his eyes. Encouraged, Agnes continued. "And while we're here, we can learn from him."

They passed some of the new barracks. "I've been working on those for the past two weeks," Jacob said.

"You built those in two weeks?" Agnes was impressed, but Jacob shook his head.

"They look more impressive than they are. They're drafty, and there's hardly any space for whoever needs to sleep there."

"So now that you're done with those, what's next?"

Jacob shrugged his shoulders. "I don't know. I am to report to my SS overseer tomorrow morning, and I'm sure he'll have new orders for me." He looked distracted as they walked on. *Something's weighing on his mind.*

He guided her to a bench, and they sat down.

"But tell me about you, Agnes. What was your life like before you arrived in Westerbork?"

Agnes smoothed her skirt. "Before the Nazis invaded, I was in my second year of nursing school." She told him about the underground classes and the Blackshirts. "I felt ashamed for leaving them behind at first, but now I realize things could've turned out much worse if I had fought them."

"You did the right thing. Mario did the right thing by telling you to bring the rest of the class to safety. Tell me about your parents. Your father was a doctor, right?"

"Yes, and even when he wasn't allowed to practice medicine anymore, he continued to help people in our home. They were often part of the resistance, but he would help anyone. That is how I ended up in Westerbork."

The sun crept toward the horizon, and they got up from the bench. Walking back to the barracks, she told Jacob about that fateful night they were picked up by the Grüne Polizei. As she did, she felt a tear rolling down her cheek. *Poor Papa, Mama.*

Jacob was shocked. "You were betrayed?"

"That's what we think now."

"I'm so sorry, Agnes."

She wiped her eyes and looked at him. "You're the first person I've told about this, Jacob."

"Your secret is safe with me."

They reached her barracks, and she looked at Jacob. She felt a sudden surge of affection for the man she'd only met the day before but with whom she already had so much in common. On a whim, she hugged him. "See you in class tomorrow?"

The following day, Agnes was instructed to report for roll call before starting her shift at the hospital. Usually, when she had the early shift, she was exempt from roll call, but this time her block elder was adamant; everybody had to receive an important message from the camp commander.

She and Yvette entered the yard, where almost all of the one thousand camp inhabitants had lined up. Their barracks was one of the last to arrive. There was movement in the front, and they quickly fell into place. Agnes looked to the group to her left, making out Hermann Kagan and his wife, but not Jacob. She frowned. *Where is he?*

As the small group of SS officers moved to the front of the group, Agnes recognized commander Deppner. She had no interactions with the man. He hardly ever left his spacious villa outside the fence, preferring to let his underlings carry out the day-to-day tasks. From what she'd heard, the man had a drinking problem, and even from her position in the back she saw his eyes were puffy.

Deppner mounted the small platform at the front and tapped the microphone. He appeared pleased and nodded at one of the men next to him, who shrieked his whistle. The crowd went silent, and after about ten seconds, Agnes heard boots entering the yard behind her. She didn't dare turn. She kept her gaze on Deppner, whose eyes were focused on the group marching in.

Before long, the group passed her, and she risked a glance. She was surprised to see not the neatly dressed SS in their crisp uniforms but a group of tired-looking men in baggy green uniforms. They marched to the front of the group and lined up next to Deppner. The SS officer leading them barked a command, and the men turned around, now facing the crowd of prisoners. Agnes' heart skipped a beat when the last of them turned around. It was Jacob.

Agnes met Jacob outside the camp commissary that evening. After he'd been introduced as part of the first *Ordedienst*—order squad—of Westerbork, she'd been dismayed. Jacob had been picked to police his own people.

They strolled past Barracks 35, the camp's orphanage, and spoke with Salo Carlebach for a few minutes. He was a teacher and friend of Jacob's, and Agnes enjoyed talking to him while the children vied for his attention. After they had walked for a while, they sat down on a small tree stump along the camp's edge.

Jacob let out a sigh. "I can't believe I'll be part of the squad transferring people through. When I arrived, I thought this would be a very temporary home."

"Transferring?"

"Those one thousand new people arriving from Amsterdam that Deppner mentioned won't be staying here. They'll be processed and sent to the next camp the same day."

Agnes was stunned, at a momentary loss for words. "You mean they won't get to rest here? Use the new barracks?"

He shook his head. "Those barracks we built aren't good enough to house people in for more than a few days."

Agnes stood up and paced in the direction of the moat, making sure to stay clear of the edge. The guards in the towers were instructed to shoot anyone straying too close to the moat. "Do you know where they're taken?"

"Deppner didn't say. He just told us they're going to work camps."

"Do you believe him?"

He thought for a few seconds. "The only work camps I remember hearing about were terrible. They weren't any better than prisons. I can't expect that has changed for the better."

Agnes stopped pacing and sat next to him. "I'm sure some of those people coming in tomorrow will be sent to the hospital as well. And when they are, I'm going to make sure we do everything we can to keep them here a little longer." She gave him an encouraging smile.

He nodded. "I had the same idea. I'm worried about some of the other men in the OD. They were talking about how they're going to impress the SS." His voice was shaky, and he cleared his throat before continuing. "I want to make sure the people in the camp see I'm not siding with the Germans. I'm not wearing this uniform by choice."

Her heart swelled listening to him, and she wrapped her arm around his shoulder. "I know you'll use your new position to help people; it doesn't have to be all doom and gloom."

"Let's get through tomorrow first," Jacob said with little confidence. "At least it's good to know you, Dr. Brunner, and my father will be waiting in the hospital."

"Not just me," she said, gently correcting him. "The doctors and nurses all have their hearts in the right place. We'll make their time in the camp bearable, however short it is."

Agnes put her head on his shoulder and as the sun nearly disappeared out of sight, she felt she could face anything as long as she had Jacob by her side.

# Chapter Fifteen

Samson sat on a crate in the empty crematorium yard. Fischl and some of the other men walked out, smoking cigarettes and chatting. For a day in the crematorium, it was as good as it got. There were no transports planned today, and they'd spent the morning working on various maintenance tasks. Samson had been assigned to scrub the floors, and dirty as it was, it was much preferable to cleaning out the ovens. Apart from the ash getting everywhere, there were always bones and other human remains that hadn't been completely incinerated. Samson had done it once and since did his best to be assigned a different job—any job.

There was movement at the gate as a small work detail carrying tool-boxes entered the yard. They were led by two guards who looked like they would rather be somewhere else. After reporting to the guards at the gate, they were directed toward the crematorium, and Samson watched them climb onto the roof. A flatbed truck arrived carrying wooden planks in different sizes. It pulled up close to the building, near the men inspecting the chimney.

Samson crossed the yard to the guard at the gate. In the weeks working at the crematorium, Samson had found some of the guards were quite willing to talk. When they did, they were a good source of information on what was happening inside and outside the camp. Today it was Jonas, a serious man around the same age as Samson. They'd spoken before, and Samson reached inside his pocket and held out a pack of cigarettes. "Want one?"

Jonas took a cigarette, and Samson lit it. "Say, do you know what they're here for?" Half the group stood about the chimney, talking animatedly, while the others started unloading the truck.

"Here to work on the chimney." Jonas took a drag. "They're going to be working on it today and tomorrow. Something about making it bigger."

Samson nodded. There were usually two to three transports per day, and the small crematorium struggled to keep up. A few times, they had had to shut down one of the ovens as the chimney bricks started crumbling from the heat. Expanding it would probably fix that. *Until they come up with a way to cram even more people into the ovens.*

"I think someone's looking for you," Jonas said, pointing across the yard. Samson turned and saw his Kapo, Mietek, exit the crematorium. He shielded his eyes as he scanned the yard, yelling at Fischl's group and then, spotting Samson at the gate, waving him over. "Thanks for the cigarette," Samson heard Jonas say as he reluctantly walked to the Kapo, who stood impatiently at the crematorium's entrance.

Mietek had been assigned to lead the crematorium crew after Aumeier's optimization. Stark occasionally came around to check on them, but he no longer bothered with the details of running the crematorium. Initially, Samson's crew had only been involved in stripping the corpses. Then, when they'd finished, another team of stokers came to burn the bodies. The SS must've decided that took too much time, and they had been merged into one unit, the crematorium now running 24 hours a day.

To make sure the men reached the required quotas, the young political prisoner Mietek had been assigned as their Kapo. Even though he was Polish, he was no Jew, and that set him apart. He had an unhealthy obsession with violence and pleasing his SS overlords—everyone working in the crematorium was a target.

On the first day under his command, an unfortunate prisoner bungled the loading of the oven. As he tilted the cart to dispense the corpses, he failed to notice the bodies had moved during transport. Two landed on the floor instead of in the oven. Mietek had been standing nearby and had exploded with fury. He'd beaten the man to death in front of the other stokers before stuffing the man's body into the oven.

"They need us at Birkenau," Mietek started without preamble. He looked rushed, his eyes shooting between them. *He's counting us.* "Okay, this will do. Come with me."

Mietek led them out of the yard to a large shed, where a truck stood waiting. Two guards stood by idly. "Took you long enough," one of them remarked to Mietek.

"Sorry about that, gentlemen. We'll be quick," Mietek said, his voice dripping with deference. They entered the shed, and his demeanor quickly changed. "Grab those barrels, quick. Quick. We don't have a lot of time."

Samson and Fischl together lifted one of the 50-liter barrels and awkwardly carried it outside. The other men helped them load it into the truck, and they repeated this for another four barrels. Mietek then jumped into the truck, and they followed as the guards secured the rear.

The drive to Birkenau took less than five minutes, and the men were quiet as the countryside rolled by. It was the first time since his arrival three months ago that Samson saw anything of his surroundings. There was little beyond the vast fields surrounding them until they passed a row of barracks. They had arrived in Birkenau. The truck rumbled past the gravel pits, where men wearing the same striped uniforms looked up before a shout from a Kapo returned their focus to their task. They had driven for another half kilometer when the truck stopped in front of two farmhouses. The driver shut off the engine, and Mietek banged on the tailgate.

"Everybody out, get those barrels to the back of the bunkers!"

Samson hadn't seen the bunkers before, but he'd heard of them. As the number of trains from all over Europe increased, the capacity of the gas chamber in their crematorium had proved insufficient. Two remote farmhouses near the Birkenau camp had been turned into makeshift gas chambers—bunkers. As Samson gazed at the innocent-looking buildings, he found it hard to come up with a less appropriate name. *What are we doing here?*

Mietek stood by as they unloaded the barrels. He snapped his fingers. "You can roll those to the back of the buildings." They struggled with the heavy barrels as they followed him. Samson caught Fichl's look as they neared the corner: there was apprehension in the big man's eyes.

Turning the corner, Samson smelled them before he saw them. He gagged and only just managed to control the wave of nausea rising in the back of his throat. He focused on keeping control of his barrel as he bent over and waited for the feeling to pass. When he looked up, the rest of his party stood about ten meters ahead.

"Hey! What are you waiting for?" Mietek yelled, as he patted the truncheon dangling from his waist.

Samson continued rolling the barrel, the smell of rotting flesh intensifying. As he joined the other men, he gasped at what was in front of him. The ground had opened up, and a mass of sprawled, partly decomposed bodies had risen as if from the depths of hell. It was hard to make out where one body ended and the next started. Flies greedily buzzed overhead.

Mietek seemed unshaken. "Let's open those barrels and spread that chlorinated lime over the pits."

*Chlorinated lime, so that's what it is.* Samson stood in a daze, not responding to the order as he looked at the remains in front of him. The fields of death stretched for some 200 meters, and he shivered at the task ahead.

"Hey, get moving," Fischl hissed as he opened his barrel. "Don't give him an excuse. You don't want to end up like them, do you?"

Samson snapped back to the present and helped his friend open the barrel. "What happened here?" The smell of chlorine stung as he breathed in.

"Isn't it obvious? They didn't bother burning the bodies but dumped them into these graves after they were killed in the bunkers," Fischl said, wrinkling his nose in disgust. "But they forgot about the summer temperatures. They didn't bury them deep enough, and now the dead are rising."

Samson searched desperately for some way to scoop the white powder from the barrels. He wasn't the only one, as the men looked around in confusion.

Mietek caught their looks. "What are you waiting for?"

"Our skin will burn away within minutes if we don't have any protection. Can we have gloves, please?" It was Fischl who spoke, and Samson held his breath. Even though his request was reasonable—they would be of no use to Mietek here or in the crematorium with severe skin burns—their Kapo was anything but.

For a second, Mietek looked on the verge of another rage, but caught himself at the last moment. He went inside one of the farm-houses and returned with gloves, flinging them at them. "No more excuses; get to work!"

Samson went about his task, generously sprinkling the white powder on the field of death. He prayed this would be the final denigra-tion of life in Auschwitz but knew not to count on it.

# CHAPTER SIXTEEN

I t was almost noon when Joel and his mother left their home. Today was Sabbath, and his only day off. It was usually spent with his mother on Friday evening, and even though they weren't very religious, she insisted on lighting candles and saying their prayers. Before the war, a hearty meal followed, but these days they made do with whatever they could find. On Saturday morning, he usually played football with Piotr.

Today, however, the game had been canceled. The main thoroughfare leading to the center of the ghetto was busy with people heading in the same direction. Most spoke softly, but they all looked as apprehensive as Joel felt. Today's summons could only bring bad news.

"What do you think they want to tell us?" His mother said, interrupting his thoughts as she gently took his hand.

"We talked about it at work yesterday, but nobody knew anything." He'd asked his overseer Andrzej after work, but he only told all the Jews in his detail that they were to report to the main square the next day. His mother looked worried, and he thought of something to calm her. "They can't take much more from us now, can they?"

She looked unconvinced. "It wouldn't surprise me if more people are moved into the ghetto. We may have to share our home."

"Where would the people come from? They've already collected

97

everybody from the nearby villages," Joel said, but his mother had a point.

A hum of voices greeted them as they turned onto a moderate square, where most of the ghetto's population had already gathered. There was a noticeable space at the front. A gallows had been erected. People kept their distance from the five ropes dangling menacingly.

His mother gasped. "An execution on the Sabbath. Savages." She whispered under her breath. She needn't have bothered, for no one would've heard her over the noise of the crowd.

In the distance, the bell tower announced it was noon, and a truck approached from the other side of the square. People made way as it honked its horn. In an elevated position in the back sat five men. Their hands were bound behind their backs, their clothes torn, eyes puffy, and noses bloodied. They looked apathetic; their spirits had already left their broken bodies. Men who knew they were headed for death. All the way in the back, Joel recognized his neighbor, Mr. Tannenbaum.

A *Kübelwagen* followed closely behind, the driver accompanied by two men who sat in the back. Around the gallows, SS troopers pushed people farther back, making room for the truck, which stopped directly at the steps. The men were hauled from the truck. Mr. Tannenbaum missed his final step and landed face-first on the square's cobblestones. It was so quiet on the square that even Joel heard the dull crack of his nose breaking from a distance. He stayed on the ground, and it took two troopers to lift him to his feet. The fall had rendered him unconscious, and he was dragged up the platform. Joel's heart ached for the man. As the nooses were slipped around the necks of the condemned, one of the SS troopers held the unconscious man in place. These were the men he witnessed being dragged from Mr. Tannenbaum's home in the middle of the night a few weeks ago.

The SS officers mounted the platform, steps creaking as they did. The largest held up his hands. It was unnecessary: the square had been stunned into silence.

"Jews of Ciechanów. You're here today to witness justice." The man's voice was deep, his words audible even at the back of the square. "Standing before you are criminals who thought they could steal from the stores outside the ghetto." He paused, letting the words sink in.

"Leaving the ghetto without permission is strictly prohibited. But these bold criminals went a step further. They went and robbed one of the stores in the center. As a result, a good man trying to earn an honest living, a good German, was robbed of his livelihood. We cannot have this; I'm sure you all agree."

There were murmurs in the crowd but not of assent. "I know, I know. You're all hard-working people, and you're just as outraged by the actions of these men as I am."

"Lies! Filthy lies!" The man on the far right of the gallows looked directly at the SS officer, then at the crowd. "Don't believe this filthy Nazi pig! We did no such thing!"

In a flash, the SS officer was on the man. He bent forward, his back to the crowd as he whispered something in the man's ear. Then, with a swift motion, he kicked the stool keeping the man's feet balanced from underneath him. The crowd gasped as he now dangled on the rope, his feet kicking as he struggled in vain to regain a foothold.

The SS officer stepped away and calmly spoke. "As I said, justice will be served. But, unfortunately, this man could not go more gracefully."

Joel's eyes went between the German and the man on the rope. As the noose tightened, his face quickly turned red. His legs threshed for another thirty seconds, his eyes bulging, cheeks turning blue. Then, in a final death struggle, his entire body tensed before his eyes closed, and his body went limp.

"Anything you would like to say?" The SS officer looked at the other three men on the gallows, who appeared too terrified to respond. The fourth man was still unconscious. *That fall was a blessing in disguise.*

The SS officer waved his arm at the men as he looked at the crowd. "Well then, let this serve as a warning to you all." He approached the first man, who closed his eyes as the stool flew from under his feet and off the platform. The second man looked at the sky, and the third found his courage in the end. "Glory to Poland!" His cry was quickly cut off as the noose tightened and the rope cut into his throat. As the men struggled and thrashed, the German moved to the unconscious man.

Joel looked to his mother, who kept her eyes on the ground. He looked to the people following the macabre spectacle unfolding on the scaffold with looks of horror and disgust. *It could just as easily have been them or their husbands and sons up there.*

The German paused and studied Mr. Tannenbaum. He spoke to the trooper holding him upright, who pointed at the side of the gallows. There, another trooper climbed the steps with a bucket of water.

*Oh no.*

As the officer nodded, the trooper took one of the overturned stools from behind the lifeless bodies dangling next to them. He placed it beside Mr. Tannenbaum and stepped onto it. He then poured the water over the head of the older man, who returned to his senses. Mr. Tannenbaum turned to the crowd first, then his eyes shot to the horrifying sight of his expired friends. Tears welled up in Joel's eyes as he forced himself to watch his old neighbor. Before Mr. Tannenbaum could say a word, the SS officer viciously kicked the stool from underneath him. He struggled for less than a minute, surprise etched on his lifeless face.

An hour later, Joel was back at home. He and his mother had left the square as quickly as they could. He could still see the broken men dangling on the nooses when he closed his eyes.

His mother placed a cup of tea in front of him. "Here, this will make you feel somewhat better." She sat down opposite him and wrapped her hands around her mug.

Joel picked up the tea and took a small sip. "We've never had hangings like this."

"Not this brutal, no." She took his hand and squeezed it. "But it's not so different from what they've been doing in the ghetto in the past weeks."

"They didn't make us attend them in the square," Joel said. "Or make those poor men witness the executions of the others." He stared into his tea for a minute. "Did you look at the faces of the people on the square?"

"I tried not to look at anything or anyone."

"People were horrified. When we walked home, I heard their anger. They said the Germans went too far this time."

His mother looked at him with sad eyes. "There's nothing we can do about it. They decide what goes."

Joel nodded, but his mind was racing. He'd seen the fury in the eyes of his fellow ghetto dwellers. Beyond the anger, horror, and desperation of their situation, the flames of resentment and insubordination were now being fanned by the Germans. If innocent people were hung for supposed, unproven infractions, who was to say the Gestapo or SS didn't knock on their door next?

Now was the time to try and garner support for their uprising. *If not now, when?*

# CHAPTER SEVENTEEN

A month had passed since the first transport from Amsterdam arrived in the morning. Agnes had started her shift in the hospital early, along with the other doctors and nurses. When the group arrived from Hooghalen train station—a two-hour walk, as Westerbork did not have its own station—people soon found their way to the hospital. Most sported minor injuries, and Agnes lost count of the number of blisters she treated. It pained her that she had only managed to save a handful of people from the train leaving later that afternoon. Despite Dr. Brunner's best efforts, the SS had insisted that everybody who wasn't in a life-threatening condition would board the train heading east. Those who couldn't walk were taken back to the train station in trucks.

Jacob had been responsible for those who could walk, escorting them to and from the station. He'd told her about the overflowing cattle cars as the train departed for a place called Auschwitz-Birkenau. He'd been especially shaken about putting 50 children from the orphanage on the train, along with his friend Salo Carlebach. Agnes couldn't fathom what use those children would be in a work camp.

Since that transport, the camp population grew steadily, with Jews from all over the Netherlands arriving in Westerbork. On Mondays, the camp inhabitants would be on tenterhooks as the dreaded transport list for the next day's train east was announced. The new arrivals, especially those without special skills, hardly lasted longer than a few weeks. Despite knowing that deportation was inevitable, she felt relief when the OD man left her barracks without calling her—or Yvette's—name that morning.

She met Jacob outside the camp canteen. "How did it go?"

"I was lucky. I didn't have many names on my list. But, I think Ethan had a tougher day."

Ethan was Jacob's best friend. They escaped Berlin with their parents in 1938, when the Nazis took Jacob's father's pharmacy from him after *Kristallnacht*. They hadn't waited for the Nazis' next move, and Jacob and Ethan had been part of the first group of people arriving in Westerbork. Ethan's cheeky nature was the perfect foil to Jacob's more serious character.

"I'm sure it weighs heavily on him." She took Jacob's arm and gently stroked the back of his wrist. "What does the rest of your day look like?"

He shrugged. "Probably keep an eye on the people in the new barracks. Ethan told me he's having trouble controlling some of them on Mondays. Often, entire barracks are on the transport list, and Deppner doesn't want any trouble. Said it would be on us if anything went wrong."

"Better get going, then. I'll see you tonight, yes?"

His face lit up. "Absolutely."

They kissed, and Agnes watched him disappear down the main road. She was impressed by how Jacob handled his duties. His job was the most unenviable one in the camp. On one side, he had to dance to the tune of the SS by keeping order in the camp. On the other side, he found himself part of the normal prisoner population while bringing the ill tidings of who was to disappear on the trains to Germany and Poland. Despite that, Jacob and Ethan had found a way to keep the other prisoners on their side. Unlike some of the OD, they were always polite and respectful.

She arrived to find the hospital buzzing. Nurses raced past her in the hallway, and as she passed the small reception area, Marion called out to her. "Agnes, I need you to help in ward three. A woman's going into labor."

Agnes felt flushed. "I have no experience delivering babies."

"That's fine; they just need someone to keep her calm. She's delirious. You can do this."

She was about to protest again when Dr. Brunner passed by. "Good, there you are, Agnes. Come, follow me."

They entered the ward, which had been cleared to make room for the delivery. A young woman lay in bed, and Agnes quickly sat next to her. She took her hand. "What's your name?"

The young woman looked up at her with big eyes. "Maria."

"Okay, Maria. I'm Agnes and will be with you until your baby arrives."

"Please make it come quickly," Maria moaned. "I've been here for three hours already. It's too soon. It's not supposed to be here for another three months."

She glanced at the far side of the bed and saw Dr. Brunner put on gloves. "It will be okay, Maria. Dr. Brunner knows what he's doing. He's the best doctor in the camp. Maybe the whole country. He's almost ready."

Dr. Brunner appeared on the other side of the bed and softly spoke. "Maria, you're going to be fine. I know your child is a bit early, but we have everything in place for your little boy or girl to be just fine, okay?" Maria nodded, pearls of sweat dripping down her forehead. "Good girl. Now listen. I'm going to complete a C-section, for your child's safety, okay?"

Maria's eyes went wide with fear, and she started shaking her head. "No, no, no. I want to be in control. I need to deliver my baby myself."

Agnes gently squeezed Maria's hand. "You need to listen to Dr. Brunner. He knows what he's doing, Maria. You want your baby to be healthy, right?"

The young woman turned to her and nodded.

"It will be over in a pinch," Agnes said. "I'll be here with you all the time, taking care of you. If you need anything, you tell me, and it's yours. Do you want some water, juice maybe?" Maria's grip relaxed a little, and Agnes nodded at Dr. Brunner. On his signal, another nurse administered the local anesthesia. Maria barely reacted to it, as Agnes continued talking to her.

"Have you already decided on names? Tell me all about it, Maria."

Less than five minutes later, Dr. Brunner held a tiny baby in his hands. He showed the little boy to Maria, who held out her arms. Dr. Brunner shook his head. "He's too fragile, Maria. We need to put him in the incubator immediately. I promise you'll see him in a few hours."

Maria started crying and tried to reach for her baby. With no feeling in her lower body, she was unable to move, and Agnes quickly grabbed her hands. "It's all right, Maria, you did great. Your little boy will be back before you know it," she said soothingly.

Maria was too tired to protest further, and she fell asleep in Agnes' arms.


Agnes quickly changed after her shift. The baby's delivery had been emotionally draining, and Marion had noticed. She'd told Agnes to take the rest of the afternoon off; she would cover the final round of medication in her ward later that day.

As Agnes headed for the exit, she walked past Dr. Brunner's office. His door was open and he looked up just as she passed. "Agnes, a quick word, please?" She stepped in hesitantly. "Close the door, please."

He waved her to a chair. She'd never been here before. It was sparsely decorated. Even though he was a doctor, he was still a prisoner.

"I was very impressed with how you handled Maria this morning. You really calmed her down and made my job a lot easier." He adjusted the glasses on his nose. "How long have you been a nurse?"

She fumbled with her hands. "I was in my second year of nursing school when the Germans invaded." She told him about her classes in Amsterdam. "And then I arrived in Westerbork. I'm sorry if I deceived anybody. I just want to help." *He's going to be mad.*

He looked at her for a moment, then a smile appeared. "That's quite all right, Agnes. I have to say I'm surprised all your practical training has been here. You're a natural."

She looked at him dumbfounded. *He's not going to fire me?* "Thank you."

"I'll make sure the other nurses help you with more training. I'll talk to Marion about it." He stood, signaling the conversation was over.

"Can I ask you something, Dr. Brunner?"

"Sure." He took off his glasses and placed them on the desk in front of him.

"I told Maria her baby would be fine, but I didn't know for sure. I just wanted to comfort her."

Dr. Brunner looked thoughtful and didn't immediately answer. Then, he stepped away from his desk and opened the door. "Follow me."

He led her to a dimly lit room housing an incubator. Dr. Brunner signaled for her to come closer. "This is Jonathan," he said. "Maria named him about an hour after delivery when she held him in her arms for a few minutes."

Wrapped up in a soft blanket, Jonathan looked even tinier than she remembered. "Will he be okay?"

"It's too early to say, but his chances are good. When Maria had her first contractions yesterday morning, I immediately reported it to the camp administration. I told them we needed an incubator for the baby to have any chance of making it."

Agnes frowned and looked up. "We didn't have one?"

"No." Dr. Brunner shook his head. "And to be honest, I don't know how they managed it so quickly. I didn't expect them to care about a baby, but here we are. They brought it in this morning."

Agnes was confused. Tomorrow morning a train carrying people in horrific conditions would leave the station, tearing families apart, and none of the SS in the camp would give it another thought. But here in the hospital, an incubator is rushed in to save the life of one prematurely born baby. She looked first at Jonathan and then Dr. Brunner—they also didn't understand what stars had aligned to provide this blessing. *We'll take it, though.*

# CHAPTER EIGHTEEN

It was still dark when Joel stood in a small alley in the ghetto. The streets were deserted, and he'd turned every corner with his heart in his throat—would this be when he ran into a patrol? Thankfully, he'd made it to the alley, and his heartbeat slowly returned to normal. He slowed his breathing as he waited for the others. *What's taking them so long?* He crept closer to the wall, hiding behind a garbage container.

After a few minutes, there were footsteps on the street. They slowed and turned into the alley. Joel sneaked a quick peek and was relieved to see Aleksy.

"Over here," Joel whispered. Aleksy had recently joined their group, and Joel had liked him from the start. Moshe had introduced him, and even though he was a fair bit younger than the others, at sixteen, he was extremely driven. When he joined, he said he wanted revenge. For Joel, that was plenty of motivation.

Aleksy crouched next to him. "Sergey isn't here yet?"

"I thought you were coming together," Joel said.

"No, he said he'd meet me here with you."

"He's probably overslept. Let's wait a few more minutes. Did you bring your knife?"

Aleksy lifted his shirt, revealing a large hunting knife tucked into his pants. "It was a bit bigger than I remembered."

Joel was impressed. "Where did you keep it?" A knife of this size should've been handed over to the Germans, just like all other weapons.

"We hide a few things in our attic," Aleksy said with a grin. "My father likes to make sure we're prepared."

Another man cautiously entered the alley, and Joel immediately recognized Sergey's bulky figure. He stood and approached the final member of today's mission. "No trouble on the way?"

Sergey shook his head. "There was no one on the streets. I was more worried about standing out too much." He patted the pocket of his pants. "Didn't want to get caught carrying this." He took out a small butterfly knife, flipping it open, its metal glinting in the faint light of the alley, before putting it away again.

"Great. Let's get moving."

They slipped out of the alley and onto a larger street. It was lined with narrow two-story houses, which were like most other dwellings in the ghetto. These buildings now housed anywhere between two and five families. In some, two families were even forced to share a single room.

Before long, they reached the ghetto perimeter, where in other cities there would be a wall or gate.

Joel turned to Sergey and Aleksy. "Last chance to turn back. Are you sure you want to do this?" They nodded, their jaws clenched in determination.

"We volunteered for this, Joel," Sergey said. "Let's go."

They crossed the street, and Joel navigated them to a house about five blocks away. Joel had been in this middle-class neighborhood many times, mainly before the war, although he'd driven through a few times while working for Kesler. Even though that was less than half a year ago, it felt a lifetime.

"This is it," he said as he pointed at a large house. "We should hide over here." As in many of the nicer neighborhoods in Ciechanów, there was a small park almost directly opposite the house. Joel had scouted the area the week prior, guiding them to a spot between thick bushes with a good view of the front door.

They crouched and settled in for the wait. On the surface, Borys

Zieliński appeared to be just like any other Volksdeutsche trying to survive, leading a work detail outside the city. They had run into Zieliński's group a few times, and the man had always spoken affably with his detail leader Andrzej.

Two weeks ago, Moshe came to their weekly meeting with news. He'd heard word of a Polish informer to the Gestapo. This wasn't uncommon, there were plenty of people looking to garner favor with the Gestapo by ratting out fellow citizens. This man was different, Moshe said. He served not merely as an informer but as an accomplice. He would willingly point out people the Gestapo selected, falsely confirming he'd seen or heard them admit to whatever crimes the Gestapo accused them of. From what Moshe had heard, the men publicly hung in the square a few weeks ago were victims of Borys Zieliński's lies. He was the Gestapo's top agent in Ciechanów.

Even though the group's plan for a ghetto uprising was gaining little traction, Joel and Moshe felt they couldn't ignore Zieliński's crimes. Joel felt his hands tingle. *Excitement or fear?* He turned to his accomplices. "Remember the plan?"

They nodded, and Aleksy said, "I'll remain on the lookout once he turns the corner. You will make it quick, right?" He looked at Sergey, calm and composed as he took out his knife again.

"It won't be the first time I use this. It won't take more than a few seconds."

Joel swallowed hard as he listened to them speak matter-of-factly about their plan.

Across the street, the soft creaking of a door caught their attention. Joel's heart beat faster—Borys Zieliński was a tall, lanky man, and he looked rushed as he locked his front door. He stepped into the street and headed east. *Exactly where we expected him to go.* The three men stood and emerged from their hiding place and silently fell in step a good fifty meters behind Zieliński.

Joel had followed Zieliński a few times prior, and he knew he would take a shortcut through a small alley farther up the street. He signaled to Sergey to up his pace and followed him, holding his breath. If Zieliński didn't take the shortcut, they would have to abort the mission—they couldn't ambush him in the middle of the street. Even though there were hardly any other people out yet, they couldn't risk witnesses.

Zieliński entered the alley, and Joel and Sergey sprinted the final few meters. He must've heard them, for he turned around and realized something wasn't right. They stood frozen for a few seconds as they eyed each other up. Sergey unsheathed his knife and locked it into position, and before Joel knew it, they were running at Zieliński.

Zieliński hesitated only for a split second before bolting for the other end of the alley. If he made it out, it was over. It was a fifty-meter sprint, and Joel was impressed by Zieliński's pace.

He was, however, no match for Sergey, who caught up with him halfway through the alley. He launched himself at Zieliński, grabbing his legs. Zieliński went to the ground face-first, and Sergey was immediately on top of him. Zieliński recovered quicker than expected, and he landed a punch to Sergey's ribs. He dropped his knife but recovered by grabbing Zieliński's wrists.

"Joel, the knife!" Sergey shouted as he struggled to keep Zieliński under control. Joel picked up the knife and looked at the men on the ground. He held the knife, unsure what to do. "Stab him! Stab him!" Sergey yelled. Zieliński was stronger than he appeared, and with an effort, Sergey pinned him to the ground, his knees digging into the man's chest.

Joel stepped closer and knelt, now inches from Zieliński. He focused on the man's exposed neck and saw the fear in his eyes. Joel wavered for a moment, but then he saw the faces of the men on the gallows and brought the knife down with force. His hands felt warm and sticky as he extracted the knife. Zieliński let out an ear-piercing shriek as the blood splurted from his neck. Then, without another thought, Joel stabbed again. And again. And again, until he felt a hand on his shoulder. He looked up to find Sergey looking at him, no longer holding down Zieliński. He looked down at the man on the ground. Terror-filled eyes stared back at him.

"It's done." He heard Sergey's voice in the distance and looked at his blood-soaked hands, still clasping the knife. Sergey took the knife and said, "This is your first time killing a man, isn't it?"

The question brought Joel back to his senses. He looked at the lifeless eyes staring up into the sky as the traitor's blood spilled between the cobblestones of the alley. He turned his gaze to Sergey and nodded. "We did it. We killed the bastard."

"Let's get out of here," Sergey said. "Best get back to the ghetto before anyone finds him." He looked at Joel's hands and pointed at Zieliński. "Wipe your hands on his shirt."

Joel cleaned his hands as best as possible before they left the alley together. Aleksy stood across the street, indicating all was clear. As they walked back to the ghetto, Joel found his hands shaking. He'd killed a man in cold blood. Oddly enough, he felt no remorse, no pity for the traitor Borys Zieliński. *He had it coming.*

# CHAPTER NINETEEN

Agnes met Jacob behind the barracks in the back of the camp. It was their favorite spot, providing some privacy as they overlooked a stretch of fields. The guard tower was just out of sight, hidden behind one of the barracks, and they sat down on a large tree stump.

"These transports are only getting worse," Jacob said. He frowned as he handed her a piece of chocolate. She loved it when he brought treats from the camp commissary. It was the one big advantage of his job: his wages were far superior to hers, and he could afford the store's outrageous prices.

"Our barracks are getting emptier every week," she said, taking a tiny bite of her chocolate. "It seems even the old guard isn't safe anymore."

Jacob shook his head. "I don't know about that; I haven't seen many of the German and Austrians on the list yet." He looked at her and raised his hands. "Sorry, I didn't mean it that way. I realize it's upsetting to see your countrymen and women being shipped off in these numbers."

"It's okay, Jacob. I know you mean well." Agnes sat a little closer and rested her head on his shoulder. He took her hand and placed it on his lap. They sat looking at fields beyond the barbed wire for a moment. *Freedom is so close, yet so far.*

"How do you think the people outside are doing?" Jacob asked.

"What do you mean?"

"Do you ever hear anything from the new arrivals? They must be anxious to talk in the hospital. Do they tell you about what's going on in the cities?"

"Most people usually ask about where they've ended up. They want to know what Westerbork is, how long they'll be staying, and after they've experienced transport day, they're asking for jobs in the hospital." She sighed. "Or any job, really."

"But not much about what's happening outside?"

"A man came in yesterday and asked me if anybody in the camp was connected to the resistance. I told him I didn't know, and he seemed disappointed. He told me he was part of the resistance in Amsterdam, but that he'd been betrayed." She paused for a moment, the memories of her father's betrayal flooding back. Jacob gently squeezed her hand. "He said most of the police have joined the Germans. They're helping them seek out people in hiding."

"The Grüne Polizei?"

"No, that's what I thought as well, but it's the regular Dutch police. The bounties for bringing in people in hiding, Jews and students, are so high that it's swayed most of the police. It's horrible, isn't it? People can't even trust their own police anymore."

"They had a choice, and they chose the wrong side," Jacob said as he fumbled with his uniform. They were silent for a moment, and then Jacob spoke, his voice soft. "Agnes, when all this is over, we will find each other, right?"

She turned to him. "Of course. But we'll still be in Westerbork together when the war ends."

"I hope so." He smiled, but he looked uncertain, his eyebrows twitching. "We need to make sure we remain useful. As long as there's a job to do, I'm sure we can stay off the transport lists. They need experienced people to run the camp."

"I know. Dr. Brunner has moved me from the elderly ward to help out in the intensive care unit. And I have additional training every Wednesday morning. I'm doing everything I can to stay useful."

"I'm so proud of you, Agnes. Look at you, you're fearless. You applied for that job without qualifications, and here you are, taking over the hospital."

She felt herself blush. "I'm just trying to help."

"My father says the patients love you and that wherever you show up, people get better. You have a gift, Agnes." He looked at her lovingly, and she felt butterflies in her stomach.

She leaned in and kissed him, enjoying the rugged evening stubble on his face. When they broke their kiss, Jacob looked at her seriously.

"But just so you know, I was serious about us being together after the war. So no matter what happens, tell me you'll find me. I promise I will do the same."

She smiled and held his face in her hands. "Of course, silly. But we're not going to lose each other. We're going to stay right here in Westerbork."

Agnes walked out of the intensive care unit and checked the clock. She had fifteen minutes to spare before they expected her at the maternity ward. On a whim, she decided to stop by the elderly ward. She'd built up friendships with many of the people in the ward, and she enjoyed catching up with them whenever she could.

Marion at the front desk waved her over.

"Agnes, when you have a minute, can you check up on Maria and Jonathan?"

"Sure, I'm scheduled there in fifteen minutes anyway."

Marion looked grateful. "That's wonderful; I overheard Dr. Brunner saying that Jonathan is strong enough to move to the regular ward."

Little Jonathan spent the first month of his life mainly in the incubator, but he had soon grown strong enough to sleep in a crib next to Maria. Maria and Jonathan would soon be allowed to sleep with the other mothers and children—it was a small group, but it would be good for Maria to have other mothers nearby.

Agnes entered the elderly ward. "Nurse Agnes! What a lovely surprise! Are you here to hand out some magic pills?" Mr. Janssen said.

Agnes smiled. "Not today; I'm just coming in to see how you're doing." She sat on the side of his bed. "Are they taking good care of you? Are you sleeping well?"

"Nothing quite like when you were in charge, but it will have to do, I guess." He winked at her. "When are you coming back to us?"

"I'm here now." She brought the pitcher to his bedside table and refilled his glass. He took a sip and smacked his lips. "You see, Agnes, this is why we love you so much. We don't even have to ask for anything."

She stood and walked across the room to Mrs. De Groot, a 68-year-old lady who was still quick as a fox. As Agnes hugged her, she heard a commotion in the hallway. Alarmed, she went to the door. Her heart sank when she saw half a dozen SS guards approaching. *Tuesday morning, transport day.*

Agnes remained in the doorway, eyeing the SS men, almost daring them to tell her to step aside. They marched past without as much as a glance. *Where are they going?* She followed them down the hallway and, to her dismay, saw them headed for the maternity ward. A nurse she didn't recognize must've heard them, for she stepped out of one of the wards. "Can I help you?"

"Where's the private room?" one of the guards barked.

The nurse looked confused. "Private? I'm not sure what you mean."

The guard shoved her aside and looked into the ward where the mothers and children stayed. Agnes closed in on the group. Her head throbbed, her blood pressure rising. *What are these brutes doing in my ward?* Before she could ask, one of the troopers barked a familiar name, and Agnes froze in place.

"Maria Prins, make yourself known."

There was silence from the ward.

*It can't be.*

The man's beady eyes shot back and forth between the women and the nurse. When all remained quiet, he took a step closer to the nurse. "Where is Maria Prins?"

She looked terrified and didn't answer. Agnes stepped forward. "Maria Prins isn't in this ward," she said calmly as the men turned to her. "And this is my ward. What do you want Miss Prins for? She's in isolation with her son."

The trooper looked confused for a moment, then quickly recovered. "She's on the list. She's coming with us." He shoved a piece of paper in Agnes' face.

To her horror, she saw Maria's name on the list. More shockingly was the name underneath. She looked at the trooper in utter astonishment, then realized the only way she was going to accomplish anything was by staying calm. She cleared her throat. "There must be a mistake. Maria and her son can't possibly board the train today. He's only just gained enough strength to join the others." She waved at the three terrified women clasping their babies to their chests.

The trooper tapped his foot. "Look, you're either going to show us where Miss Prins is, or I'm taking all these women instead. Your choice."

Agnes held his gaze as she tried to devise a way to stall the trooper. *I can't give up Maria, or these poor women in the ward.* Then it hit her. "Give me one minute," she said as she sprinted down the hallway. She made her way to Dr. Brunner's office, but when she knocked and tried to open the door, she found it locked. *Shit, where is he?* Then she remembered: Dr. Brunner would be at the train, overseeing the loading of the prisoners. Agnes' frustration started to boil over, her temples throbbing as panic gripped her.

"Agnes, are you all right?"

She had never been more relieved to see the soft, concerned eyes of Hermann Kagan.

"Herr Kagan, I'm so glad you're here. Please come with me." As she guided Hermann to the maternity ward, she gave him a quick recap of what had happened. By the time they reached the troopers, he was fuming.

"Who ordered for Maria Prins to be on the list? This is absolute madness," he said as he snatched the paper from the trooper's hands. Agnes had never seen him like this before.

"Who are you, exactly?" the trooper who towered over Hermann responded.

"I'm Dr. Kagan, in charge of the hospital when Dr. Brunner is away." Hermann wasn't a doctor, but the SS men didn't know this.

"Which would, in fact, be now." He scanned the transport list, his eyes widening as he spotted Maria and Jonathan's names. He flung the paper back at the trooper. "They're not fit to go on the transport, and that's final."

The trooper's eyes narrowed. He looked at Hermann, then at Agnes, then back at Hermann. "That's quite all right. As I told your nurse, we'll just take her replacements from the women in this ward." He stepped into the ward menacingly. "All right, ladies, pack your things; you have five minutes."

Hermann looked ready to explode and opened his mouth. Before he could say anything, a voice spoke from across the hallway. "That won't be necessary. I believe you're looking for me."

Agnes' knees felt weak. Standing in her hospital gown, carrying her tiny baby, was Maria. "I'm Maria Prins."

The trooper turned to her, ignoring Hermann and Agnes. "Very well. Get your things. You're coming with us. You and the baby."

"Where are you taking us?" Maria asked, not moving. *Brave woman.*

"You're going on the train. Better wrap him up warm. It's a long journey to Sobibor." The trooper spoke without emotion as he looked at his watch. "Four minutes left, better hurry."

"What use does a newborn have at a work camp?" Agnes said, her voice breaking. "Have you lost your minds?"

The trooper turned to her in a flash. "Watch your mouth, missy. One more word, and you're joining her." His tone was icy, and Agnes shrunk away from him. She looked at Hermann, resignation in his eyes. He shook his head. *It's no use.*

Agnes caught up with Maria as she entered her room. She placed Jonathan in his crib, and then started packing her belongings. Agnes awkwardly stood near the door, unable to find the right words.

Maria must have sensed her unease, for she turned and took Agnes' hand. "It's not your fault. You've done everything you could and more for us. Look at him. He probably wouldn't even be alive if it wasn't for you."

Agnes' eyes stung, and she swallowed hard, fighting back the tears. "But Maria, I don't understand how your name ended up on the transport list. Jonathan is in no state to travel."

"We both know the transport lists have no logic." There was determination in Maria's eyes. "But it isn't fair to those three other women and their babies to be taken in my place instead. I must go."

She slung a small bag over her shoulder and picked up Jonathan. He cooed a little, then closed his eyes contentedly as Maria pulled him close to her chest. She looked at Agnes with her big brown eyes.

"Agnes, take care of yourself and the people around you. My next step in my journey starts now, and although I don't know what we'll find east, I know it is the path God has set out for us." She gently hugged Agnes, and Agnes kissed little Jonathan's forehead. Then, Maria stepped out and walked to the SS troopers waiting for her. As Agnes looked on, the last thing she saw was Maria—surrounded by six large men in uniforms—escorted out of the hospital, holding onto tiny Jonathan. Agnes stepped back into the privacy of the small room and buried her face in her hands.

# Chapter Twenty

Agnes woke up early. She shivered as she pulled her blanket a little closer and listened to the sounds of the other women sleeping. Looking through the thin curtains in front of the windows, she saw it was still dark outside. Their barracks were one of the oldest in the camp, built by the first inhabitants in 1939. Even though it was sturdier than the hastily-built dwellings, it was far from comfortable.

The October cold had set in a few days ago, and the cracks in the building that provided welcome ventilation in summer now gave the cold free rein. She turned to return to sleep, but her mind had other plans.

The past month in the hospital had been tough. As the trains east increased in size and frequency—there were now often two trains a week—the number of people in the hospital shrank considerably. When Maria and Jonathan were selected, Agnes convinced herself it had been a terrible mistake. A week later, some of the sweet old people from the elderly ward were selected. Even Dr. Brunner had no explanation. The SS visited the hospital more often, questioning diagnoses and selecting people for transport almost at random. It was as if they didn't care if people were of any use in the work camps, as long as they reached the quotas supplied by Berlin.

Jacob noticed the same happening across the camp. He told her he didn't understand how some people ended up on the list while others didn't. He was concerned about the increased number of families being split up. When this happened, those left behind often volunteered to come on the train. Agnes suspected that was precisely why the camp command did this: it made reaching their quotas easier, and it almost looked like people willingly boarded the trains.

Yvette stirred and opened her eyes. She gave Agnes a sleepy smile. "Morning, sis. Why were you staring at me like a creep?"

Agnes suppressed a giggle. "I wasn't, silly." She looked at her sister with affection. *She looks more like Mama every day.* Her mother still visited in her dreams, and Agnes' heart ached at the memory.

The barracks came to life as the other women slowly awoke. Before long, the block elder switched on the lights, and the women climbed down from their bunks. Some dressed quickly to brave the cold to the washing block, but Agnes dressed and remained inside. It was Monday morning, so they would have to wait for the OD to announce the unfortunates who found their names on this week's transport list.

The atmosphere in the barracks was tense, and Agnes tried to stay out of everybody's way as she lay in her bunk. The OD man would be here any minute now.

"Hey, are you almost done with that?" Yvette asked as she pointed at a book on the side of the bunk.

Agnes handed it to her. "I've finished it. You can have it. It's pretty good. You'll probably finish it within a few days."

"Thanks." Her sister flipped through the pages. "Small print, great!"

The front door opened, and Agnes knew it was their OD man, Frans. He had a very peculiar gait, and his heavy boots amplified it. She closed her eyes and heard him clear his throat. The voices in the barracks died down, and all eyes were on Frans. Agnes didn't envy him; somehow, he always had extensive lists, and the rotation in their barracks had been brutal in the past few weeks.

"Ladies, I'm sorry, but I'm afraid I have quite a big list. If you could please remain quiet while I read out the names, we can hopefully get through this quicker." He slurred his words; he'd been driven to drink.

It was quiet as Frans read out the names. As he moved down the list, the murmurs, stifled cries, and sobs intensified. Frans' eyes stayed fixed on the piece of paper.

"De Leeuw, Amelie. Leopold, Ingrid." Frans turned the page, and Agnes' heartbeat increased. Even though she was an essential worker in the hospital, she knew that didn't give her any guarantees.

"Levie, Cathelijne. Levie, Judith. Markx, Yvette. Meijer, Gertrude."

The words came as a punch to the gut. In the background, Frans' voice droned on, but his words no longer registered. She turned to Yvette. Her sister sat wide eyed, her bottom lip quivering. Agnes opened her mouth, but no words came out, her head spinning. *This can't be happening.*

Agnes wiped the tears from her eyes as she led Jacob into the hospital and headed straight for Dr. Brunner's office. Navigating the corridors with Jacob was a balm despite her worries and fears for her sister.

After Frans left their barracks, Agnes and Yvette sat in their bunk, holding each other tightly. Agnes had tried to be strong, but her emotions had gotten the better of her, and together they had cried. Agnes couldn't let her sister go like that, and if anyone could help her, it would be Jacob.

Agnes knocked on Dr. Brunner's door and waited a few seconds. When there was no response, she knocked again and tried the handle. It was locked.

"We can't wait for him," Agnes said as her chest tightened. *We have no time to lose.*

Jacob looked thoughtful, then nodded. "Follow me. My father will help us."

They reached Hermann Kagan's office, and he stood up to greet them with a smile. It vanished when he saw Agnes' puffy red eyes. "What's wrong?"

"Yvette is on tomorrow's transport, Papa."

"We need to find a way to get her off the list." Agnes took a step closer to Hermann, who looked back at her sympathetically. "And we think her best chance is to be admitted to the hospital."

Hermann cocked his head, looking pensive.

"If we can convince the SS she's too sick to travel, she gets to stay, right?" Jacob said.

"We've tried this a few times before. You remember, Agnes?"

She nodded. Even people who could hardly walk were still taken to the morning train. Berlin's quotas were nonnegotiable. "But we've managed with a few."

Jacob looked to Agnes, then to his father. "Are you saying it's impossible, Papa?"

"It's not impossible. For Yvette to stay, she would need to be brutally ill, and that's hard to fake."

"Hard, but possible?" Agnes asked, feeling hopeful.

Hermann picked up a book from a small shelf next to his desk. He leafed through it, then pointed at a paragraph. "Here it is. This is a mix of medicines we use to clear someone's stomach. Look at the warning at the bottom."

Agnes gasped. "Internal bleeding possible? Isn't that dangerous?"

"Yes, but just taking these pills will make her look very sick. It's a risk we need to take."

Agnes turned to Jacob. "What do you think?"

"I think it's not up to us. Yvette should decide."

Hermann stepped to the door. "I'll get the pills, so Yvette can take them if she decides to go with our plan. She'll need to take them as soon as possible, so we can admit her and prepare her file to show she's too sick to travel. I'll be right back."

Hermann disappeared down the hall, and Jacob took Agnes' hand. "This is going to work, Agnes, I promise."

It took little effort to convince Yvette. She swallowed the pills in one gulp. "I'll do anything that gives me a chance to avoid the transport."

Fifteen minutes after taking the pills, Yvette started to feel nauseous, and Jacob and Agnes had barely gotten her to the hospital before she collapsed.

Agnes had stayed with her the entire night, and as morning came, she sat next to her sister's bed, gently stroking her hair. Yvette was still asleep, and she listened to her shallow breathing. *I'll never abandon you, sis.*

Yvette opened her eyes and looked alarmed. She sat up quickly, and Agnes took her hand. "It's okay; I'm here with you," she said as she gently squeezed her sister's hand.

"Oh, yes, okay," Yvette said as she sank back into her bed. "How long have I been out? I feel horrible."

"We got you to the hospital, and then you passed out. The nurses had a real scare, and you slept through the night." She handed Yvette a cup of water, which she gulped down.

"But I'm off the list, right?"

"Dr. Brunner reported you as unfit to travel last night. He's let the camp administration know."

Yvette sighed deeply, and Agnes smiled. "Now we just need to find a way to make sure you don't end up back on the list next week. But I think we might be able to get you a job in the hospital as Hermann's assistant."

Yvette didn't respond, drifting off again. Agnes adjusted her pillow and pulled up the covers.

With her sister softly snoring, she heard her stomach grumble. She left the room and went to the nurses' station to see if she might find something to eat.

In the hallway, she was surprised to find the head of the Ordedienst, Arthur Pisk, accompanied by a nurse Agnes didn't recognize, making his way toward her. The big Austrian hardly ever came to the hospital, and she stepped out of his way. From what she'd heard from Jacob, Pisk was a man to be avoided. Even though he was Jewish, he considered himself above the rest of the camp population and took to his job with zeal.

Pisk brushed past her without a word, and as she walked in the other direction, a chill washed over her. She glanced back and saw Pisk stop. Her heart skipped a beat—he stood at her sister's door.

Before she could say anything, he went inside.

"So, you're too sick to travel?" The words hit Agnes like pellets as she rushed back.

"Please lower your voice—she's in a lot of pain," the nurse said, but Pisk ignored her.

"She doesn't look in such a bad state," he said as Agnes rushed into the room. "I've seen people in worse conditions make the journey just fine."

"What's going on?" Agnes asked, her voice firmer than she expected.

Pisk turned to her in surprise. His eyes narrowed as he looked her up and down. "What are you doing in the hospital? You're not allowed in here, get out of here," he said.

Agnes realized she wasn't wearing her uniform. "I work here, but I'm looking after my sister. She's very sick. Dr. Brunner took her off the transport."

Pisk took a step toward her and raised his eyebrow. "Did he now?" He took a sheet of paper from his jacket pocket, handed it to Agnes and pointed at a name down the list. "Here's today's list, updated this morning. The camp administration rejected Dr. Brunner's *suggestion*. Your sister seems perfectly fine to me."

Agnes scanned the list and looked at the nurse, who seemed paralyzed by fear. *She's going to be of no use.*

"What's happening? What's going on?" Yvette had woken up and looked terrified.

"She's too sick. She can't even walk," Agnes said. "You can't put her on a train like this."

"Don't tell me what I can or can't do." Pisk spoke to Agnes with surprising venom. He turned to the nurse. "Get a gurney."

The nurse disappeared, and Agnes knew she couldn't win this battle alone. It would take the nurse a few minutes to get the stretcher. "I'll be right back," she said to Yvette, who looked ready to protest, but Agnes knew she didn't have time to argue.

She ran through the hallways to Dr. Brunner's office, and she caught him just as he was closing his office door.

"Agnes? What's wrong?" He looked surprised to see her. "Shouldn't you be with Yvette?"

"Pisk is here to take her to the train! He says the administration rejected your assessment. Did you know about this?"

Dr. Brunner looked horrified. "Of course not! She is in no state to travel."

They hurried through the hallways and reached Yvette's room just as two nurses moved Yvette onto the gurney. She was crying, trying to hold onto her bed but failing as the women lifted her. Pisk looked on with his arms crossed in front of him, a smile on his face at the grim spectacle.

"Put her back in her bed immediately." Dr. Brunner's voice boomed through the small room, and the nurses looked unsure. Then, after a few seconds, they moved back to the gurney.

Pisk stepped between the gurney and the bed. "She's coming with me."

"You don't have the authority in my hospital," Dr. Brunner said, taking a step closer to Pisk.

The Austrian looked perplexed for a moment, then cocked his head and smiled. "Doctor, don't overestimate your power. It's not my decision, nor yours." He pointed at the sheet of paper. "Commander Gemmeker personally signed the orders this morning. Do you want me to tell him you blocked his orders?"

Dr. Brunner held Pisk's eyes, then took the sheet of paper. He studied it, and shook his head. He turned to Agnes with sorrowful eyes. "I'm sorry, Agnes, I can't do anything else. I can't stop him from taking her."

Pisk looked at Agnes challengingly, holding her gaze until she looked away. He scoffed. "Take her to the train," he said to the nurses.

"Agnes, please, stop them," Yvette cried as the women rolled her out of the room. Agnes followed and held her sister's hand. She racked her brain as she thought of a way—any way—to stop her sister from reaching the train. She looked at Yvette, her eyes filled with terror as they rolled down the hallway. Her sister's hand gripped her tighter, and Agnes suddenly knew what she had to do. She stopped and turned to Pisk.

"She's not going anywhere without me."

# CHAPTER TWENTY-ONE

J oel stepped into the cold November morning and quickly closed the door. His mother was still asleep, as was the Novak family. The parents with two young children were moved to the Ciechanów ghetto a month ago, and this time Joel and his mother had to give up space in their home. Even though it was now more crowded, Joel had come to like the Novaks, especially the children. As an only child, he had never experienced what it was like to grow up with a sibling. The Novak children were five and seven, and he looked forward to playing with them when he came home from work.

He neared the ghetto perimeter, where his work detail was waiting. It had been well over a month since he'd assassinated the Gestapo informer, but every time he neared the edges of the ghetto, he felt a flutter of excitement as he relived that morning. During the first week, he'd been worried there would come a knock at his home, with Gestapo men ready to take him away. When that didn't happen, he started to believe they'd gotten away with it. So now, Moshe and he were busy planning their next step. More people had joined their organization, and he felt confident they could convince the Home Army in Warsaw to help them in their uprising, perhaps even by supplying them with weapons.

Joel was so caught up in his thoughts that he didn't immediately notice the group was smaller than usual. He searched for Moshe but didn't find him. They were supposed to leave any minute now. Scanning the faces, he saw the other men also looking slightly surprised. They were also missing friends. There was restless energy in the air as they talked among themselves.

"Gentlemen, please listen up." Andrzej stood slightly elevated on a small crate as he held up his hands. The murmurs subsided as Andrzej waited, looking uncomfortable. Joel felt the hair on his arms prickle up. "We won't be heading out today. You've probably noticed a number of our regulars are missing. They were told the news yesterday."

Joel shifted on his feet.

"You are to go home and gather your belongings and report to the castle outside town by seven tomorrow morning. There, you will receive more instructions." Andrzej climbed down from his crate and looked unsure what to do with himself. The men looked at each other, and for a moment, nobody spoke.

"What are we supposed to pack?" one of the men asked, and more men nodded, turning to Andrzej.

Their overseer looked like he'd just remembered something. "Just the essentials. Warm clothes, shoes, and any tools that might be useful."

"Where are we going? Should we bring our families?"

The questions kept coming, and Andrzej looked overwhelmed. Finally, he said, "Just report there with your families, and you'll be told what to do next. I'm sorry, that's all they've told me."

With that, he turned away and left them standing there. As they continued talking, speculating about what would happen tomorrow, Joel decided he was going to find Moshe. He would know what was happening.

"The Germans are emptying the ghetto. We're all going to be reassigned to work camps."

It made sense. Joel's work in the fields could easily be taken over by other people in the city or abandoned altogether. The work in

Germany's war industries would have priority, and they could use all the cheap labor they could get.

"But where would they take us? Have you heard anything?" Joel asked Moshe, who always knew a little more than most people in Ciechanów. It was Moshe who had found out about the Gestapo informer. Joel hadn't asked him how, but he was grateful his friend was always a step or two ahead of the regular chatter.

This time Moshe shook his head. "I've only heard of people who feel we shouldn't leave."

"Stay in Ciechanów?" The option hadn't even occurred to Joel.

Moshe nodded. "They'd rather stay here and fight than be taken from their homes."

"What do you think?"

"I think it's foolish. These people were nowhere to be found in the past months, when we were looking for them, and now they want to fight, without any preparation? I think they're just desperate."

Joel was relieved. "We need to make sure we stick together tomorrow. Wherever they're taking us, we'll be stronger together."

"Your house is on the way to the castle. I'll come and pick you up."

Joel nodded and shook Moshe's hand. "Be safe. See you tomorrow."


At almost five in the morning, Joel and his mother left their home. Moshe and Piotr stood waiting for them, each carrying a duffel bag.

"Where are your parents?" Joel asked Piotr as he closed the door, making sure it was locked. The Novaks were still asleep. They hadn't been ordered to report that day.

"They're meeting us at the castle entrance," Piotr said. "They weren't ready yet. So I told them to hurry."

Joel had stopped by his best friend's home after he spoke with Moshe. As expected, Piotr had also been sent home, and Joel had been oddly relieved. At least he would make this journey with his two best friends and mother. Whatever happened next, they had each other.

They started the short walk to the castle, and the streets were busier than usual as people carrying sacks, suitcases, and bags headed in the same direction. They were of all ages, ranging from families with small children to elderly people who would play checkers in the street on sunny days. They reached the castle to find a mass of people already gathered around the foot of the hill.

"My God, this must be half the ghetto," his mother said. "And so many children."

Joel made a quick estimation. "If I had to guess, there are at least a thousand people here." He turned to Moshe and Piotr. "It looks like they're not taking any chances today, though."

SS soldiers stood at regular intervals. They had their rifles out as they scanned the crowd. Joel noticed some people moving toward the castle while others moved in another direction, toward a small patch next to the hill. Some twenty trucks were parked there, their drivers hanging around chatting and smoking cigarettes while more troopers guided oncoming people toward the trucks.

"Come, we should report and find out what's going on," Piotr said, pointing to a row of tables. They joined the queue, and Joel turned to Moshe.

"Are you seeing what's happening up there?"

Moshe nodded. "They're sending the old people and children to the trucks. The younger people are sent up the hill."

"We need to make sure we're sent up the hill." He looked at his mother. "Mama, you need to make sure you stay with me, with the group going to the castle, okay?"

His mother nodded as they reached the front of the queue. Joel stepped forward, holding his mother's hand, and reported to the man sitting behind the table. He checked their papers, handed them two documents, and informed them without emotion, "You're going to the castle, your mother to the trucks." Then, with a wave, he dismissed them, but Joel intervened.

"We want to stay together. My mother can work."

"Not my decision. Your mother is going to Mława. To the trucks, now." He looked beyond Joel to the people in the queue. "Next!"

Joel's mother pulled him aside. "It's okay, Joel. I'll go to Mława. It's probably better for me. There won't be much I can do in a work camp."

"No, Mama, you have to come with me." He looked at the people heading toward the castle. Then, he spotted a woman struggling to get up the hill. "Wait here," he said to his mother and sprinted after the woman.

"You look like you're having trouble getting up," Joel said as he caught up with her. "Do you want to go to Mława instead of the work camp?"

The woman stopped and sighed. "I told the man down there I have a bad knee, but he didn't care. Instead, he said I needed to go to the work camp."

Joel produced the paper his mother was given and pointed at the trucks. "If you show them this, they will let you board the trucks to Mława."

"Are you sure?"

"They don't care about who you are; they just want to have the right numbers." Joel was bluffing, but the woman was keen to believe him.

She looked up the hill, the entrance to the castle still a good climb away and then at the trucks at the foot of the hill. She nodded, and they exchanged their pieces of paper. Before she left, she asked, "Why are you doing this? Who would want to go to a work camp instead of Mława?"

"I want to stay with my mother."


Fifteen minutes later, they entered the castle grounds, where they were told to line up. Joel stood with his mother. Piotr and Moshe were in the next line. They waited for half an hour and were told to stay quiet. As the last people entered the yard, an SS officer appeared at the front.

Without introducing himself, he barked at them: "You've been selected to work in service of the *Reich*. This is a great honor, and everybody who does their bit will be rewarded. But the time has come to leave Ciechanów. You will be well paid in the work camp, but you must leave your valuables here. We will keep them safe for your return." SS troopers with large sacks appeared at the front. "You will hand all your valuables and currency to these men. You are to keep no more than 20 marks. Anybody found with more will be shot."

Gasps went around the yard as people looked at each other. Joel glanced at Moshe, who frowned.

The first of the soldiers approached the people in the front. The people looked unsure, reluctant to hand over their valuables. The SS trooper realized this and without delay, smashed the back of his rifle into the ribs of the man closest to him. The man screamed in pain as he doubled over and collapsed on the sand, clutching his chest. The soldier kicked out at his head, which the man then tried to shield, exposing the rest of his body. The SS trooper kicked furiously until the man stopped moving.

A hush fell over the yard, interrupted only by a few people softly crying. The SS man then looked up and held out the empty sack in front of the next person, who quickly reached into her pockets. Less than fifteen minutes later, everyone in the yard had been relieved of their valuables.

Two hours later, after a short march from the castle to Ciechanów's small train station, Joel found himself squeezed between sixty other people in a cattle car somewhere south of the city. His mother was next to him, and he'd seen Piotr and Moshe board the car behind them.

The air in the car was heavy. The small ventilation holes in the roof did little to provide fresh air in the overcrowded space. A man coughed, and on the far side of the car an argument erupted over someone taking too much space.

"Are you all right, Mama?" He turned his face to his mother's. She looked pale and tired. Joel hoped they would reach their destination soon.

"Don't worry about me," she said softly. "I'm glad we stayed together."

Joel sighed. When they left the castle, one of the SS troopers had stopped his mother and asked her for her papers. When she'd shown him the slip Joel had exchanged with the woman earlier, his heart stopped. He'd waited with his mother as the trooper inspected it, expecting him to ask for her identity papers as well. To his surprise, the trooper was satisfied with her small slip of paper, and they continued.

As the train drummed on, Joel wondered where they were headed.

The train stopped a few hours later, but nothing happened. Joel couldn't distinguish anything but fields through the cracks in the car's walls. People cried out for water, to be let out to relieve themselves, but their words fell on deaf ears. The SS troopers climbed off the train and stretched their legs, smoking cigarettes and chatting. They stood in the field for two hours as two large trains roared past, heading east.

After a third train passed, the troopers climbed back aboard, and the train slowly resumed its way south. As the sun set, the train continued, and Joel closed his eyes, drifting into an uncomfortable sleep sandwiched between people he barely knew.

The train didn't stop the next day, either. A number of people had fainted, and some of the arguments had turned into fights. Other passengers had intervened, but some of the men stood with blood-crusted faces. The smell in the car had also worsened. The empty bucket provided for people to relieve themselves had overflowed and had spilled into the car. People no longer bothered using it.

It was dark when the train stopped, and the engine let out a long, almost content sigh, followed by a long, sharp whistle they hadn't heard before. Joel was instantly alert, forgetting his hunger and thirst. *Something is happening.* The troopers jumped off the train and were soon joined by more. Excited barking was all around them. *Dogs.*

In a flash, the darkness was replaced by bright lights. More voices, and then the doors of the car opened. The light was even brighter now, and Joel squinted as he struggled to make out the faces of the men yelling at them. "Everybody out! Now! Quick! Quick! Come on!"

The first people jumped onto the platform, instantly herded away to form rows of five. The platform transformed into a hive of activity, with dozens of armed SS troopers crowding around, harrying people into position. Joel was grabbed by the arm and pulled to a group of four young men, completing their row. His mother stood two rows behind him, and as their eyes met, his heart broke. His mother looked terrified, tears in her eyes, hands shaking.

He looked across the rows but didn't see Piotr or Moshe. As the train cars emptied and the neat rows of five stretched down the platform, men in striped uniforms boarded the cars. They started unloading the bodies of the dead, and for the first time, Joel realized it hadn't just been the smell of human excrement that had tainted the air.

Then, things moved very quickly. An SS man wearing an expensive-looking coat stood in the middle of the platform. He was surrounded by a number of troopers and the rows of people were marched by him. With a flick of the wrist, he sent the person ahead of him left or right.

Joel saw that stronger men and women were sent to the right. Other women, children, and the elderly were sent to the left. He saw trucks waiting for them beyond the rows of people marching left. Those who struggled to climb aboard were beaten by the troopers crowding around, yelling at them to get in.

When Joel approached the man, his heart was in his throat. His best chance of survival was to be sent to the right. He stood behind a man of about fifty, who looked in poor health. He could see the man shaking at the selection process.

From close by, Joel could see that the man in the expensive coat was much younger than he initially thought. He was in his early thirties, with a strong jawline and brown hair perfectly brushed backward. He looked like an intellectual, out of place on the ramp of a work camp. He swiftly jerked his thumb left as the fate of the man ahead of Joel was decided.

Joel stepped forward and looked into the man's eyes. There was no emotion as he appraised Joel, taking his arms and legs in a fraction longer. Then, the flick of his wrist. Right.

He walked away slowly, feeling no relief. As the man continued his selection, Joel looked at his mother in the next row. Their eyes met, and he saw resignation on her face. *She knows.*

Joel slowed his pace even more, carefully checking on the troopers, who looked eager to beat anyone stepping out of line.

His mother walked forward, facing the man who would decide her fate. As the man's eyes inspected his mother, Joel gritted his teeth. *Why did I insist in Ciechanów that she join me ?* He looked at the ghoulish scene surrounding him. More bodies were carried from the train cars; families were torn apart as husbands and fathers were sent to the right, watching helplessly as their wives and children disappeared to the trucks on the left. Joel felt his eyes sting, but he knew he was powerless to do anything.

The man flicked his wrist, and Joel closed his eyes for a second. When he opened them again, his mother stood in front of the man—she hadn't moved. One of the troopers yelled something, but she ignored him. Joel met his mother's eyes, and he could see she was struggling to contain her emotions. She had her hands balled into fists.

"Be strong, my son. I love you." She mouthed the words before the trooper roughly pulled her away. She held her head high as she was marched to the trucks on the left side of the platform.

# PART II

AUSCHWITZ-BIRKENAU
CONCENTRATION CAMP,
POLAND
JUNE 1943

# Chapter Twenty-Two

S amson was ready before the cell door opened. He sat on his bunk with a small bag containing all his belongings. He treasured his well-worn toothbrush most of all. There were few things he could control in the hell of Auschwitz, but at least he always had a toothbrush.

Today's guard was new and calmly told them to get out of the cell. The men opened their bags for a cursory inspection, then followed a second guard down the hallway and stairs before stepping through Block 11's front door. Samson savored the warm June sunshine as he was led to the truck parked outside. The driver stood talking to two guards. They ignored Samson, and he wondered if they realized the men walking out had been the block's longest surviving residents. For most people entering Block 11 it meant one of two things: torture and death, or torture and a return to the regular camp to die from exhaustion a few weeks later. It had been neither for Samson and the four men walking alongside him. Their cell in Block 11 had been home for over a year.

Now, climbing aboard the truck, Samson wondered what was waiting for him beyond the gates of Auschwitz. Feliks was last to board, entering just before the engine roared into life.

"Can you believe we've survived Block 11?" Feliks asked over the engine's rumble as they pulled onto the camp's main thoroughfare.

Samson glanced at the gallows, used more frequently than when he arrived and shook his head. "After all the death we've witnessed, I thought we would go down with the crematorium. But it seems they have other plans for us." They approached the camp's main gate and Samson looked to his right. The large, red-brick chimney of the place he'd spent most of his waking hours stood abandoned. No longer did the fires of the ovens below burn almost continuously, nor were hundreds of people crammed into the small gas chamber daily. Crematorium 1 stood as if nothing had ever happened, weeds spreading from the grass-covered roof.

The truck pulled onto the main road, heading east. It had been months since Samson had been in Birkenau, and he blinked hard as it came into view. Rows of neatly aligned barracks stretched as far as Samson could see. A double layer of barb wire fences surrounded the camp, creating a 50-meter-wide no-man's-land surrounded by watchtowers. Atop each tower, eagle-eyed guards trained their rifles on the prisoners below. The truck passed through the camp's main gatehouse, the guards waving them through without delay. They drove along the camp's main passageway, separated from the barracks by barbed wire. To his right, on the largest side of the camp, men wandered around pretending to focus on an invisible task.

On the left, Samson had to look twice to ensure his eyes weren't deceiving him. Behind the barbed wire stood groups of sorry-looking creatures. It was hard to make out from their gaunt faces, shaved heads, ragged clothing, and malnourished bodies that these were in fact, women. Samson looked at them in shock as his throat tightened.

The truck slowed and turned into the men's camp. As it did, Samson caught sight of two enormous chimneys at the end of the road. One of them belched dark plumes of smoke; the other stood idle.

Feliks was looking in the same direction. "I think I know where we're going."

The next morning, Samson awoke early to a lively barracks. The men around him climbed down from their bunks, not trying to be quiet or keep their voices down. Some shouted across the room to their friends, urging them to hurry. A few washed at the water station in the front, but most didn't bother. Samson rubbed the sleep from his eyes and found Feliks standing next to their bunk.

"You better hurry if you want to clean yourself up before roll call. We're expected in ten minutes." Feliks was dressed and looked remarkably fresh.

The crew working in the crematorium were Poles, and Samson had talked to a few of them. They were happy to have reinforcements, explaining the workload had gone up dramatically in the past weeks. When Samson told them he spent over a year in the old crematorium, he saw respect in their eyes. They asked him all sorts of questions, but mostly how he'd survived for so long. He admitted he didn't have an answer to that question other than simply doing what he was told.

After he washed his face and brushed his teeth he stepped out of the block. The sun shone brightly, and he shielded his eyes as he looked into the yard. Their block was surrounded by a ten-foot-high fence. A single gate, manned by a bored guard, separated them from the rest of the camp. This was no Block 11. Their barracks housed over 200 men, and he was encouraged to see plenty of room for interaction. No longer were his evenings and nights confined to a small cell.

"They finished construction on the crematoria last week. You'll be in number 2 and 3, most likely. They're low on stokers." A man with a confident demeanor was talking to Feliks, and Samson joined them. "And they're the largest of the four crematoria, so I'm sure they've sent you here because of your experience."

"How long have you been in the camp?" Feliks asked the man.

He frowned. "I came in early 1942, and, unlike you, I was immediately placed in Birkenau. I've seen it grow from a few barracks to what it is today. Of course, they had us work in the bunkers first." His mouth twitched as he continued. "The horrors I've seen there. The endless stream of people led into the farmhouses. And when you couldn't burn them quickly enough in the crematorium anymore ... well, we had to be creative."

"The pits?" Samson asked. He shuddered as the bloated corpses of last summer came to mind.

The man nodded. "After last summer, we were told we needed to burn all the bodies behind the bunkers. Can you imagine? Those people waiting outside could see the smoke only fifty meters away from them. We had to use all sorts of excuses to explain what was happening as we led them into the bunkers." The man's gaze was distant, reliving the scenes. Then he snapped back to reality and held out his hand. "My name is Kaminski. Just reach out to me if you need anything. We can use your experience here in the *SK*—the *Sonderkommando*."

*Sonderkommando. So that's what we're called here?* Samson introduced himself and opened his mouth when there was a sharp whistle from the gate.

"Better get ready for your first day," Kaminski said as he turned to the source of the sound. The other men in the yard did the same, and before long, 200 men stood neatly lined up. Samson was surprised to see a modest number of guards near the gate—it didn't look like they expected any trouble. But, as the Kapos inspected the prisoners, Samson's heart skipped a beat when he saw a familiar face—Mietek.

He hadn't seen the young Pole since the start of spring as operations in their crematorium wound down. Even though Samson had suspected Mietek would be moving to Birkenau, he'd hoped the cruel man would be assigned to a different area.

Samson turned to Feliks, standing next to him. "Do you see him?"

"Mietek, yes," Feliks hissed back. "Maybe we won't have too much to do with him. Keep your head down."

Roll call was mercifully quick, and the Kapos called their men to head out. Samson was relieved to see Mietek leaving with a different group. *Hopefully I won't see him anytime soon.* Samson followed the rest of his squad of 50 out the gate. As they marched through the men's camp for the first time, he eyed the other groups. He realized he'd missed most of Birkenau's prisoners when he arrived in the truck yesterday. Looking at the men in the work details, many looked just like the apparitions of the women's camp. They shuffled after their Kapos and SS overseers in a stupefied manner, their eyes fixed on the ground, each following the feet of the man ahead. The few that made eye contact had a lifeless expression, no doubt the result of a combination of grueling six-day workweeks and too little to eat. Every day was another closer to the day they would either collapse or go to bed never to wake up again.

Samson's detail turned right, where most others headed left in the direction of the gatehouse. Those details would spend hours marching to the mines, fields, and factories. Samson's destination loomed up a mere 500 meters in the distance. The chimneys of all but one of the crematoria belched thick, dark smoke into the morning sky. The men around Samson looked much stronger than the regular prisoners: the Nazis needed those working in the Sonderkommando to be as strong as possible. They were carrying out the Reich's essential work.

The work detail ahead of them passed crematoria 2 and 3. One of the men walking next to Samson caught his look. "They're off to the bunkers and pits. There's still plenty of work to do there. Cleaning up, mostly," he said, grimacing. "Just be glad you're not assigned there. Now that we no longer have to burn people there, the SS decided all traces of their existence must be removed."

Samson nodded but said nothing. He had a good idea of what was happening behind the bunkers. They turned left and entered a barbed-wire-enclosed yard. The large red-brick chimney he'd seen from a distance rose into the sky. Attached to it was a building built with the same red bricks.

"That's crematorium 2," the man who spoke earlier said. "We haven't used it yet, but I'm sure that will change now that you're here."

The building was three times larger than Auschwitz's crematorium 1. "How many ovens?"

"Fifteen."

Samson looked at him open mouthed. *Fifteen ovens?* He made a quick calculation. If the setup was comparable to the old crematorium, they would be able to burn close to 1,500 corpses a day. That was five times what the old crematorium could handle. And there were four crematoria in Birkenau. Samson winced, his hands shaking.

"Listen up, prisoners!" A loud, clear voice boomed across the yard, attracting the attention of the assembled men. They crowded closer to the man wearing an SS officer's uniform. "We need to prepare crematorium 2 for operation, and Marek here will oversee the duties of the men working outside. I'll be inside, inspecting the ovens and changing rooms."

Two men stood on either side of the officer, and Marek gestured for the men on the left of the group to follow him. Samson and Feliks were among them and followed the young Kapo.

They were handed shovels and directed toward a mound of dirt next to the crematorium. As they got closer, the sand under their feet made way for concrete.

"Spread out the dirt, so the roof isn't visible anymore," Marek said as they walked over the concrete slab. Samson immediately recognized the cylinders sticking out at regular intervals—an underground gas chamber.

They spent most of the morning covering the gas chamber's roof with sand and dirt. The sun was high in the sky and Samson was sweating when Marek called for a break. There was a water faucet by the side of the crematorium, and Samson queued up along with the other men. After he drank his fill, he sat near the pile of dirt. There was nowhere to hide from the scorching midday sun.

"It's unbelievable, isn't it?" Feliks sat next to him. "How big do you think the chamber is?"

Samson had thought about it as he was shoveling dirt. "At least three times bigger than the entire crematorium in Auschwitz. And there are fifteen ovens in the crematorium."

"Fifteen? That's insane." Feliks was quiet as his eyes went over the building, then to the opposite crematorium. "And I suppose that's a copy of this one?"

"I would think so."

# Chapter Twenty-Three

The journey had been hell. Only half of the sixty people in Agnes' car made it to Auschwitz alive. The October weather had been brutal, the cold wind buffeting people in the car through the many cracks, slicing through their clothes as the train thundered on. The older people had been the first to perish. Acute pneumonia without treatment had taken many overnight. The train stopped on side tracks in open fields for the night, exposing its occupants to the elements. When a snowstorm blanketed the train on the second night, many people rested their heads for the last time, not rising in the morning. Agnes had only survived because she had hastily stuffed several blankets in a bag upon leaving the hospital. She had kept Yvette and herself warm throughout the journey and had fought off anyone trying to take their lifeline.

On arrival, nearly four days after leaving Westerbork, the doors had opened, and the bodies of the dead spilled onto the platform. There, Agnes had caught her first glimpse of the hell she'd arrived in. Stepping onto the platform, she had supported Yvette as they lined up. Between the chaos of the soldiers barking at people to move along and the dogs straining on their leashes, baring their fangs at anyone who came too close, a man suddenly appeared in front of her. He wore a striped uniform, and he simply said, "If you want to live, you can't stay with her."

The man's ominous words rang in her ears, and she looked around for someone to help her, to take Yvette to a hospital or anywhere she could get medical aid.

As she stood in her line of five, a man wearing a doctor's coat passed by. She broke from her line and spoke to him in German before the trooper accompanying him could do anything. "Sir, please, my sister is very ill. I'm a trained nurse; she needs help. Can I please take her to the camp infirmary?"

The trooper took a step toward Agnes, but the doctor stopped him. He looked at Agnes curiously. "A trained nurse, you say? And you came from Westerbork?" His pronunciation of the camp's name was off, but Agnes nodded.

"Me and my sister. The people in Westerbork said there would be care for her once we arrived." She held her breath as the doctor looked at Yvette and then returned to Agnes. To her relief, he nodded and spoke to the trooper.

"Take her sister for a check-up in Birkenau. And make sure she has a shower before she is placed in quarantine." The doctor turned back to Agnes. "Don't worry, they will take good care of her, and you can visit her once she's properly recovered. Now, for yourself."

Agnes had trouble keeping her eyes focused on the doctor as the trooper summoned two of the men in striped uniforms carrying a stretcher.

"Your German is rather good, from what I can tell. I assume you also speak Dutch?"

"Yes, I speak both languages. I'm from Amsterdam."

He clapped his hands sharply. "Then you're perfect. We have a lot of Dutch patients in the hospital in Auschwitz. You would be a true asset." Then, without waiting for her response, he whistled sharply at a nearby trooper. "You, take this woman to the hospital in One. Tell Dr. Wirths I sent her."

The trooper clicked his boots. "At once, Dr. Mengele."

Agnes blinked her eyes and focused on the man in the bed. His lips were moving, but his voice was distant. "I'm sorry, what did you say?"

"I said, I guess you also know what happens to people who are sent left on the ramp. Working in the hospital, you must talk to many different people."

Agnes nodded. She hadn't seen Yvette since she was carried away on that stretcher. She stood and forced a smile. "I best be on my way. I need to check on the people in the other wards. Stay strong. I'm sure you'll be fine in a few days."

She picked up her tray filled with cups of water and entered the ward at the end of the hallway. Putting the tray down, she remembered her face mask. This ward contained mostly people with contagious diseases; she shouldn't spend too much time here.

She approached a new patient in the back. He was a few years older than Agnes and looked remarkably well. She handed him some water and checked his chart—early-stage malaria symptoms. Checking the name of the treating physician, she smiled. Dr. Wójcik usually found a way to have prisoners needing some time to recover admitted to the ward.

"Why are you smiling?" the patient asked in German. From his chart, she saw his name was Michal Ziemba.

Agnes looked up at him, surprised he spoke German. Most of the patients were Poles, and few spoke German. "I was just looking at your diagnosis. I suspect you have mild symptoms?"

"Why would you say that?"

"Because you look fine to me. You've either recovered remarkably quickly or found another way to be admitted here." Agnes' voice was neutral.

He sat up in his bed. "I know Dr. Wójcik from Kraków. We used to go to school together."

Agnes sat at the foot of his bed. "We all need a little help to survive. How did you end up here, if you don't mind me asking?"

Michal shook his head. "Just like everybody else, I suppose. I lived in the Kraków ghetto, and one day the Gestapo came to take my wife and me away. It was in the middle of the night, and before we knew it, we were on a train. The journey was just a few hours, then—" He lifted his hand to his eye and choked. "I haven't seen my Ewa since. At first, I was hoping I could find her, but then I found out what happened to those who are sent to the left."

A heavy silence fell between them, and his story triggered the memory of Agnes' own arrival at the camp, now half a year ago. Her departure from Westerbork had been swift. After telling Pisk she wouldn't abandon her sister, he'd shrugged and told her she could join her. On the ramp, she had run into Jacob. It had been the hardest goodbye of her life. Jacob had tried to convince her to stay, but in the end, he understood that she couldn't let Yvette make the journey on her own. *My sweet Jacob. I hope you're well. I hope you're alive.*

Agnes finished her rounds and headed to the nurses' room when Dr. Wójcik stopped her in the downstairs hallway.

"Do you have a minute for me?" he asked, his eyes fierce. "In private?"

Agnes followed him into the empty nurses' room. All the other nurses were making their rounds. Dr. Wójcik closed the door and turned to her.

"They're preparing another selection tomorrow. It's bad, Agnes."

Agnes swallowed hard. The selections were a regular part of life in the hospital. Every week a number of SS physicians and officers inspected the patients. Every chart was checked and the physician would decide which patients had good chances of recovery, and which were lost causes. The latter would be loaded into a truck bound for the back of the Birkenau camp, where they would perish in one of the gas chambers. Everybody knew the only way to avoid the gas chambers was to be strong enough to work in the slave labor pool of the camp. Anyone unable to work after minimal time in the hospital was dispensable.

"How bad? Who's coming?" She feared some of the SS doctors. Some didn't even bother looking at the charts and picked entire wards at once.

Dr. Wójcik shook his head. "I'm not sure, but I know who they are after. It's everybody with malaria on their chart."

"That's madness. We're getting the best recovery rates from malaria patients!"

"I know, I know. And that's why we're not going to let them empty our wards like that."

Agnes raised an eyebrow. "How so? What are you going to do?"

"Not me. Us. We'll make sure nobody in the hospital is diagnosed with malaria when the SS comes tomorrow."

She looked at the doctor, scrambling for a solution. Agnes found her composure. "What are we going to do?"

That evening Agnes sat in Dr. Wójcik's office with him and two other nurses. They were gathered around a large desk; files were stacked high between them. At regular intervals, one of the nurses pushed a file toward the doctor, who duly signed at the bottom.

Agnes finished another chart and handed it to Dr. Wójcik. He glanced at it and pushed it back to her. "Make sure you backdate the first pages. We need it to look authentic." Frustrated, Agnes carefully adjusted the dates before sliding the chart back to the doctor.

They worked for hours, and Agnes' wrists hurt when Dr. Wójcik signed the final file. She stood and checked the clock on the wall. It was almost three thirty in the morning. The SS doctors would be here in a few hours. They made it with time to spare.

Dr. Wójcik stood and stretched. "You've just saved the lives of all these people," he said, gently patting the files on his desk. "But you can't speak a word of any of this. If anybody finds out we did this, we will go with these people to Birkenau."

The women nodded solemnly, but Agnes couldn't resist feeling slightly euphoric. Even though it was a small act of disobedience—no, resistance—against the camp administration, her work saved these people. She looked at Dr. Wójcik and smiled. He looked confused at first, then smiled back. He also felt it, she was sure.

That morning, the SS delegation arrived for their inspection. As Dr. Wójcik predicted, they asked to see all files of patients with malaria symptoms. Agnes stood next to Dr. Wójcik as he told them they currently had no cases, but he would be happy to provide them with the files of prisoners who had recovered.

"Our recovery rates have been remarkable, really," he said with a hint of pride.

No patients were selected for Birkenau that morning.

# CHAPTER TWENTY-FOUR

Joel lifted the heavy suitcase from the platform onto the cart. The supply of suitcases and duffel bags was never ending, much like the trains arriving every day, spitting out the condemned from all over Europe. He sighed and bent to grab another bag when a familiar voice interrupted him.

"Remember, this is always better than where those sorry sods are taken." Piotr stood next to him, his gaze on the procession of people disappearing in the distance. "Have some water. Strache just called a five-minute break." Piotr handed Joel a container, and he drank thirstily. They sat on the ramp where a train with 30 cattle cars stood just five minutes ago, half of its cargo scattered on the ramp, the other—human —half now walking toward death in Birkenau's ever-operational machine of death.

Joel had lost count of the number of trains he'd seen arrive at the *Judenrampe*, the platform between the main camp and Birkenau, where trains stopped to unload people from all walks of life. While the SS separated the people headed straight for the gas chambers from those deemed useful for another few months of slave labor, Joel stood at a distance, waiting for those people to clear the ramp.

"You seem half a world away," Piotr said, and Joel turned to him. "Can I join you?"

Joel smiled sadly. "It's been six months, and I'm afraid I'm not even seeing the faces of the people getting off the trains anymore. They're ghosts."

"I try not to look at them."

Joel still felt a sinking feeling every time he heard the heavy rumble of the approaching locomotive—utterly powerless to stop what was happening, along with the knowledge that he could be next any day.

It was also this ramp where his mother had been sent to the left. The only way out of Auschwitz was through the chimney. He still dreamed of his mother, her face appearing briefly and vaguely as she spoke to him in words he didn't understand. He looked up at the sky and into the sun. He hoped his mother was looking back at him from a better place.

A shrill whistle indicated it was time to return to work. Joel reluctantly lifted himself to his feet and moved to the next suitcase. He prayed there wouldn't be a second train today.

No second train arrived, and they finished loading the trucks three hours later. They were led back to Birkenau by their Kapo Strache. As a criminal prisoner, he'd spent most of his life in various prisons around Germany. The Nazis had been keen to recruit these lowlifes to lead the work details in Auschwitz. Strache had turned out to be surprisingly mild. Joel had heard the stories of murderous, sinister, and cruel Kapos attacking the men under their command, but Strache was content to stand by and allow them some leeway. That was, as long as there was no SS around. Once they made one of their inspections, Strache would move into overdrive, harrying and shouting at them to work faster. He hardly ever hit anyone, and because of this, Joel and the other men in his detail worked at an acceptable pace. He reminded Joel of Andrzej in Ciechanów.

They entered Birkenau through the main gate, and as they reported to the men's camp, there was a delay at the gate. The guard pointed at a sheet of paper, and Strache nodded and turned around. "Bartnik, Kozak, report immediately!"

Unlike the SS, who exclusively used the prisoner numbers tattooed on their arms, Strache called the men by their last names. Joel and Piotr rushed to the front of the column. With trepidation, they stood in front of their Kapo. It was never good to be singled out, and Joel's heart beat in his throat. He tried to control himself by taking deep, long breaths, but the anxiety remained.

"It appears you're needed in the main camp. Don't ask me why, but here are transfer orders for you to report immediately." He handed them a sheet of paper each. Joel scanned the words but couldn't make out anything from the overly bureaucratic wording. He looked back at Strache, who seemed to consider what to do next. They wouldn't be able to walk back to the main camp alone, but he had to take the rest of the work detail back to their barracks.

"Wait here, and I'll be back to take you there in half an hour," Strache said, already signaling for the other men to continue.

"This is Block 26, your new home." The SS man's voice was without emotion, and Joel decided the man considered them a burden, taking him away from more important duties.

He led them upstairs to a room filled with bunks. The building was a former Polish army barracks built using stone instead of the hastily— and flimsily—constructed wooden sheds that served as living quarters in Birkenau. There was enough space for the men not to be stacked like sardines.

"Find a free bunk, and report to the block elder when you've settled in. You'll need to collect the block's rations soon, so hurry up," the SS man said as he left.

A man who sat in a bunk near the door looked them up and down. "You're the new block supervisors, then?"

"Apparently," Joel said, scanning the room for a free bunk. "We were told an hour ago. Do you know if there are any free spots?"

The man pointed to the back. "Should be plenty of room there. We had some people moved to a different camp a few days ago."

Joel and Piotr found adjoining top bunks and sat down, taking in their new surroundings. The door opened and a group of men walked in, likely returning from the day's labor.

"Why do you think they picked us? I have no idea what it means to be block supervisor. Who are we supervising, exactly?" Piotr said.

"It doesn't sound like supervising anything. I think we just need to make sure we collect food for these men twice a day."

"It's not even that." A voice came from the bunk across. Joel was startled as a man emerged from the bottom bunk. He hadn't seen him when they picked their bunks. "We don't need that nasty excuse for food they serve here. We've got our own supplies." He pointed to a box on his bunk: it was filled with canned food. Joel's mouth watered.

Piotr climbed down from his bunk and looked closer at the cans. "Where did you get that?"

"I've got friends and family outside the camp. They send me these every week. It's the same for most of the others in this block."

*That explains why he looks relatively healthy.*

"What kind of work do you do?"

"I work in the camp bakery."

*So he has his own food and access to the bakery. No wonder he's doing all right.*

More men walked into the room, finding their bunks. Joel scanned their faces. Even though they looked tired, they all seemed well fed.

"Joel Kozak, is that you?" A familiar voice called out from across the room, and Joel looked up to find none other than his friend Moshe Kolko at the end of the aisle.

He jumped down from his bunk and embraced him. They then looked at each other. Apart from the customary Auschwitz shaved head, Moshe looked much the same from when he'd last seen him board the train in Ciechanów.

"I can't believe you're here. I looked for you on the ramp when we arrived, but it was such chaos that I feared you might've been sent to the wrong side," Moshe said.

"I was sent to Birkenau, but not on one of the trucks going to the bunkers." Joel could still see the procession of trucks passing him by. Back then he hadn't known what he knew now, and his heart still ached for his mother. *The horrors she'd had to go through in her final minutes.* "I worked on the ramp sorting luggage for almost half a year."

"Well, thank heaven you've been sent here!" Moshe spread his arms wide. "In the hell of Auschwitz, this is the best block to be in." He then spotted Piotr sitting on the bunk below. "Hey, Piotr, I didn't see you there!"

The two men embraced, and Moshe asked them, "What brings you to our block?"

"We've been made block supervisors."

Moshe's face broke into a wide grin. "That's great! I assume they told you what you'll need to do?"

"Sort of. The SS guard wasn't too helpful, but we know we're supposed to fetch food twice a day."

"Don't worry too much about the food. The men in this block all receive their rations from outside the camp."

"So we've heard."

"Just pick up the food every morning and evening and see if anybody wants anything extra. Then you can just do with it whatever you want," Moshe said, looking serious. "The other supervisors decided to share it with those less fortunate in the blocks around us."

Joel nodded, then a thought struck him. "But what about you? You don't have anyone on the outside sending you anything, do you?" From what Joel had heard Ciechanów's ghetto had been emptied.

Moshe shook his head. "I don't, but these men are often willing to trade. And if you worked on the ramp for six months then you know how to *organize* things in the camp, right?"

*Organizing* meant taking valuables found within the camp. Joel had been careful on the ramp. The guards watched them like hawks, and Joel had witnessed more than a few on-the-spot executions of prisoners caught pocketing valuables from the suitcases.

"One more thing about your new job." Moshe looked at him with a frown. "You'll also need to report to the SS on anything happening in here."

"Like what?"

"If someone is sick, needs to miss work, any concerns, that kind of thing."

"Okay, sounds about right."

Moshe looked at him intently and shook his head. "You need to make sure no one is reported sick unless there is absolutely no other way. We all have good jobs in this block. These men are tailors, bakers, butchers." He pointed at a group of twenty men making their way into the room. "You see them? That's the camp orchestra, the ones playing those god-awful marching songs every morning and evening."

"So, we need to stick together, make sure no one is picked off for selections, or considered useless to the camp."

"Exactly. And if you look after them, they will look after you."

# CHAPTER TWENTY-FIVE

Agnes finished her rounds early that morning and was ready for her break in the nurses' room. She had been up early, her wards overflowing with people. More than half of the people in the contagious diseases ward showed signs of malaria, which was making her anxious.

Even though she spent her days looking after people with horrible diseases, she had been fortunate enough not to catch any. She was convinced it was down to Dr. Wójcik's strict policy of good hygiene and facial masks. It also helped that he rotated the staff regularly, making sure Agnes didn't spent weeks working the same ward. She had to admit it was frightening to see how many patients passed through the hospital. Despite their best efforts, the circumstances were suboptimal at best— there was hardly any proper medicine, and Agnes often found herself using regular handkerchiefs or even toilet paper to bandage people.

She had just opened the door to the nurses' room when someone called out from down the hallway. "Agnes, wait a minute." Dr. Wójcik took large strides toward her. A smile formed on her face, but it quickly faded when she saw his furrowed brow. *Something's wrong.* "Walk with me, please."

They sat in his small office and he put his hands on the desk between them. "I'm sorry, but there's no easy way to say this. You're being transferred to another block."

Agnes felt a chill run down her spine but kept her composure. "Have I been selected?"

He quickly shook his head. "No, it's nothing like that. You're moving within the hospital. Dr. Wirths has asked for you specifically."

"Really?" She felt a little faint. Dr. Wirths was the SS' head physician in charge of the entire hospital operation. She couldn't imagine why he would be interested in a simple nurse like her. Her head was spinning and she grabbed the sides of the desk, closing her eyes.

"Are you okay?" Dr. Wójcik stood and put his hand on her shoulder. She looked up at him and blinked hard, the stars disappearing from her vision.

She felt embarrassed and nodded. "Sorry about that. I'm fine."

"It's okay," he said, his hand still on her shoulder. "I understand it must be a lot to handle. I'm afraid you need to report to your new block immediately. The orders just came in, and Wirths requested that you report to him at the start of the afternoon shift."

Agnes looked at the clock on the wall. It was almost twelve, which meant she had a bit over an hour before she had to face Wirths. "I'll pack my things. I'll be ready to leave in ten minutes."

"There's an SS guard waiting for you outside. He'll take you to the new block."

She felt deflated. If she was escorted, she knew there was only one place she could go. "Am I assigned to Birkenau?"

Dr. Wójcik hesitated, looking at the floor before meeting Agnes's eyes again. "No. Block 10."

Agnes had never been to Block 10, but she'd heard of the things happening there. They seemed too horrific to be true, even for Auschwitz. Up until now, she assumed whoever spoke of Block 10 had mixed up the stories coming from the adjacent Block 11, the penal block.

As she followed her SS escort through the front door, she was struck by the atmosphere. Even though it felt similar to the other hospital blocks—the white-washed walls, the smell of fresh detergent, and the hurried footsteps of nurses in the hallways—something was different. She couldn't quite place it, but her stomach flipped while she followed the man to an open door at the end of the hallway.

The guard stopped and indicated for Agnes to continue. Dr. Wirths was waiting, sitting behind the single desk. The office wasn't unlike the one in her previous block, where she had just spoken to Dr. Wójcik. Dr. Wirths was reading a file but heard her come in, glanced up, and motioned at the chair opposite him. "Sit."

Agnes did as she was told and folded her hands on her lap. The guard closed the door, and she felt uncomfortable in the silence of the small room. Dr. Wirths made no move to start the conversation as he leafed through the file, picking out the last page and studying it.

She studied him. If it wasn't for the SS uniform, he could pass for a regular doctor, his hair parted neatly to one side. *I need to be careful.*

"So, you are the Dutch nurse who has been in my camp for almost a year?" He shoved the papers aside as he looked up.

"Yes, sir. I arrived in October of last year."

"Very well. And from what I hear, you've been doing a good job with Dr. Wójcik."

She shifted in her seat. "If you say so, sir."

He folded his hands on his desk, his small eyes observing Agnes for a moment. "You must be wondering why I asked you to come here." He didn't wait for her answer. "It's very simple."

"Yes, sir."

"Now, some of the procedures are quite complicated, and the patients don't always understand what's about to happen. This results in somewhat ..." He paused for a moment and looked as if he was unsure what to say next. "Unpleasant situations I'd rather avoid. You speak both German and Dutch?"

"I do." *Unpleasant situations?*

"And you're a trained nurse?"

"I am." She decided this was not the time to split hairs over her qualifications.

"Do you have any experience assisting in surgery?"

157

"A little bit." She had none.

Dr. Wirths didn't pick up on her hesitation or simply ignored it. "Very well. You are just what we need. You'll report to Dr. Samuel. Tell him you're here to assist him with the Dutch girls. You can find him in the operating room down the hall. He knows you're coming." He picked up a sheet of paper and signed it, handing it to Agnes. "You can hand this to him when you start; this confirms your transfer." He picked up another file and started reading, indicating the meeting was over.

Agnes found a middle-aged man talking to a nurse in the hallway. Underneath the well-worn white doctor's coat Agnes caught a glimpse of the camp's striped prisoner uniform.

"Look, I need this to be ready in fifteen minutes. Dr. Schumann insisted on us carrying out the operation today." The man spoke in crisp German, and Agnes had no trouble following him. The nurse nodded but looked flushed.

"I'll make sure we have everything ready as soon as possible, Dr. Samuel," she said as she hurried away toward the stairs on the far end of the hallway.

The doctor mumbled something as he leafed through some of the papers in his hands. As Agnes approached, she saw that he looked a little unsure. His eyes shot across the sheet of paper, but not in the calculated manner she'd seen with Dr. Wirths earlier. "Can I help you?"

"Are you Dr. Samuel?" When he nodded, Agnes stepped forward and introduced herself. "Dr. Wirths sent me. He said you require assistance with the Dutch patients?"

Dr. Samuel stared at her outstretched hand for a moment, his eyes distant, then shook it. "Ah yes, of course. Agnes, welcome. I'm glad you're here. I can certainly use your help. Did you say you speak Dutch?"

"Dutch and German."

"Good, follow me." Dr. Samuel stepped into the operating room, which was only slightly larger than Dr. Wirths' office. In the middle stood a single gynecological table next to an X-ray machine. A side table on wheels carried syringes and hypodermic needles. Dr. Samuel placed the files he was carrying on a small desk in the corner. Agnes took in a deep breath, as she looked around. She'd last been in an operating room in Westerbork, and those had been well stocked. This room looked more like the makeshift hospital one would expect near a battlefield.

"I know what you're thinking, and you're right." Dr. Samuel was looking at her sympathetically. "When did you arrive in Auschwitz?"

"October."

"And you've worked in the hospital since?" Agnes nodded and he sighed. "Then you must've heard something about what's going on here."

"There are many rumors in the camp." Agnes tried to read the older man's face. His eyes were kind, and despite his accentless German, he was a prisoner of Auschwitz, like her. Jewish as well, considering his last name. She decided to chance it. "What is happening here, Dr. Samuel?"

"Upstairs, we have around two hundred women in the wards. More than half are Dutch, many having arrived in the camp in recent weeks."

"What kind of procedures?"

A shadow crossed his face. "You'll find out in a bit. There's one scheduled in a few minutes. You're here because you speak Dutch. You won't need to do anything other than keep the girl calm." He picked up a chart. "This will be the girl's first procedure. She will likely be scared. Just tell her everything will be okay and that she will be back in her bed within the hour."

Before Agnes could ask anything else, there was a knock on the door. The same nurse she'd seen in the hallway earlier came in with a girl wearing only a hospital gown. She looked no older than sixteen, and her eyes shot across the room before focusing on the needles next to the gynecological table. She shrieked.

"It's okay, calm down," Agnes said in a soothing tone. "You will only be here for a little while. You'll be back in your bed before you know it." Speaking Dutch again after speaking only German for so long felt awkward, but the girl responded well. Agnes placed the small bag with her belongings underneath the desk and approached the girl, taking her hand.

"Just sit down here for a minute while the doctor prepares everything."

Agnes managed to appear calmer than she felt. Looking around, she was disappointed to see there was little she could do. There were no blankets or pillows, not even a pitcher of water.

"Can I get her some water?" Agnes turned to Dr. Samuel, who measured the girl's blood pressure and heartbeat.

"There will be no need for that. This will only take a minute." The other nurse closed the door and turned to the girl on the gynecological table. "Take off your gown."

Agnes gave her a hard stare but remembered Dr. Samuel's words. *I'm here to keep her calm.* She helped the girl out of her gown.

"Lie down." The nurse was preparing one of the syringes, drawing a milky substance into it.

Agnes helped the girl down. "What's your name?" she whispered.

"Juliette."

"Where are you from, Juliette?"

"Rotterdam." Her eyes shifted to the other nurse, who put the syringe on the table. "What are they going to do?"

"It will all be over soon. Do you see the doctor? He's ensured me he's going to be gentle."

Dr. Samuel appeared, and as he looked at Juliette, Agnes could see sympathy in his eyes. "Sylvia is going to give you an injection. It will sting a little, and we need to run some tests with the X-ray machine." He stepped away and signaled for the other nurse to proceed.

Agnes was horrified when Sylvia inserted the syringe between Juliette's legs. The girl gripped Agnes's hand tightly and squeezed her eyes shut. When Sylvia withdrew the needle, Juliette's grip loosened, and she appeared to relax a little. "It's okay, it's okay." Agnes whispered, not quite believing herself. Dr. Samuel adjusted the X-ray machine over Juliette's abdominal area and said to Agnes, "Better keep holding her hand. It's about to get much worse."

A minute after he switched on the machine, Juliette's body tensed. With her free hand, she reached for her stomach but then violently jerked backward in her seat. A piercing scream came from her lips as her face turned red. Tears streamed from her eyes as she howled in pain. "Agnes, what are you doing to me?" She fixed her eyes on Agnes with a look of pain and betrayal.

Agnes forced herself to hold on to Juliette's hand as she spoke soothing words to the girl, who was trembling violently, tears running down her face. *What are they doing to her?* She looked to Sylvia, who stood by impassively. Juliette let out another howl, her grip tightening around Agnes' hand. She felt the girl's pain as she looked into terror-stricken, bloodshot eyes. Dr. Samuel's attention was switching between the X-ray monitor and Juliette. Even though he looked calm, Agnes could see Juliette's pain unnerved him. Agnes felt powerless as Juliette's body convulsed, sweat pouring down her face. She put her face close to Juliette's and closed her eyes. She whispered soft words and prayed the girl could hear her.

After ten minutes, Juliette was so exhausted that she no longer struggled. She softly whimpered as she held onto Agnes's hand, her clammy grip so weak Agnes worried the girl might pass out. Another ten minutes passed before Dr. Samuel switched off the X-ray machine.

The poor girl looked utterly broken, her eyes glazed over. Agnes supported Juliette's head in her hands as she looked at Dr. Samuel. He nodded, and Agnes whispered, "Juliette, it's done. You can go back to bed now. Would you like me to take you?"

Juliette barely acknowledged her, a soft moan the only thing she was able to muster. Agnes stood to grab Juliette's gown when she saw the blood: she had been so focused on Juliette's face that she had missed what had happened during the procedure. Juliette's thighs were covered in blood. The floor was covered in excrement. Agnes felt faint. Sylvia tried her best to clean the girl's legs and pelvic area, but the rags and toilet paper hardly sufficed. *What kind of hospital is this?* Sylvia quickly wiped the floor while Agnes changed Juliette into a fresh gown.

"I'll take her back to the ward," Sylvia said. Agnes opened her mouth, but Sylvia shook her head. "You can check on her later. This is my job." She opened the door and called out to another nurse. She must've been waiting, for she entered with a stretcher almost immediately. Together, they took Juliette, now asleep, away from the room.

Agnes stood near the bloodied gynecological table and looked at Dr. Samuel, who sat at the desk scribbling in the file.

"What is going on here, doctor?" Agnes said, exasperated and struggling to process what she had just witnessed. "What did you do to her?"

He looked up over the rims of his glasses. His face was a little paler than earlier, and she saw defeat in his eyes. "Agnes, before I say anything else, you need to understand I'm not doing this work because I want to. I'm forced."

Agnes nodded silently, stepping closer to Dr. Samuel.

"You felt her pain," he continued. "Unfortunately, you will soon become used to this."

She doubted it but bit her tongue. "What did you do?"

"These experiments are carried out under the orders of Dr. Wirths, and managed by my superiors, Dr. Clauberg and Dr. Schumann. When they're not able to do them themselves, or when it's the first injection, like today, they ask Sylvia and me to carry them out. We have no choice."

Agnes ground her teeth. *Answer my question.* "Dr. Samuel. Please tell me. What are we doing to these girls?"

He took off his glasses and sighed. "We are mutilating them, Agnes. We are running experiments to see if we can sterilize them."

Agnes felt sick as Dr. Samuel confirmed her suspicions. All the rumors she'd heard turned out to be true and a little worse. She'd heard about experiments on men and women in this block, but she'd never imagined they would be this atrocious. She closed her eyes and rubbed her temples. When she opened her eyes, she found Dr. Samuel observing her with a curious expression.

"Agnes, when you arrived in Auschwitz, did you consider yourself lucky not to be sent to the gas chambers?"

She frowned, surprised. *What an odd question.*

He stood and took a few steps closer. He lowered his voice as he spoke the following words. "You've been here long enough to know the ones that go to the gas chambers were the lucky ones. For us, it's a slow, tortured death. They grind us down until we're completely worn out, of no further use. For the girls picked for these experiments, it's many times worse." He looked downcast as he met her eyes. "The only thing you and I can do is make things as comfortable as possible for them."

Agnes nodded. As he opened the door to the hallway, he turned back and said, "And sometimes, the only way to do that is to be kind, gentle, and show compassion. It's everything we have, and they'll never be able to take it away from us."

# Chapter Twenty-Six

S amson walked with the rest of the Sonderkommando, having finished his day in the crematorium. He'd been assigned to the oven room of crematorium 3 today, one of the toughest jobs in the death factory. He'd spent the entire day carrying coke from the storage rooms to the ovens, making sure not to spill any while avoiding the heavy carts transporting corpses. There was constant harassment from Kapos and stokers alike. The former group concerned with looking good for their SS overseers, the latter group desperately needing the ovens to remain hot enough to meet their daily quotas. Samson could now barely lift each foot to take a step, completely drained as he entered the yard of the Sonderkommando block.

He went inside and climbed into his bunk, closing his eyes for a moment.

After fifteen minutes, he got up and swung his legs out of the bunk as he heard noises outside. The men bringing their evening rations had arrived, and soon a queue snaked through the yard. They held tins and spoons in hand, ready to collect their dinner. Even though the food was hardly appetizing, Samson knew they received some of the best rations in the camp. The SS needed the men of the Sonderkommando to be strong and able to last throughout the day, and he ate slowly but heartily as he sat on a small bench in the yard.

"Where were you assigned today?" Feliks sat next to him.

"Stokers team. Carrying the coke. You?"

"Ouch, rough assignment." Feliks let out a low whistle. "I had to inspect the changing area."

"I'm sorry, that's even worse."

"I don't think I'll ever get used to that. I always feel like a traitor standing in the room with them, helping them hang their clothes on the numbered racks, helping elderly people tie their shoes together." Feliks studied some of the men playing a football game in the yard as he held his bowl of soup at his chin. "Have you ever thought of just stepping into the next room with them?"

Samson looked at his friend in dismay. "Never, but then I'm usually near the ovens. I guess I've been fortunate, I'm hardly assigned downstairs."

"I'm not sure how much longer I'll be able to keep my mouth shut, Samson. We had two shipments of people today. I saw more than two thousand enter the room alive, only to be on their way to the ovens less than an hour later. I've seen too many accusatory eyes of the dead looking up at me while I strip them of their hair and hidden jewelry. And you know the only way out of here is to follow them."

Samson looked at Feliks, who had set his almost full tin of soup on the ground. He'd never seen his friend so downcast, although he wasn't alone. Many of the men in the Sonderkommando suffered survivor's guilt. Unlike people who'd once lost their friends or families in an accident, the men in the Sonderkommando refreshed their guilt every day. In addition, they were forced to keep the gruesome secrets of what happened in the death factory of Auschwitz-Birkenau.

"They're never going to let us get out of here alive. You've seen what they've done to the men before us," Feliks said, picking up his soup and taking his first bite.

His friend was right. Samson had seen his fair share of comrades dying. The men around him were just as susceptible to dying of a typhus infection as the rest of the camp. He remembered his friend

Fischl, who had passed away almost a year ago. *Taken down by one of those nasty lice.*

"The best we can do is keep our heads down and try to organize extra rations however we can," Samson said, putting his empty tin away. "I don't see any other way."

"Hmm." Feliks slurped some of his soup.

"What, you have an idea?" Samson sat up. Feliks wasn't normally this enterprising.

"It's just an idea, but some of the men on my squad were talking about it."

"Tell me."

"Well, there's only two hundred of us, so there's no way we can rise up against the guards. Not without weapons, anyway. We wouldn't have the numbers."

"Right."

"But what if we convinced the people in the changing room to revolt? They have nothing to lose. They're going to die when they step into the next room. So why not fight and give themselves a chance of survival?"

*That's not a bad idea.* "But how? When would you tell them? And they would be unarmed."

"We could only tell them when they enter the changing area when they go down the steps. That's where we're always standing around, instructing them, telling them to remember where they left their belongings. That's when we would tell them they're about to be killed." Feliks looked confident, and Samson realized his friend had given it serious thought.

"How long have you been planning this?"

"For about two weeks. There's not much to plan, but we needed to make sure everybody is on board with it."

"And when you get those people to rise up, what is your next step? Let's say you overpower the guards at the door; where will these people go?"

"We would take over the crematorium, take out the guards and grab their weapons. With more than a thousand people, we could get the rest of the camp on our side." Feliks looked annoyed. "You don't believe in the plan?"

Samson held up his hands. "No, no. I don't think it's a bad idea. I agree you need the numbers because we sure as hell don't have any weapons."

"We're taking it to Kaminski tonight."

*So they're serious about it.* "What if he says no?"

Feliks shook his head. "He won't. He's been saying he wants to do something for months. This is our chance."

Samson looked at Feliks as his friend inhaled his soup. Feliks looked confident, a man with a mission.

The leader of the Sonderkommando didn't like the plan one bit. He flat out refused to give it his blessing, telling the group to be patient. Kaminski had hinted that the camp resistance was reaching out to the Home Army—the Polish resistance—cells outside the camp. They were planning an armed uprising, potentially storming Auschwitz in the future.

Needless to say, Feliks and his men weren't impressed.

"He's too cautious and thinks we have all the time in the world," Feliks had said the morning after the meeting. "What if the SS decide they no longer need us, or that we know too much, and take care of us? We would die without having even tried."

Samson had attempted to calm him down, but Feliks and his friends wouldn't abandon their plan that easily—so he approached Kaminski the next evening.

"I fear they're going to go ahead with the plan, with or without your blessing," Samson said. They stood near the fence, which meant nobody could eavesdrop or sneak up on them.

"Damn fools. It's suicide." Kaminski was normally calm and collected, which was how he'd become the head Kapo of the Sonderkommando. He was smart and deferential to the SS, and fair but uncompromising to the rest of the Sonderkommando. Most of all, he was an experienced head who knew how the camp functioned. He made sure the men working in and around the crematoria were efficient in keeping the fires stoked and the ovens at capacity, and that was what mattered most to the SS. Despite his Kapo status, he was still very much one of the prisoners, always looking out for the men in the barracks. That earned him everybody's respect, and going against his wishes was ill advised.

"We'll need to keep an eye on them, but it won't matter a bit if they're set on carrying out the plan." Kaminski looked troubled. "What do you think?"

"I know Feliks. He wouldn't do something like this unless he believed there was no other option. He's not been himself the past days." Samson felt uncomfortable. "I think they're going to take the first opportunity they get. They think they have nothing to lose."

"I agree with you, but a lot of those boys are quite new. They haven't seen what you and I have seen."

"Work hard and do as you're told."

"Exactly. Feliks should know better."

Samson nodded. "I think he's seen too much death around him. And I can't blame him for worrying. Last week they transferred the men clearing the pits behind the bunkers to some unknown camp. What do you think happened to them?"

Kaminski looked thoughtful. "I think we all know. They served their purpose."

It wasn't the first time large groups of the SK were suddenly transferred to new camps. At first, the SS had asked for volunteers to move to a different camp, and some men had jumped at it. Then, in an uncharacteristic oversight by the SS, the bodies of the supposedly transferred men had been delivered to the crematorium. They were riddled with bullet holes. That put an end to the volunteering, and now the SS simply selected entire squads for *reassignment*.

Kaminski got up. "Look, Samson, we're not going to stop them if they're as determined as they seem. Just be smart when it happens. Don't be among those actively rising up. Wait for the camp resistance to come up with a better plan. We won't stand a chance unarmed against the SS. They'll wipe us out, and it will all have been for nothing."

"I know."

"And try to talk some sense into Feliks. Maybe he can stop it."

Samson watched Kaminski walk away, and he very much doubted he would be able to stop Feliks.

Four days later, Samson stood near the door of the changing room. It was his second day in a row in this area, and even though it meant a reprieve from the heat of the oven room above, he couldn't wait for the day to end. The faces of the people streaming through the door had the usual mix of emotions. Some looked hopeful as they undressed, no doubt wanting to believe the lies they'd been fed on the way. Others appeared apathetic, too tired from the train journey to care about what would happen next. And then there was always a group of brave, defiant people who'd heard the rumors of what happened in Auschwitz. They would stand in the middle of the room, not making an effort to undress. It was up to Samson and the rest of the SK to convince them to do otherwise before the SS came in with more persuasive measures.

Samson felt something was different today. More people seemed on edge, and he spotted a group in the corner, fully dressed as they looked around pensively. He had sighed and walked over to the small crowd when someone raised their voice behind him.

"Stop undressing! Don't let yourselves be fooled!"

Samson froze and turned to find a woman on the opposite side of the room. She looked panicked, her eyes bulging as she went around the room, clasping on to people. *Shit.*

"They're going to kill us in there! Don't believe them!" She spotted Samson and pointed at him. "You! Tell them the truth. We're going to be murdered in the next room, aren't we?"

Samson looked at her and barely managed to keep his face straight. He looked around and saw some people looking at the woman, then turning their attention to him. He was relieved to see most people were ignoring her as they continued undressing. "Please get ready for the showers," he said as he turned his back to the woman. *What is happening?*

He continued toward the people in the corner. They still hadn't undressed, their eyes following the woman with interest. Samson reached them, and, with an effort, asked them to undress. "You really don't want the guards to come in here and see you fully dressed. They're not very patient." He put on a conciliatory and almost apologetic tone. It was the best thing he could think of: both for keeping those poor people calm and for his own conscience. The people in the corner stared at him but said nothing.

Meanwhile, the woman was screaming and grasping at people now. Something had to be done, and Samson looked around for help. To his horror, he saw his colleagues looking on, almost encouraging her. That's when it hit him. *Someone told her. It's happening.*

Samson studied the people in the room. Most of them continued undressing, ignoring the woman. Some stopped and stared, fascinated by the display of madness as the woman dug her fingernails into her cheeks. She drew blood, and as it trickled down her face, she unwittingly made for an appropriate sight in the underground chamber of death.

*Should I stop her?* By now people were turning away from her, shielding their children. Some of the little ones started crying and their parents told her to stop making a fuss.

"We're all going to hell! We need to fight back!" The woman was frothing at the mouth. "Don't undress! Come to the door with me; we can't let them shut us inside!" After a few more moans, the woman collapsed onto the floor, exhausted from her struggles and no doubt demoralized by the lack of support.

Samson shook his head and felt an odd sense of relief. He walked back to the door. Two SS officers had entered the room. They stood talking, paying little attention to the people undressing. He recognized one of them: Franz Hössler, a particularly brutal *Obersturmführer* who'd shown up in the old crematorium 1 in Auschwitz many times.

Something had changed again. People were no longer undressing. Mothers started buttoning up their children's shirts. Within minutes, more people again stood wearing their shirts, pants, and skirts. Some sat on the ground, putting their shoes back on. The woman's words had cast enough doubt.

The SS finished herding the last of the condemned through the front door, and Hössler and the other men became aware of what was happening. In a few minutes, a thousand people had fully dressed and inched toward the exit. The guards coming down the steps saw the unusual—and dangerous—situation and quickly disappeared upstairs.

The crowd continued to push forward, and more of the SS bolted up the stairs. Hössler barked orders at the remaining SS men, forming a human barrier around the exit. Hössler remained where he was, his face pale but his eyes calculating. Samson imagined what was going through his mind. Those outside would sound the alarm, and backup would be here soon. Would it be soon enough for Hössler?

People moved forward, some shouting. Hössler tried to wave them back, unsuccessfully telling them to get back to undressing. "You won't receive any tea and soup if you're not properly bathed," he shouted to little effect as the first men and women reached him. As they did, Hössler reached inside his coat and pulled out a whistle. The short, shrill blasts were deafening in the confined space, and the crowd went silent. "Please, everyone, stay calm and get back to undressing. What madness has come into you? We just want to get you bathed and ready for your midday meal."

Samson eyed the people around him, and he saw some nodding, keen to believe Hössler. Most appeared unsure, and then the woman who'd started it all appeared at the front of the crowd. She looked like an apparition from another world: her face covered in blood, eyes bulging, her hair disheveled.

"You're a lying piece of shit! You're going to kill us with gas in there! I know it!" she roared in fury, spittle flying.

Hössler recoiled at the sight and took a few seconds to respond. "Now, now, woman, have you lost your mind? Who told you this nonsense?" He tapped his forehead.

"It's true! You want to kill us with gas!" The woman took a step closer to the Obersturmführer. The room fell silent, and Samson heard the people around him breathing hard. They looked confused, worried, and undecided. He glanced around and saw some of the SK close to the front. From their faces, Samson could make out they were nervous but hopeful. He didn't see Feliks.

"Please, ladies and gentlemen. I'm shocked at what I hear here. From what I've read in the reports, you are all hard workers and behaved exceptionally well in the ghetto. Are you really going to believe this madwoman?" He waved his hand at the bloodied woman dismissively. "Or are you ready to serve the Reich? I give you my word of honor that you will be treated well, and paid well."

There was a rumble of engines outside, and soon the sound of barking dogs was clear as SS soldiers with guns raised came down the steps. Hössler glanced back and Samson thought he detected a hint of relief on the man's face.

"Now, please make your way to the showers. There is a war going on, and everybody has to do their part. There are severe consequences for anyone who refuses these orders."

More soldiers appeared behind Hössler, some with dogs baring their teeth while they barked menacingly. The people in the front cowered back, and the children started crying. The resistance of the crowd was broken as people realized there was nowhere for them to go.

Samson heard people sobbing around him as husbands and wives comforted themselves and their children. There was still a slight bit of hesitation in the air, quickly ended by Hössler. "Get to the showers, now! You want to live and work, don't you?" He purposefully glanced back at the show of force behind him.

Slowly, the people turned around and started undressing. It took twenty minutes to clear the changing room, and the last person walked through the door to the gas chambers. Half an hour later, there was only silence.

Samson was sorting the clothing in the changing room when Hössler entered. "All prisoners report upstairs, now!"

When Samson reached the oven room, he found the stokers already lined up. He joined them, and soon the 50 men on duty in crematorium 3 stood in the heat of the raging fires behind them.

The door opened, and Samson had to look twice to recognize the crumpled mess of the woman who had tried to prevent today's gassing. She had been badly beaten and was dragged in by two SS guards. Her legs and arms were bent unnaturally—more dead than alive. His heart sank. *Oh no.*

"This woman knew what was about to happen." Hössler wasted no time as she was placed before them. "And there is only one way that she could have known. One of you told her." Hössler marched past them. He was met with silence. None of the men dared look the German in the eye. "But don't worry, we'll find out who it was soon enough." He snapped his fingers, and the woman was dragged past the line.

She was forced to look at every man in the line, and as she approached Samson he felt his heart beat faster. *What if she remembers seeing me and points me out?*

Their eyes met, and there was a sparkle of recognition as the woman strained to look at him. Samson struggled to keep his composure but forced himself to look at her without fear. They stood facing each other for what felt like an eternity, and then she slowly shook her head.

"Remember what I told you, woman. We'll kill them all if you don't tell us who it was." Hössler spoke without emotion, Samson's life in the hands of this condemned woman.

The woman continued, and as she reached the end of the line, Samson felt gripped by fear. *She's going to get us all killed.*

Someone was pulled from the lineup. The woman collapsed on the dirty floor, shaking and sobbing, and was momentarily ignored by the SS guards. Samson dared a glance in that direction and saw a young man he didn't recognize dragged to Hössler.

The Obersturmführer looked at him with contempt but didn't say anything. Instead, he nodded at two guards, who tied up the man's wrists and ankles.

"Let this be an example to anyone with the same idea," Hössler said as they dragged the young man toward one of the ovens. As he realized what was happening, he started crying and pleading. His fingernails scraped the concrete floor.

One of the guards opened the oven door, and the roaring fire muffled the man's screams. It took four guards to lift the bound man struggling for his life. They looked to Hössler, who nodded. Samson closed his eyes as he heard the screams of agony as the man was thrust into the oven. The man's howls intensified and Samson closed his eyes.

The screams ended abruptly, and one of the guards closed the oven door.

Samson stood shaking and felt his knees buckle. He controlled himself as Hössler dismissed them without another word. As he walked out of the room, a single gunshot ended the sobs of the woman on the soot-covered floor. Samson didn't look back.

# CHAPTER TWENTY-SEVEN

Joel and Piotr struggled along the camp's main road. It was hard work despite using two sticks to distribute the weight of the vat containing forty liters of soup from the kitchen to Block 16.

"Just be glad we don't have to take it to our block," Piotr said. "That would be even farther."

They approached the block entrance, and one of the men idling outside hurried to open the door. "It's our turn today?" he said with a smile as he held the door.

Joel and Piotr entered the block, and the men erupted in a chorus of cheers. Joel smiled. This was a thankful job, bringing additional rations to the blocks in the camp. The first two days Joel and Piotr had dutifully carried the heavy vats of morning tea and evening soup to their own block. They were quickly reminded it was unnecessary—the men had plenty of their own supplies. Joel and Piotr decided carrying the full vats between their block and the kitchen four times a day was not the best use of their energy. Now, they took their rations to other blocks in the camp, strengthening the men who didn't have the luxury of supplies being sent to them every week.

They placed the vat in the middle of the room, and soon men were scooping their second dinner of the day into their tins. Joel recognized a man he'd worked with on the ramp. "I'm going to catch up with Antoni for a second," he said to Piotr.

"Sure, I'm heading back to the block. Moshe asked me to help him with some things."

"I'll find someone to help carry the vat back later."

Joel approached Antoni and, as he did, saw that the men in the block really needed these extra rations. Some of them were skin and bone, and he suspected more than a few of them worked in the fields or, worse, the mines. He counted his blessings for having been assigned to the Polish block.

"Joel, the bringer of life!" Antoni said as they shook hands. Antoni had joined Joel on the ramp about a month after he arrived in Auschwitz. They were around the same age, and Joel had shown him the ropes.

"It's been a while," Joel said as he crouched in front of Antoni's bunk and looked around. "How are things on the ramp? Keeping busy, I assume?"

"The trains keep coming; it's hard to keep up sometimes. But you know all about that." Antoni looked him up and down. "Looks like life in the Polish block is treating you well."

Joel felt awkward; he knew he was lucky.

Antoni picked up on his unease and waved his hand. "Sorry, I didn't mean it like that. I'm just glad you're doing well, friend."

Joel put his hand on Antoni's shoulder and smiled. "I know, I know. It's okay. Just glad I can help." He changed the subject. "What's it like on the ramp? Are most of the men hanging in?"

Antoni shook his head, frowning as he looked troubled. "Hardly. You wouldn't recognize most of us on the ramp these days. Some days we have two trains coming in, carrying close to two and a half thousand people each. Some of the men just give up."

Joel was shocked. *Twenty-five hundred people per train?* "How do they make it fit? I remember our transport from Ciechanów wasn't even half that, and it took us a full day to sort through all the luggage."

"There's more of us now, and the SS make sure we get just enough of a break to eat something at midday. Other than that, we're lugging suitcases all day."

"But they must see the men dropping out, right?"

Antoni scoffed. "To them, it's just one more dead Jew on the ramp."

Joel picked up Antoni's food tin and walked to the front of the queue for soup. The other men let him pass without protest. He filled the tin and returned to Antoni, handing it to his friend. "Eat up. They need an experienced man like you on the ramp. Take care of those new boys, and take care of yourself."

Antoni nodded at him. "I'll return the vat for you," Antoni said as he took a sip of his soup.

"Appreciate it." Joel walked past the rows of bunk beds where some men were already fast asleep. His eyelids were getting heavy, and he looked forward to returning to his bunk soon.

He was ten meters from the exit when the door opened. Three SS men and a Kapo purposefully walked in.

"Everybody to their bunks, now!" the tallest of the SS men shouted. "Line up!"

The men who'd stood around chatting and eating their soup so amiably seconds ago now hurried to their spots. Joel stood in the middle of the aisle running directly down the room. As everybody found their spot, he realized he had nowhere to go. He could pretend to be part of the block but didn't know what the SS were here for. There would be trouble if they found out he was pretending to be part of this block. He made a decision and slowly approached the men at the door.

"Get to your bunk, now," one of them barked at him.

"This is not my block; I was just visiting a friend."

"Sure, that's what they all say. Get to your bunk; you're not going anywhere."

Joel took a deep breath. "I'm sorry, but I'm a block supervisor in the Polish block. I was just leaving."

The group leader looked up from a sheet of paper he was studying. His face was twisted in a snarl. "You're lying. Why wouldn't you be in your block now?"

Joel remained silent: there was no point in arguing with the man. He feverishly racked his brain for a response, but his mind was blanking. He glanced around the men lined up near him, but all kept their eyes averted. Joel suddenly realized this wasn't a routine inspection, and his heart sank. This was a selection.

The SS leader turned to the Kapo. "Do you know this man?" The Kapo shook his head, and the SS man flashed a nasty smile as he clasped his hands together. "Perfect. Then I believe we've found our first prisoner for the quarantine block. He does look a little pale, doesn't he?" He took a step closer to Joel and hissed, "Outside. Now."

Joel dropped his head. He knew nothing he said would change the man's mind.

"Herr *Unterscharführer*," said a familiar voice behind him. *Oh no.* It was Antoni, who had stepped away from his bunk and made his way forward. *Don't do this, Antoni.* "I can vouch for this man. He really is who he says that he is. We used to work on the ramp together."

The Unterscharführer turned to Antoni, surprise on his face. "Is that so? So you're saying we shouldn't select this man for the quarantine block tonight?"

Antoni blinked, and it was clear he realized his mistake. Joel looked at his friend and shook his head, but Antoni continued. "I just wanted to say that his *Rapportführer* would be able to clear up this misunderstanding. He's not part of our block."

"So you're saying I'm wrong," the SS man said matter-of-factly.

Antoni's face turned a shade paler, as he struggled for words. He'd walked straight into the Unterscharführer's trap. "No, sir, absolutely not. I wouldn't—"

"Take him outside as well." The SS man pointed at the door, spotted Joel, and shouted, "What are you still doing here? Get out before it gets worse than the quarantine block!"

As Joel hurried out into the heavy July evening air, he turned to Antoni. "What did you do that for?"

Antoni looked at him in surprise. "You didn't think I was going to abandon you like that, did you?"

They entered the quarantine block an hour later with thirty other men selected from Antoni's block. It was crowded, and Joel immediately knew he was in trouble. More than three-quarters of the men staring back at him were emaciated *Muselmännern*. These creatures were the condemned, and the quarantine block was their last stop before the gas chambers of Birkenau tomorrow.

Joel and Antoni found a bottom bunk in the back of the room and sat down.

"We need to find a way out of here," Joel said. "If we don't, we'll be dead this time tomorrow. Have you looked at who we're in here with?"

"How could I miss them? But how are we going to get out? The block is surrounded by barbed wire and guards. There's no way to escape. And even if we did, our own blocks will be locked by the time we get there. We can't be found wandering around the camp outside. The guards will shoot us."

Joel nodded. Antoni was right; escaping now wouldn't help them. But they couldn't just wait for death in the morning.

"What if we fight the SS when they come for us? We have nothing to lose," Joel said.

"Fight them? We have no weapons, nothing to defend ourselves with."

"But we'll have our dignity. We'll die with honor, not led to our deaths like sheep."

Antoni opened his mouth, then closed it. He looked thoughtful as he scanned the room. Joel could see his friend was sizing up the men in the room, just like he'd done moments earlier. After a minute, Antoni turned to him. "How much use are most of the men in here? They have no strength left; that's why they're here."

"Don't underestimate what people can do when they really want to," Joel said.

"How are you going to convince them to do something? They all look like they just want to hide in their shells for their final night."

"By telling them the truth." Joel stood and walked to the front of the room. He looked at Antoni, who watched encouragingly, his eyes urging him on.

Joel took a deep breath and raised his voice. "Men! Can I have your attention for a moment?" A few nearby faces turned to him in surprise. They looked indifferent but curious to hear what this stranger had to say. Joel turned to the other side of the block, repeating his request. Soon, he had the attention of all but a few men in the block.

"What I'm about to say shouldn't surprise anyone, but it needs to be said. Tomorrow morning, the SS will come for us and take us away to the gas chambers in Birkenau." The gaunt faces around him remained impassive. *I have to convince them somehow.* "The Nazis have decided we are no longer of use to them, and they will expect us to come willingly, without protest. That we step into their trucks and step into the gas chambers to fill our lungs with poison. To take our final journey up the chimney and out of the camp."

Some of the men became slightly restless and murmured. Despite that, Joel felt he had their attention. "Are we going to let them take us like that? Are we sheep? No!" He waved his fist in the air. "We are still men, and we have our dignity. We shouldn't let them take that from us after everything they've done to us. To our families." That last remark hit a nerve as he heard some voices agreeing.

"What do you suggest we do?" someone nearby asked.

"What *can* we do?" another asked. "Most of us can hardly walk, let alone resist armed soldiers."

Joel nodded. "I know, the odds are not on our side. But we must resist all the same. When they come for us, we need to be ready. We will attack the guards in the morning. They won't expect it, and we'll have the element of surprise. We'll take their weapons and set this place on fire. We'll take down as many as we can. They won't take us so easily!" He felt the adrenaline rising as he spoke the words, the plan forming in his head. His heart was beating fast as he envisioned the carnage they would inflict on their unsuspecting tormentors in the morning. They would go down in a blaze of glory.

"You don't know they're going to kill us tomorrow." Joel turned to find a large man standing next to him with his arms crossed. "You're just kicking up a fuss."

Joel was stunned. Did this man not know what happened to people who ended up in this block?

The man spoke to the rest of the block. "Don't listen to him. We will be reassigned to the new camp tomorrow, just like the SS told us. That's why we're here."

"You don't believe that, do you?" It was all Joel could muster in his state of shock.

The man shook his head. "They showed me the papers. The train leaves tomorrow morning, and I will be on it. I won't join in your folly."

Joel looked at the faces around him. To his dismay, the men looked back at him with the same apathetic looks he'd seen earlier. The Muselmännern shrugged and turned away their bony faces. He then realized what was going on in the block. These men had nothing left but hope the SS' lies were the truth.

Joel stood alone in the middle of the room as the men returned to their bunks, settling in for what would be their final night in this life.

The morning came too soon, even if Joel hadn't slept a wink. He was awake when the door opened, and a bulky man wearing a Kapo's armband walked in, carrying a sheet of paper. Joel sat up as the man went around the room, ignoring the Muselmännern, still fast asleep. Instead, he approached some of the stronger men. A few got up and waited by the door. Joel's heart pounded as the Kapo approached him and Antoni.

"Name and number," the Kapo said, glancing up from his paper only momentarily.

Antoni rang off his details, and the Kapo ran his finger down the shortlist. After a second, he nodded. "Get up and wait for me by the door." He then looked at Joel.

"Kozak, 731135." Joel held his breath as the Kapo checked the list. *I have to be on there. Someone must've realized I was missing last night.*

The Kapo looked at him. "If someone had asked me, I would've bet you would be on the list. Sorry." He walked on to the next bunk. Joel felt like he'd been hit in the gut with a sledgehammer. *Something must be wrong.* He looked to Antoni, standing at the door with his mouth agape. *He can't believe it, either.*

Joel felt in a daze as the Kapo rounded up the men on his list. When he opened the door, and the men filed out, Joel looked around. It was only him and the Muselmännern left.

The men of the Sonderkommando were kept from the rest of the camp, and even though it was possible to speak with them, very few people did. Some of the prisoners said the men of the SK were cursed, others said they were collaborators, saving their skin while they killed their fellow prisoners.

*Will they pity me, or hurry me to the gas chamber like an animal?*

Joel prayed death would at least take him quickly.

"Prisoner 731135, report!"

Joel sat up and saw a tall man wearing prisoner garb near the door, impatiently scanning the room, tapping his foot. He looked out of place.

"Kozak, 731135, are you here?" The man looked ready to leave, and Joel jumped to his feet.

"Right here!"

"Come with me." The man's voice was calm, but his eyes showed urgency.

Joel hesitated only for a second. In any other situation, he wouldn't have volunteered to come forward. But here, in the last stop before the gas chambers, there was nothing to lose. Besides, the man wore the same uniform as him and was no Kapo. Joel hurried forward as the man held the door for him. "Stay quiet. I'll explain in a minute."

The sun's warmth had never felt so good as Joel stepped outside. The man motioned him to follow, and Joel's relief grew with every step from the quarantine block.

They walked for another ten minutes, when they neared the repair shed. The man opened the door and pointed to a pair of stools in the corner. There was no one else inside.

"You must be wondering what's going on," the man said. His face was open, and now that he sat inside he appeared more at ease.

"You took me from death's footsteps. I'm most grateful," Joel said. "How did you get me out of there?"

The man scratched his head. "Everything I tell you from now onward, it needs to stay between us, okay?"

"Sure."

"I heard you used to be a block supervisor." *Used to be?* The man smiled wryly. "When you didn't show up in your block last night, you lost that privilege. I'm sure when your Rapportführer investigated your disappearance and found you were marked for crematorium 2 today, he found a replacement."

Joel nodded. It made sense. "I hadn't considered how it would look in my block." Piotr and Moshe must've been so worried. He hadn't even given them a second thought as he pondered his bleak future. He felt a tingle of guilt.

"So, how did you find me? And who are you?"

The man smiled again but ignored his questions. "I heard about your speech last night. That was quite impressive."

"We had nothing to lose. Who told you?"

"Your friend Antoni came to me this morning. He told me you needed to be saved, no matter what. He told me about the speech and said you would be a valuable asset to my team."

"Asset?"

"In your speech, you spoke about fighting the SS, rising up. Did you mean it? Would you still want to do this now that you're out of the block?"

"Yes," Joel said without hesitation. "They killed my mother, and everyone I cared about."

The man looked at him hard for a few seconds. Joel held his stare. Finally, the man spread his arms. "I'm in charge of the repair shed. I requested your transfer this morning, pulling some strings with the camp administration. Antoni told me you're a handy guy to have around. Please tell me he wasn't lying."

Now it was Joel's turn to smile. "I'm pretty good with electrical things. Engines, machinery. Anything with a motor or wire, I can fix."

"Good. Because we could use someone like you." The man held out his hand. "Welcome to my team, Joel. My name is Bruno. I think we're going to get along just fine."

As Joel shook his hand, he felt an energy that betrayed there was more to Bruno than met the eye.

# Chapter Twenty-Eight

Agnes was in the operating room with Dr. Samuel. A young woman of only eighteen lay on the table between them. Agnes had escorted her down from the ward two hours earlier; this was the third time Marieke found herself on Dr. Samuel's table.

"Please hand me those scissors," Dr. Samuel said as he finished sewing up the incision he'd made earlier. Agnes had assisted Dr. Samuel during the operation, and besides handing him the correct instruments and checking on Marieke's vitals, she had studied the man's precise work.

Dr. Schumann led the sterilization experiments, and Agnes had learned that, in addition to the X-rays, they often involved removing the patient's uterus. Schumann was especially interested in the women's recoveries. If they did, they were sent back to Birkenau to work. Sadly, most women died from severe radiation burns from the X-ray experiments.

When Schumann was present, Dr. Samuel dutifully executed the lead doctor's instructions. Today, however, she noticed some discrepancies during the operation and wondered if she had missed something.

The doctor took a few more minutes to finish up, then told Agnes she could leave and return to take Marieke back to the ward in about an hour. She hesitated as he sat down to write his report. Dr. Samuel looked up. "What's on your mind, dear?"

She looked at him, the kind eyes of the older man looking at her in the bright lights of the operating room. "Today's operation seemed different from the past two I've witnessed."

He put down his pen. "How so?"

"Well ... It was a lot shorter than the others, and it looked different when I emptied the surgical tray with the residue."

Dr. Samuel didn't immediately respond, instead taking off his glasses and placing them on the desk. He studied Agnes, and she felt uncomfortable as she fumbled with her hands. *Have I spoken out of turn?* "I'm sorry, I have no right to question you." She moved for the door.

"Agnes, wait."

She turned around to see him leaning forward in his chair.

"You're right. Today's operation was different. Can you make sure the door is closed?"

Agnes pushed the door shut.

"Please sit down." He pointed at the chair opposite him. "I remember when you joined the block a month ago. We've both seen enough suffering for a lifetime. But you and I both know there's little we can do about it without endangering ourselves."

Agnes nodded. "We can't stop it. But I'm struggling with my conscience. Every time I'm sent upstairs to fetch one of the girls, I feel part of the horror. Like I'm on the wrong side."

"I know that feeling. I wake up every day dreading the horrible things I'll have to do, but I also know I have no alternative. They have my daughter, Agnes. She's in the camp. I don't know where they're keeping her, but they let me see her once a week." He sighed as his eyes went moist. "Dr. Wirths is only keeping her alive to make sure I keep doing what he asks. Wouldn't you do the same?"

Agnes felt for the man opposite her. She would probably do the same in his position. *If Yvette was still alive.* She thought of her sister, her sweet sister, as they took her away on the ramp, now almost a year ago. *I would've joined her if I had known where she was headed.* She shook her head at the thought. There was no sense in what-ifs. She needed to stay alive now more than ever. She couldn't—wouldn't—allow the Nazis to finish off her entire family. *I need to stand strong.*

"But today, you did something different." Agnes focused on Dr. Samuel, who raised his head, his eyes meeting hers.

"I did. I made sure she has a chance to have children if she ever makes it out of here alive." His gaze shifted to Marieke, who lay motionless on the operating table. The only movement came from her chest, gently rising and falling. "I know it's too late for me anyway. I won't get out of here alive. I know too much, and they will dispose of me once they find a more willing doctor."

"Don't say that."

He raised his hand. "It's the truth, Agnes. They will find out about me sabotaging the experiments. I shouldn't even be talking to you about it, but I've seen how you talk to the girls and comfort them. You're a good nurse. I'm just trying to survive. I'm a fraud."

The tall doctor sat in his chair, hunched and defeated, and suddenly looked years older than he was. On impulse, she reached out and gently brushed his hand.

"I don't think you're a fraud at all. These women would not receive proper care if it wasn't for you. Can you imagine if Dr. Clauberg or Dr. Schumann did these operations? The girls wouldn't stand a chance." He looked at her, the shame still evident on his face. "Every girl you save is one. And one day, when this is all over, their children will be born, and it will be thanks to your bravery." She handed him a paper handkerchief, and he wiped his face.

On the operating table, Marieke stirred, looking around groggily. Agnes let go of Dr. Samuels' hand. "I better see how she's doing and take her upstairs."

He looked at her. "Thank you, Agnes. I'm sorry to burden you with this, but I trust you. I believe you and I can make a small difference."

She gave him a sad smile. "So do I, Dr. Samuel, so do I."


It took a bit longer than usual for Agnes to get Marieke back to the ward. The girl was exhausted from the surgery, and Agnes made a mental note to double-check the amount of tranquilizer used next time. She shrugged. *Better to make sure they don't wake up halfway through the operation.*

As she stepped back into the hallway, Dr. Samuel's words echoed in her head. At first, she had been relieved to hear he was purposely sabotaging the experiments, but the doubts crept in as she helped Marieke up the stairs. What if someone found out what he was doing and connected it to her? They might think she was in on it, and she didn't doubt it would mean a one-way trip to Birkenau for her. She tried to calm herself: she was just a nurse following orders. Still, the thoughts lingered as she descended the stairs and headed for the front door. She needed some fresh air, having spent the entire morning indoors.

"Agnes, can I have a word, please?" Sylvia caught up with her as she opened the door.

"Sure." She held the door for the tall blond nurse. *What does she want?* Since their first encounter in the operating room, Agnes had tried to avoid Sylvia. The pretty Czech nurse seemed eager to please Dr. Clauberg. Despite that, Agnes had kept her thoughts to herself, and spoke to Sylvia cordially as they stepped outside. "What's on your mind?"

"I just wanted to clear something up." She placed her hands on her hips. "I saw the way you looked at me at yesterday's experiment."

Agnes feigned ignorance. "I'm not sure what you're talking about."

"Yesterday, when Dr. Clauberg asked me to administer the injection."

"Oh, that." Agnes had flinched at the enthusiasm shown by Sylvia, but she didn't think she had noticed. "I'm sorry. I guess I still find it difficult what we're doing sometimes, you know? It had nothing to do with you."

Sylvia raised an eyebrow. "I felt you were judging me."

*I was.* "Of course not! I know you're doing the best you can looking after these women and making sure the experiments are carried out properly."

"I know I can seem tough on the girls sometimes, but they need to understand that if they refuse the experiments, they'll be killed."

Agnes nodded but said nothing. In truth, Sylvia could be unnecessarily heavy-handed with the girls. She reminded her of some of the Ordedienst men in Westerbork, letting their power go to their heads.

"I'm only doing this to survive, Agnes. Dr. Clauberg is very observant, and I want to make sure he's pleased with me."

*I'm sure he's very satisfied with you.* The girls in the ward called her the Death Announcer, for she was often the one to pick them up for their experiments.

Sylvia turned her face to the sun as she continued. "And I need to think of my mother. You've seen her in the block, right? She wouldn't survive a day without me. I care about the girls, Agnes. I detest what I do, I really do." Her voice was flat and devoid of emotion.

Agnes wanted to ask her more about the experiments, and her relationship with Dr. Clauberg. "I'm sorry if I gave the impression that I judged you. I know you mean well. We're all just trying to survive here."

As Sylvia flashed a grateful smile, Agnes decided she needed to keep her wits about her when Sylvia was around.

# CHAPTER TWENTY-NINE

I t was the end of the afternoon when Joel made his way from the Kanada warehouses back to the maintenance shed in Birkenau. There were a couple other men handing in their toolboxes, and Joel headed their way to do the same. He was looking forward to returning to the barracks. It had been a hot, sunny day and the air was sweltering in the packed warehouses of Kanada. Before he could put down his toolbox, he heard Bruno's voice from the other side of the barracks.

"Joel, when you're done packing up, can you come to see me?"

The foreman had a stern look on his face as he walked to the back, where he had a makeshift desk. Besides being responsible for making sure none of the men ran away, Bruno also needed to make sure the men had the required passes to go between the different areas of the camp. The group was not large—there were about 40 men reporting to Bruno —but they worked in every part of the camp, including the subcamps, and were often alone. It required meticulous planning, as permission was granted by the camp administration. Joel didn't envy him, and having worked for Bruno for over a month now, he had a lot respect for the man.

After double-checking his toolbox was in order, he walked over to the foreman, who waved him to a stool. He waited for the other men to saunter off and soon it was only Joel and Bruno in the shed.

"Remember what I said when I asked you to join us?" Bruno started without preamble, something Joel liked about his boss.

"You said a few things," Joel said noncommittally. "I recall something about me being a handy guy to have around. Do you still feel that way?"

Bruno smiled. "Sure, you haven't made me regret my decision. I can send you anywhere and you just get things fixed. But that's not what I meant, and I think you know that." Joel returned his smile, and Bruno continued. "Look, the reason I asked you to join was firstly because Antoni vouched for you. He may not have told you this, but Antoni and I arrived in the camp on the same day, just a different train. We were in the same block and worked the fields first. Then, as the camp grew, the Germans realized they needed a larger team taking care of repairs, and I was moved here and to a different barracks in Birkenau. I believe you and Antoni met shortly after at the ramp."

"We did. I remember when he joined. He was keen to show his worth. Smart."

"Exactly. So, when Antoni tells me someone is in trouble, and I can help them, I will do just that. But when he mentioned your impassioned speech in the quarantine block that night, I knew you could be even more useful. I suppose we lucked out in the end. A hard worker with a good attitude."

"I appreciate what you've done for me. If it wasn't for you and Antoni, I'm sure I would've died that day."

"No doubt. But you don't need to thank me. I want to ask you something else." His eyes narrowed. "Do you still feel the same as that night when you thought you had nothing to lose? When you believed you were going to die the next day?"

"Are you asking if I would still fight the SS?"

"Fight, resist, sabotage."

Joel looked at the leader of his work detail. Bruno's jaw was clenched, his hands shaking a little, but he looked at Joel calmly, holding his gaze. *He's serious.*

"Yes."

Bruno's jaw relaxed as a smile appeared on his face. "I was hoping you'd say that. It would've been awkward if you didn't."

"What's the story? Are you with the camp resistance?" Joel had heard of the underground organization but had never spoken to one of its members. There were always rumors about another escape attempt, and some prisoners even claimed the camp underground had ties with the Polish resistance, the Home Army. Talk about the Home Army storming Auschwitz had intensified in recent weeks, exciting prisoners and generating rumors. Joel tried to ignore the chatter: there was no sense in harboring false hope. *But maybe Bruno knows more.*

"We're in a unique position, Joel," Bruno said, ignoring his question. "We get to move around the camp freely, and we have access to places regular prisoners would never get to. Just consider how many prisoners not working in Kanada would be able to get inside. None."

"Are more men in the work detail involved?" Joel thought of the men working with him. They all seemed so normal.

Bruno held up his hands. "You know I can't answer that question. But there is something you can do. Since you're still in the Polish block, I need you to establish contact with someone there. My sources tell me he's recently joined the camp resistance, and he would be a valuable connection to have, considering you live in the same block."

"It would make exchanging information between Auschwitz and Birkenau a lot easier." Joel's skin tingled—he still remembered that morning in Ciechanów. It had felt good.

"Yes, and we need this connection." Bruno looked troubled. "The SS have been purging the resistance more successfully in recent weeks."

"How so?"

"Sometimes we're caught. It happens. People get careless, talk too much, talk to the wrong person, or they're ratted out. But recently, the SS have caught somewhat of a lucky streak. A lot of our assets have been selected for the gas chambers, and there's only so much we can do when that happens. Most of the time, it means recruiting new people, but that takes time. We've lost especially many men in the main camp in the past weeks." He eyed Joel carefully. "Remember, don't speak to anyone about this. For now, it's just me and the man you're about to meet in your block. Be very careful when speaking with him, and always find a quiet spot where no one can sneak up on you or overhear you."

"When do I meet this man?"

"Today. He'll be waiting for you outside the block after roll call. Just wait for the other men to enter, and be one of the last to return to the block."

"How will I recognize him?"

Bruno smiled. "Don't worry. He'll recognize you."

The evening roll call had been quick. It appeared the SS guards and Kapos were keen to wrap up for the day, and it was still light when Joel shuffled back to the barracks. Even though he was tired, he felt a buzz of excitement about meeting his contact. He knew most of the men in the block, and he was curious who it could be. On the way from Birkenau to Auschwitz, he'd gone through the faces of the men in his barracks, and he'd narrowed it down to about half a dozen. They had all been in the camp for a longer time, were a good fifteen to twenty years older than Joel, and had an air of confidence about them. Joel was confident it would be one of those six Poles.

He looked for Piotr and Moshe, but they were well ahead, talking to some of the older men in the front. Joel was keen to talk to them, but he remembered Bruno's instructions and lagged in the back.

Walking down the camp's main road, he considered how joining the camp resistance would change his life. When he was in his small underground group in Ciechanów, things had remained very much the same: he went to work every day and met up with his friends in the evenings. The only time he'd felt actively part of the resistance was when he murdered the traitorous Gestapo agent. Joel passed the gallows—it would be quite different in Auschwitz. Here he was surrounded by SS guards looking to snuff out any form of resistance, active or passive. He would have to be intelligent and covert, but he also realized Bruno had only given him a messenger's job for now. *I can do that, and no one has to know.*

His block came into view, a small group stood outside, smoking cigarettes as they caught the last rays of the setting sun. He recognized all of them: it was always the same group. He joined them and was surprised to see Moshe among them. His friend didn't smoke. Moshe seemed entirely at ease, laughing at one of the jokes.

"Hey, Joel!" He waved him over. "Grabbing some more fresh air before turning in?"

"Not a lot of fresh air around here, though," Joel said, raising an eyebrow.

Moshe smiled. "They're good company."

They listened to the men chatting about their days, most of them complaining about the poor conditions of their stations, before they went inside, one by one. Moshe and Joel remained outside, and Joel got a little anxious. *My contact isn't going to approach me if I'm standing with Moshe.*

"Say, maybe it's time to go inside? It's getting a little chilly," Joel said, even though he wasn't cold.

"Sure, in a bit," Moshe said as he gave Joel an inquisitive look. "You look uncomfortable. Is something wrong?"

"No, not at all."

"All right, then," Moshe said as he peered over Joel's shoulder. "I'd swear it looks like you're waiting for someone."

"Who would I be waiting for?" Joel fumbled with his hands as he turned around. The streets behind him were almost deserted as the last men hurried inside their blocks. When he looked back at Moshe, his friend had a smirk on his face.

"I don't know. Me, perhaps?" He looked at him deadpan, then the smirk turned into a smile as it finally dawned on Joel.

"No." Joel took a step back, feeling lightheaded as he stared at his friend. "It's you? You're my contact?"

# CHAPTER THIRTY

Agnes exited the post office empty handed. Even though she'd gotten used to it, she still fostered a tiny bit of hope every time she went to check if there was any mail for her. When she arrived in the camp, she'd been told she could send two postcards a month. In the first months, she thought her postcards must've simply gotten lost in the mail: there was a war going on, after all. But now, almost a year later, she was starting to think there were other reasons Jacob wasn't responding to her. Perhaps he had been shipped out of Westerbork shortly after her, and her mail was simply tossed into the trash upon arrival in Westerbork's small post office. Every week without a response, her hopes of the man she loved being alive dwindled.

As she entered the nurses' room, she tried to put the morbid thoughts out of her head. *Jacob is still alive. When this is over, we'll find each other again.* She closed her eyes as she splashed water on her face and saw his handsome face smiling before her. Her eyes stung as she choked back tears and took a deep breath before opening them again. Agnes looked at herself in the mirror: she looked as bad as she felt. The door opened, startling Agnes.

"I'm sorry, I didn't think anyone was in here," a woman entering in a white doctor's coat said.

Agnes smiled at her. "It's fine, Dr. Brewda. I was just freshening up a little."

"Rough morning?" Dr. Brewda stood next to her, talking to her via the mirror. "I can only imagine what's going on with you. I've only been here for two weeks, and I'm already struggling. You've been working with Dr. Samuel for what, four months now?"

"Almost four, yes. It's tough, but I guess you get used to it on some level." Agnes tried to be brave as she wiped the water and tears from her face.

Dr. Alina Brewda had joined Block 10 a couple of weeks ago, and Agnes instantly liked the Polish doctor. Dr. Wirths had recently announced Block 10 was to become a female-only block, which apparently meant he also wanted female doctors. Dr. Brewda had since joined a number of the experiments, and even though Dr. Samuel still carried out the surgical procedures, Agnes had been impressed by Dr. Brewda's response. Instead of condemning or trying to stop the experiments—she appeared smart enough to realize that was beyond her powers—she focused on the girls during the procedure and stayed in the ward with them long after. She had insisted on better bandages, and Dr. Wirths had, surprisingly, acquiesced.

"I can't imagine ever getting used to that. As soon as I get a chance, I'm going to see what I can do about changing some more things around here. From what I've seen, these experiments are doing more harm than good."

Agnes suppressed the urge to tell her Dr. Samuel had been trying for months. "I've seen how the girls in the ward respond to you. They feel protected. I've not seen that before."

Dr. Brewda smiled sadly. "I wish I could do more, but unfortunately, it looks like kind words and making sure they don't bleed to death is all I can do for now. That, and making sure the nurses behave."

*So she's noticed Sylvia's behavior as well. Good.* "If you don't mind me saying, you remind me a bit of my father. He was a doctor, too."

"Well, that certainly explains why you're so dedicated to the girls, Agnes. I may not have been here for long, but I've seen you work with Dr. Samuel. You care. I'm not so sure about him, though."

Agnes frowned. "Dr. Samuel is a good man." She put her hand before her mouth.

Dr. Brewda raised an eyebrow, looked thoughtful, and then said, "Perhaps I need to give him some more time. But anybody who carries out these experiments for the Nazis, I have a hard time trusting."

"He tries his best. He's got a daughter in the camp."

"I see." Dr. Brewda looked uncomfortable as she washed her hands. Agnes turned away, but then the doctor spoke again. "Agnes, have you thought about what you'll do when this is all over?"

Agnes was surprised by the question. She had expected the doctor to reproach her, but she seemed to become even more human. "Take my formal nurses exam."

The other woman turned off the tap and dried her hands. "That sounds like a great idea. Judging from what I've seen, you will ace it."

"Thank you."

"I'm serious. If you can perform your job in these circumstances, an exam will be easy."

"We just need to make sure we're alive by the end of all of this."

Dr. Brewda turned and gripped Agnes' shoulders with both hands. Her eyes shot fire. "We will be, Agnes. When these Nazi bastards are defeated, we'll be the ones left standing. Just remember not to forget anything you've seen here. The world needs to know." With those words, she turned and left the nurses' room.

Agnes felt herself shaking at the doctor's words. Dr. Brewda was right. She was going to survive and tell her story.

A week later, Agnes was cleaning the upstairs hallway when something happened downstairs. The front door to the block opened, and there was the familiar sound of stomping. Heavy boots worn by one group in the camp—the SS. Agnes' heart skipped a beat. That sound always brought her back to the night her everyday life ended. In her mind, she was back in her bedroom in the home she grew up in, in Amsterdam. She waited for the men to make their way up the stairs, as they always did when they came for the girls in the ward, but to her surprise, the sound ebbed away farther down the downstairs hallway.

A few faces peeked from the doorways. The ears of the girls in the ward were trained for the sound as well. *Poor things.* "I think they're not coming upstairs," Agnes said, hoping she was right and the soldiers didn't change their minds or hadn't made a mistake looking for the ward. She clutched her stomach, as if something horrible was about to happen. Against her better judgment, she placed her mop against the wall and headed toward the stairs. The shuffling of chairs and footsteps echoed on the far end of the hallway, and she carefully trod down the steps.

She reached the bottom and stopped as she caught two SS soldiers stepping into the operating room. That was odd: there was nothing scheduled for this morning. *And there's no reason for them to go in there. Unless.* Agnes looked up the stairs and considered getting out of sight, but the urge to see if she was right was too strong, and she remained rooted to the floor, holding onto the railing of the stairs.

The door to the operating room was open. Raised voices came from within. They barked orders in German, and then Agnes heard the voice she'd hoped she wouldn't. She didn't have time to respond before the first soldier exited the room. Next came Dr. Samuel, wedged between two soldiers tightly gripping his upper arms.

The doctor kept his eyes on the ground, stumbling along as the men forcefully dragged him toward the front door. As they passed Agnes, Dr. Samuel looked up. In the flash that their eyes met, she saw resignation.

The soldiers took no notice of Agnes as they roughly manhandled him toward the exit. She looked at Dr. Samuel's back, his feet dragged along the smooth concrete floor, his head down: the figure of a man defeated. Gripping the railing of the stairs tighter, Agnes whispered her goodbye—she knew she would never see him again.

Dr. Samuel's departure had shocked Block 10. Not just the patients, but the nurses as well. Although none of them had worked as closely with him as Agnes, he had been kind to all of them. The news of his arrest had spread through the block within minutes, and by evening, every-body appeared to have their own version of what had happened.

Agnes lay in her bunk. The sun was setting outside, and it was almost time for lights out. The girls around her were still talking about Dr. Samuel, and one of them turned to her.

"Is it true that you saw it happen, Agnes?" It was Mary, a young Polish girl Agnes got along with well enough but didn't consider a friend.

Agnes answered without turning her face away from the wall. "I did."

"Did you hear where they were taking him?"

"No, I don't know, and I don't want to talk about it."

"I've heard it's because he refused to carry out Dr. Clauberg's orders the other day," another nurse, Rosalie, said in a hushed tone. "Apparently, Dr. Clauberg was furious." She raised her voice a little. "Weren't you in the operating room, Agnes?"

Agnes shook her head without speaking. It had been one of the few times when Agnes hadn't assisted Dr. Samuel for an operation. Dr. Brewda had insisted on taking her place. Did Dr. Brewda have anything to do with Dr. Samuel suddenly finding the courage to go against Dr. Clauberg's orders?

The next morning Agnes woke up to find Sylvia next to her bunk. Her expression was neutral as she said, "Dr. Clauberg wants to see you immediately." She walked off before Agnes could respond.

She rubbed the sleep from her eyes and looked around the dormitory. Most of the other nurses were still asleep. Despite the growing fear forming in the back of her throat—all she wanted to do was curl up under her covers and hide—she rose and dressed. She quickly stopped in the bathroom, splashing her face with ice-cold water, before she headed to Dr. Clauberg's office.

The door was open, and he sat at his desk. She knocked and he looked up, casually waving her in. "Close the door, and sit down."

He looked at her through his round glasses, his ratty eyes studying her as the harsh light reflected on his balding scalp. "This is only going to take a minute." He started their conversation reassuringly, as he did with his experiments.

Agnes felt a shiver run down her spine: this was her first one-on-one interaction with the doctor, and it was only now she noticed the details of his face.

"I'm sure you're aware Dr. Samuel was removed from our hospital yesterday, hmm? I believe you may even have witnessed it happening?" He looked at her, and Agnes simply nodded. She hadn't seen Dr. Clauberg in the hallway, but he must've heard from someone else. *Sylvia.* "Considering you worked with him on many occasions, I have decided that you will also need to leave. Dr. Samuel was a troubled man, and his performance was inadequate." He looked over the rims of his glasses. "A properly trained nurse would've seen this, and reported it to me."

Agnes felt her throat constrict. Dr. Clauberg was blaming her for what had happened? She couldn't believe it. In the world of Block 10, no nurse would ever dare speak ill of a doctor, and Clauberg knew it. She bit the inside of her cheek to fight the tears welling up in her eyes.

Dr. Clauberg appeared not to see her distress as he continued. "Because of this, I've decided you will be taken to Birkenau this morning."

Birkenau meant death. She dropped her eyes and studied her feet. *So this is how it ends.* She looked back up at the doctor sitting across from her. He said nothing but simply regarded her. *Is he done?* She felt the urge to say something, anything. To show some defiance, but words failed her.

"Be ready to leave in half an hour. There will be an SS escort waiting for you downstairs." He waved his hand, indicating the meeting was over.

Agnes stood and turned, still failing to think of something to say to this monster. *Am I really just going to be dismissed like this?* As she opened the door, she heard Dr. Clauberg clear his throat. "Good luck in the clothing commando."

She gripped the door handle and turned around, but the man had already returned to his papers, oblivious to her presence.

She stepped into the hallway and closed the door, almost bumping into Sylvia. The Czech nurse was leaning against the wall next to the door. Agnes glared at her. "What do you want?"

"I wanted to tell you I'm sorry about what happened to you."

"I'm not surprised you already know what he told me in there." Agnes snapped at her, brushing her aside as she walked toward the stairs. "Now if you don't mind, I need to grab my things."

"Agnes, wait." Sylvia's voice sounded odd, and Agnes paused. "I wanted to tell you Dr. Clauberg initially wanted to use you as a test subject for his latest experiment."

Agnes turned around. "He wanted to do what?"

"It's true. When he found out about Dr. Samuel, he said the doctor would be sent to Birkenau, and his assistant, that's what he called you, would be a good test subject for the new man coming in."

Agnes put her hands on her hips. "So why didn't he?" *Enough healthy test subjects coming in every day saved me.*

"I told him you were infertile. I said you told me in confidence." Sylvia avoided eye contact as she stared at the floor.

"And he believed you?" Agnes tried to hide the feelings raging inside her. She didn't trust Sylvia, but her explanation was perfectly plausible. Of course, Agnes wasn't in her prime fertile years like some of the younger women here, but at 25, she would still be a interesting test subject.

"I added some details to your files."

Agnes stared at Sylvia, trying to work out this tall blond woman. *Is she speaking the truth?* "It doesn't explain why I'm sent to the clothing commando, though. Wouldn't it have been easier just to send me to the gas chambers?"

Sylvia shuffled on her feet. "That was my suggestion, actually."

Agnes frowned.

"I said working you to death would be a better punishment than a quick death."

Agnes didn't know what to believe anymore. From walking into Dr. Clauberg's office half-asleep, assuming she would die that morning to

Sylvia telling her she saved her from the horrible experiments. *Have I completely misjudged Sylvia?* She shook her head. Sylvia had done evil things; she had seen the beatings she gave the poor girls in the ward upstairs. But had Sylvia stepped in to save her? It was certainly possible. Perhaps the Czech woman's relationship with the deplorable doctor had saved Agnes in the end. She looked Sylvia in the eye and said, "If what you're saying is true, I thank you. I don't know why you saved me; I didn't think we were friends."

Sylvia flinched, but recovered and nodded. "We're not. But you don't deserve to die for following orders, or the incompetence of someone else. I know you don't think much of me, but I hope you won't forget what I did for you today. I told you I'm just trying to survive." With that, she walked away and into the nurses' room, leaving Agnes alone in the empty hallway.

# CHAPTER THIRTY-ONE

S amson sat with Feliks in their barracks. They had just returned from the crematorium, after a grueling twelve-hour shift. Samson had barely made it to the arrival of the night shift, and he wasn't alone. On the way back from the crematorium, the men of the Sonderkommando were silent. There was none of the usual chatter, no occasional laugh as they tried to cover the horror of their daily lives with nervous and dark humor. Samson could see it in the eyes of the men around him: most of them were close to breaking. In the past month, two trains daily had become the norm. Today, three trains had arrived, carrying more than five thousand souls. The gas chambers and crematoria had not been able to process that many people, and Samson had seen people queuing up outside the crematoria yard. He felt a tap on his shoulder. Feliks had gotten up from the bunk, but Samson hadn't even noticed.

"Come, we should get something to eat. There will be plenty of time to sleep later."

Samson followed his friend and they collected their food. As they sat down to the side of the building, Feliks glanced around quickly, then produced two pieces of hard cheese. "Here, I found these on some of the people coming in today. I'm pretty sure it's Dutch."

One of today's transports had come from the Dutch camp of Westerbork. He took a bite and savored the rich taste as the cheese melted in his mouth. He sat for a moment and stared out through the barbed wire surrounding them.

"Aren't you meeting with your friend in the women's camp tonight?" Feliks asked as he took a bite of his soup. His face was neutral, but his eyes sparkled.

"I am, and it's nothing like that," Samson said. "We're no more than friends. I don't have the energy for anything romantic. And I'm sure she doesn't, either."

"How long have you been seeing her now? Two months?"

"Month and a half, ever since Kaminski told me about our connection with them."

Feliks looked unconvinced. "I don't know, Samson. Are you sure she feels the same way? No expectations from her side?"

"Feliks, can you please stop?" Samson put his soup down. "She works in the clothing detail, and by the time we meet in the evening, she's as tired as you and I. With all the death around us, I don't even want to think about doing anything romantic. And where would we do it, if we wanted to? There's no privacy in this camp, you know that."

"People find ways." Feliks slurped his soup.

Samson shook his head. "We are just friends." He finished his soup and stood. "I better get going if I want to have some time with her before roll call. I'll see you later."

Samson approached the gate to the women's camp and was relieved to see Anton on guard. Anton had been part of the Hitler Youth since he was fourteen, and when he turned eighteen his father had sent him off to the SS. Anton claimed he had no say in the matter, and Samson believed him. Unlike most of the guards, Samson had never seen Anton use violence against prisoners. *The women are lucky to have him.*

"Hey, Samson, I thought you might show up today," Anton said, getting up to open the gate. Samson handed him a pack of cigarettes and a small piece of chocolate he'd traded for earlier that week. The young SS guard gave him a nod of thanks as he quickly stuffed the goods in his pockets.

"Any news?" Samson asked as Anton closed the gate. Even though the prisoners sometimes picked up news from the Polish workers coming into the camp every day, the SS guards were often better informed.

"Not much. I haven't been on leave for a few weeks, and the news coming from the party is always the same. The war is progressing well, despite some setbacks on the eastern front." He shrugged. "You know how it goes—we never hear the full truth, either."

Samson continued into the women's camp. It was only the fourth time he visited, and it still amazed him that he hadn't known about the possibility earlier. About a month ago he overheard other men in the Sonderkommando talking about visiting the women's camp. They boasted about girlfriends, and Samson had asked how they managed to get out of their own block and then into the women's camp. Both sections were separated from the men's camp.

He had been nervous on his first visit, wandering around anxiously near one of the blocks, when Roza approached him. She had cheekily asked him if he was lost. They had talked about their pasts, successfully blocking out reality for an hour.

"Samson, over here!"

He turned to find Roza waving from a nearby barracks. She looked tired, her clothes hanging loosely around her body, but she managed a radiant smile as he approached her. They hugged, and she said, "Come, let's sit over there." She pointed at a space near two barracks, mostly out of sight from the guard towers. Even though Samson was officially not allowed in the women's camp, it was Anton's responsibility, and the guards outside the women's camp hardly cared. Samson had heard of only one instance where an overzealous guard had dragged one of the SK from the women's camp. He had been returned to the SK block with a bloodied nose, but that was it. Kaminski had told the other men to be careful.

Roza and Samson sat on two rocks between the barracks. Their spot was out of the way, and they were alone.

"I brought you something," Samson said as he reached into his pockets and handed her some salami and cheese. "The cheese is from Holland."

"Thank you, I'll share it with some of the girls later." Roza placed the food in her own pockets. They were almost the same age and had arrived around the same time, but Roza had aged more quickly in her years in Auschwitz. Her work in the clothing commando of Kanada was hard, and she had recently been made a supervisor. She had to oversee the work of about a dozen other female prisoners sorting the clothing.

"I know it's a bit odd to say this," Roza continued, "but I'm glad we have some new faces. We keep losing the older women, the ones that have been around for longer. With so many new transports coming in, it's good to have some relatively healthy replacements." She caught herself and put her palms up. "I'm sorry, that sounds horrible."

"No, it makes sense. I feel the same about new people joining the Sonderkommando," Samson said, waving his hand in a conciliatory manner. "When I see strong men walking through our gate, I'm glad. It means my chances of surviving increased a little. I welcome them and pray that they will be part of my team the next day. We had some new arrivals a few days ago, and more than half of the young men were assigned to my unit."

"Are you still mostly working in the oven room?"

"Yes, and to be honest, I prefer it that way. I know it sounds morbid, but I prefer working with the dead, rather than downstairs. At least I can give them a somewhat dignified send-off."

They were silent for a moment. Samson fumbled with his hands and looked at the barracks around them. Cracks in the walls were large enough to stick a hand through.

"Say, Samson, do you mind if I ask you something? It might be a little personal." Roza was looking at him pensively, her eyes studying his face.

"Of course, go ahead."

"When you talked about the people in the crematorium, you sounded a little, hmm, how would you say. Apathetic?"

He sat up and thought about her words for a minute. "You're right. Sometimes it's easier not to overthink. That's probably why I prefer working in the oven room. The dead don't talk. I'm sorry, I know how it sounds. I think my humanity is being chipped away day by day."

To his surprise, Roza took his hand. "Those feelings don't make you a bad man. I don't know you that well yet, but it shows that you're trying to hold on to your humanity more than ever. You've faced death in the crematoriums every day for a year and a half, and you're still here. You haven't given up; you've not gone mad. Not many others can say that."

"I don't know how much longer I'll be able to keep my sanity, though. Sometimes I think about sneaking into the gas chambers and end it all."

"But what good would that do?" Roza's tone was sharp. "That means they win. And we can't let them win, Samson. Don't you remember Kraków? Don't you remember what your life was like before this? I remember my life in Ciechanów. We were free, and we will be free again."

"I wish I could do something about it, though." Samson looked away.

"What do you mean?"

"I'm just a cog in their machine of death and destruction."

"If you could do something about it, what would you do? Would you fight back if you had the chance? Would you rise up if it meant a chance for freedom?"

"Of course," he said without hesitation. "I would do whatever it takes."

"Do you think more of the Sonderkommando share your feelings?"

Samson looked at her. Roza's eyes were sparkling, a fire burning within them. *There's something she isn't telling me.* "We're all tired of death. And there's one more thing about us."

"What's that?" Roza reached into her pocket and broke off two pieces of cheese, handing him one.

"We know we're only useful to them as long as the transports come in. Four crematoria are working at full capacity. I've been lucky to survive for as long as I have."

"So you think your comrades would stand up and fight?"

He nodded. "Some of the men have connections with the camp

resistance, but from what I hear, they're not making much progress." He took a bite of the cheese. "By the time they're ready to lead an uprising, it might be too late."

"So you think it would be easy to convince your fellow SK men to revolt if the circumstances were right?"

"I think so. But tell me what you're thinking. You're being very vague."

She wiped her hands on her shirt and clasped them together. "What if I told you I may have found a way to fight back?"

The hairs on his neck pricked up. Samson looked at Roza in wonder, studying her face to see if she was joking. She held his gaze, the sides of her mouth rising into a smile. "We could fight back, Samson. But we'll need the support of the Sonderkommando."

"Tell me what to do."

# PART III

AUSCHWITZ-BIRKENAU,
POLAND
OCTOBER 1943

# CHAPTER THIRTY-TWO

Kaminski scratched his chin. "This is very interesting, Samson. Very interesting. But there is one problem with her plan."

"What is it?"

"We need help. Having only the Sonderkommando involved is not going to be enough to overcome them."

Samson nodded.

"How confident are you that she can pull this off? I mean, I don't want to be pessimistic, but it sounds risky."

"She's determined, and her friends all work in the factory. They come back to the women's camp every day, so they would be able to smuggle the gunpowder in that way."

"Have they done it before?"

It had been Samson's first question as well. "Not yet. Roza only came up with the idea when one of her friends was appointed forewoman of the gunpowder room a month ago. Until Roza and I met, she had no idea who to approach with this information. Yesterday she felt comfortable enough to involve me." He noticed a frown forming on Kaminski's face. "She insisted her friend wanted to help. She'll do it." *I hope she's right about this.* Even though Roza had been persuasive,

Samson counted on Roza and her friends to come through. To his relief, the leader of the SK slowly nodded.

"Okay, Samson. If your friend can provide gunpowder to the resistance, it would be a serious breakthrough. But I'll need the camp underground to agree. Either way, we'll need their help with logistics."

"Are they still planning a camp uprising?"

"They're always talking about it, but they keep moving the date. From what I hear, they have had trouble persuading the Home Army to join. Without them and their weapons, the camp resistance isn't confident enough to try."

"Do you think the gunpowder might change their minds?"

Kaminski smiled. "I think it just might. Give me a few days to talk to them and see what they think. Make sure you're ready to meet with her soon. Can you do that?"

"Of course. I'll be waiting."

It was busy in the oven room of crematorium 3. The people from the day's first transport had made their way down the steps to the changing area about an hour ago, which meant the first corpses would show up in the oven room within half an hour. Samson was assigned to the stokers unit and heading to the storage room when Obersturmführer Hössler blocked his path.

"You! What are you doing?"

"Supplying the coke, sir."

Hössler nodded and jerked his thumb back. "Not anymore. Wait here." He stepped into the oven room and soon returned with six more prisoners. Their soot-covered faces shared Samson's surprise. It was never good to be singled out in the crematorium, especially by Hössler. "Quick, come with me."

They followed him downstairs, and Samson's heart sank when he realized where they were going. Hössler was taking them to the gas chamber. Samson had become adept at avoiding this particular selection in recent weeks, but today his luck had run out. The officer pointed to the open door of the gas chamber. A sweet, tangy smell lingered in the air as they neared it.

"All of you, get in there and help carry the corpses to the lifts. I want this room empty within the hour."

Samson entered the gas chamber, and even though he thought he'd become used to it, the sight of more than a thousand bodies piled in heaps still horrified him. He suppressed a wave of nausea as he passed through the small clearing between the bodies at the door. On the other side of the room, the door was blocked by a mass of bodies reaching almost to the ceiling. As soon as the gas canisters were dropped down the chutes, people rushed for the doors. They would try to claw their way out, the strong trampling the weak. The strongest men were always found at the top of the pile, the elderly and children crushed underneath. The pillars in the middle were always free of bodies. Even in the pitch-black room, people soon realized the origin of the deadly gas.

Two of the Sonderkommando were hauling bodies from the pile at the door, and Samson joined them. He pulled at the arms and legs of the mangled heap without registering their faces. Most were still warm. They went through the motions almost mechanically, performing the functions required to clear the room as quickly as possible. It took them half an hour to reach the final layer of the pile, and when Samson pulled at a young girl's legs, she coughed. Samson dropped her feet in shock. It wasn't unusual for sounds to emerge from the corpses, but this was different. As he moved a little closer, his heart stopped. The girl was moving, her chest rising and falling: very slowly, but she was breathing.

Samson's throat went dry and his heart pounded in his chest. Across the room were two other SK men but no SS. "Guys!" They looked up without interest. "This one's alive." The men turned around, mouths agape, and they hurried over.

"Holy shit. I've never seen this before," the youngest of the two said. His face was flushed, his eyes betraying panic. "What are we going to do with her? If Hössler sees this he's going to throw a fit."

"Why don't we take her upstairs?" said the other. "We might be able to hide her in the overseer's office?"

Samson shook his head. "And then what? We can't keep her hidden there. Besides, look at her, she's in no state to go anywhere."

"So, what do you suggest we do?" the other man said, looking annoyed. "There's nowhere we can take her. Hössler will find out soon enough."

"We have to try," Samson said. "We can't just leave her here."

More men returned to the room and, overhearing the conversation, joined the group. They were as stunned as Samson was.

"Isn't Pawlak a doctor?"

"I think he's a pharmacist."

"Good enough for me. He's working next door today, right?"

"Yes."

"Go get him, quick!"

Samson focused on the girl. She couldn't be older than fourteen. He put his hand on her forehead. She was cold, but she didn't shiver. Her breathing was so shallow that he had to put his hand on her chest to make sure she really was alive. He turned to the men behind him. "We should get her some water."

A minute later, one of the men returned with a bucket of water and a washcloth. Samson dipped it in the water and squeezed it above the girl's mouth. *Come on, you need some of this.* As the drops landed, she licked her cracked lips. Samson felt a sense of victory and gave her some more. When it seemed like she had had enough, he placed the washcloth on her forehead. Her breathing improved, her chest rising slightly higher.

There were footsteps behind Samson, and he turned to see Alexi Pawlak making his way over. The man looked overwhelmed as two other SK men accompanied him. As soon as he spotted the girl, his eyes watered. "Oh my God. Why?" He crouched down and snapped his fingers. The girl didn't respond. He gently slapped her cheeks, and she stirred. "More water," Pawlak ordered.

Samson took the washcloth and draped it in the bucket. Pawlak took it from him and gently patted the girl's face. It took a few minutes, but then her eyes opened. She looked terrified and managed a croak from the back of her throat.

"Stay calm, don't say anything," Pawlak said as he took her hand. He turned to Samson. "We need to get her out of here."

"Yes, but where?" Samson had racked his brain for the past fifteen minutes, but there was nowhere to take her. There was no way they could smuggle a girl from the crematorium yard without the guards noticing. He could hear voices on the other side of the door. The next group of condemned had arrived.

"What's going on in here? Why are you all standing around doing nothing?"

Obersturmführer Hössler quickly crossed the room, and when Samson looked up, the other men had parted for the SS officer to make his way to Samson and the girl. It was the first time Samson had seen Hössler flustered as he spoke the next words. "How did she get in here?"

It was an absurd question. The girl was naked and perched against the closed door of the gas chamber. She was battered and bruised from the death struggle only an hour earlier. "We found her alive at the bottom of the pile," Samson said.

Hössler's demeanor changed as he crouched next to the girl. He looked fascinated. "But how, how did she survive?" he muttered under his breath. "Remarkable." Then he snapped back to his usual self, realizing the girl posed a problem.

If this girl beat death in this room, against these incredible odds, perhaps even Hössler realized a miracle had happened. Hössler looked at the girl, then scanned the room to focus on the pillars in the middle. She was now shivering on the cold concrete floor, her arms wrapped around her legs pulled tightly against her chest.

All was quiet, and Hössler appeared to consider his options as he closed his eyes for a second.

"She's coming with me," Hössler said.

Hössler instructed two men to carry the girl outside. When they lifted her, she didn't protest. Her body was broken, her mind was too hazy to understand what was happening. They left the gas chamber, and Samson wanted to scream. He wanted to tear the girl away from Hössler and run away. Save her from this hell. *She beat death, for God's sake!*

Instead, he dropped his head and closed his eyes as hot tears streamed down his face. The girl's bright blue eyes stared at him, ingrained in his brain.

A single shot rang out in the yard outside, and Samson opened his eyes. The men dragging the final corpses out of the room stopped and looked up at the windowless, white-washed walls and ceiling. As Samson slowly got up, his knees aching, he wiped the tears from his eyes and clenched his fists. *One day I'm going to burn this whole place to the ground.*

# CHAPTER THIRTY-THREE

Agnes carried the large basket to the rows of tables where five women waited. She put it down with a sigh before Marta, a Polish woman she'd gotten to know in the past month.

"All women's undergarments again, Agnes?" Marta said, inspecting some of the pieces on top. Her German was very good.

"Yes, it's all of good quality. You can check it if you want."

Marta waved her hand. "No need, I trust you." She looked at Agnes with concern. "You know, you should take a break. You look like you're about to collapse."

"I'll take a break when the guard tells me I can." The women working in the warehouses had earned a few privileges. Even though they arrived roughly around the same time as Agnes, they had survived, worked their way to the top of the chain in Kanada, and now reaped the rewards.

Agnes turned around with an empty basket, ready for a few more hours of sorting clothing. As long as she worked hard, or pretended to when the guards were looking, she found they weren't too brutal. They occasionally found fault with some of the sorting: a few guards were more involved, and Agnes suspected they simply wanted a bribe. Agnes had found keeping her head down helped in the beehive of Kanada.

She returned to one of the piles, took a suitcase and found a free spot. The name and address on the suitcase was that of a Dutch family from Haarlem, a city not far from Amsterdam. Agnes' mind wandered to the days when she would bike there with her parents and Yvette. It was a pretty route that they cycled through the countryside, passing small boats and rows of cultivated fields. The memory warmed her momentarily, but she was quickly overcome by the chill of the void in her heart. *Even if I get out of here alive, those bike rides will never be the same.* She quickly went through the clothing and added the suitcase to the empty pile. She returned to her spot and overheard two women chatting in Dutch. They looked surprisingly well, without the haggard look of most of the women in Kanada.

"Sorry, I couldn't help but overhear you talking." The women looked up, startled at first, but then they both smiled at Agnes. "Did you arrive in the camp only recently?"

They nodded, and the smallest of the two said, "We arrived a few days ago. I'm Trijntje, and this is Johanna."

"Agnes, nice to meet you. Are you from the south?"

Johanna smiled and answered, "Ha, what gave it away?" She spoke with the softly-pronounced *g* of the Dutch south. "We're from Venlo, arrived through Vught three nights ago. How about you? I can't place your accent."

Agnes was surprised. She was always told she had a very distinctive accent. "Amsterdam. But I've been here for a year now."

Trijntje and Johanna looked surprised, and Agnes could see their eyes scanning her face and body. Despite her winter clothing, she didn't have the gaunt face many women around her had.

"Hey, what do you think this is, a teahouse?" a Kapo barked at them, waving his truncheon. "You can talk when you're in the barracks!"


"Markx, Agnes! Report!"

At first, she wasn't sure she'd heard correctly, but then she heard her name again.

Despite her apprehension, she stood and raised her hand. "Here!" The guards waved her over. She pointed at her basket of clothes. "What about these?"

"Leave them; you're needed somewhere else."

She slowly walked through the chaos of the people sorting clothes. Some glanced up and gave her looks of encouragement, while others kept their heads down. Whenever guards showed up for transfers, people stayed out of sight. Transfers away from the clothing commando were hardly ever good. Agnes had seen plenty of people taken away, never to be seen again.

She reached the guards. "Arm." Agnes lifted her arm and rolled up the sleeve of her coat to expose her tattoo. One of the guards checked the paper he was holding and nodded. "Follow us."

Agnes felt her heart in her throat as they navigated through the maze of activity in Kanada. As they reached the road connecting Kanada to the main thoroughfare, she saw crematoria 2 and 3 only a few hundred meters ahead. Their chimneys belched out ominous dark plumes of smoke. The guards walked in the same direction. Agnes felt her heart beating in her chest. She wiped her clammy hands on her trousers. *Is this it?*

They continued for another fifty meters until they reached the intersection with the main road. There stood a small army car and much to Agnes' surprise, they opened the door and told her to get in. The engine roared to life, and soon they were headed toward the camp's gatehouse, past the women's camp where she'd spent the past month. Soon they cleared the gatehouse, leaving Birkenau and the deadly crematoria behind.

Ten minutes later, the jeep stopped in front of a familiar building. Agnes blinked hard as the driver shut off the engine and opened the door. "Get out."

Block 10 looked the same. Little appeared to have changed in her month of absence as they made their way down the hallway. The sanitizer smell wafted from one of the operating rooms, and Agnes resisted the urge to look inside. To her horror, she was back in the hallway leading to Dr. Clauberg's office, where he had banished her from the block a month ago. *What am I doing here?*

The door was closed, and one of the guards knocked. A voice answered, and Agnes was shocked to see the person sitting behind the desk—Dr. Brewda hurried to get up and embrace Agnes.

"Thank you, that will be all," she said curtly to the guards standing by awkwardly.

"We need you to sign this."

She signed and dismissed the guards with a grunt. Agnes stood in awe. She'd never seen a prisoner treat the SS guards like this and get away with it. Dr. Brewda must've caught her look, for she grinned as she sat down, waving Agnes to the chair opposite. "A few things have changed since you were last here. One of the guards tried to bully me a few weeks back, and I told him I wouldn't stand for it in no uncertain terms. He hit me, and I reported him to Dr. Wirths. He took care of it."

Agnes struggled to understand what Dr. Brewda was saying. *Is this Block 10? Am I still in Auschwitz?* "But how?"

"I don't know what changed exactly, but Dr. Wirths made it clear all the doctors within the block would be treated with respect. Even the non-German ones."

"I guess it helps you're not Jewish." Agnes put her hand before her mouth, instantly regretting what she said. "I'm sorry, I didn't mean it like that."

Dr. Brewda brushed off her apology. "Don't apologize for speaking your mind, dear." She switched on a desk light and studied Agnes closer, lifting her eyebrows as she did. "How did they treat you in Birkenau?"

"It was rough and a lot of hard work."

"You look like a ghost."

"Did you get me back to Block 10?" Agnes said softly.

Dr. Brewda looked surprised. "Why, of course! When I heard you were transferred I was furious, but there was little I could do against Dr. Clauberg at the time. He was convinced you and Dr. Samuel worked together in botching the operations." She looked at Agnes curiously. "And I think he was right." Agnes said nothing and glanced at the papers on Dr. Brewda's desk. "I'm just going to take that as confirmation. Which is why I wanted you back here."

Agnes looked up. *Dr. Brewda approves of what we did?* "But how did you convince Dr. Clauberg to take me back?"

"I didn't. I talked to Dr. Wirths. I told him you are essential in the operations of the ward, in addition to your experience in the operating room."

"But didn't he know about my dismissal?"

Dr. Brewda shook her head. "Dr. Clauberg slipped it past him. When I told Dr. Wirths, he was furious and was more than happy to grant my request. Before we get you some food and back to the wards, I wanted to ask you something."

"Anything."

"In Kanada, what was it like? Where were you positioned?"

She told Dr. Brewda about her work in the clothing commando, and as she did, she saw a hint of disappointment on the physician's face. "Why?"

"I was hoping you knew more about the situation around more valuable items."

"Such as?"

"Medication."

*Of course.* "Any medication found in the clothing or suitcases had to be handed in to the women in charge of the medication *Lager*. They would take it inside a guarded barracks."

"Did you find a lot?"

Agnes nodded. "Every suitcase has medication. Most people brought basic painkillers, but plenty of people came with specific medication."

Dr. Brewda's face lit up as Agnes went through some types of medicine she encountered in people's clothing. "It is as I expected. Do you know how much medication would be in that part of Kanada?"

Agnes thought for a moment, making some calculations. "It's safe to say the other people sorting through the luggage and clothing would have the same experience as me. I think the cabinets in Kanada are well stocked."

"Well stocked. I'd say that's putting it mildly."

"Probably, yes," Agnes said.

Dr. Brewda looked thoughtful for a moment. "Agnes, you know we have a medication shortage in the hospital, right?"

"Of course."

"Would you be up for a quick inspection of the medication area of Kanada?"

"Sure," Agnes said. "But how would I get in?"

Dr. Brewda put her hands on the table and smiled. "Just let me worry about that."

# CHAPTER THIRTY-FOUR

The block was bustling when Joel walked in cradling his tin of morning soup. He sat on his bunk, taking a bite from the small piece of bread he'd saved the prior evening. It was hard and dry, and he dipped it in the watery soup.

He looked around at the other men. Most were also eating their soup: in Auschwitz, you ate whatever you could. Fewer received their weekly rations from the outside. Joel had spoken to some of the guards, and they told him the war on the eastern front was not going well. Hitler was worried about an assault from the west, and the rumors of the Nazis abandoning the eastern front became more frequent. It gave Joel and the other prisoners hope—perhaps Hitler had finally overextended himself by trying to fight on two fronts simultaneously.

"That was a pretty tough roll call, wouldn't you say?" Moshe knelt next to Joel's bunk and sat on the floor, taking a bite of his hunk of bread.

"The guards seemed a bit nervous," Joel said.

"The Kapos even more so. You'd almost think they're expecting something to happen.

Joel shrugged. "Kapos come and go. They think they're safe when they're appointed, but then they realize their problems have only just started." The prisoner-guards of the camp needed eyes in the back of their heads. If they were too soft on the prisoners, they'd attract the attention of the guards. If they were too rough, they could find themselves in an unfortunate accident when nobody was watching. "I'm glad I don't have anything to do with them working for Bruno."

"You're lucky. You can go around the entire camp without anyone constantly watching you." Moshe took a bite of his soup and looked around; the bunks surrounding them were empty.

Joel thought Moshe looked a little on edge. "Anything on your mind?"

"I received some exciting news last night." He set his tin down and glanced over both of his shoulders. They were alone but for a few men on the other side of the barracks, well out of earshot. "The camp resistance is preparing an escape."

Joel leaned forward. "When? How?" There had been talk of escapes since he arrived, but nothing had happened.

"Soon. There's been contact with the Home Army, and they are confident they can ambush a work detail traveling between two camps."

"I've heard this before. How is this different?"

"I know, I was hesitant, but this one is straight from the top. The leadership believes the only way we can fight back is by having escaped prisoners tell their stories to show proof of what's happening here."

Joel sat up. "Do you think the Brits and Americans would help?"

"I don't know. But I think it's worth a shot. Either way, we need to do everything we can, and if they don't believe people who've experienced this hell, who would they believe?"

Thousands of prisoners marched to the fields, factories, quarries, and mines around Auschwitz every day. If they planned it well, they might just succeed. "So, what do you need? I suppose you need me to tell Bruno in Birkenau?"

"Bruno already knows about the plan."

"I'm sure you're not just telling me this for no reason." As Joel spoke the words, he noted the expression on his friend's face. Moshe's head was slightly cocked, the corners of his mouth up in a smile.

"They want you to escape the camp."

Joel felt lightheaded. "Me?"

"You're perfect. Think about it. How often do you have to go between Auschwitz and Birkenau in a week? Three, four times?"

"Something like that."

"And you usually only have one or two guards with you? They could pick them off easily. I've heard an escape trail takes you farther south, avoiding villages. Or maybe farther north even, to Warsaw. Or Kraków—it's only ninety kilometers from here."

Joel nodded, and he could see why the leadership had picked him. "But when I get out, what will I do?"

Moshe shook his head. "I don't have the details on what will happen, but we should be ready to move in a few days. First, I wanted to make sure you were on board. This is a huge opportunity, Joel. You could join the resistance outside, and fight the Nazis. Maybe you could even join when the assault on the camp happens."

Moshe's optimism was contagious, and Joel found himself nodding along. Of course, an escape would be dangerous, but he agreed he was in the best position to attempt it.

"Tell them I'll do it."


Four days later, Joel sat in the back of a Kübelwagen. In the front, a young driver and guard talked about how long it had been since they'd been given some time off. Joel scanned the road ahead as he blocked out their voices. Moshe had come to him as they walked to the roll call area. Today was the day.

When the guards arrived to escort him, Joel felt an odd sensation. He no longer feared the SS men as he sat in the back although freedom was still far away. Ambushing a single car between the camps wasn't the biggest challenge. However, getting him away from the camp without someone raising the alarm would be a different story. A truck and another Kübelwagen passed them in the other direction as the drivers almost mechanically acknowledged each other. Whoever was looking to free Joel would need to time their ambush perfectly: there was plenty of traffic between the camps.

They were halfway between the camps, where a stretch of trees lined both sides of the road. Unfortunately, they had lost their leaves, and there was limited cover. Joel sat up straighter, scanning the tree line. The only place the ambushing party could hide was in the ditch next to the road, behind a row of bushes that retained some leaves. The car entered the cover of the first trees, and Joel held his breath.

He waited for the sound of—well, of what exactly? He expected men stepping onto the road with rifles raised, forcing the Germans to stop. Or would they simply shoot at the SS men in the front? He looked at the back of their heads. They seemed confident and utterly unaware of any impending danger. Joel didn't want to be caught by any stray bullets and sank a little lower in his seat. *It's taking too long.* He looked to the side of the road, but there was no movement in the bushes.

A few seconds later, they cleared the trees and were back in the open. Fields stretched out ahead, the town of Oświęcim in the distance. Five minutes later, they pulled into the main camp. Joel felt deflated. He had been sure he would be stomping through the fields by now. Had something happened along the way? He tried to hide his disappointment as they pulled up at one of the medical blocks.

The driver opened the door, and Joel shivered as the cold air hit his face. His well-worn coat was better than what most prisoners had, and despite wearing more layers of clothing than usual, he still felt the icy Polish winter air seeping through the holes in his coat.

"What are you waiting for?" The guard stood at the entrance of the block. "Get in; there's work to do. We don't have all day!"

Joel quickly made his way up the steps. Then he noticed the block number and hesitated. He'd heard the stories of what happened inside and almost felt he shouldn't enter. Then he saw the guard's face darken even more. He took a quick breath and entered Block 10.

The nurse closed the door, leaving Joel's guard standing outside. He expected him to come in, but all remained quiet as she led Joel to a table surrounded by all sorts of medical equipment.

"I suppose you know how these work?" she said as she pointed at a machine with a long iron bar arched over the operating table. At the end of the bar was an element that Joel didn't recognize. His confusion must've been evident, for the nurse frowned and then smiled. "Do you know what this machine does?"

Joel looked at her. At first he thought she was mocking him, but her smile was genuine. "I'm sorry, I'm just a technician. I can fix anything, though," he said, regaining a bit of confidence. "As long as it has wires."

"All right, this X-ray machine stopped working yesterday, and we need it back as soon as possible." She tapped on one of the buttons on the controls console. "I can still switch it on, but that's it." She pushed another button, and a faint clicking sound emerged from the element on the end of the bar.

"I'll see what I can do." He tried a few more settings on the machine, each resulting in the same sound. Finally, the nurse sat down on a chair in the corner. He could feel her gaze on his back and turned around. To his surprise, she didn't flinch.

"Just let me know if you need me to help or if I can test something," she said as she picked up a stack of papers.

Joel worked on the machine for half an hour, and much to his relief, found it was something he could fix. It wasn't without a hint of pride when he replaced the cover of the element and announced, "It should be good to go now."

The nurse got up and pushed a few buttons. This time, a high-pitched wheezing sound was followed by a distinctive click. The nurse looked up and raised her thumbs.

"That's what it should do." Her green eyes sparkled, although Joel thought he caught some sadness in her face as well.

He started packing up his tools. "This must be the cleanest block in Auschwitz. The hospital barracks in Birkenau aren't anywhere near this nice. How do you manage it?"

"We do what we can to ensure the people here are as comfortable as possible. With the operations going on here, ensuring this room is clean is the very least we can do for these poor people." She then stopped and quickly covered her mouth. "Sorry, please forget I said that."

Joel looked at her with interest. *So it's not just rumors.* "Don't worry. I'm not telling anyone about what's happening or what you've said. I've already seen the women arriving from Block 10." He sighed as the image of the limping and traumatized women flooded back into his conscious-ness—clutching their stomachs as they shuffled into the barracks.

The nurse's eyebrows shot up. "You've seen them return to the regular population?"

"Well, only a few, and then they're usually in the quarantine block." He hesitated before continuing, her eyes urging him on. "That's normally the last stop before the gas chambers." He remembered his close brush with death in the same block. The nurse nodded but said nothing. She looked slightly paler than before. "But some of them avoid the quarantine block," he added quickly. "It's a miracle they managed to survive, considering the state of the hospital blocks in Birkenau. But now that I see this, it makes sense."

The nurse shook her head. "It could be better, but the patient's health isn't the priority of the people running Block 10. So we, the pris-oners, do our best instead."

Joel stood up and, on impulse, held out his hand. "My name is Joel. It's been a long time since I've spoken to someone who seems to care so much."

She didn't immediately respond, and Joel felt awkward with his hand outstretched. He was about to withdraw it when she shook it more firmly than expected.

"I'm Agnes, and I'm glad to meet you. Even though you knew what was happening here, you didn't judge me when I asked you to fix it."

"Why would I? You don't have a choice, either. We have to do what-ever they tell us."

"We all have a choice. It's only our fear for what might happen when we resist that drives us to do what they tell us."

They were silent as her words sank in. *I suppose she's right. Even more reason to get out of here. I need to tell the world what's going on.*

There was a knock on the door, and the guard peeked his head in. His eyes went to Joel's closed toolbox. "Looks like you're done." He turned to Agnes with a questioning look.

She nodded. "We were just finishing up; I need to run one more test. You may want to close the door." She turned back to the control panel of the machine. "It will only take a few minutes."

"Five minutes." The guard closed the door.

"I suppose I'm heading back to Birkenau. It was nice to meet you."

"Maybe I'll see you again some time," Agnes said with a sad smile.

"Perhaps."

Joel stepped into the hallway, where the guard looked bored, and jerked his head toward the exit.

They reached the car, where the driver stood, smoking a cigarette. Joel climbed into the back and looked at Block 10 as the engine sputtered to life.

They approached the tree-sheltered area. There was movement in the bushes, and the driver slowed down a little. Joel's heartbeat pulsated in his throat as he looked through the windshield. *This is it.* He moved his hand closer to the door handle, ready to jump out of the car. The leaves rustled, and Joel leaned forward. The driver almost stopped the car; the guard reached for his holster. *I'll take them out myself if I have to.*

The eyes of the occupants in the car were fixed on the bush, and a figure carefully emerged. Joel dropped his eyes as a deer crossed the road.

Five minutes later, they were back in Birkenau.

# CHAPTER THIRTY-FIVE

The car was moving slowly, but Agnes didn't mind. She enjoyed being outside the camp, and the block for that matter. It had been almost two weeks since she'd seen anything but Auschwitz, and even though she was grateful for Dr. Brewda's efforts in getting her out of Birkenau, she felt very much like the prisoner she was in Block 10. She spent most of her time indoors, working long shifts with the rest of the nurses in the understaffed block. Dr. Brewda had asked Dr. Wirths if they could have some more nurses in the block, but her request had been denied. They needed all the hands they could get in Birkenau these days.

Despite their lack of nurses, the experiments continued, and Agnes often found herself escorting and supporting young women from the wards. It was exhausting, and she had jumped at the chance to collect medication from Birkenau. This was how she now found herself in the back of the car heading to the larger camp. Dr. Brewda had convinced Dr. Wirths that, to keep his test subjects healthy and useful for as long as possible, they required additional medication. She had hinted at the medication area in Kanada, and to her surprise, Dr. Wirths had agreed.

They entered the camp, and Agnes caught the walking skeletons staring from behind both sides of the barbed wire. She shuddered. *If it wasn't for Dr. Brewda, I would be one of them.*

It took only a few minutes before the car stopped near Kanada. The guard opened the door. "Do you know where you're supposed to go?"

Agnes nodded. "I worked in Kanada before."

"Good. Just be quick; we have more assignments today. I want you back here in half an hour." He handed her a piece of paper which afforded her entry into the medicine warehouse.

"That won't be a problem," she said as she hurried toward the hive of activity around the warehouses. She was excited the guard had sent her into Kanada alone—it was liberating to move without an escort.

She passed the clothing commando and looked for familiar faces. There were none, and even though she was a little disappointed, she knew she would draw unnecessary attention if anyone recognized her.

The medical warehouse was on the far side of Kanada, and it was slightly less crowded. Fewer prisoners working in Kanada were finding medication in luggage these days. She knew it was because many new arrivals tried to hold on to their medication for as long as possible. Most of the medication would be found in the crematoria changing rooms, and that would be delivered to Kanada by truck each day. Two guards stood near the entrance, and she approached one of them, holding out her piece of paper.

"Excuse me; I'm here to pick up medication for Block 10."

The guard was at least five years younger than her, and his fresh face made him look like he'd just come from the Hitler Youth. He inspected the paper, and Agnes held out her arm for him to check her prisoner number. He nodded and handed back the paper. "I'll come inside with you."

She followed him into the warehouse, where it was oddly quiet. A few prisoners carrying baskets milled about, sorting boxes. The inside of the warehouse was smaller than she'd expected, but the racks of shelves lined up neatly through the room were full. She marveled at the amount of medicine available.

"How much time do you need?" the guard said, interrupting her thoughts.

"No more than twenty minutes."

"Fine with me. I'll be over here. Let me know when you're done, and then you'll need to register what you took with her." He pointed at a young woman wearing prisoner garb sitting in the corner behind a small table. "If you need help finding anything, ask her." The woman looked at Agnes without emotion on her face, and Agnes noticed the woman's high cheekbones and striking blue eyes. Even with her shaved head, the woman was attractive.

Agnes thanked the guard and walked along the rows of neatly stacked medication, occasionally stopping to take a box on her list. She was at the back of the room when an older woman restocking the shelves approached. The woman pretended to place some boxes on the shelves near Agnes.

"Where are you taking those?" she whispered as Agnes put a box of sulfonamides in her small pouch.

Agnes glanced over her shoulder and saw the guard smoking a cigarette and chatting with the striking woman behind the desk. "What's it to you?"

"How many prisoners do you think are sent here to pick up medication?" The woman looked hard at Agnes. "That guard was very lenient with you. I suppose you found some way to get in here?"

Even though her tone was stern, her eyes revealed her anxiety. *Why did she approach me?* Agnes decided to share the truth. "I'm here to collect medicine for Block 10 in Auschwitz."

The expression on the woman's wrinkled face changed. Her features softened as she stepped closer to Agnes. "Are you? I've seen those poor wretches. Is it true what they say about what's going on in there?"

"It is. That's why I'm here." She studied the woman, who appeared to have forgotten the guard at the front. Agnes looked back; the guard was in casual conversation, leaning on the young woman's desk. *We don't have to worry about him.* "How long have you been working here?"

"Almost six months."

Agnes smiled. "Tell me, how often does the SS come here to collect medicine?"

"Twice a week—we have so much coming in every day that we sometimes run out of space."

"Has it always been like that?"

The woman shook her head. "No, I can tell there are more transports these past few months. And a lot more medication. It's almost as if people are told to bring their medication."

*Wouldn't surprise me.* "What can you tell me about the administration? Is she the only one checking the comings and goings?" Agnes nodded at the young woman near the entrance.

"She is, officially." The woman hesitated, and Agnes gave her an encouraging smile. "But she's also a prisoner, like you and me."

"Anything extra from this list would save lives in Block 10." Agnes pointed at her piece of paper, showing the required amounts of medicine.

"We should keep moving. Follow me."

They walked along the shelves, and Agnes picked up a few more boxes. If the woman walking next to her was being truthful, they may have found a way to supply the hospital with additional medicine.

"Do you think she would help?"

"Without a doubt."

Agnes was surprised. "How can you be so sure?"

She placed some more boxes in Agnes' pouch and smiled. "Because we've done it before."

Agnes returned to Block 10 in high spirits. She couldn't wait to share the good news. When she left the medicine warehouse, the young woman at the desk had been cordial. She'd carefully cross-checked Agnes's supplies against Dr. Wirths' order sheet. While she did, Agnes noted the guard paid little attention to the administration. Instead, he was more interested in the young woman behind the desk, cracking bad jokes while she worked.

The woman refilling the shelves—who had introduced herself as Lena—ensured her that she would have a chat with the gatekeeper. They would be ready for her the next time she visited.

She found Dr. Brewda in her small office and entered without knocking. The doctor frowned until she saw it was Agnes, and a smile appeared on her face. "How was Kanada? Did you get everything we needed?"

Agnes closed the door and emptied her pouch on the desk. Around twenty boxes of different sizes poured out, and Dr. Brewda inspected a few. She mumbled to herself in Polish, then nodded. "Well done, these are perfect." She picked up one of the boxes of sulfonamides. "I didn't expect these; they're not very common in Germany."

"I know. I even saw some English-labeled penicillin. I wanted to take some, but I didn't know how strictly the guards would check me."

"And did they?"

Agnes shrugged. "I could've easily taken more. This guard was more interested in the woman's records than the medication itself. He didn't as much as glance at what I took and hardly checked my papers."

"So you think you'd be able to take some extra boxes next time? Imagine what we'd be able to do with penicillin."

"I can do better than a few boxes." Agnes sat opposite Dr. Brewda. "When I searched for the medication on the list, a woman approached me." She told Dr. Brewda about her encounter with Lena.

"She said they'd done this before?"

"Her exact words. She said they would smuggle medicine in through a subcamp named Raisko earlier this year."

"Never heard of it."

"Me neither, but apparently, it's very small and not heavily guarded. She worked in the camp in the daytime and returned to Birkenau in the evening. People from nearby cells would bring in food and medicine in the evening, leaving it near a window for the morning shift of prisoners. Then, they would deliver the medicine to the hospital in Birkenau."

Dr. Brewda looked at her, perplexed. "I've never heard of this before."

"That's because it's not operational anymore, and it wasn't when you arrived. They were caught last March, but by then, Lena and the other woman had already been transferred to the medicine warehouse in Kanada. She told me she knows nothing about the connection now but believes it's been abandoned."

"A lucky escape." Dr. Brewda looked thoughtful. "Do you believe her?"

Lena had shared enough details about the smuggling operation at Raisko to make it plausible. "I don't see another reason for her to take the risk in approaching me. She's obviously keen to help, and when I showed her Dr. Wirths' orders, she knew I wasn't lying. She could've stopped there, thinking I might turn her in, but instead, she said she would talk to the woman keeping record.

Dr. Brewda smiled. "All right, I have to admit it sounds very promising. Let's try again soon. Did this Lena tell you when to come back? When would she have things set up for us?"

"She's there every day except on the Sabbath. We just need Dr. Wirths to sign off on another order."

"That won't be a problem. I'll prepare an overview of what we need in two days. He seemed happy enough to sign my previous request."

"I'll be ready whenever you need me."

Agnes' breath bottled up inside her chest for a moment as she stepped out of the office and headed upstairs. She couldn't wait to plunder the medicine warehouse next. She entered the ward and looked at the bunks filled with young women recovering from the gruesome experiments. *They're finally going to get proper treatment. We're going to defy those Nazi butchers.*

# CHAPTER THIRTY-SIX

S amson didn't look back as he exited the crematorium yard. His soot-covered hands were filthy, and despite the cold air, he was sweating. The day had dragged on despite the endless stream of corpses coming up from the gas chamber.

He felt a nearby presence and looked up to find Kaminski walking next to him. The leader of the Sonderkommando walked purposefully, keeping his eyes fixed on a couple of nearby guards escorting them back to their block.

"I talked to our friends in leadership," Kaminski said in a low voice, and Samson strained his ears to make out the following words. "They're keen to hear how your friend plans to acquire the gunpowder."

"They like the idea?"

Kaminski nodded. "They do, but they're skeptical. They're wondering how one woman can do it and be so confident about it. I told them you spoke to her and trusted her."

"She said the women working in the factory were ready to start smuggling out the gunpowder as soon as she gives them the word."

"And you still believe she can deliver?" Kaminski turned his gaze to Samson, his eyes boring into him.

Samson swallowed and thought of Roza. She had been so determined. There was no trace of doubt when she spoke of the plan. "Yes."

"Very well." Kaminski returned his focus to the guards as they turned into the men's camp. "Then you should meet with her as soon as you can. I have more instructions."

"I can visit her tomorrow morning."


It was an October Sunday morning, and Samson and Roza sat in their usual spot between two barracks. With no wind, the weather was surprisingly mild, and Samson wiped his forehead, the warmth of the sun on his face. Roza was off from her work in the clothing commando. For Samson, it was a rare day off from the crematorium. Even though the chimneys continued to belch their black smoke, no transports were scheduled for today, and Samson was not among the smaller contingent of Sonderkommando making their way to work today.

"So the underground is on board with our plan?" Roza said, her voice trembling.

"That's what my contact told me. He proposed it to them a few days ago, and even though they still have some questions about the logistics, they want to give it a shot. To be honest, I'm surprised. There's no downside for them. You're taking all the risks."

Roza nodded. "Yes, but only for the first part. I can get the gunpowder from the factory to the women's camp, but I haven't thought about the next steps. Who would build the bombs? And how would we distribute those around the camps? That's where the underground comes in."

"You need not worry about that. I spoke to my contact about this. There's someone in the Sonderkommando who has previously worked with bombs."

"That's unbelievable." Roza sat up. "Have you talked to him yet?"

Samson shook his head. He didn't want to tell Roza he hadn't spoken with anyone but Kaminski yet. He realized he was making a lot of promises on both sides, and suddenly he felt flustered. Roza and the women in the factory were going to take tremendous risks to acquire gunpowder. He regained his composure. "I haven't spoken to him directly. We must keep the people who know about the next link in the chain as small as possible. You know, in case someone gets caught."

"I understand. We did the same back home in Ciechanów when I joined Hashomer Hatzair. Even though we had many members, we all worked in our independent cells. I didn't know anyone beyond the six or seven people in my cell." Her eyes went glassy. If she had been a member of the Hashomer Hatzair movement, she knew the risks in fighting back. He looked at her with different eyes, confident about the plan, and he held out his hand.

"What happened to the people in your cell?"

She looked up and stared at his hand for a moment. Then she took it, the touch of her skin soft but her grip firmer than he'd expected. "I don't know. When the Germans started emptying the ghetto, we agreed we needed to split up into smaller groups. All the cells tried to stay together, but when we arrived in Auschwitz, I lost sight of many of my friends on the ramp. It was mayhem." She looked sad as she squeezed his hand. "When we lined up, I tried to stay with my family, with my mother. But she was too frail, and we were soon separated. That was the last time I saw her."

Samson was quiet. It was a familiar story, and there was nothing to say.

"I'm sorry, I got distracted." Roza let go of his hand and wiped her eyes. She looked at him fiercely. "If you're confident this man can build the bombs, I can ask the women to start taking the gunpowder from the factory. I guess I could give the powder to you, but it seems risky having you transport everything?"

Samson shook his head. "I don't know where the bombs should go once they're built. And you're right; we can't do this on our own. We need the underground. But they want to be sure they can trust you."

"Why would they question that?" Roza's eyes spat fire. "I came up with this plan while they're waiting around for the Home Army to make up their minds. We should do something, Samson."

"I know, and I don't doubt you." Samson held up his hands. "And neither does my contact. He's already vouched for you." *For us.*

"So, what do they need?"

"I don't know, but I suspect they want to see if you can deliver."

"Then I will get the powder," Rosa said confidently.

"Hold on. The underground wants to meet with you first. I suppose they would want to hear your plans. Perhaps you could also ask them about theirs?" He was certain Roza would have plenty of questions for them as well.

Roza raised an eyebrow, then quickly recovered. "All right, that seems fair. What's next?"

"They said they'll reach out to you in the next few days. That's all I know."

"I'll be ready."

# CHAPTER THIRTY-SEVEN

Joel and Piotr walked back from roll call together. Roll call took longer than necessary, as one of the guards had found fault with how one of the blocks was lined up. They had beaten two men to death in the yard and taken another five to Block 11. They would probably see these men hanging from the gallows soon. He scanned the faces of the men around him and reassured himself that hardly anyone knew what he was doing. Only Moshe and Bruno knew about his connections. They would sooner die than reveal their secrets.

"I still feel sick after watching that," Piotr said. "It seems like the roll calls are getting more brutal. There have been deaths at every one since Monday."

Joel nodded, and even though he'd looked away while the guards rained their deathly blows on the two men, roll call executions were only a tiny percentage of the killings happening farther down the road. "They're trying to scare us; keep us in line."

"Well, it's working. Did you see the faces of the others?"

"Of course. But I think it has to do with the large number of new men arriving last week. They don't know all the rules, and the SS enjoy scaring the others. Come, let's pick up breakfast."

After making a detour past the camp kitchen, Joel and Piotr

returned to their block and put down the heavy vat of soup. The men of the block gathered around, and soon a line had formed. Supplies from the outside had dwindled ever further, and by now, the once privileged bakers and butchers of Auschwitz's Polish block were eating the same soup as everyone else. What a difference a few months made, Joel thought as he looked around at the men who had been so well fed and privileged when he arrived. He was slurping from his own tin when Moshe appeared next to him.

"Joel, we need to chat." He looked restless. "Now."

He followed his friend to a quiet spot in the corner. They hadn't spoken much since the day he was supposed to escape. A few days after Joel returned to the block, Moshe explained that the Home Army had changed their minds at the last minute. They had been waiting early in the morning at the tree-lined spot Joel had passed but had been put on alert by increased patrols. After a close brush with a heavily armed SS regiment, they'd decided to abandon the mission.

Moshe had been apologetic. "I'm sorry, Joel, there won't be another escape anytime soon. Our friends on the outside are worried the SS might be setting traps, and they want to hold off for a while."

*Typical. So much talk, hardly any action.*

"I know you're disappointed, and it will happen sometime. We just need to be patient."

"It's all right, Moshe. I know you're just the messenger," Joel had said.

Now standing with Moshe in the corner, Joel took a quick sip from his soup. "What did you want to talk to me about, then?"

Moshe looked around. There was no one nearby. "I spoke with the leadership, and they've discovered a very interesting connection in the women's camp."

Joel cocked his head. "That would be our first in the women's area, wouldn't it?"

"I don't know." Moshe shook his head. "They don't tell me much more than what I share with you."

Joel suspected that wasn't entirely true, but he let it go. "So, who's the woman? It's a woman, I assume?" It could be a guard or a Kapo, but that would be sensational, and Joel doubted it.

"I don't know her name, but get this. She's from Ciechanów."
Moshe's face lit up. "And from what I've heard, she was also involved in
the resistance. She was part of one of our cells!" His voice rose an octave.

Joel almost choked on his soup. "She was in the Hashomer Hatzair
in Ciechanów?"

"Hard to believe, isn't it?"

"If she's really from Ciechanów, it means she's been in Auschwitz
for as long as you and I." Joel placed his tin on the floor. "What does the
leadership want with her?"

"They want you to check on her story. She says she can contribute
to the uprising."

"Contribute how?"

"She claims she has connections at Union."

"The ammo factory?"

"The very one. She has a friend in the Sonderkommando who
reached out. She says she can smuggle gunpowder into the camp."

Joel was quiet for a moment. Access to gunpowder would be huge.
"We could build bombs," he muttered under his breath while he looked
at Moshe. "What do they want me to do?"

"Find out how she's planning to do it. Talk to her and see if you
think she can actually do it. They have their doubts. It's quite a claim."

"It sure is." *How would they smuggle out enough gunpowder for
bombs?* "I'm not sure I can get into the women's camp. It's usually two
other guys who do the repairs in there."

Moshe nodded. "Don't worry about it. Bruno will take care of it."

Joel nodded and looked at his friend. Moshe was beaming. "This
could change everything, couldn't it?"

"We might finally be able to fight back."

"When do I visit her?"

"Today. Bruno will tell you everything you need to know."


Joel found Bruno in the back of the repair shed.

"Big day today, Joel." Bruno made his way over, waiting for the last
of the other men to leave the shed. When the door slammed shut, he

motioned for Joel to sit down. "You're heading to the clothing commando this morning."

Joel raised an eyebrow. "Really? I thought I was needed in the women's camp?"

"Change of plans. I received complaints about the lights not working properly at the clothing commando." He looked at Joel intensely. "You'll need to find the forewoman of one of the groups there. Have you been there before?" Joel shook his head, and Bruno continued. "She won't be hard to find. She'll be the one inspecting the baskets."

"And what do I tell her?"

"That you're there to inspect the faulty lights. She'll show you what to do next."

"Do you know her name?"

"They didn't tell me. But Joel, listen." His face turned serious. "All I know about this mission is that the leadership is torn on whatever this woman is offering, and they want you to verify her intent."

"I'll get the information."

The masses of people sorting through never-ending piles of clothing were overwhelming. Joel had been to the Kanada warehouses before, but the scale of operations seemed to have gone up again. He walked around the Kapos, careful to stay out of their way.

Making his way from the chaos, he saw a row of tables lined up before one of the warehouses. The mood was very different here, with women carefully inspecting baskets of clothing before handing them off to other prisoners carrying them inside the warehouses. Joel had studied them for a moment when his eye fell on a woman going back and forth between the others. She occasionally inspected some of the baskets before they were hauled off. Her area was calm in the chaotic surroundings, and she even spoke a few words to the SS guard at the head of the row of tables. He appeared bored but nodded as she pointed at some of the baskets on the tables. *That must be her.*

Joel waited for her to walk clear of the guard. He gripped his toolbox tighter and approached her when she went from one woman to the other. "Excuse me, are you in charge here?"

The woman looked up, her dark brown eyes showing little surprise as she looked him up and down, her eyes lingering on the toolbox. She looked confident as she answered. "As much as anyone can be in charge." She waved her arms in an arc at the frenzy. "Can I help you with something?"

Joel was sure there was a hint of a Ciechanów accent in her voice. So he decided to risk putting on a slight accent of his own. "I was told you have trouble with some of the lighting around here?" As he spoke, the woman shifted her weight, the corners of her mouth lifted ever so slightly, and her eyes narrowed a little.

"I'm glad you could come by so quickly. It's been difficult to find our way around the back of the warehouse. Come, I'll show you." She walked toward the guard and said something Joel couldn't make out, but the man nodded. Joel followed her to the wooden structure serving as a warehouse. The inside was packed with clothing, neatly sorted in racks reaching the roof. The woman caught his look as she turned around.

"And this is just one of the warehouses. Every other week this building is emptied, only for us to fill it up just as quickly again." She sighed. "It's hard to imagine the previous owners disappeared within the past two weeks."

Joel nodded, not knowing how to respond. The air in the warehouse was suddenly heavy, and he was glad when she continued onward. It became darker in the back; one of the lights was flickering.

The woman stopped near the broken light. "I assume this is easy enough for you to fix?"

Joel opened his toolbox and nodded. "Not a problem." He picked out some tools, then looked at the woman. "You're from Ciechanów, aren't you?"

She looked around, and Joel followed her gaze. They were alone. "Yes. And you're not just here to fix the broken lights, are you?"

"Maybe not." He closed his toolbox and looked around. "Do you have anything I can use to reach that?" He pointed at the light bulb. She walked to the front of the warehouse and returned with a crate. "Now we can pretend I'm working on this when someone walks in." He put on foot on the crate and looked at the woman. "I'm told we have a common goal."

The woman put her hands on her hips. "What's your name?"

"Joel."

"I'm Roza. It's nice to meet someone from Ciechanów. There used to be more of us in Kanada, but you know what happens to people in this camp."

"I saw the Kapos earlier. It looks like you've got a tough job here." It was clear Roza wasn't ready to share just yet. "When did you arrive at the camp?"

"November 1942. I was on one of the first transports from the ghetto. I can't remember where we stopped along the way, but when the doors opened, I found myself on the ramp."

*So we'd just missed each other.* "If you don't mind me asking, I heard you were also part of the resistance in Ciechanów?"

She cocked her head. "Also?"

Joel smiled. *She's smart.* "I know Hashomer Hatzair had a few cells in Ciechanów. I was also part of one of them."

"Did you do anything while you were in the ghetto?" Roza fixed her eyes on his.

"What do you mean?"

She rubbed her nose, hesitating. "I couldn't get anyone to join me in fighting back. I wanted to fight the SS, but I never got the chance. Nobody listens to a sixteen-year-old girl."

"If it helps, nobody listened to me, either." He considered telling her about his act of resistance in the ghetto. "I wish we would've met in Ciechanów; maybe we could've helped each other."

Roza nodded, and they were silent for a moment.

"I think we can do something here, though, in Auschwitz."

"I think so, too."

"You were sent by the resistance leadership—right, Joel?"

"I'm told you can play a big part in the planned uprising."

Her eyebrows shot up. "The underground is planning an uprising?"

Joel nodded. Even though he didn't know the exact plans, an uprising couldn't be far away. "If you can do what you're promising, it could be the final piece of the jigsaw needed to convince the Home Army to attack the camp while we fight from the inside." He was speculating now, but he could see the excitement in Roza's eyes. "Tell me about your plan. Can you really get the gunpowder from the Union factory?"

"Yes." There was no trace of hesitation in her answer. "I have friends working in the powder room of the factory." She took in Joel's blank look and quickly explained. "This is where the gunpowder is weighed and portioned before it's distributed further along the production process. The women check the quality of the gunpowder. The forewoman is my friend, along with a few others."

Joel was impressed. "Did you talk to them about taking the gunpowder out?"

"They are keen to help, and we've discussed how we'll take it out several times."

"Have they taken anything out before?"

"Not yet. But they're waiting for me to tell them to start. So we know the plan will work."

"How will they smuggle it out? Aren't they checked when leaving the factory?"

"Every evening, they're taken back to the women's camp. There are inspections, sure, but not always. Whenever the SS inspect the women, they start at the front or the back of the group. My friends will make sure they're always in the middle."

"And what will they do when the inspection happens?"

"They'll scatter it." She looked confident now. "It looks much like the sand and gravel on the ground and road around the factory."

"Let's say you get the gunpowder to the women's camp. What's next?"

"You mean, how will we make bombs out of the powder? I'll need help from the camp underground. And the Sonderkommando."

Joel saw a sparkle in her eyes at the mention of the Sonderkommando. Roza exuded confidence as she spoke about her plan. Everything she told him sounded plausible as far as plans in Auschwitz went. They all knew the risks: if any of the women were caught, the plan would be foiled. He scratched his chin. *But it's worth a shot.* He was keen to help Roza, and he wanted to vouch for her. But before he could do that, he needed one more thing.

"You look hesitant," Roza said, interrupting his thoughts. For the first time today, she looked worried.

Joel shook his head. "I'm not. I like your plan, and if you succeed, it will make a huge difference."

"But?"

"I need you to show me you can really do it."

"You need me to bring you the gunpowder." Roza met his eyes, and without flinching, she said, "I'll contact my girls. Come find me in three days."

Exactly three days later, Joel and Roza stood in the warehouse again. Joel had been more confident entering the clothing commando, and as soon as Roza spotted him, she'd led him inside.

Without a word, Roza reached into her shirt and bra. Joel moved from one foot to the other, but Roza stood firm as she produced a tiny container no bigger than a shirt button. She opened it and carefully handed it to Joel. He gasped as he looked at the small amount of grayish-yellow powder inside, then back to Roza.

"This changes everything."

# CHAPTER THIRTY-EIGHT

S amson wiped sweat from his brow as the three other men set the water pump down. Each was panting heavily, relieved to take a short break.

"Are you sure this is going to work?" One of the men asked, his eyes shifting nervously as a Kübelwagen passed them. The guards didn't give them as much as a second look. Samson shielded his face from the dust as the driver sped away.

"I've done this many times before. Trust me, it will be fine." The man who spoke up had been with the Sonderkommando for almost as long as Samson. His name was Jan, and Kaminski had arranged a spot for Samson on the work crew lugging the camp's only water pump from the crematorium to the women's camp. For the other two men accompanying Samson and Jan it was their first time visiting the women. Samson felt conspicuous transporting the heavy pump, but Jan looked confident.

Samson would've preferred heading to the women's camp on his own to see Roza, but Kaminski had insisted he would go under the guise of transporting the water pump. "She has something important for you." Kaminski had said, and Samson had a good idea of what it would be.

They lifted the water pump and continued down the road. They soon reached the gate to the women's camp.

"Okay, do you all have your cigarettes handy?" Jan asked, reaching into his own pocket to show a full pack. The others nodded. Even though they were technically allowed into the camp with the water pump, they needed the guard's permission to hang around a bit longer. It was a game played by the men of the Sonderkommando and the guards of the women's camp, and they all knew the rules.

The guard took their *donations* and waved them through. They quickly installed the water pump and soon found themselves surrounded by women. Most were interested in what the men had brought, while some used the water pump. Water was scarce, and the water supplies in the barracks hardly ever worked. Samson snuck away while the others handed out chocolate, cheese, and other goods they had organized.

He found Roza at their usual spot. It had been over a week since their last meeting, and he was relieved to see her this unseasonable mid-October day. Despite her position at the clothing commando, life in Auschwitz could change at the slightest whim of a guard.

"I'm so happy to see you," Roza said as she hugged him. He smiled, breathing in the smell of her hair. She was using the soap he'd brought her last time.

"You too," Samson said. "I've missed you. How are you holding up at Kanada?"

"It's much of the same. There are so many clothes coming in these days that it's almost impossible to find enough room for all of it. One of the guards said they may soon expand Kanada." She shook her head, her expression darkening. "But it's still nowhere near what you're going through."

"I don't really want to talk about it. I'd prefer to leave that at the crematorium's gates."

Roza looked around and lowered her voice. "The camp under-ground reached out to me."

"I expected as much."

"Really? How would you know?" Roza looked genuinely surprised. "They seem so covert about everything."

"Kaminski's never put me on the water pump crew before. It's a popular job in the Sonderkommando. He said I urgently needed to meet with you. That's when I thought something must've happened." He smiled. "So what did they say? How did you meet them?"

"One of their messengers came to Kanada when I was at work."

"That's bold."

Roza shook her head. "No, it was smart, actually. He came in to do some repairs, and it gave us some time to speak in one of the warehouses."

"Were they keen?"

"They had lots of questions, but that's not what I wanted to talk to you about."

Samson raised his eyebrows. Roza appeared impatient, and her face flushed. "Okay, what is it?"

"I need to show you something." She reached into her dress, produced a small weathered matchbox. She handed it to him. "Be careful when opening it."

Samson's hand shook as he slid the little box open. His mouth went dry when he saw its contents—inside was a good portion of grayish-yellow powder. Gunpowder. He looked at Roza, who stood observing him with a smile.

"We've done it, Samson. We've started getting it out."

He quickly closed the box and held it in the palm of his hand. Even though the box was light, he could feel the weight of its contents as he marveled at Roza's accomplishment. "I'm so proud of you. How did you do this? We only spoke about this last week."

"Don't ask too much. Just take the box to your contact. We need to know if he can make the bombs."

Samson didn't immediately respond. He thought of the potential of the little bit of powder in his hands. If they could set up a steady stream, the possibilities would be endless. "We could finally fight back. Maybe the uprising will really happen," he mumbled to himself.

"That's certainly what the messenger from the camp underground thought," Roza said, startling Samson. "He said this might mean the Home Army will attack the camp."

Samson scowled. "I'll believe it when I see it. They keep putting any support off, much like the underground."

"If anything is going to change their minds, this surely will." Roza gently stroked his arm. "We need to keep the faith, Samson. Soon, we'll be able to fight back, with or without the support of the Home Army."

As they sat in the afternoon sun, Roza resting her head on Samson's shoulder, he wished for only one thing: that they would survive this hell together, somehow.

On the way back, Samson could almost feel the matchbox burning in his pocket. The other men were in no hurry to return to their block, and they took frequent breaks. Every passing patrol made Samson feel his heart in his throat. The guards could decide on a surprise inspection any time they wanted; they needed no excuse. He wondered what would happen if they found the gunpowder. In the best case, he would be shot on the spot. More likely, though, he knew he would be taken for interrogation. He wasn't sure how much torture he would be able to endure before he would give up names. Samson clenched his jaw—he would never give up Roza's name. *They'll have to kill me before I tell them anything.*

He was relieved when they reached the gate to the Sonderkommando block, and the guard let them in. Glad to leave the heavy pump behind, he scanned the yard, where a number of men stood chatting, idling, and smoking cigarettes in the setting sun.

Samson forced himself to calmly enter the block. He found Kaminski reading a tattered book in his bunk. As soon as the Kapo saw him, he tossed the book aside. He looked at Samson in anticipation. Samson nodded toward the door and, together, they exited the block. They steered clear of the smokers and reached a spot on the side of the building, out of sight of curious onlookers.

"And?" Kaminski could barely contain his curiosity. "Did she have it?"

Samson produced the matchbox and handed it to the Kapo. He slid it open and looked at the powder for a few seconds. Then he closed the box and put his hand on Samson's shoulder.

"Incredible! She really did it!" Samson had never seen Kaminski this excited. He almost felt the energy coursing through the man's hands as he gripped his shoulder tighter. "This changes everything, Samson!" Kaminski looked into the distance, where the crematorium chimneys bellowed their smoke uninterrupted. "In a few months, we should have enough of this to blow up those houses of death."

When the big man finally let go of his shoulder, he looked him in the eye. "Did she tell you how often she'll be able to get this?"

Samson nodded. Before he left, Roza had assured him she would have gunpowder available for him every other day. "The only thing I'm worried about is the guards becoming suspicious of me visiting so often."

Kaminski shook his head. "Only on the way in, I would suppose. Just make sure you always bring them something."

"Don't worry, I wouldn't get in without that, anyway," Samson said, slightly annoyed. *I know the rules.* Despite his annoyance, he agreed Kaminski had a point—the guards had never checked him on the way out.

"But you're right to be careful," Kaminski said, scratching his head. "We'll need to find a better way to transport it here. I'm sure I can find some volunteers to bring back the powder when they're going to visit the women's camp." He smiled. "I decide who gets to go, anyway. So it shouldn't be too difficult."

Samson felt his shoulders unknot—they were in this together.

# CHAPTER THIRTY-NINE

The hallway was empty when Agnes stepped out of her office. Technically it was Dr. Brewda's office, but Agnes spent a lot of time in there as well these days. She headed up the stairs, holding on to a couple of files. Dr. Brewda was waiting for her at the top.

"Are those the new arrivals?"

Agnes held up the papers. "Just four last night. They're all in the back." She hurried to keep up with Dr. Brewda, who took big strides toward the women. They found them fast asleep. None older than sixteen. Agnes gasped at their tired faces, malnourished bodies, and cracked lips.

Dr. Brewda looked around and summoned one of the nurses tending to the women in the room. "Have they had enough water?"

The nurse looked slightly overwhelmed. "They've slept ever since arriving last night. We've given them water and some weak tea. They ate some bread this morning, but they couldn't hold it down. They're very weak, Dr. Brewda."

The doctor took the files from Agnes and jotted down some notes. The girls had arrived from the Greek city of Thessaloníki, more than 2,000 miles away. The journey must've taken at least a week. It was a miracle the girls had survived.

"Wake them up and give them some sugar water," Dr. Brewda said to the nurse, before turning to Agnes. "Come, to my office."

They entered the office and Agnes closed the door. Dr. Brewda sank down in her chair with a heavy sigh. "Those girls are in no state for an examination, but I don't know how I'm going to stop it." She looked at Agnes, exasperated.

"We could keep them sedated?"

Dr. Brewda looked at her for a few seconds, her face thoughtful. "It's worth a try. Dr. Clauberg prefers to be able to talk to the young women on the first examination. Can you take care of it?"

"Of course."

Dr. Brewda reached for a notepad on her desk and scribbled something. She ripped the piece of paper from the pad and handed it to Agnes. "Make sure they're properly out so Dr. Clauberg can't talk to them."

Agnes noted the high dosage on the note. It reminded her of something. "Have you noticed we're starting to run low on some of the medication coming in from Birkenau?"

Dr. Brewda took on a pained expression, holding her head in her hands. "I know. We can't keep up with just you and Margie going between the warehouse and here. There are too many girls in need of medication."

Agnes had made the journey back to the Kanada warehouses three times in the past month. The problem wasn't obtaining the medicine— it was getting it to the hospital without arousing suspicion. Margie, the other nurse who had volunteered to go between Kanada and the hospital, had been stopped on her first visit, and only her quick thinking had saved her from further interrogation. "We need more girls going between the camps."

Dr. Brewda nodded. "I know, but I'm not sure who to trust. We have so many new girls working in the wards these days."

"I know. I'll keep an eye out." In truth, Agnes had identified some of the new girls as potential conspirators, but she wanted to make sure they were trustworthy before promising anything. Dr. Brewda had enough on her mind. Agnes walked to the door and as she reached for the handle the door burst open. It was Dr. Wirths. Agnes stepped back as he barged past her. The head physician looked rushed as he sat down opposite Dr. Brewda.

"I'm quarantining everybody in the Birkenau hospital. No interaction with any of the prisoners here." He turned and pointed at Agnes. "Including the nurses."

Dr. Brewda looked worried. "Is the typhus infection not under control?"

"No, and if we don't keep those people quarantined, it's going to spread through the entire camp." Dr. Wirths' face was flushed. "Before you know it we'll have an epidemic on our hands. And I certainly can't have it spreading to our hospital. We can't have our important medical research interrupted. Not while we're making such great progress."

Agnes bit her lip. The fatality rate had greatly increased since Dr. Samuel's departure. Dr. Clauberg and Dr. Wirths seemed undisturbed by these deaths. Dr. Samuel had been replaced by a butcher of a man called Dering. He claimed to be a doctor, but Agnes had seen precious little proof of his supposed credentials. She'd seen young women bleed to death on the operating table.

"Agnes? Are you paying attention?" Dr. Brewda's voice interrupted her thoughts, and she found both doctors staring at her.

"I'm sorry?" Agnes stammered.

"I was just telling Dr. Wirths we're a bit short on good nurses here. Do you have the actual numbers?"

"Of course." Agnes recovered and made her way swiftly to one of the filing cabinets. She quickly found the file she was looking for and handed it to Dr. Brewda. "I believe we have seventy-eight nurses working here."

"Just for Block 11?" Dr. Wirths asked.

"No, in the entire hospital."

Dr. Wirths looked pensive for a moment. "We could use more help, but to be honest, we don't have enough trained people coming in these days. They're not suitable for work here. We have standards."

What Dr. Wirths was really saying was that the people on the incoming transports were sent directly to the gas chambers, but Agnes again held her tongue. Dr. Mengele still stood on the ramp, but he was only interested in finding very particular subjects for his own experiments. Agnes was rooted to the floor and tried to stop her legs from shivering.

Dr. Wirths got up. "No one goes to Birkenau until I tell you otherwise. You're to stay here for now." He didn't wait for a response but left the room, slamming the door behind him.

"We can forget about getting more medication in now, that's for sure," Dr. Brewda said as she replaced the file in the filing cabinet. "It could be a month until we're allowed to go to Birkenau again."

"It doesn't change our main problem, though," Agnes said. "Once Birkenau is open again, we need more nurses to smuggle medication from Kanada."

"Yes, but we won't see any new nurses arriving soon, Dr. Wirths made that clear enough."

They sat in silence for a while, and then Agnes looked at Dr. Brewda. "What if we try a different approach?"

"What do you mean?"

"Do you think it's Dr. Wirths' call whether people are selected from the ramp?"

"I think he has some say," Dr. Brewda said hesitantly.

"But it's probably not up to him. The camp command cares more about making the quotas of deaths in the crematoria, wouldn't you say?"

Dr. Brewda nodded. "Unfortunately, yes. The hospital in Birkenau, and ours to some extent, is more for show than anything else."

Agnes stood up. "Exactly. But Dr. Wirths cares about his experiments."

"More than anything."

"So what if we tell him we may have a way to fix our shortage of good nurses to assist in the experiments without involving the incoming transports?"

Dr. Brewda sat up, her expression one of disbelief. "How?"

"We train our own nurses from the women in Birkenau. The work in Block 10 isn't that difficult. But if we have women coming in from Birkenau every day—"

"They could smuggle medication."

Agnes smiled. "Exactly."

# CHAPTER FORTY

The sun was setting behind the rows of barracks to Joel's right as he walked along the road. He tried to ignore the wails from the women to his left as he picked up his pace—he couldn't help them. With every step he came closer to the place he wanted to avoid most of all. He gripped his toolbox tighter, reminding himself this was his last job of the day. As he reached the end of the road, he stopped and turned to the gate. He looked at the large chimney, seeing it up close for the first time. The guard at the gate stopped him.

"Where do you think you're going?"

Joel pointed at his toolbox. "They need help fixing some of the lights inside. I'm an electrician."

The guard eyed him suspiciously. "Papers."

Joel produced the work order and handed it to the man. The guard took his time, shuffling between the two sheets multiple times. He wasn't much older than Joel, yet his perfectly tailored uniform, polished boots, and clean-shaven, somewhat pudgy face gave the guard an air of confidence Joel had long since lost.

"You can go in," the guard said as he handed back the papers. Joel stepped through the gate and immediately felt a sense of dread as he entered the yard. Death was in the air, and he knew he could and probably would end up here one day soon. He put the thoughts from his mind as he approached the first door leading into a large red-brick building. A prisoner wearing soot-covered overalls stood outside.

"Who are you looking for?"

"I was told to report to Kaminski."

The man nodded. "Right in here. He should be near the ovens."

Joel entered the building, and the first thing he noticed was the darkness and heat. He continued toward the sound of roaring flames as the heat intensified with every step. Then, all of a sudden, he found himself in a large room with a low ceiling. Men were busy pushing carts stacked with dead bodies along narrow tracks. Other men, covered in soot and with sweat running down their faces, ran between the ovens, dumping coal into the flames.

"Hey! Get out of the way!" Joel turned to find two men racing toward him with a cart. He quickly jumped out of the way as they narrowly missed him. They stopped near one of the ovens, where another man opened the oven door just in time for the bodies to tumble from the cart into the oven. Joel looked away in horror.

"You lost?" a tall man asked, seemingly undisturbed by the horrors around him. Instead, he eyed Joel with a curious expression, hands in his pockets. He wore the armband of a Kapo, but he didn't fit the profile. A regular Kapo would have his baton out and ready.

"I'm looking for Kaminski," Joel said meekly. He focused on the man, keeping his gaze averted from the carnage.

"I was hoping you were," the Kapo said as he extended his hand. "I'm Kaminski. You must be Joel." Joel shook his hand, relieved. "Come, let's talk in the other room."

Kaminski guided him to a smaller room and closed the door. "This is the overseer's office, but he won't mind me using it. I'm glad to meet you, Joel. I hear you've been involved in quite a few operations."

Joel nodded. "Just happy to do something." The man opposite him made a formidable first impression. "What do you need from me?"

"Getting right to it, I like it," Kaminski said with a grin. "Have you been to Raisko before?"

Joel raised an eyebrow. "Can't say that I have. What is it?"

"It's a small subcamp to the south of Birkenau. It's used mostly for botanical experiments."

"Botanical? Seems an odd place for such research."

"Hey, what do I know." Kaminski raised his hands. "I imagine the Germans have their pick of Jewish scientists from all over Europe, and they must've figured it would be useful to have them working on plants as well. But that's not the reason you're going there." He lowered his voice. "Tonight, a group of Polish partisans are delivering an important package to the camp's laboratory. The women working there are in on the delivery and will retrieve it in the morning. They'll wait for you to pick it up. You'll then bring it to me in the afternoon. Bruno has already prepared all the work documents. Your cover will be to fix a machine in the laboratory."

"How will I know who to approach?"

"You'll look for a female scientist called Felcia. She'll be expecting you. In fact, she'll probably approach you."

"What's in the package?"

Kaminski smiled. "Are you sure you want to know?"

"I ..." Joel hesitated but then found his composure. "If I'm going to risk my life carrying something into the camp, I'd prefer to know what it is."

"Fair enough." Kaminski clicked his tongue. "A pistol."

Joel studied Kaminski's face for any hint the man was not being serious. The tall man looked back at him with a deadpan expression. "You think you can do that?"

Joel held his gaze. "Yeah, I think I can do that just fine."

The road to Raisko was oddly quiet when Joel set off in the morning. Bruno had told him it would be busier in spring and summer when more workers were sent to tend the gardens. Now, in November, only the greenhouses and laboratory were operational. Joel had been told to expect a small, permanent conclave of female scientists and assistants at Raisko.

He breathed in the fresh morning air; walking down the tree-lined road at a leisurely pace, his life almost felt normal. Joel shook his head; he would be shot for being outside the camp's perimeter if he wasn't carrying the papers clutched in his right hand.

In the distance, small houses and the faint glint of the glass roofs of the greenhouses appeared. He was surprised at the absence of barbed-wire fences—the camp was surrounded by picket fences no higher than his waist. It felt as if entering a village. Then Joel realized that was exactly what it was. The houses in which the offices, laboratories, and kitchen were located used to belong to the villagers of Raisko.

"Halt!" A tall guard appeared from one of the houses. He looked relaxed, his pistol holstered as he approached the small fence. "What brings you here?"

Joel handed the papers to the guard. "I'm here to repair the machinery in the laboratory."

"Sounds a bit vague." The guard inspected the papers and looked up at Joel with a frown. Are you sure you know what you're doing? Where's Florian? He normally takes care of everything around here."

Joel felt his hands get slightly clammy. "I'm not sure, I was sent here this morning. I'm just doing what I'm told, sir."

The guard sighed and shook his head. "Your papers appear to be in order. Carry on. Do you know where to go?" He handed the papers back to Joel.

"Not really."

"Just go past that row of greenhouses. It's the building on the left— the one with the red roof. You'll find the scientists working there. Try not to touch anything." The guard walked away, and Joel breathed a deep sigh of relief as soon as he entered the house. Passing the greenhouses, he was startled by the abundance of crops: peppers, cucumbers, and neatly aligned rows of Brussels sprouts. The greenhouses closest to the laboratory were filled with flowers that looked very similar to dandelions. *What use do flowers have in Auschwitz?*

The door to the laboratory building was open, and Joel hesitantly stepped into a hallway. He stepped through another door and was immediately blanketed by comfortable, humid, warm air.

"Close the door, please!" a woman's voice shouted from the back.

Joel closed the door and looked around. There were plants—more of the dandelion-like flowers—scattered on desks everywhere.

"Hey, who are you?" A woman in her midthirties appeared from behind a large plant in the corner. She wore a white lab coat over her camp uniform. From what Joel could see, both were spotlessly clean, a rarity in Auschwitz. She looked at him with curiosity as she adjusted her glasses. "How did you get in here?"

"The door was open, and I was told this is the laboratory? I'm here to carry out repairs. I'm Joel, I was sent by Bruno."

The woman eyed him, then smiled. "If Bruno sent you, I'm glad you're here. I'm Felcia, and I run this laboratory." She held out her hand. "I hope the guards didn't give you too much trouble?"

Joel shook her hand, startled by the woman's confidence. *Is she a prisoner as well?*

"I know, this is an odd place, isn't it? We're growing crops and doing research while people down the road are, well ..." Her smile faded as her voice trailed off. "I don't need to tell you."

"What are these flowers I see here and in the greenhouses?" Joel pointed at one of the dandelion-like plants on the nearest desk.

Felcia looked relieved to talk about something else. "These are experimental flowers brought in by the Germans. They're called Kazakh dandelions, and we're trying to optimize their growth."

"Optimize for what?"

"Rubber. The Germans need it for the war. They hope this is a cheap and quick way to grow it."

"And is it?"

Felcia shook her head. "It seems to be working, judging from our experiments. But I doubt we have the space to grow enough plants for the quantities they need."

"What about the crops in the other greenhouses?"

"For the SS and their families." She looked at Joel with something resembling pity. "I know they don't care about feeding us in the camp, but they certainly don't want their guards starving. Most of the greenhouses on the other side of the camp are filled with crops and flowers for German consumption."

"Flowers?"

There was a hint of pride in Felcia's voice as she answered. "We've managed to create some of the best flower species in Europe here. Although it's not surprising when you have some of the best botanists in the world in one place." She walked to the back of the room and picked up a small device that looked like a pocket watch. "But you're not here to listen to me talk about what's happening in Raisko. This hygrometer is acting up a bit. Can you take a look?"

"Sure." Joel was relieved. He opened the hygrometer and studied the delicate network of dials. Felcia sat down at a desk behind him, and they both worked in silence for a good fifteen minutes.

"I think I've got it," Joel said as he closed the back of the hygrometer. Care to test it?"

"Sure."

They entered the next-door greenhouse. Joel enjoyed the humidity and watched Felcia stick the hygrometer into the soil and add some water to the ground. She waited a few seconds, then nodded and turned around. "I think you've fixed it. It's responding as expected."

She retrieved the hygrometer and spoke to him in a hushed voice as they walked back to the lab. "Now, let's get you what you came here for. It's in the drawer in my laboratory. Make sure you hide it in your toolbox as soon as I take it out."

Joel nodded, and they quickly entered the laboratory. He was relieved to see there was no one there. Felcia walked to her desk and handed him a tightly wrapped paper package. It felt heavier than he'd expected, and he quickly opened his toolbox, shoving his tools aside to place it in the bottom. Closing the toolbox, he said, "Thank you for this, Felcia. You're taking quite a risk looking after this."

"Not as much as you are carrying it into the main camp," she said, waving her hand dismissively. "I hope I'll see you again some time, Joel."

He turned to leave, then turned back to face her. "How often do you receive these packages?"

She smiled. "Home Army people come to the camp maybe twice a week. But they usually don't bring weapons. More often than not, they bring news, food, and a bit of medicine when they can."

"Don't they ask for anything in return?"

"We keep them informed of what's happening in the camp. They're quite interested."

Joel felt encouraged. *Perhaps they do care.* "Do you ever talk to any of them?"

"No." Felcia shook her head. "They come early in the morning when it's still dark. We hide whatever messages we have for them, and they leave the supplies."

"And then you pick it up when you start work?"

"Yes, one of us usually sneaks out just before roll call to make sure the packages are retrieved."

Joel nodded; he had no idea of the scale of the operation. *Perhaps I should have a bit more faith in the leadership.*

"I best be on my way," Joel said, turning to the door. As he did, it opened and an SS guard walked in. His eyebrows shot up when he saw Joel in the room.

"What are you doing in here?" he bellowed as he reached for the pistol on his belt, and Joel's heart froze. "Put your hands up, now!" The man had unholstered the pistol and pointed it at Joel. Then he noticed Felcia, who stood looking at the scene in horror. Joel put the toolbox down and raised his hands.

"You know no unauthorized prisoners are allowed in here!" The man's eyes went between Felcia and Joel, but his surprise had made way for anger. "The plants are too delicate to have people coming in and out."

Felcia found her voice and composure. "He was here to carry out repairs. He has papers."

The man eyed Joel and nodded, keeping his pistol trained on his chest. "Okay."

Joel took out his papers and took a step toward the man, carefully keeping his other hand in the air. The man glanced at the papers and appeared to relax after a few seconds. Then, he lowered the pistol and holstered it. He handed the papers to Joel. "You should have reported to me when you entered the laboratory area."

"I'm sorry, sir, this is my first time in Raisko."

"I'm sure it is." The man looked at Felcia. "What did he fix?"

She pointed at the hygrometer. "This wasn't giving me proper readings. It's good now."

"Interesting." The German eyed Joel suspiciously and then looked at his toolbox. "And you need a toolbox that size?"

"I always have the same toolbox with me, sir. I also repair larger machines."

"Open the toolbox."

Joel felt his heart pound in his ears as he slowly opened the top compartment of the toolbox. The German looked at the various tools.

"Open the bottom part."

Joel did as he was told, and he felt the blood in his veins freeze as the man glanced inside. Joel focused on taking deep, calming breaths as the man picked up a large hammer and inspected it. Joel saw the paper wrapping at the bottom of the toolbox and prayed. The German dropped the hammer back in the toolbox and flicked his wrist.

"Okay, all in order. Was there anything else he needed to do?" The guard looked at Felcia.

"No. He was just leaving."

"Good," he said without looking at Joel.

Joel calmly closed the toolbox—he wanted to slam it shut—and made for the door in a relaxed manner. As soon as he closed the door and exited the laboratory he exhaled deeply. *That was way too close.*

## CHAPTER FORTY-ONE

The changing room was empty. Samson and Feliks walked along the rows of benches and hooks, collecting shoes and clothing. Samson quickly checked the pockets for anything of value. Even though people were instructed to hand in their jewelry before stepping down into the changing room, many decided to hold on to their most precious belongings: photos or notes from loved ones, necklaces, rings, banknotes, and even gems. They reached the end of the row and Feliks looked at him. "Find anything?"

Samson shook his head. "Just a pocket watch, but it's too big to hide." He held it up. "I'll just put it in the basket and hand it over to the SS."

"Always stings to hand anything to them. It's been a while since we've had any luck."

"Are you running low on merchandise?" Feliks coped with life in the Sonderkommando by smoking. Cigarettes were obtained by bartering with other prisoners or guards. Feliks had been able to fuel his addiction by salvaging the belongings of the recently departed.

Feliks shook his head. "No, I'm fine. It's just frustrating to go through these clothes and not find anything useful."

"Just be happy they're not your clothes." Samson couldn't hide his irritation. "At least we're still breathing."

"I'm sorry, you're right. I'm just tired, Samson. I keep hearing rumors of an uprising, but it never happens. I don't know how much longer we can survive or when they'll decide it's our time."

Samson bit his tongue. He wanted to tell his friend about the gunpowder, but he had promised Kaminski to be quiet about it. The fewer people who knew, the better. When he last saw Roza, she had even more gunpowder, and his nerves had been frayed on the way back to his own block. He had been relieved when Kaminski announced he'd found more men to transport the gunpowder.

"You two, what are you doing standing around? Get moving; we have more Jews waiting outside. Hurry, hurry!" The shrill voice of a guard cut their conversation short. Samson looked up and recognized Fritz, a middle-aged guard who was generally easy on the men of the Sonderkommando.

Samson resumed his work until he felt a presence next to him. It was Fritz.

"Did you find anything interesting?" The guard spoke in a low voice, which was amusing because everybody in the room knew why he was speaking to Samson.

"Not really. I've got a pocket watch here." He handed it to Fritz, who inspected it against the dim ceiling light.

"It'll do. Same deal?"

Samson nodded. "Do you still have French salami and cheese, as well?"

"Yes, I'll bring it to your block this evening. Kanada is bursting with food. Do you need some cigarettes as well?"

Samson was about to reject the proposal but looked at Feliks and changed his mind. "Yes, two packs, please."

"Done. Always a pleasure, Samson." The guard scurried off, and Samson continued his work. As he did, he fingered the tiny gems in the inside pocket of his shirt.

Samson found Kaminski waiting for him as he entered the yard of the Sonderkommando block. The Kapo waved at him urgently, and he approached his friend. "What's wrong?"

"I need to talk to you," Kaminski said as he pulled Samson to the side of the block, near the fence. His voice was higher than usual. "There's good news from the outside. The Home Army can supply us with weapons."

Samson was shocked. "Into the camp?"

"We've already smuggled the first guns in this week. Don't ask me how, that's not important right now. You realize what this means, right? If we can get outside weapons in, we're not just relying on your friend's gunpowder." There was excitement in Kaminski's voice.

"That's great, but where will we keep them?"

Kaminski shook his head impatiently. "We can hide them in the crematoria. It's acquiring the guns that will be challenging. They're expensive."

"How expensive?"

"From what I'm told, they'll take any valuables we have."

"So, it's much like the other outside workers do with food and medicine?" The day laborers coming in from nearby towns often traded with the prisoners. They charged exorbitant prices, but prisoners privileged enough to be able to afford the additional supplies were happy to pay whatever price. It was often the difference between life and death.

"Yes, but this time we have a well-established and safe route in and out of the camp. I tested it a few days ago, and it worked. I talked to the leadership, and they want to acquire as many guns as possible."

"We'll never know how long the route will last."

"Exactly."

"What do you need?"

"You've been assigned clothes duty recently, along with a few of your friends, right?"

"Mostly Feliks."

"I need you to collect all valuables from there. Cash, jewelry, gold, anything. Of course, you can still keep some of it for yourself, but we need to pool our resources to get those guns in as quickly as possible. This could be our way out."

Kaminski's enthusiasm was infectious, and Samson nodded. "Anything to get out of here. But there's one thing that bothers me."

"Tell me."

"Has the leadership told you anything about their plans?"

Kaminski's face dropped, but he recovered quickly, responding confidently. "They want to attack from multiple places in the camp. Our quarters and the crematoria will be some of the most important areas. We'll have most of the weapons and bombs. Crucially, we'll decide our own fate." He placed his hand on Samson's shoulder. "I promise you will make a difference. You will have a gun."

Kaminski's eyes burned with fiery determination. Samson trusted Kaminski with his life.

# CHAPTER FORTY-TWO

There was a knock at the door as Agnes was working in Dr. Brewda's office. She put down her pencil. "Come in." The door opened, and she was surprised and happy to see a familiar face peek in. "Joel, right?"

He smiled. "Agnes."

She was pleased he remembered her name. "You must be here to help in the operating room." He nodded and she skipped past her desk and to the door. "That's quick. I wasn't expecting you today. Dr. Brewda said everyone in the maintenance department is very busy these days."

"We are, but I suppose the hospital gets priority. Or, well, Dr. Brewda does."

They made the short walk from the office to the operating room. "Dr. Brewda gets priority treatment?" Agnes asked as she opened the door and switched on the lights. The room smelled like disinfectant, which was rarely the case within these walls.

Joel put down his toolbox and shrugged. "I don't know, but my foreman said it was important everything in Block 10 function as well as possible." He pointed at the X-ray machine. "I was told this needs to be looked at, again?" He emphasized the last word.

"Yes, please. It's still being used a lot." She decided she wanted to know more about Joel and sat down on one of the stools beside the machine. Before she could ask another question, he beat her to it.

"I assume the experiments are still going on?"

"More so than ever. The doctors keep saying they're close to finishing their research. They're expecting breakthrough results."

"But you're not so sure?"

"I see too much pain and misery to believe that something good will come from their experiments. Least of all for the women involved."

Joel hummed his agreement. "I'll take your word for it. Unfortunately I'll have to make sure this keeps functioning, or I'll be in big trouble."

Agnes waved her hands. "I know, I didn't mean to make you feel bad about it. Trust me, I know what it's like. I've been witness to this for over a year now."

"I'm sorry you have to go through this every day," Joel said, his voice slightly softer. He picked up a wrench and undid some screws, exposing the inside of the machine. Agnes was quiet while he untangled some wires—fascinated by the ease with which Joel carried out his work.

"Do you mind if I ask you something personal, Agnes?"

She was taken aback, but nodded. "Sure."

"Do you have any family in the camp?" He looked at her with an open face, his eyes compassionate.

"No." She swallowed hard as she remembered Yvette's face. "I lost my sister on the ramp on arrival. She was very ill."

Joel looked pained. "I'm sorry I asked."

*Jacob.* She thought of the man she left on the ramp in Westerbork. She wished he was here with her. No, she corrected herself. She would settle for knowing he was still alive, that there was some sort of hope to cling onto. Her letters remained unanswered, and she had stopped sending them every week. She suddenly felt very alone, and shuddered. She felt a hand on her shoulder.

"Are you all right? I'm sorry I upset you." Joel stood next to her, his brown eyes full of concern.

A tear rolled down her cheek and she quickly wiped it away. "I'm okay, Joel. I'm normally not like this."

"That's all right. I feel quite alone myself at times. The pain comes and goes, doesn't it?"

"Do you have any family left?"

He shook his head. "No. My mother was sent to the gas chambers on arrival as well. I didn't even get to say goodbye. I didn't know back then."

"Me, neither," Agnes whispered.

Joel took her hand and they sat in silence together. Even though it was the touch of a stranger, she felt kindness in his touch. She looked up at him and saw his eyes were glassy and moist as well. *It's better to grieve together.*

She was reluctant to let go when he pulled his hand back and returned to work on the X-ray machine. Suddenly feeling awkward, she said, "How is the situation in Birkenau with the typhus outbreak?"

Joel secured some of the screws before answering. "They didn't tell you?"

"We haven't heard anything since they were put into quarantine, and we couldn't have any interaction with them until the situation was resolved."

"Well, they resolved the situation," Joel said grimly. "They rounded up everyone with even the mildest symptoms from around the camp, and put them in the isolation barracks."

Agnes felt dread build in her stomach.

"They were then loaded in trucks and sent to the gas chambers. They killed almost ten thousand people in one day." Joel closed his toolbox. "That's how they reined in the typhus epidemic."

"My God. All those people." Agnes put her hand before her mouth.

"I'm sorry, Agnes. I know what happens in this block is barbaric, but at least these people have you and Dr. Brewda."

"People talk about Dr. Brewda?"

Joel nodded. "You can't change everything overnight, but you're not in this fight alone. I promise you that." He picked up his toolbox and made for the door.

Agnes was confused. "What do you mean?"

He grabbed the door handle. "If you ever need anything, just ask me. I will see you again soon, Agnes. Look after yourself."

# CHAPTER FORTY-THREE

Moshe's words rang in Joel's head as he approached the crematorium. "You can trust them, they're Poles, just like us. They want to help."

Despite his friend's confidence, Joel was skeptical. The Home Army weren't the ones inside the camp, taking the most significant risks. He wanted to make sure Kaminski was truly convinced these people could be trusted.

He entered the crematorium yard after being waved through by the guard. Joel had become used to passing even into the most restricted areas of the camp—working for Bruno really opened all areas of the camp to him. He couldn't imagine the camp's resistance functioning at even a fraction of its efficiency without their connections in the repair shed.

Crematorium 2 was as hot as ever—smoke and death was inescapable. Kaminski was talking to some men near the coke storage room. Joel kept his distance as he waited for them to finish their conversation.

It didn't take long, and Kaminski spotted him almost immediately. He shook his hand, again guiding him to the small overseer's room.

"You did a great job bringing that first package in."

Joel nodded. "I could hardly believe the freedom those scientists have."

"They're anything but free. Everything they do is monitored, and if their research isn't producing what the Nazis want, they are replaced."

Joel wondered how Kaminski knew but didn't ask. "You want me to go back there today?"

"I need you to provide payment for more weapons. That first gun was a test, a show of good faith from the Home Army. We're paying for that now, along with an order for more guns."

Joel nodded, but a small voice sowed doubt in his mind. "How are we going to pay them?"

Kaminski pulled the cord from a small pouch and turned it upside down into the palm of his hand. A handful of sparkling gems fell out, and Joel softly gasped. "How many guns does that buy?"

"Four," Kaminski said. "And they're just pistols for now, but it's better than nothing."

"And you're sure we can trust them?"

Kaminski smiled. "Trust me, Joel, I've had the same doubts. But if the leadership is comfortable with this, I'm not going to argue. Not at this point, anyway."

Joel frowned. "At this point?"

"Look, if we hand these over and we receive nothing in return, I will look for another way. But for now, there is no other option."

Joel nodded, seeing the sense in what Kaminski was saying. The large man carefully put the gems back in the pouch and handed it to Joel. "Hand it only to your contact, and no one else. It's the same woman from last time."

*Felcia.* He already felt better knowing he would be dealing with the smart scientist again. He carefully hid the pouch in a pocket he'd sewn into the inside of his pants. "Don't worry, I'll make sure this is delivered safely. Do I need to bring anything back from Raisko?"

Kaminski shook his head. "Not this time. Just deliver the gems. We'll worry about picking up the merchandise once we get the signal. Good luck."

As Joel stepped out of the suffocating heat of the crematorium and into the cool winter air, he felt the weight of the gems tugging inside his pocket. He approached the crematorium gate as casually as possible, his cheeks burning. Thankfully, the guard was distracted as he let him through. Only a few hundred meters down the road a large procession slowly approached. Joel picked up his pace and avoided eye contact with the people making their final journey. He comforted himself knowing he was doing everything he could to stop these murders.

The road to Raisko was even quieter than before. Joel looked at the outstretched fields around him. In summer they would be bustling with activity as prisoners would be cultivating potatoes and other vegetables. Now, they were deserted. How easy it would be for him to walk into the fields and disappear. He shook his head. His disappearance would put the camp on high alert—no, it would go into lockdown. There would be consequences. Bruno would be the first to be killed, for he was responsible for Joel. Joel shivered; he couldn't have the man's death on his conscience.

Raisko came into view. If everything went to plan today, he would be laying the foundations for a more organized escape, one where he and the rest of the underground would stand a chance to survive. *Us and the Home Army.*

He reached the perimeter of the camp, where two guards stood chatting near one of the small gates. Joel raised an eyebrow; they looked like they were waiting for someone. There would be no other reason to for them to be outside in the cold weather. He warily approached them. The men noticed him and addressed him without surprise.

"You're late," one of them said. He had a long face and looked at Joel with hazy, bloodshot eyes. "You're here to carry out repairs to the greenhouses in the back, aren't you?" He pointed at Joel's toolbox.

"I am. I was sent over here just now—I came as quickly as I could."

"You've kept us waiting in the cold. You were supposed to be here half an hour ago."

"I'm very sorry, sir. It wasn't easy to get out of Birkenau. I was caught in one of the arriving transports."

The man gave a crooked smile. "Ah, another transport arrived? At least those are on time." He laughed, and the other guard joined in half-heartedly. He looked uncomfortable. "Well, we're not going to change anything now. Show me your papers." Joel did as he was told and waited while the man's eyes quickly scanned the work order. He handed it back within seconds. "That all looks in order."

Joel was about to walk on when the guard stepped in front of him.

"Not so fast. We've had reports of illegal activities between Raisko and Birkenau."

Joel felt his ears burn. He cleared his throat. "Illegal activities?"

The guard squinted at him and took a step closer. "You wouldn't know anything about that now, would you?"

Joel shook his head. "I just fix things around the camps."

"Hmm." The guard eyed him suspiciously. "Why don't you let me have a look into that toolbox?" He turned to his colleague. "Seems like a good place to hide something."

Joel put the toolbox in front of the guard and tried to control his shaking hands. The guard took the toolbox, opened it, and turned it upside down. The tools clanged as they spilled on the sandy ground. The guard picked up a hammer, tossed it aside, and searched through the rest of the pile. After a minute he grunted, finding nothing. Joel kept his expression neutral as the German looked him up and down. The man's eyes glistened as he turned to the other guard. "Pat him down. I'm sure he's carrying something."

Joel felt his heart drop. The gems were still in his pants, and even though the pocket was lined on the inside, anything more than a casual pat down would expose them.

The other guard stepped forward with a sigh. "Is this really necessary? It's cold, let's go back inside and just let him get to work. He seems harmless."

"Just do your job and search him." The guard with the long face scowled at his colleague.

Joel slowly spread his arms and legs, desperately praying the man wouldn't find the gems. He would have no excuse for having such wealth on him, and even these two guards would understand he was up to something bringing them to Raisko. He bit the inside of his cheek as the man started at his shoulders and moved his hands down the sides of his chest and groin area. He was now close to where the gems were. *Should I run? Attack them?* He wouldn't be able to fight off two trained, well-fed guards.

Joel closed his eyes; there was nothing to do but wait.

The guard's hands were now only inches from the gems, and Joel could feel them move in his pocket as the man pushed the fabric. Joel tensed and the man looked up. The guard opened his mouth when a loud bang near the greenhouses drew their attention.

They all turned their heads toward the source of the sound. At first, everything was still, but then a man wearing a prisoner's uniform sprinted between the greenhouses. A few seconds later, two guards burst through the doors of the same greenhouse, their pistols raised.

"Halt! Halt! Stop that man!" the guards shouted. Joel's eyes focused on the prisoner, who had cleared the first row of greenhouses and sprinted into the field. The two guards—who had been so interested in Joel seconds ago—looked keen to join the chase. The man with the long face took his gaze to Joel and then to the excitement in the field. "You know where the laboratory is? Go report there; they'll send you to the right greenhouse. Come, Fritz, let's catch ourselves an escaped prisoner!" The guards ran off.

Joel decided not to risk being asked what he was doing again and rushed toward the laboratory building. As he opened the door, the first shot rang through the air, and he paused. He looked back, but the greenhouses blocked his view. Another shot. Joel shook his head and quickly stepped inside. He knew how this would end.


He found Felcia inside, and she made him sit down for a minute.

"What happened out there? I heard shots."

Joel shook his head. "Someone tried to escape. I don't think he made it. The guards were on him immediately."

"That's the third person trying that this week. People are getting desperate," Felcia said, her face sad.

"Why? Compared to Birkenau, this isn't so bad."

She looked him in the eye and nodded. "You're right, it isn't. As long as you're allowed to stay."

"What do you mean?"

"Some of the results have not been, how should I say this ... satisfactory to the Germans."

Joel remembered Kaminski's words earlier. "What happens to them?"

"They're sent to Birkenau." She was silent for a moment. "I can't blame some of them trying to make a run for it. At least they're giving themselves a chance."

"Are you in danger?" Joel asked softly.

She shook her head resolutely. "My plant research is going well. They'll let me stay a bit longer, for now."

Joel let out a sigh of relief. If he was going to come to Raisko, he hoped he could work with Felcia more often. "I've brought the payment for the weapons." He reached inside his pants and handed the precious gems to her.

She eyed them appreciatively. "I'm sure our contacts in the Home Army will be very happy."

"Do you think we can trust them?"

Felcia's attention shifted from the gems to Joel's eyes. "Well, we don't really have another choice. But they did provide us with that pistol a few days ago. And they've certainly smuggled in plenty of extra food and medicine. So I suppose, yes, I do trust them. For now. We have a common enemy."

That was enough for Joel. "Okay, I best pretend to do some repairs in the greenhouses. When do you think we will receive the weapons?"

Felcia shrugged her shoulders. "They'll pick up the payment today, and then it could take anywhere between days and weeks before they have the weapons. Just be patient, Joel. They'll deliver."

Joel nodded and left the laboratory. Patience was the one thing he was running out of.

# CHAPTER FORTY-FOUR

A gnes awoke early. She lay in her bunk, listening to the soft snoring of the women around her. The nurses' dormitory had never been emptier, with many sent to Birkenau. Most had become too weak to perform their duties, and even though there was a shortage of nurses, the selection was brutal. They had lost their value and were taken along with the weaker patients. Dr. Brewda had protested to no avail.

That morning, life returned to normal in Block 10, with experiments carried out as if nothing had happened. Agnes knew she was lucky that she had been appointed Dr. Brewda's assistant when the doctor was made head physician of Block 10 earlier that month. She no longer needed to assist with the experiments, and it put her in a position where her contact with the sick women in the wards was reduced. Even though she missed caring for the women, she realized she could make a bigger difference from Dr. Brewda's office.

She swung her feet out of bed and headed for the bathroom. After a very quick—and cold—shower, she slipped into her uniform and headed for Dr. Brewda's office. She opened the door and was surprised to find Dr. Brewda was already there. The doctor looked up, her face betraying the same surprise at seeing Agnes.

"You're up very early! Did you not sleep well?"

Agnes sat down. "No, I just felt rested, oddly enough. I couldn't sleep any longer, so I thought I'd prepare some of the files for today's experiments." She glanced at the papers on Dr. Brewda's desk. "Or did you beat me to it?"

"I did. I was looking for ways to keep some of them from the operating room today."

"And, did you?"

"Not really. But I can make something up." She winked at Agnes and put the file away. Her face turned serious. "Agnes, there's something I want you to know before anyone else hears about it."

Agnes sat up. "Sure."

"Dr. Wirths came into my office late last night and had news about our plan to train our nurses in the camp. I think he also heard about the women being taken away to Birkenau."

"I'm sure he realized he would run out of nurses soon." Agnes dropped her eyes immediately. "I'm sorry, I spoke out of turn."

Dr. Brewda waved a hand. "You're probably right. But the important thing is that he brought good news. Berlin approved our proposal."

A burst of energy shot through Agnes' body. "Really? We're going to train our own nurses? From Birkenau?"

"Yes, Dr. Wirths said he was enthusiastic about the plan from the start, but Berlin was taking its time to decide. He even got Dr. Mengele involved. Apparently he leaned on some people in Berlin."

"Mengele." Agnes felt a shiver run down her spine at the mention of the man's name. She quickly put him out of her mind. "So what will happen next?"

"I'm going to the women's camp tomorrow to pick out some of the girls."

"How many?"

"Wirths said we could start with about twenty."

"That's a good start. Will they stay in Birkenau, or will they come live here?"

"They'll stay in Birkenau for now. Dr. Wirths didn't think it was a good idea to move them right away. But that's not bad, Agnes. They'll be able to bring medicine from Birkenau every day once they've finished their training."

"Maybe we could find a way to do that before they do." Agnes was thinking of the possibilities. This opened a consistent supply line between the camps again. "I'll think of something. We need the medication sooner rather than later. We also need to make sure the nurses in Block 10 receive proper care, Dr. Brewda."

The doctor put her hand on Agnes' wrist. "Patience, Agnes. We need to be careful. This is a big opportunity, but we need to make sure we don't overplay our hand. We need to prepare everything perfectly."

"I understand." She looked at Dr. Brewda for a moment, then said, "I'd like to help. Is there anything I can do?"

Dr. Brewda smiled. "Yes, I'd like you to accompany me to Birkenau tomorrow. Help me with the selection."

"Of course." Agnes was delighted as she got up, energized.

Dr. Brewda held up her hand. "There's one other thing I'd like to discuss with you, Agnes. And you need to be very discreet about it."

Agnes sat back down. "Anything."

"When I say discreet, I mean don't tell anyone about this. Not even people you consider friends, okay?" Dr. Brewda looked serious, her eyes boring into Agnes'.

"I won't tell a soul."

"Forging the files of the girls upstairs only helps so much." Dr. Brewda tapped on the folders on her desk. "And I know you've been doing that since you joined. I've heard the story of how you and that young doctor spent the whole night removing the malaria diagnoses for all the people in Block 20. It was very brave."

It felt a lifetime ago. "I did what I thought was right."

The woman across from her nodded vigorously. "And you've never stopped doing that. Look at us today—we're still trying to come up with medical reasons why the experiments should be stopped." She paused for a moment. "But the truth is, there's only one way we can really make these experiments stop. We need the outside world to know. They need proof."

"But how will we do that?"

"Now that I'm head of the block, I have access to all the files, and you, as my assistant, do too. So I want you to start keeping track of the experiments, and—" She paused again as she searched for the right words. "And they need to be the worst examples you can find. The ones where the girls didn't survive." There were tears in Dr. Brewda's eyes. Agnes had never seen her like this before. "Can you do that, Agnes?"

"I can," Agnes whispered.

They were silent for a moment, the footsteps of the first nurses making their way down the hallway to the bathroom the only sound.

"And you need to keep those copies in a safe place, where no one else can find them. And if someone ever finds them, they can't be traced back to you or me." Agnes opened her mouth but Dr. Brewda raised her hand and shook her head. "Don't tell me where you'll keep them. If anything goes wrong, I can pretend I knew nothing about it."

"How will we get the files to the outside world?"

Dr. Brewda didn't immediately respond, instead keeping her eyes on the files on the desk. When she looked up, there was an odd expression on her face, one Agnes couldn't place. There was a faint smile, as if Agnes asked a question to which the answer was obvious to everyone but her. "We'll find a way. Trust me."

"Okay, Dr. Brewda. I will do this. For the girls. For you."

The Polish doctor took Agnes' hand in hers. "Please call me Alina. We're in this together now."

Agnes smiled through the tears forming in her eyes. "Okay, Alina. But we've never not been in this together."

Agnes and Dr. Brewda arrived at Birkenau's women's camp midmorning. Most of the work details had already departed, and the only women left were those either too weak to work or those in charge of the barracks. Dr. Wirths had sent two guards along from Auschwitz. Agnes suspected he wanted his men to keep an eye on them. Agnes and Dr. Brewda had been quiet on the ride over.

They were greeted by a woman in her late thirties, Marlena, a block elder of the women's camp. As they walked through the camp, Agnes realized there were very few women older than Marlena capable of taking on the job—all wandered about hopelessly, with no life in their eyes.

"I was happy to hear of your new project, Dr. Brewda," Marlena said. She spoke German with a heavy Polish accent, and she only did so for the benefit of the guards, who followed closely behind Agnes and Dr. Brewda. "It is an exciting opportunity for many of the younger women here. I think you'll find I've selected the strongest, brightest women for your consideration."

Agnes frowned. The block elder had made a preselection? That seemed odd. She glanced at Dr. Brewda, who seemed unfazed, almost as if she'd expected this. *Did she already know?*

They continued past a few more barracks until they reached a small clearing between four barracks. Agnes counted three rows of ten women lined up, surrounded by half a dozen bored-looking guards.

"All these girls have something of a medical education," Marlena said. "Although they're not all trained nurses, most of them should be able to pick up the work at the hospital quite quickly."

Dr. Brewda looked at them, running her eyes across the lines of young women nervously trying to look as capable as possible. Suddenly, she strode forward and addressed one of the girls in German. She asked her some standard questions: her age, place of birth, education. The girl answered quickly enough.

"Have you ever seen someone die?"

The girl flinched and didn't immediately answer. She fumbled with her hands, then her hair as she averted her eyes. Dr. Brewda repeated the question, in a softer voice this time. "It's all right if you haven't."

The girl looked back up, her eyes now shooting fire. "My father, my mother, my brothers," she said in Polish. "I watched them all die in the ghetto of Warsaw." She spoke quickly, but Agnes could understand enough to make out what she was saying.

Dr. Brewda nodded to Marlena. "She's coming with us."

Suddenly, the other women in the rows started to speak in Polish as well. They had all lost someone; their family, or their friends. The guards sprang to life, shouting at them to be quiet unless spoken to. The murmurs died down, but Agnes could see a smile forming on Dr. Brewda's face. She knew enough.

# CHAPTER FORTY-FIVE

Joel found Agnes sitting on the steps outside Block 10. Even though it was chilly, he could imagine her needing some fresh air, and the sun made it feel less cold than it was. He approached her and thought she seemed different today. Her shoulders were pulled back, and as she looked up she flashed a smile. Agnes seemed confident, and Joel was glad. He'd felt a little down leaving her the last time they met, having gone through both of their losses on the ramp. With Agnes facing death and abuse in Block 10 every day, he worried about her. Seeing her smile gave him hope. If she could find a reason to be upbeat, so could he.

"I didn't expect to see you back here so quickly." Agnes stood from the steps. "There's nothing scheduled for you to work on today, is there?"

He shook his head. "No, I was needed in the kitchen and thought I'd pass through here."

"So you came to see me?" Her voice was a little playful. She sounded pleased.

"Maybe," he said with a grin. "You look like you're having a decent day?"

"As good as can be in this place." Agnes turned away from the block. "I have another fifteen minutes off. Want to take a walk?"

"Sure. My foreman isn't expecting me back for another hour."

They walked toward the main road, where a few cars left the SS quarters at the end of the camp. They appeared in a rush, wheels throwing up dust from the gravel road.

"How are the experiments going?" Joel asked.

"Still happening, but now that Dr. Brewda is in charge, we're able to delay more of them. She's also appointed more Jewish doctors."

"So I've heard. I guess they need their own doctors at the front lines?"

"Who told you that?" Agnes looked at him with a surprised expression. "I thought the rest of the camp knew little about what was happening in the hospital."

"News travels quicker than you think. Especially now that you've got women from Birkenau working in your hospital." Joel grinned and held up the palms of his hands. "They're all very impressed with Dr. Brewda. They're calling her a hero." They turned off the main road, looping themselves back toward Block 10. "That also makes you a hero, Agnes."

She waved dismissively. "I'm just supporting her. I do what she tells me to. It's all Dr. Brewda and the doctors. They take the big risks deceiving the SS."

"You don't really believe that, do you?" Joel stopped, and Agnes took a few more steps before turning to face him. "You've been with her every step of the way. You were the one going to Kanada, smuggling medicine and finding other nurses to do the same."

Agnes's eyes grew wide. "How do you know—"

"And you were the one who suggested recruiting the women in Birkenau." Joel felt his heart beat a little faster. "You're just as important, Agnes."

She looked back at him in stunned silence, her mouth agape. Joel realized he'd come on too forcefully, and he took a step toward her. She didn't flinch as he took her hands. "Agnes, I'm not here by chance. I'm here to help."

"Just like you've been saying all along," she said, her voice uneven.

He nodded. "But you've never asked for my help, so now I'm volunteering it, again."

"But ... how did you know about what I've done?"

Joel gently pulled her along. "Let's keep moving before the guards get suspicious."

Block 10 was still a good five-minute walk, and Joel slowed his pace. He glanced at Agnes, who still looked confused, even though he could see her mind working at a frantic pace. He smiled reassuringly.

"Don't worry. We're on the same side. I'm sorry I startled you."

"You didn't." Her voice had returned to normal. "You've always been pretty frank with me." Joel wanted to speak but she held up a hand. "But now things are falling into place. You were always very interested in what was going on in the block. You had lots of questions, and you were always in the right place at the right time. The other time you were here, you seemed very aware of what was going on."

Joel nodded. "I do know what's going on, and we want to put a stop to it."

"We." It was a statement. "We do."

He took a deep breath. "I was sent to pick up your notes."

Agnes paused before answering. "What notes?" She walked on toward Block 10, nodding at some of the other prisoners who went between the different barracks. Joel felt she was purposely averting his eyes.

"The ones you and Dr. Brewda are compiling on what's happening in the block. The underground sent me. They want to hand over the evidence to the outside."

Agnes stopped in her tracks, her calm exterior dissolving as she turned to him. Her eyes were burning with excitement, the corners of her mouth up. "Really? They think they can get the information out?"

"They don't just think. They know." He hesitated. "I know."

She held his gaze as they stood looking at each other for a few seconds. Joel could see the thoughts racing through her mind as she processed everything. He knew the camp resistance could just as easily have asked Dr. Brewda to hand over the papers to him, but that would've defeated the purpose. Agnes needed to be on board. They couldn't rely on Dr. Brewda alone. He felt his pulse quicken as she slowly nodded.

"You've been testing me all along, haven't you, Joel? It was no coincidence you were the one sent to fix things in the block." Joel said nothing, and Agnes continued. "How long has Dr. Brewda been working on this?"

Joel shrugged. "I wouldn't know; they don't tell me much more than you."

"Sure." The smile on Agnes' face widened. "It all makes sense now. Tell me something. When did I pass the test?"

"Does it really matter?"

Agnes turned around and walked back to Block 10. She looked back over her shoulder. "It does to me."

He picked up his pace to catch up with her. "Honestly? The first time we met."

# PART IV

## Auschwitz-Birkenau, Poland April 1944

# CHAPTER FORTY-SIX

S amson awoke to find someone tugging at his arm. He opened his eyes and saw Feliks. His friend held a finger before his lips. Samson sat up and rubbed his eyes. The rest of the men were still asleep, and Feliks spoke in a low voice.

"Kaminski wants to see you outside. Hurry."

Samson followed Feliks to the door. When Samson stepped outside, he realized it was still dark. Kaminski stood near the door wearing a heavy coat—Kaminski must have traded something precious to obtain such an invaluable piece of clothing.

Samson shivered as he wrapped his ragged coat a little tighter. For Kaminski to summon him well before reveille, something important must be happening. *Is the revolt on?*

"Sorry to wake you like this, but I couldn't have anyone overhearing us." Kaminski didn't sound apologetic, and Samson didn't care. "But there are some developments we need your help with."

"Anything. What can I do?"

"You know about the documents and news that are being smuggled out of the camp, right?"

Samson nodded. "I don't know the details, but I've heard we've had good contact with the Home Army."

"Decent contact." A shadow passed over Kaminski's face, and Samson thought he spotted the Kapo biting his lip before answering. "They say they've been sending the documents about what's happening in the camp to London, but they're having trouble getting them to believe it."

Samson frowned. "They're questioning the documents? That's absurd."

"They think it can't be as bad as it seems. The Home Army connections say they think the government maybe doesn't want to see what's happening here. Or they really don't understand."

"But why would we make this up? With all the trains arriving, there should be hundreds of thousands of people in the camp. Or millions, even?" Samson was aghast. "How can they question what's right under their noses? Don't they have airplanes taking pictures of the camp? They can't ignore the smoke."

Kaminski held up his hands. "I know, I know. But sometimes it's impossible to believe something unless you've seen it with your own eyes. Whoever is looking at the documents in London must think it can't be that bad."

Many of the men and women in the camp had gone through so much collecting the documents. Once outside the camp, they had somehow managed to get them to London, and now some bureaucrat deemed the story a lie? "No, I can't accept this, Kaminski! What else do they need before they believe us?" Samson heard his voice waver, but he didn't care. "Are they waiting until we're all dead?"

Kaminski grabbed his shoulders and looked him in the eyes. "Samson! You need to be calm. Focus." He looked around. "Don't forget where we are. There are guards just outside the gate."

Samson looked into the Kapo's dark eyes and realized he hadn't been summoned only to hear what wasn't working. "You have a way to convince them?"

"We might." Kaminski let go of his shoulders. "If documents don't convince them, we need to send people who have experienced what is happening here firsthand."

"Prisoners?"

Kaminski nodded. "Yes. Two men have volunteered to escape the camp at the first opportunity."

Samson swallowed hard. "How many successful escapes do you know of?"

"One or two," Kaminski said unflinchingly. "But we have to try."

"I've only heard of failed escapes, of people being caught even after making it through no-man's-land." Samson involuntarily looked toward the west, to the city of Oświęcim. Between where they stood and the city were kilometers of electrified fence, and even if one managed to get past the first fence, no-man's-land consisted of 50 meters of open space, where guards simply picked off whoever got that far. "How would they manage?"

Kaminski shook his head. "That's not for us to know. The only thing you need to worry about is obtaining the evidence they need."

"You're hoping they can deliver the evidence themselves."

"I can see how they can question information coming via the Home Army. But who would question the word of an escaped prisoner?" Kaminski pointed at the tattoo on his wrist. "I think this would make quite a convincing case."

Samson nodded. "What do you need me to do?"


The men were going to attempt their escape the week after, and Samson needed to provide some of the most damning evidence.

His chance came three days later. He was assigned to the undressing area of crematorium 2, and when he opened the door to the yard, he saw the familiar Red Cross ambulance parked to the side. The ambulance was further proof that the wickedness of those running Auschwitz knew no bounds. Instead of using it for its intended purpose, the vehicle was used to transport the canisters of the deadly Zyklon B crystals to and from the gas chambers. Two guards returned to it, gas masks dangling from their necks as they carried a small bag from the crematorium.

Samson had been waiting for this, and he was ready. The guards reached the ambulance, opened its doors, and tossed the bag in the back.

The clanging sound was unmistakable: used canisters. The guards closed the doors and walked toward the gate. They lit up cigarettes and chatted with the guard there.

Samson's heart pounded in his chest as he crossed the yard. He had practiced what he would say a hundred times in the past days. *Keep it together. They're not going to kill you for asking.*

He reached the guards, who ignored him. Samson cleared his throat as he kept his head down.

The man guarding the gate noticed him first. "What are you doing here? Don't you have work to do?"

"I'm sorry. I just needed to ask these gentlemen something." He kept his eyes focused on the ground.

"What is it?" a new voice asked.

"I was hoping I could perhaps take one or two of the cans from your car," Samson started. He felt his ears burn, but continued. "We're using them to collect the gold teeth, and the ones we have, well ..." Samson faced the guards. "Well, they're full of holes."

The guards looked at him in silence. One of them dropped his cigarette and shook another from his pack. Samson couldn't read the guards as they looked to each other. The one who had addressed him started laughing.

"You need cans to collect the dead Jews' teeth?"

Samson fumbled with his hands. "We don't have anything else."

The man laughed even louder, and his companions joined in as he shook his head. "Yeah, take as many as you need. Just be sure to take the empty ones. Don't want you killing yourself before your time." He waved at the ambulance. "The doors are unlocked."

"Thank you, sir, I'll be quick." Samson scurried off before they changed their minds.

He reached the ambulance and opened the doors. The smell was oddly sweet; some of the canisters perhaps still contained crystals. Even though the gas wouldn't be deadly in such small quantities, he kept the doors open for a minute before picking up one of the cans. He looked inside, relieved to find it empty. He picked another one and held both upside down. He looked to the guards, who were happily chatting. He closed the car doors—two he could convincingly argue he needed.

As he made his way back to crematorium 2, he felt adrenaline course through his veins. He left the bright sunlight behind and stepped into the changing room—never more relieved to step into death's anteroom. His colleagues had opened the door to the gas chamber, and the same sweet scent he'd faintly smelled in the ambulance entered his nostrils. He clutched the canisters tighter as he walked into the gas chamber, avoiding the corpses. He needed to get to the darkness of the oven room.

Half an hour later, Samson had secured a dark spot in the oven room. He was impatiently peeling away at the label of one of the gas canisters. The warning sign was unmistakable, as the skull and bones with the ominous wording "Zyklon. Danger, poison gas!" screamed at him in the roar of the fires.

It was hard work in the heat of the crematorium, with men yelling and hustling around him. Samson tried to concentrate, knowing that he'd be unable to explain what he was doing here if a guard caught him. He'd almost peeled the label off the first canister when it ripped, tearing the skull and bones into two parts. *Shit.* That wouldn't do.

It took him another half hour to successfully peel the label off the other canister. He was sweating from exertion, but held the label up proudly. He stuffed it into his pocket, and then took the canisters through the oven room to the dental area. Here, three men stood with pliers as they inspected the corpses and pulled out any valuable teeth. Finally, he handed them the new cans. "Here, so you don't have to use the old ones anymore."

They looked at him without a word, their faces showing no emotion. Samson shook his head and headed back to the changing room. He hoped nobody had missed him.

A few days later, Samson walked toward the steaming cauldron. Roll call had just finished. The men of the Sonderkommando were all accounted for—as usual. He took out his bowl and spoon as he lined up behind Kaminski. He was near the front when a siren pierced the quiet evening air. Soon, another joined on the other side of the camp, and then another.

The guards at the gate suddenly looked nervous, and one of them sprinted off. Another guard appeared near the cauldron and instructed the man to stop serving soup. There were complaints from the men in the queue, but they were quickly silenced. The line dispersed and Samson and Kaminski drifted away, moving closer to their barracks.

"It's happening, isn't it?" Samson asked.

Kaminski simply nodded. "They were ready. I handed over your label just in time."

"What do we do now?"

"We wait, and we pray."

The lockdown lasted three days as search parties scoured the camp and its surroundings. Samson spent his nights worrying and thinking of all the horrible things that would happen to him. If any of the guards near the crematorium remembered Samson asking about the cans, they would surely make the connection.

After three nights and days, Kaminski's booming voice sounded through the barracks. "Get ready to get back to work. Lockdown is over!"

Samson had to control himself not to rush to the Kapo instantly. Instead, he waited for everyone to collect their breakfast before catching up with Kaminski.

"Did they find them?"

Kaminski shook his head. "They found their hiding place last night, but from what I've heard it was empty. They made it out."

Samson felt his knees buckle as a wave of relief washed over him. Kaminski grabbed his arm. "They still have a long way to go, but it's a start. I can't remember the last time someone successfully escaped, let alone with all that evidence."

"And the world can no longer ignore what's happening here."

Kaminski shook his head. "No, they can't."

# CHAPTER FORTY-SEVEN

Samson and Feliks sat in the yard outside their block, limbs like lead after a shift at the crematorium. Samson counted at least a hundred new faces milling about, unsure where to sit or stand. One group of about twenty stood out in particular. Some wore the blue clothing of the Sonderkommando, but Samson didn't recognize any of their faces—and he knew all the men in the SK by now. He turned to Feliks.

"Those men over there, do they work with you?"

His friend shook his head. "I don't know any of them."

"Don't you think it's odd they're wearing tattered SK clothes? And look at those boots." The Sonderkommando were provided with better footwear than regular prisoners—the Nazis didn't want them cutting their feet while working in the crematorium.

Feliks squinted. "I suppose you're right. That is odd."

"Let's go talk to them." Samson was on his feet and walked purposefully toward the group. Feliks followed, mumbling something. One of the men saw him approach, a curious but wary expression on his face.

"Hey, did you arrive today?" Samson spoke to him in Polish, his voice turning the heads of the other men.

The large man facing him shook his head and turned away. Then, a smaller man wearing glasses approached. Even though he wasn't as tall as the man at the front, his bulging muscles betrayed many months of hard physical labor. "We come from Lublin camp." He spoke Polish with a thick Russian accent. "We are Russian soldiers."

Samson looked to Feliks in surprise. The last time they'd heard of Lublin was in February, when 200 of their Sonderkommando comrades were hastily sent to assist. But why were these Russians sent to Birkenau, and why now? He asked the Russian, who shook his head.

"We heard the artillery approach from the east in the night. The next morning, the SS were in a frenzy. They evacuated the camp within a day, and we were sent here. When we arrived they split us from the other prisoners." The man scratched behind his ears as he looked at Samson. "I suppose we're in the same place we were in Lublin. This is the SK, isn't it?"

Samson nodded. "How long were you in Lublin for?"

"I'm not completely sure, but well over a year."

"So you must've worked with our brothers who were sent in February?"

The Russian gave him a hard look, then his features softened as he looked away. His gaze focused on the chimneys behind Samson. He seemed to be far away for a moment, and Samson waited for the man's focus to return. "I'm sorry, but I'm afraid they were given little chance to assist us. They were sent to the gas chambers on arrival. I spoke to them when they handed in their things. They knew what was about to happen."

Even though the man's words confirmed his suspicions, Samson closed his eyes. *So we were right. They were murdered.*

"I'm sorry," the Russian continued. "But your brothers were very brave. They handed their good coats and boots to us before meeting their maker." He pointed at his own boots. "If it wasn't for them, many of us wouldn't have made it this far. We were not treated as well in Lublin as you are here."

Samson didn't respond as the man scanned the yard. He would've done the same. The dead don't need boots.

"Did they tell you why you were transferred?" Feliks asked, bringing Samson back to the present.

The man nodded. "We were separated on the ramp a few hundred meters from here. The other people were sent toward the chimneys, and we thought we would follow them. Then the SS guards on the platform told us to follow them in the other direction. They took us here. They said there would be plenty of work for us before we followed them up the chimney ourselves."

"You said you arrived on the ramp in Birkenau?" Feliks asked.

"Next to the crematoria."

Samson and Feliks shared a look.

"So, they finished the ramp and tracks, then," Samson said. "Whatever they were building it for, it wasn't for a few hundred prisoners arriving from Lublin. Something's happening."

The Russian frowned. "This ramp is new?"

"They started work on it a couple of months ago. We didn't understand why, for the number of people arriving has only gone down in the past months. With you and the other newcomers in the yard arriving, I'm sure things will change very soon."

"And it won't be for the better," Feliks said.

"Thanks for letting us know what happened to our friends. If you need anything, let me know. We need to look after each other."

The Russian nodded, and Samson and Feliks strode back to the barracks.

"To Kaminski?" Feliks asked.

"To Kaminski."

The leader of the Sonderkommando looked troubled. "This is really bad. Even though I suspected the men sent to Lublin were in trouble, I didn't think they would be gassed on arrival. The Russian was certain?"

"They were wearing their clothes." Samson looked at Kaminski, who appeared composed but his words suggested otherwise. "It could be us next. What if the SS decide they want to replace us? What if those men in the yard are our replacements?"

"What are you suggesting?" Kaminski's voice was ice cold. "That we revolt today?"

Samson had trouble containing his excitement. "Yes! As soon as possible. We've been assembling and hiding bombs for months now, thanks to Roza and the women from the factory. We must have at least a dozen guns hidden. We can blow up the crematoria at night and surprise the SS."

Kaminski stared at him for a few seconds. His face was passive, giving away nothing. Samson turned to Feliks. His friend looked on with interest, but didn't say anything. *Shit. Did I misjudge the situation? No. We need to do something.* Before Kaminski could say anything, Samson continued. "I'm sick and tired of waiting for the SS to decide when our time's up. We're on borrowed time." Feliks was now nodding along. "We need to do something before it's too late."

"Are you done?" A joyless smile appeared on the big man's face. "You're right about the guns and bombs. We have a good number stashed away. We even have some ammunition, and plenty of men who know how to use them." Kaminski sat down on a stool in the corner of the room. "But even if everything goes exactly as planned, and we manage to do as you say—blow up the crematoria, where would we go? There are maybe four hundred of us, armed with a dozen guns, against a force of well-trained, armed soldiers. As soon as the first bomb goes off, they'll mobilize every soldier in the camp. We'll be dead within the hour."

Samson felt his adrenaline rise and fall as he listened to Kaminski. "But when will we do something? We've been talking about this for over a year now."

"We can't do anything without the camp underground," Kaminski said in a soothing tone.

"I'm tired of waiting for them. They're not in the crematoria. They're waiting for the Soviets or the Americans to show up. But the Nazis won't let us see any liberation. We know too much. You know this, Kaminski. We all know we'll be the first to be shot when the Allies close in on Auschwitz."

"Nobody knows where the Americans and Soviets are. Those are just rumors. The underground is in contact with the government."

"Screw the government! They don't give a shit about us, either! They're just letting us die here. It's been over a month since the escape, and we've heard nothing. Absolutely nothing." Samson took a deep breath and held up his hands. "I'm sorry. I'm just scared, and angry. I feel we're being abandoned by everyone." He dropped his head and closed his eyes.

Kaminski stood from his stool and moved toward him, putting his hand on his shoulder. "We can't lose our faith now, Samson. We're so close. We will move soon, but only when we know the rest of the camp underground moves with us. And we need the men on the outside, we need the Home Army to support us. Otherwise, where will we go when we break out of here?"

"I know."

"Listen to me. We will move when the time is right. But, for now, we stick together, do our job, and lay low. You mentioned not many of us have survived for this long." Samson looked up into the fiery eyes of Kaminski. "There is a reason we're still alive. And I sure as hell don't intend on letting them kill me just before we break out of here. Have faith, Samson. We will get out of here."

The next morning, Samson reported for roll call. To his relief, the new arrivals were added to the existing work crews. Over 450 men lined up in the yard. *They won't be killing us just yet, then.* As the guards moved the new members of the Sonderkommando to their crews, there was movement at the gate. A host of SS officers entered, and Samson squinted against the rising sun to scan their faces. As he focused on the man at the front, his heart dropped. *It can't be.*

Leading the group was none other than *Hauptscharführer* Otto Moll. The same man who'd overseen the burning of the corpses who'd risen from the ground behind the bunkers almost two years ago. Moll had made sure every single man involved in that operation had been executed, never to tell their story to the world. Samson had escaped death only because he wasn't part of the burning of the corpses. He'd only joined for a day, when Moll thought the use of lime would be enough to dispose of the bodies. He'd seen Moll around the camp a few times after that, but he'd been relieved never to have any direct contact with him. Until now.

Moll confidently strode to the front of the group, where he signaled to one of the guards. A piercing whistle silenced all murmurs. Moll looked pleased when the eyes of the Sonderkommando focused on him.

"Listen up, dogs. I'll keep this brief so you can follow." He grinned, and the men surrounding him did the same. "Commander Höss has entrusted the operations of the crematoria to me. There will be some changes as we return to full capacity. Make no mistake, things will get busy, and I expect you all to carry out your jobs as expected." He gazed at the men lined up in front of him with one good eye, the other a glass replica. Samson made sure to keep his gaze firmly ahead.

Moll called out the names of a number of Kapos, and Samson was dismayed to find his foreman was also called out. "You will work on the pits behind crematorium 5," he said as he casually flicked his wrist toward the gate. The Kapos sprang into action, shouting at their men to get moving.

Crematorium 5 had been idle for months, and there were no pits there. Those had been emptied by Moll himself. Samson passed the building and exited the camp. Within minutes, the small farmhouse known as bunker two came into view. It looked innocent from the outside, but Samson knew the horrors inside. Thousands of people had been gassed in previous years, before the larger crematoria and gas chambers were built. *God help us if they're thinking of putting the bunkers back into operation.*

Their Kapo led them past the farmhouse and to the meadows behind crematorium 5. A truck filled with spades, shovels, and other excavation tools awaited them.

One of the SS officers—thankfully not Moll—had followed and spoke in a loud voice. "You'll have two weeks to dig five pits, following those markings." There were five areas, each the size of about half an Olympic swimming pool, marked off throughout the meadow. "They'll need to be two meters deep."

Samson looked on in shock. *It's impossible.*

It soon became apparent, even to Moll, that they would never finish the five pits within two weeks. He changed tack the following day, ordering them to focus on two pits instead. For the next week, the men were worked to exhaustion every day. Moll oversaw the work himself, inspecting every little detail.

After a week, the rough outline of the first pit was done. Samson stood by the side of the pit when Moll climbed down with an assistant, each carrying a measuring tape. They marked out a narrow, 25-centimeter-wide area running through the middle of the pit.

"Pigs, you see those markings? You'll dig out a trough down the length of the pit. It needs to slope down from the middle to both sides, you understand?" The men nodded. "You'll find everything you need over there." Moll pointed at a jumble of tools at the end of the pit. To his surprise, there were sacks of cement.

Samson started digging, and they soon finished the narrow trough. As he helped mix the cement, the others went to work with spirits levels, making sure the troughs sloped down correctly. Suddenly it hit Samson. They were constructing a drainage channel. His blood ran cold. The drain would be used to channel the fat exuding from the corpses to the sides. It would serve as fuel for the fires.

After spending an entire day adding boards to the fences, Samson walked back to his barracks, desperate to get some rest. Feliks walked next to him, his friend as exhausted as he was. Samson was too tired to speak and focused on putting one foot in front of the other. As they returned to the Sonderkommando block, he saw most of the others had returned before them.

After wolfing down his inadequate dinner he sought out Kaminski. "How much longer?" Samson asked, his voice trembling from fatigue.

Kaminski looked at him. "It's almost time. I promise. Go to sleep. Rest. Tomorrow they arrive."

"Who?"

Kaminski sighed deeply. "The Hungarians."

# Chapter Forty-Eight

J oel was sorting his tools in the shed when he felt a hand on his shoulder—Bruno. "Come with me," the foreman said, his face serious. Joel reached for his toolbox, but Bruno shook his head. "Just leave it there."

The rest of the shed was empty. The others were still at work. Bruno pointed at a chair.

"Did you hear about the trains being sent away from the camp?" Bruno asked without preamble.

Joel shook his head. "What do you mean? The ones leaving after bringing people in?"

"No, no." Bruno sounded a little frustrated, his voice rising. "They're shipping people from Auschwitz to other camps."

"Why?" Joel was confused.

"Wish I knew. I've already lost a few men, and I've heard other work details around the camp are also losing valuable people. The bakery, the hospital, and now us."

"What do you mean?" Joel had a bad feeling.

Bruno looked at Joel for a moment. "I spoke to one of the guards earlier, and he said a large number of my men will be put on transport in the next few days."

"Do you know who?"

"I do." He looked uneasy. "You're also on the list."

Joel's chest tightened. "Who told you?"

"The guard said those with the low prisoner numbers would go first. You're the lowest number here. I'm sorry."

Joel leaned forward, resting his hands on his knees. Even though it wasn't certain, he needed to prepare for the worst. "How bad do you think it will be? Do you think I will go to the same place those Sonderkommando men were sent?" Before Bruno could answer, he added, "But why don't they just kill me in Auschwitz?"

"I don't know." Bruno spoke in a voice unfamiliar to Joel. It was softer, lower than usual—less confident. *He also doesn't know how to handle this.* "There's a good chance you're just needed somewhere else, and they want the most experienced heads moving."

"I'm not so sure about that," Joel said. He looked to Bruno and saw his foreman was also having trouble believing his own words. "I can't leave Auschwitz; people are counting on me."

Bruno nodded. "I know, which is why we need to know for sure if you're on the list. And if you are, we need to get you off it."

"But how?"

Bruno smiled wryly. "We may not have much, but at least we have the connections around the camp. And there's only one way to get what you need in Auschwitz, just like anywhere else."

"What's that?"

Bruno stood up. "Gems, gold, money. In that order. And luckily for you, we know someone who can get us enough of it to convince the SS to take you off that list."

"And why would he do that?"

"Because he needs you here."


"Of course I'll help, Joel." Kaminski looked at him with a serious expression. "After everything you've done, how can we abandon you now?"

They stood in the oven room of crematorium 2. Joel had never seen it so busy, and it seemed even more men than usual were running around stoking the fires and feverishly shoving corpses into the ovens. He tried to ignore the mayhem.

"What if you're unable to convince them?"

"I won't fail you. Trust me." Kaminski's voice was firm.

Joel reported to Bruno the next morning. Despite Kaminski's confidence, he hardly slept that night.

"You feeling all right, Joel?" Bruno said, raising an eyebrow. "You look like hell."

"I'm okay, don't worry about it." Joel walked to the row of toolboxes and picked out his own. "Am I going to Raisko?"

Bruno handed him a slip of paper. "Your morning assignment. You need to be back before noon. Can you do that?"

"No problem. I'll fix those lights and be on my way back. Anything planned for the afternoon?"

"Not yet. But I'm sure something will come up. It always does. Better get going if you don't want to have to run."

Joel did a last check of his toolbox and then headed for the door. As he did, it opened and he froze. Two guards walked in, one of them carrying a piece of paper. He looked at Joel and waved his hand in a backward motion. "Move back to the bench, you're not going anywhere."

Joel felt the blood drain from his face as he turned and walked toward Bruno. The foreman stood motionless, keeping his face composed, fear etched in the man's eyes. The hum of the voices of the other men packing their toolboxes died down—eyes darting between their toolboxes and the SS men.

"When I call out your name and number, step forward," the guard carrying the piece of paper said. "You will leave your tools here."

"What is this about?" Bruno asked. *Brave man.*

"This doesn't concern you," the guard said, his mouth twitching.

Bruno didn't back down that easily. "I'm the foreman of this work detail. I have a right to know what's happening."

The SS guard shot forward and thrust his finger in Bruno's face. "These are not your men. These are the men of the Reich. You best keep your mouth shut, or I'll report you to your superiors. Let's see how long you'll be a foreman after that."

Bruno swallowed hard and dropped his head.

"That's what I thought." The guard looked smug as he turned back to face the group. "Now, pay attention." He started calling out names and men stepped forward. Soon, about half of the men's names had been called. Joel had trouble controlling his hands, and he clenched them into fists. He bit his lip as the guard's voice droned on.

"Kozak, 731135."

Joel didn't immediately respond, and the guard repeated his name, this time with unmistakable annoyance. "Kozak. Report."

Joel stepped forward as in a haze. The guard looked at him, took a step forward, and Joel braced for the imminent beating. Then the guard changed his mind and called another half dozen names.

Joel looked at Bruno, who appeared utterly defeated. More than half of his men were about to be taken away, and he would have no say in it. When Joel met the man's eyes, he saw surprise and guilt, as if Bruno was apologizing for what was happening. Joel shook his head almost imperceptibly. Nothing is ever certain in Auschwitz.

Joel and the other men were escorted to the ramp between the men's and women's camps. Crematoria 2 and 3's chimneys belched dark plumes of smoke in the background.

He was surprised by the relatively orderly manner in which they were directed toward the ramp. There was none of the chaos he remembered from when he arrived on the old ramp between Auschwitz and Birkenau. Instead, the SS guards stood patiently waiting as prisoners approached from different sides of the camp.

Joel's group was told to wait. He looked around and saw a young officer flanked by two guards at the top of the ramp. Every person entering the ramp was checked off the list before boarding the train. If they cared enough to keep records of the men and women leaving, perhaps they really were being reassigned. Joel shook his head—it was wishful thinking. He shouldn't delude himself. He was going to die soon.

The man ahead of him moved forward. They were up next. As he ascended the ramp, Joel looked back to the place that had been his home for two years now. The desolate plains had made way for hundreds of barracks stretching as far as the eye could see. He thought of the people he left behind and prayed they would find a way to survive. To rise up and deal a blow—any blow—against the death and destruction of Auschwitz. Moshe, Piotr, Kaminski, Roza, and Agnes.

"Name and number!" The harsh voice jolted him from his thoughts and he looked up into the stern, impatient face of the SS officer.

"Kozak, 731135." It was an automatic response conditioned by two years of camp life where people were reduced to numbers. He waited for the officer to wave him through. When it took longer than expected, he glanced to the paper. The officer's finger was frantically going through the list. When he didn't find Joel's number on the next page, he looked at him in annoyance.

"Are you sure that's the right number? Show me your arm." Joel held out his wrist, exposing the same combination tattooed there. The officer sighed in frustration. "You're not on my list. Who brought you here?"

The guard who had escorted him from the repair shop appeared. "Something wrong, sir?"

"What is this man doing here? He's not on the list." His voice was strained.

"Sir, he was on my list." The man grabbed Joel's wrist, then pointed at the entry on his list. "Kozak, right here."

The officer took the page, then shook his head. "You have an outdated list. This is yesterday's." He pointed at the date at the top. "Something must've changed. Bloody bureaucracy."

"So, what do we do, sir?" The guard looked lost. Joel held his breath.

The officer looked at the guard as if he were speaking to a small child. "What do you think? You're going to take him back to where he came from. If he's not on my list, he's not going anywhere! I'll talk to those imbeciles in administration about this. How am I supposed to work like this?"

Joel could cry from relief as he listened to the words. Unable to move, he stood in stunned silence, unsure if what he heard was true.

"Come on, get down from the platform, people are waiting!" the officer snapped at him. "Quickly, before I change my mind."

The guard dragged Joel down and placed him near a cart at a short distance from the ramp. "Wait for me here and don't move. If you move, I'll shoot."

Joel nodded and leaned against the cart. He couldn't believe his luck.

Then he realized luck had nothing to do with it. Kaminski had come through.

# CHAPTER FORTY-NINE

S amson wiped his brow after dropping the corpse of a young woman on the growing pile of bodies behind crematorium 5. As soon as he did, he heard the piercing voice of Moll only inches from his ear.

"What the hell do you think you're doing? Did I tell you you could take a break, *Jude*?"

Samson jumped at the voice and turned, vigorously shaking his head. "No, Herr Hauptscharführer, I'm sorry, Herr Hauptscharführer."

Moll waved him off. "Don't let me see you dragging your feet again, or you can join them in the pits!"

Samson rushed back inside, sweat pouring from every pore. He entered the gas chamber, where more than 400 corpses still lay strewn across the room. He picked up another and hurried back outside.

On the other side of the fence, Samson heard the voices of the people waiting outside the crematorium. They spoke Hungarian, and even though Samson didn't understand exactly what they were saying, he knew what they pleaded for. Water. When the transports started two weeks ago, multiple trains a day arrived at Birkenau's new ramp. People were herded toward the crematoria, and if they were unfortunate enough to be assigned to crematorium 5, they would often spend their time waiting in an open space the Nazis called the Little Woods. If they survived the journey from Hungary, they arrived at Birkenau exhausted and parched. Moll and his henchmen promised them water and made them wait, while Samson and the other men of the SK hurried to clear the gas chamber. The wails of the children cut through everything and haunted Samson in his sleep.

Samson was on his way back into the crematorium when Moll appeared, followed by two guards and dragging a younger member of the SK with him. "Everybody, come here for a second," Moll said. Samson felt dread build in the pit of his stomach. Moll hated slowing down the process.

Moll walked to the pit closest to the crematorium. It was smoldering, red embers glowing amid the white ash. The heat was intense. Moll held up his hand, displaying a few banknotes. Samson's stomach roiled. "This man was caught stealing from the Reich! As you know, there is only one punishment for such a crime." He patted the pistol on his belt. The young man recoiled and started to whimper. Moll shook his head, tutting. "Now, now, you know I'm no monster. I've decided to give you a chance to survive." The young man looked up, hope on his face. Samson was surprised. What was Moll up to?

Moll pointed at the smoldering pit below. "If you can run the length of the pit twice barefoot, I'll forget this happened." He waved the banknotes in the man's face with a crooked smile.

Samson was dismayed. The pit was at least 50 meters long. The boy didn't stand a chance.

The young man didn't hesitate as he took off his shoes and jumped into the pit. He started sprinting, to the encouragement of the guards. Samson watched his face, and it soon became clear the poor wretch wouldn't even make it halfway through. He started screaming as his feet blackened. With a bone-chilling shriek, the young man collapsed face-first into the fiery ashes. His clothes caught fire immediately. In a desperate effort, the man rose as he tried to take off his shirt, stamping his feet as his wails grew louder. His face was covered in ash, the skin from his nose peeling from the heat. As he sank to his knees, a shot rang out, instantly stopping the wails. The man's body fell backward into the embers and within seconds caught fire.

"Well, he had his chance." Moll said as he holstered his pistol. "Everybody get back to work. And let this be a warning." He dropped the banknotes into the pit—less than twenty Reichsmarks.

Samson returned to Block 13 with the sun setting. His legs ached and his shoulders were sore. But most of all, his mind was exhausted. After Moll executed the young man, the men of the Sonderkommando had continued in silence. Even though the SS officer was known for his zeal and cruelty, this was the first time most of them had been witness to an execution of one of their own. On the way back to Birkenau, no one had talked.

After Samson had wolfed down his dinner, he found his bunk and reached for a small flask. He unscrewed the top and took a quick swig. The liquid burned down his throat, then spread as a comfortable warmth in his stomach. He sighed and felt his muscles relax. Soon, a pleasant fog engulfed his brain, and he took another sip. As he closed his eyes, he tried to block the day's images. Then, slowly, he started drifting away.

"Samson." A familiar voice spoke urgently and Samson opened his eyes. Kaminski stood next to his bunk, his eyes on the flask. "Drinking again?" He frowned. "I didn't take you for a drinker."

Samson put the flask away. "I'm not. Just having a very rough day."

"That's how it starts. Be careful, my friend." There was no judgment in the Kapo's voice. "I need to speak to you."

Samson followed Kaminski outside, where the day's warm summer air had cooled a little. They stood a few paces from the door, away from a crowd of Russians on the other side.

"I spoke to some of the men in the resistance this morning. There are rumors of the Red Army making good progress. It has the Nazis spooked."

"Any idea where they are? We've heard this many times before."

"No, but apparently the Nazis think they might be closer to Auschwitz than they thought. They're drawing up plans in case the Soviets show up sooner than expected."

That sounded ominous. "Plans?"

"To make sure nobody lives to tell the truth of what happened here."

"I see." The pleasant fog in his brain dissipated. "But they're just rumors for now?" Kaminski didn't respond, staring into the distance instead. "Do you believe they're true?"

Kaminski slowly nodded. "The news came from multiple groups on the outside. They're all saying the same thing. Moll is in charge of the contingency plan. There is talk about artillery and bombers to destroy the camp when they need to. We need to take this seriously."

Samson tilted his head. "And are we?"

"That's why I needed to speak with you," Kaminski said, his face serious. "The underground agrees the time to rise up is now."

*Finally.* Even though Samson was excited, he had a bitter taste in the back of his mouth. "So now that they see they might not live to see the liberation either, they decide it's time for action? They're no longer happy to sit and wait, wait for the Nazis to kill us?"

Kaminski held up his hands. "I know, Samson. And when this is all over, we can have this conversation with them. But now we need to stick together. The plan is complicated, and everybody needs to do exactly what they're told at the right time. You understand this, right?"

"It's for a greater good, I know," Samson spoke softly, suddenly feeling petty. The Kapo was right, it wasn't just about them. "So what are we going to do?"

"We have weapons hidden in all the crematoria, but we'll start the uprising in numbers four and five. I need you to be part of the first wave, overpowering the SS guards in four. It will be easy, as they won't expect you. There are only seven or eight guards there, right?"

Samson nodded. "Yes. How many guns do we have?"

"Just three in crematorium four, but you won't need more. As long as you attack them individually, you shouldn't even need to fire a shot. In fact, it would be better if you don't. We'll need the ammo later on."

"What happens after we take the crematorium?"

"We'll take their uniforms and we'll do the same in the other crematoria. Then we lay low and wait for the change of guards in the evening."

"It sounds like we're still doing all the work," Samson said with a frown. "Why didn't we do this earlier?"

"We're not on our own. The outside work details will overpower their guards and take out telephone lines. Then, once we're ready, we'll attack the remaining SS inside the camp. They won't be able to call in help, and we'll attack from all sides."

"How do you rate our chances? Honestly?" Kaminski made it sound so simple.

The Kapo thought for a moment, then smiled. "If I didn't think it was possible, we wouldn't be talking now."

The trains from Hungary continued to arrive, two or three a day carrying close to five thousand people in cattle boxcars. With every corpse Samson carried to the fiery pits of hell, he promised he would avenge their deaths. Soon.

On a sunny morning in June, Kaminski appeared next to him as they marched out of the yard after roll call. "Today is the day, be ready," he whispered. Samson nodded, and Kaminski made off, finding another man farther ahead. Samson's excitement rose as he kept his eyes on Kaminski. He wasn't surprised to see the Kapo approach more than a dozen men before the first group turned off to crematoria 2 and 3.

Samson's group approached crematorium 5 and he eyed the guards at the gate. They looked bored, casually glancing at the group of incoming prisoners. Samson balled his hands into fists. *Just wait.*

Samson was on his way back into the gas chambers when he saw three men with an empty wheelbarrow enter the yard. Two of them worked in crematorium 2. *What are they doing here?* Samson immediately felt uneasy. Something must've gone wrong. He stopped, and one nodded at Samson. He slowly approached them.

"What are you doing here?" he asked as he reached the men. He looked over his shoulder, but there was no one else in the yard. Yet.

"Change of plans."

"What?" Samson had a sinking feeling.

"The uprising is off. Too dangerous. Something happened outside the camp. Tell everyone to back down." The men picked up some wood from one of the piles as cover for their visit before turning around. Samson stood rooted to the ground. He wanted to scream in frustration. After all the preparation, they had called off the uprising?

That evening at roll call, Moll had another surprise for them. As Samson frantically searched for Kaminski in the crowd, the SS officer's voice boomed across the yard.

"From tomorrow onward, you won't be sleeping in Block 13 anymore. We'll have more men joining us soon, and you won't all fit here." Samson turned his head, alarmed by the words. "Instead, you will sleep in the crematoria."

There were a few sounds of disbelief across the yard, but most took the news impassively. After everything they had been through, being made to sleep in the buildings of death almost seemed like the next logical step.

After Moll dismissed them for the evening, Feliks caught up with Samson. "You know what this means, Samson?"

Samson nodded his head, embracing his friend. "They're shutting us off from the rest of the camp."

"Do you think they knew about today?"

"Oh yeah. They knew. They just can't kill all of us." He smiled wryly as they entered their block. "Not yet, anyway."

# CHAPTER FIFTY

A gnes moved through the room, carefully inspecting the faces of the young women in the beds. The ward was full, with some forty women spending most of their time sleeping and occasionally chatting to each other. The number of deaths had gone down, despite Dr. Wirths' butchers posing as surgeons still botching numerous operations. Agnes sighed, but reminded herself it used to be much worse. She recalled the days women would die from infections after surgery. At least they could treat most infections these days with the medicine she collected.

She stopped by the bed of one of the Dutch girls who'd arrived around a month ago, Hannie.

"How are you doing today?" she asked Hannie, who sat up in her bed. She had recovered exceptionally quickly from the initial experiments. Agnes hadn't told her, but Dr. Wirths had been encouraged by the results. *Poor girl. She'll never be able to have children.*

"Agnes! I haven't seen you up here for a while." A smile spread across the girl's face. "Have you heard anything about my parents?"

Agnes forced herself to keep her face straight. Hannie had been selected because of her age. Even though Agnes didn't know for sure, she was almost certain her parents had been sent to the gas chambers on arrival. She would have to break it to Hannie soon. She looked at the girl's face and decided: not today. She shook her head. "I'm sorry, I haven't had a chance to check with the administration yet. I'll let you know as soon as I hear anything." She picked up Hannie's chart and suppressed a frown. She was scheduled for another experiment the next day. That was a bit quick; her previous surgery was only three days ago. Surely this was a mistake. Agnes made a mental note to check with Dr. Brewda when she returned to the office. She had just put the file back near Hannie's bed when someone tapped her shoulder. It was one of the new nurses.

"There's someone waiting for you downstairs. A gentleman. He says he needs to see you urgently."

"SS?"

The nurse shook her head. "No, he's wearing the prisoner uniform. I told him to wait outside."

"I'll be back later, Hannie. We can chat then," she said before quickly making her way downstairs. When she stepped outside and into the bright afternoon, she was delighted to find Joel. "I was hoping it would be you!" Then she saw the expression on his face. "What's wrong?"

"It's Roza. She's sick. Very sick. She's unable to get out of bed." He spoke quickly, the words tumbling out of his mouth almost incoherently.

Agnes held up a hand. "One thing at a time. Where is she? Did she go to the Birkenau hospital?"

"No, she doesn't want to. She's hiding in her bunk. The other girls are covering for her in Kanada. But I saw her this morning—she can hardly breathe."

*Poor woman.*

"I'll come check on her."

Joel's shoulders sagged a little. "Thank you."

"Let me just check with Dr. Brewda." She headed back inside. If Dr. Brewda provided her with a pass for Roza, she could make sure no one touched her while she recovered. It wasn't foolproof, but it was the best she could do. She entered Dr. Brewda's office. "I need your help."

Half an hour later, Joel and Agnes stepped into a drafty barracks in the women's camp. Joel had bribed the guard, whom Agnes was surprised he knew, and she was secretly pleased he was with her as they moved to the back of the building. The draft creeping through the holes and cracks in the walls and roof made for a comfortable breeze in summer, but she could imagine the circumstances in winter. The barracks were almost empty. They found Roza at the back of a bunk in the corner. Even before Joel called for her to come out, Agnes could see she was in a very bad state.

"This is Agnes, she's one of us," Joel said softly. "She works in the hospital in Auschwitz."

Roza looked at Agnes with glassy eyes, her teeth chattering as her head bobbed up and down in acknowledgment. Agnes gave her best comforting smile. "I'm here to help you get better, Roza. We need you to get well soon; people are counting on us."

Roza coughed violently, and immediately put her hand to her chest as she averted her face. Joel looked to Agnes, wide eyed, but Agnes kept her composure. "Can I listen to your heartbeat and lungs, Roza?" She took out a simple stethoscope. Roza moved closer and Agnes gently placed the device on her chest, moving it around as she listened to the women's vital organs.

"You have pneumonia, Roza. We need to get it treated in the hospital."

"No." Roza shook her head as she spoke for the first time. "They'll kill me."

"They won't, I promise they won't," Joel said. "That's why I went to get Agnes. She can keep you safe."

There was surprise in the young woman's eyes as she turned to Agnes. "Really? Can you guarantee I won't be sent to the gas chambers?"

Agnes felt uncomfortable. She lowered her voice. "You know I can't promise you that. It's beyond my control. But I can promise you that if you stay here, you will die before this week is over." Roza launched into another violent cough, and Agnes waited patiently. "This will only get worse."

Roza's eyes went between Joel and Agnes, and Agnes could see she was wavering. "I promise you coming with me gives you the best chance to survive," Agnes said as she held out her hand.

With an effort, Roza reached out and took Agnes' hand. Her touch was cold and clammy, and Agnes knew they needed to hurry. She gave Joel a look. "Ask some of the women outside to help, we'll need to carry her."

That evening, Agnes sat in Dr. Brewda's office. She was startled when the door opened and the doctor walked in.

"How did it go in Birkenau?" She sat down across from Agnes.

"As well as it could. We got her to the hospital, and the girls working there will make sure she stays out of sight."

"And this woman is important?"

Agnes nodded. "If Joel says she is, I believe him."

"Me too. I'm glad he came to you about this. What's wrong with her?"

"Pneumonia."

"Did they have enough medication in Birkenau?"

"I sent one of the girls to Kanada to collect some sulfonamides. She came back with plenty." Agnes smiled. "Roza was in a bad state, but I'm confident she'll be better soon."

"Good. Let's keep an eye on her." Dr. Brewda studied Agnes intently. "Speaking of keeping an eye on, you need to get to bed. You look horrible. What time did you start today?"

"I don't really remember. It was early."

"Off you go then. I'll take care of these files. Go to bed."

Agnes got up, suddenly overcome with exhaustion. She stumbled to the nurses' room and tiptoed to her bunk. She put her head on her pillow and closed her eyes. Just before she drifted into unconsciousness, she saw Joel's smiling face.

# CHAPTER FIFTY-ONE

I
t was still early when Joel made his way toward the hospital blocks in Birkenau. Other prisoners were preparing for the day, some already forming their work details, getting ready to leave. Joel pitied them. They would soon march toward the mines, fields, or nearby quarries to carry out backbreaking labor. In the evening, they would return broken and tired, while the bodies of the fallen were carried back. Others would perish in the night, silently escaping the anguish of the camp.

Joel arrived at the hospital and was let in by the guard, who knew him by now. Most of the time, just the appearance of his toolbox was enough to grant him access to all areas of the camp. It was only at more remote areas, like Raisko, or the crematoria that he needed to show his paperwork.

He entered the block where Roza was kept and was overwhelmed by the stench. The block wasn't much different from the regular Birkenau barracks, with wooden bunks stacked three high against both side walls and through the middle. Narrow walkways provided just enough space for him to squeeze through without disturbing those withering away. More than half the bunks packed two nights ago were now empty.

A woman approached from the other direction as he walked toward Roza's bunk. She frowned as he made room for her to pass.

"What are you doing here?" She looked at his toolbox. "You must be lost. There's nothing that needs repairing."

"I'm here to visit the patient in the back. The one brought in by Dr. Brewda." Roza wasn't brought in by Dr. Brewda personally, but Agnes had told the nurses Roza was transferred on the doctor's orders.

The nurse's attitude instantly changed. "Of course, she's awake and doing much better." She pointed to a bunk and hurried on.

"Hey, Joel." Roza's voice sounded quite clear, and Joel couldn't suppress a smile. It had been a week since he and Agnes had convinced her to move to the ward. He had visited her twice since, and her condition improved every time he saw her. Today, Roza even had a bit of color on her cheeks. She looked at him with clear eyes. "Did you bring me anything?"

He crouched down beside her, reached into his toolbox, and handed her a large piece of salami. "I got this from the Sonderkommando. You can imagine there's a lot of this coming in these days."

Roza took the salami gratefully, but there was sadness in her eyes. "Are the transports still coming in at the same pace?"

"I'm afraid so. Kaminski said a minimum of two trains every day."

"It's hard to believe the Nazis are using all those trains to transport Hungarians across Europe when they're struggling to keep the Soviets at bay." Roza took a tiny bit of the sausage and looked up in surprise. "This is really good."

"It's not just the Soviets," Joel said. "I heard something's happening in the west as well."

Roza's eyes lit up. "The British?"

"Not just the Brits. Americans, Canadians, and people who escaped Europe are returning. There are rumors that they've landed in France."

"So the liberation might actually happen." Roza sounded hopeful.

"We're a long way from France."

"But if the Soviets push through in the east, they might reach us sooner than expected. The Nazis won't be able to fight the war on two fronts."

Joel nodded. "Let's focus on surviving long enough for them to get here first. You seem to be doing much better."

"There was a selection last night. The nurses hid me away when the SS came. More than half of the women in my block were taken away in the morning." Roza's mouth twitched as she cast her eyes downward.

"It's time to get you out of here. Did you talk to any of the nurses about leaving? Do you still have a fever, or any other symptoms?"

She shook her head. "After the selection I told them I wanted to return to work, and they said they would reach out to Dr. Brewda first. But I don't want to wait for that. What if the SS come back before she has a chance to check on me? They might not be able to hide me this time. And I need to talk to the girls working in the Union factory. They must be wondering what happened."

"Don't worry about them."

Roza raised her eyebrows. "What do you mean? Did you talk to them?"

"Not me. But someone in the Sonderkommando talked to one of them and let them know you were in here."

"So they've continued without me?" She looked relieved.

Joel nodded. "Kaminski told me their supply of gunpowder continued this past week. We're fortunate you set up the smuggling route into the crematoria the way you did. In a way, having the Sonderkommando confined to the crematoria helps us. It means they have access to the gunpowder and bombs all the time, even when they're not working."

"There will always be corpses to be sent to the crematoria every day. And nobody checks the corpses, certainly not the guards. It just made sense to hide the gunpowder among them." She was quiet for a moment, then looked thoughtful. "Do you know how they're doing? It must be tough to be completely isolated from the rest of the camp."

"Moll increased the number of men in the Sonderkommando. Over a thousand now work day and night to process the Hungarian transports."

Roza gasped. "A thousand? That's madness. I can't believe it. And what will happen to them when the transports stop?" Her brow creased with worry.

"Let's not think about that yet."

"Do you think you could send a message to one of them?"

"Of course, anything you need."

She handed him a small piece of paper. "I need you to deliver this to Samson Tarski. I'm sure Kaminski will know him."

Joel took the piece of paper and carefully placed it in his pocket. "He's the man who started all of this, right? He went to Kaminski, and that's how the underground got involved?"

"And that's how you got involved as well, Joel," Roza said, smiling. "Samson is a good man. I think in a different life you two would be friends."

Joel returned her smile. "Well, Samson and I might not know each other, but I can see you're fond of him." Despite the bad lighting in the barracks, Joel could see Roza blush a little. "And any friend of yours is a friend of mine."

Joel entered the eerily quiet yard of the crematorium and asked for Kaminski. One of the SK men took him upstairs into their sleeping quarters. He pointed at a bunk in the back, where Kaminski sat reading a book: he hadn't taken Kaminski for a reading man.

As he approached, Kaminski looked up. He didn't even appear surprised to see Joel as he put down the book. "Any news?"

Joel told him about the Allied forces landing in France, and Kaminski looked pleased.

"That's what the camp underground had also picked up from the government in London a month or two ago. Well, not in as many words, but the Home Army said the government was hinting at an impending invasion, and that they should be getting ready to support it."

"How are your preparations going?"

"I suppose that's what the leadership really wants to know, right? How many bombs and guns we have." Kaminski smiled and pointed at the area around them. "We haven't had an awful lot of time to build more bombs. Moll is working us to the bone, but we're making some progress. We now have three men capable of assembling bombs."

"Can I tell them the Sonderkommando is ready to fight?" Joel felt the gravity of his words. "In case they want to move ahead with the uprising?"

Kaminski held Joel's gaze for a moment, neither man flinching. *Has Kaminski forgotten about the uprising that was blown off at the last minute?* That had been mere weeks ago. Were the Sonderkommando still on board?

"Yes. Tell them we're ready."

# CHAPTER FIFTY-TWO

Agnes awoke with a start. The sound was so familiar her heart skipped a beat. She strained her ears, hoping her groggy mind was playing tricks on her. But then she heard it again—heavy footsteps and muffled voices. Some of the other women in the room stirred, a few sitting up, no doubt wondering what roused them early. Then she heard a man's voice barking orders farther down the hallway.

Agnes was now fully awake and swung her legs out of bed. She grabbed her nurse's uniform, hanging on a chair by her bed, and quickly dressed. When Agnes stepped toward the door, she froze as one of the voices was too familiar. *Alina.*

She opened the door, the brightness of the hallway lights momentarily blinding her. Agnes blinked hard and when her vision returned she felt her body tremble. Five SS guards surrounded Dr. Brewda as she stood in her white doctor's coat.

"On whose orders are you operating?" She spoke to the most senior guard. Her voice was strained and an octave higher than usual. The guard looked unimpressed.

"You can come with us quietly, or we can drag you out of your precious hospital. Your choice. But you're coming with us. Now." He jabbed a finger in Dr. Brewda's face, and Agnes gasped. She felt some of the other nurses peeking over her shoulder.

Dr. Brewda scowled, and for a moment, Agnes feared she would resist. She looked beyond the men and caught sight of Agnes and the other nurses. Her expression changed as she calmed down, holding out her hands. "All right, I'll come with you. But I want to speak to Dr. Wirths about this."

The guard chuckled and ignored her hands. Instead, he motioned at the guards standing beside her. They grabbed her arms and shoulders and pushed her toward the exit.

As Dr. Brewda passed the shocked nurses, she halted and smiled at them. "Everything will be okay, girls. I'll be back before you know it." Her attention turned to Agnes. "Take good care of them."

"That's enough, keep moving!" the senior guard yelled as the others shoved her forward. "And you." He turned to Agnes. "Get ready for work. Dr. Wirths will be here shortly."

The nurses behind Agnes shrank away, but Agnes kept her eyes on Dr. Brewda as she was manhandled to the exit.

Five minutes later, Agnes stood in Dr. Brewda's office. Files were neatly stacked on one side of her desk—the day's planned experiments. Dr. Brewda always prepared them well before anyone else was up. There were six operations scheduled for the day, and Agnes knew with Alina gone, there was no one else here to look after the girls. She took a deep breath, and she paused for thought. *What if Alina's arrest wasn't a misunderstanding at all?*

Her blood turned cold. Five guards seemed excessive, but now that she thought of it, she imagined the guards wanted to make a show of her arrest. And their leader had seemed especially cocky as he refused to answer any of her questions. Agnes gripped the side of the desk as the room spun around her. *What else do they know?*

She heard a door open in the distance, and she turned, her head still swimming. From her blurred vision she made out the figure of a tall man. He spoke to her, but his words didn't register. Then, in an instant, her vision cleared, and Dr. Wirths' voice came through loud and clear.

"Are you deaf? I asked you what you are doing in this office." Two troopers followed him inside, and the small office was suddenly very crowded.

Agnes blinked, her eyes going between the three men. "I'm sorry, Dr. Wirths, I was a little dizzy." She focused on the doctor, who stood eyeing her with his arms folded across his chest. "I was just preparing the files for today's operations." She reached for the files on Alina's desk, but Dr. Wirths grabbed her wrist and pulled her away. She looked at him with fear.

"You won't be touching anything in this office. This is now evidence." He snapped his fingers, and the two SS men approached the desk. "Search the drawers, and those filing cabinets. Anything that looks suspicious, you bring it to me." He turned back to Agnes. "You won't be seeing Dr. Brewda back here anytime soon. She's been moved next door."

Agnes couldn't suppress her horror. "She's in Block 11?"

"Yes. She violated the code of medical conduct." Dr. Wirths picked up the stack of files from the desk. "It's a grave offense."

Agnes was in shock and at a loss for words. The guards emptied the desk's drawers and moved on to the filing cabinets. Fear gripped her throat as her suspicions were confirmed. The arrest had not been a mistake.

"Oh, and Agnes, one more thing." Dr. Wirths spoke casually while flicking through one of the files. "As her assistant, did you ever suspect she was involved in these violations?" He emphasized the last word, and Agnes' hands started trembling. She quickly clasped them together. *Does he know?*

"I only prepared the files and ensured all the reports of the day's operations were up to date, Dr. Wirths. Other than that, Dr. Brewda asked me to handle the day-to-day running of the wards."

"Hmm." He nodded and put the files down before meeting her eyes. His dark eyes bored into her soul as he spoke the following words: "So you wouldn't know anything about her illegal activities? Her sabotage?"

Agnes fought to control her fear as she held Dr. Wirths' gaze for a few seconds. "I know Dr. Brewda only wanted the women in the ward treated the best way possible." She looked away and silently cursed herself. *Did I just make myself suspicious?*

She could feel Dr. Wirths looking at her for a few more seconds; then he turned toward the door. "Very well. Why don't you check on the *day-to-day running* of the wards, then? I'm sure we'll have more questions for you later." He held the door for her.

Fighting the urge to run, Agnes slowly left the room, careful not to appear rushed or nervous. She fought the urge to look back when she stepped into the hallway. Instead, she focused her eyes on the stairs at the other end of the hall.

"Agnes?" Dr. Wirths' voice echoed through the silent hallway. She turned around slowly. He stood holding two files. "While you're up there, can you prepare these girls for surgery? You'll assist Dr. Clauberg today."

Agnes walked back with heavy feet and took the files. Without another word, she walked toward the stairs again. It wasn't until she reached the top that she let go of the breath she was holding. She needed to see Joel.

# CHAPTER FIFTY-THREE

Joel arrived in the late afternoon. Mercifully, Dr. Clauberg hadn't asked Agnes to assist him, instead opting to work with his favorite, Sylvia. She had witnessed Dr. Brewda's arrest but had said nothing to Agnes. She appeared to pretend everything was normal.

Agnes couldn't. She tried to distract herself by comforting the women as she prepared them for the experiments.

"You're going to be fine; they know nothing, Agnes." Joel spoke with conviction as they sat outside the hospital block, near the fence. The closest guard tower was too far away for the guard to overhear them. "If Wirths knew about you, he wouldn't have waited. He would've arrested you right away."

Agnes picked up a small pebble and twirled it between her fingers. "I don't know. This morning I thought the same, but I'm not so sure as I went through everything today. They've got Alina in Block 11. You know what that means."

Joel didn't say anything but stared at the guard tower in the distance. The guard had his back to them.

"They're probably torturing her if she's not dead already."

"She's not dead, Agnes."

"How do you know that?"

"Because they haven't arrested anyone else. She hasn't betrayed anyone," Joel said, his voice surprisingly calm, his expression stoic. "Did she ever speak about the experiments? Or the doctors?"

Agnes thought for a minute, then shook her head. "Only to me. But she was very careful. She would never speak out against Dr. Wirths."

"Does she have any enemies in the block?"

Sylvia's face flashed through Agnes' mind, but she quickly dismissed it. Even though the Czech nurse performed her assistant's duties to Clauberg with too much enthusiasm, she had never been anything but cordial to Alina. Agnes had even seen them laugh together on occasion. "The nurses love her, as do the patients."

Joel turned to her and took her hand. "Look, I know it's scary, and Dr. Brewda was your closest friend, but you can't do this to yourself. It sounds like Dr. Wirths doesn't know much about what Dr. Brewda did exactly, and he's just testing to see if anyone breaks. Don't break, Agnes. Do you think Dr. Brewda will break in there?" He looked to the building next door, the windows facing the yard shuttered close with pieces of wood.

Agnes gripped his hand tightly. "I don't know. She's strong, but you know what happens in there. They get even the strongest to talk."

"There's no sense in worrying about something you don't know for certain," Joel said softly. "Don't let yourself go crazy. You need to be strong now. Dr. Brewda needs you to continue her work in there. The resistance needs you. We can't stop now. We're so close."

She looked up. "Are we?"

"The uprising will be any day now. The Russians are coming from the east, the Americans and Brits from the west. Hitler's days are numbered. We need to hold on just a little longer." He leaned forward and kissed her forehead.

Agnes closed her eyes, overwhelmed by emotions. She felt a tear roll down her cheek and reached to wipe it away. Before she could, Joel took her hand and pressed it against his chest.

"We're going to make it out of here together, Agnes, I promise."

She opened her eyes and looked at him. His dark brown eyes looked at her lovingly, and she felt a surge of affection shoot through her chest before she controlled the urge to kiss him. Instead, she burrowed her head into his chest and whispered, "I hope you're right, Joel, I really hope you are."

Agnes drifted into an uncomfortable sleep that evening. She was exhausted but woke up multiple times that night, unable to process the roller coaster of emotions she'd gone through.

It felt like she had only been asleep for a few seconds when a flash of brightness awoke her. She was horrified to find two SS troopers heading straight for her. They ignored the other women, who were in various states of confusion, pulling their covers over themselves as the men passed them by.

Fear gripped Agnes as her throat constricted and her palms became sweaty. *This is it. They've found out.*

The troopers reached Agnes, and the tallest spoke to her surprisingly calmly. "Get dressed; you're coming with us."

Agnes realized nothing she could say would change the outcome. She took a deep breath and steadied her fraying nerves before stepping barefoot onto the cold floor. Under the watchful eyes of the troopers, she dressed in her nurse's uniform. The man who spoke to her nodded and took her by the arm. He gently escorted her across the silent room. The eyes of the other nurses followed Agnes as she slowly walked past them. She tried to look brave, but she could feel her heart beating out of her chest. When she passed Sylvia, she saw compassion in the woman's eyes. *Yes, they finally got me.*

The first thing Agnes noticed was the air in the building. It was stale, as if no fresh air ever made its way inside. The floor was dirty, the lights dim. She was taken to a narrow staircase. She was lead down, and the air became colder, her face damp. She coughed, and the guard paused as they reached the bottom. The floor was sandy, and she had trouble seeing where they were. When her eyes adjusted to the darkness, she gulped. Rows of small, low steel doors lined the narrow walkway. As the guard pushed her forward, she was shocked to see small hatches at ground level to her right wide enough for a man to crawl through. They were spaced so close together that it seemed unlikely these were cells, but as Agnes listened closely, she heard labored breathing coming from a tiny opening at face height. The guard caught her look.

"Those are the standing cells. Better behave, or you'll end up in one of those. They're mighty uncomfortable," he said with a sinister smile.

Agnes stepped through a doorway and found herself in a cell marginally larger than a broom closet. The guard closed the door, and she was shrouded in almost complete darkness. The only illumination came from the faint moonlight filtering through the bars above her head. She sat down on the bare wooden bunk in the corner. Looking up at the small window, she realized she was on the other side of the yard between Blocks 10 and 11. A distance of 30 meters, but two completely different worlds. In the distance, the sound of electrical buzzing followed by screams of anguish reverberated around the walls. Agnes curled up on her uncomfortable bunk and closed her eyes. She had arrived in a special corner of hell.

# CHAPTER FIFTY-FOUR

Samson stood near the gate of crematorium 4. He fumbled with his hands, aware of the guard's glare.

"Five more minutes, or it's not happening—I can't risk Moll seeing you out here."

Samson nodded. "She'll be here. You'll get your cigarettes."

"I'm getting those cigarettes even if she doesn't show up."

Samson ignored him and kept his eyes on the crowded area a few hundred meters away. He could see dozens—or hundreds, perhaps—of men and women working in the Kanada warehouses. It was the one advantage of his move from Block 13 to the upper level of crematorium 4. He was closer to Roza. The problem was obvious: other prisoners weren't allowed anywhere near the crematoria, nor were the Sonderkommando permitted beyond the fence of their living quarters.

But the men of the Sonderkommando had found a way, as they always had. Samson felt for the cigarettes in his jacket pockets. Most of the guards were happy to allow them half an hour, sometimes longer, outside the crematorium gates. They were willing to turn a blind eye if they were supplied with organized goods. And with the unbelievable numbers of Hungarian Jews coming through, Moll was too occupied making sure they were all killed and burned as quickly as possible to notice the large-scale looting by the SK. Of course, some of the men got too greedy at times, and when caught, they usually ended up in burning pits.

"Samson?"

He was shaken from his thoughts to see Roza standing on the other side of the gate. She kept her distance, at least five meters from the fence, and Samson took a few steps toward the guard. He reached into his pocket and handed the man two packs of cigarettes. The guard scanned the area, making sure Moll was nowhere to be seen, then quickly opened the gate. Samson slipped through, and the gate shut behind him with a loud clang.

"Thirty minutes or I'm reporting you missing." Samson barely heard the guard as he ran to Roza. She threw her arms around him and they hugged each other tight. They stood for a few seconds, and when they broke their embrace Samson looked at her face.

"You look much better than I expected! Did they treat you well in the hospital?"

"Thank you, I suppose?" She had an impish smile on her face. "I was lucky to have some connections in the hospital."

Samson took her hand and led her south, leaving the crematorium and Kanada behind. "So I've heard. I was so happy to read your note. I was worried when I didn't hear anything for days."

"But Kaminski must've told you eventually, no?" Roza frowned.

"He did, but that was only after three days. I kept the faith because I spoke to the Russians building the bombs. He said he was still receiving new gunpowder. I assumed you were still running the operation."

They reached a row of barracks and sat down on a small tree stump. Roza shook her head. "I was in no condition to run anything. I was delirious with a fever the first few days. It wasn't until the last days that I regained some consciousness, and then I started worrying about the operation."

"But if it wasn't you, who did?"

Roza looked at him in surprise. "Joel said someone in the Sonderkommando told the girls, and they made it work together. I assumed it was you."

"I didn't know until I received your note a few days ago."

"Do you think it might've been Kaminski?"

There were only a few people in the Sonderkommando who knew about Roza. "I suppose it must've been him. But it doesn't matter. What's important is you've survived."

She leaned closer. "Tell me about the uprising. Is the Sonderkommando ready?"

"I'd like to say we are, and Kaminski says it could happen any day now, but I'm not so sure."

Roza looked surprised. "But you've been pushing for this. What's wrong?"

"I've gone through this a few times before. Last month, even when everything was in place, the leadership decided to blow it off at the very last minute. I'm afraid it'll happen again." He rubbed his temples. "I fear it might all be too late."

"It's not too late! Joel told me the Sonderkommando has grown to over a thousand men. That means they need you alive." She looked at him sternly, her eyes shooting fire. "We haven't survived Auschwitz for nearly two years to give up at the last hurdle."

Samson stared at her. He felt his heart hammering in his chest as he listened to this strong woman. She was right. He hesitated, then gently reached for her hand. He waited for her to pull it back, but instead, she slipped her fingers into his.

"You're right, Roza. I want to be here when the war is over. I want to be here with you."

She moved closer to him, their knees touching. Samson felt the warmth of her body and turned his face toward hers. He looked into her eyes and his doubts dissolved. He leaned forward and closed his eyes as he found her lips. The worries of the world melted away as he felt only Roza's soft lips on his. For the first time since arriving in Auschwitz, he felt happy.

When they reluctantly broke their kiss, they looked at each other and laughed. Roza wrapped her arms around his neck and placed her lips near his ear. "I was afraid we'd never get the chance to do this."

"Me too. I thought I'd lost you last week."

She kissed his ear and whispered, "It'll take more than that to take me from you."

They sat together for a few more minutes, savoring their time. Then Samson stood. "I'm afraid I need to return to the crematorium. The day shift will end soon. If I'm even a minute late, I'll be in for a hiding from Moll. He's killed three men this week alone."

Roza looked worried. "Be careful; it can't be long now."

He took her hand and pulled her toward him for another kiss. Their lips parted and he caressed her cheek. "I'll see you soon. I'm so proud of you." He started to turn back to the crematorium but caught her looking at him with a curious expression. Samson stopped. "What's wrong?"

"Nothing is wrong, Samson." Her eyes glistened, and the world appeared a little brighter as she spoke the next words, beaming. "For once, for half an hour, everything was wonderful."

# CHAPTER FIFTY-FIVE

Keys rattled outside her door. Agnes moved from the wall, where she had caught the first rays of sunshine filtering into her cell. It was her fourth morning, and she had soon learned to savor the morning light. She sat on her bunk just as the door opened. Two stern-faced SS guards walked in, one of them carrying manacles. Her head dropped as she held out her hands. It was so unnecessary—she wasn't going anywhere. Even if she managed to run from them, where would she go? Nevertheless, the guard fastened them securely and urged her toward the door.

As always, the men were silent, and Agnes learned it was better not to speak unless spoken to. On the first morning after her arrest, she had asked for water. They had ignored her for two days and two nights. On the third morning, she was handed a tiny piece of hard bread and a cup of weak tea. She had fought to urge to wolf it down, instead making it last until last evening, just before she went into an uncomfortable, hunger-filled sleep.

Agnes followed the men through the narrow hallway. They passed the stairs she came down a few nights ago, and continued farther into the basement. There were more cell doors on both sides, some closer together than others. Smaller cells.

At the end of the hall they reached a larger metal door, and the guards knocked. A muffled grunt came from the other side and they opened the door. The bright light almost blinded Agnes, and she squinted as her eyes adjusted. What she saw made her stop as fear paralyzed her. The room was filled with all sorts of tools she didn't recognize. In the middle of the room was a small table with leather straps on each corner, and a metal chair with the same straps on the armrests and legs. To the left a pole was mounted horizontally, with more straps and rope.

The guards pushed her toward the table, and for the first time since her arrival in Block 11, she protested. She leaned back, planting her feet firmly in front of her as she struggled against the two much stronger men. Two pairs of hands gripped her arms and legs, effortlessly lifting her. A voice spoke from a corner.

"You're only making it harder on yourself. Calm down."

While Agnes was manhandled and secured onto the chair, a man wearing an SS officer's uniform stepped into the light. "You can resist, but you're too weak." He turned away and grabbed a chair, placing it opposite Agnes. The guards tightened the straps on her wrists, and she could already feel the blood flow cut off.

The man waved the guards away. "You can leave us now. I'll call for you when we're done." The guards saluted him and left the room, closing the metal door with a clang.

The man stood behind his chair, casually resting his hands on its backrest. He studied Agnes, his eyes meeting hers before gliding past her upper body and finally her legs and feet. He appeared to have all the time in the world. Satisfied, he sat down, his feet only inches away from hers. His cologne was overpowering. Agnes hadn't smelled a man's cologne for years. Her head swam as the sweet scent entered her nostrils, making her feel faint.

The man opened a file and started reading.

"Well, then. Agnes from the Netherlands," the man said, closing the file and placing it on the table next to them. "It seems you've worked yourself into a bit of trouble." Agnes didn't respond. He hummed a little and faintly nodded his head. "All right, you don't want to talk?

How about I start by telling you what's going to happen next? Perhaps that will change your mind."

Agnes' stomach churned as the man stood up and walked to the corner of the room. He returned pushing a small table on wheels of a type Agnes knew from the operating room next door. There, they used it to keep the instruments required to perform surgeries and experiments organized. Here, the tools were slightly different. The man held up a pair of pliers.

"This is for ripping out fingernails. That's usually my first move. Tends to get people talking," he said as he waved it in front of her. He put them back down and picked up a large hypodermic needle. "This is another favorite."

Agnes was shaking in her restraints. She tried to move her legs, but they were strapped so tightly that she had trouble even wiggling her toes.

The man placed the needle back on the small table, moved his chair closer, and sat down. Their feet were now touching. "Or, we can just talk, and there's no need for all this unpleasantness." He folded his arms and leaned back. "Your choice."

Agnes' nerves were frayed, and she felt the skin at the back of her neck flare up. "What do you want from me?" she whispered.

"Ha!" The man clapped his hands and veered forward in his chair. "You don't know why you're here? Let me remind you, and you can just tell me what's true." He reached for the file and started listing off the accusations. "Supporting medical malpractice, sabotaging important research and, my favorite, assisting prisoner escape."

Agnes looked up at him in disbelief. "I've done none of those things."

"Ah, but this is where we differ in opinion."

Agnes shook her head, her eyes wide. "How? I don't even know about these things myself."

"Your good friend Dr. Brewda, of course. She's already confessed to everything, just last night." The interrogator looked triumphant. "She didn't seem to remember either, but then I jogged her memory a bit." His eyes went to the small table.

*Alina would never admit to those accusations.* The interrogator stood and started sorting some of the tools. Her eyes followed his hands, his earlier words still echoing in her mind. She bit her lip. *Stay strong.*

He turned back to her. "Why don't we start with the escape?"

Agnes looked up wide eyed. "What escape?"

In a flash, he stepped forward and viciously slapped her cheek. The force of the blow jerked her head right and a sharp pain spread through the left side of her face, crawling up to her ringing ear.

"Don't lie to me! Don't think because I speak in full sentences that I will hesitate to use everything in this room, you filthy Jew! You did it! You helped them escape!" The man's earlier calm had disappeared. A vein on the side of his forehead had popped out, his eyes bulged. Agnes looked at him in terror; his earlier demeanor had been an act. *This man will kill me.*

The man's hand swung back again and Agnes closed her eyes. Seconds later, she felt the impact on her other cheek. Both of her ears were ringing now, and she felt dizzy as she fought the pain. She could no longer contain herself as tears streamed down her face.

"I swear I wasn't involved in any escape! I only wanted to help the people in the hospital. That's all!" She cried as she looked up at him, her vision blurred by tears. She closed her eyes and braced herself for another blow.

She heard the scraping of the chair and reluctantly opened her eyes. The man sat on the table, his feet resting on the chair. He looked down on her without emotion.

"How did you help these people?" he asked in a normal voice.

She sniffled, surprised at the sudden change in attitude. Agnes swallowed the lump in her throat. "Dr. Brewda and I were in charge of the women in Block 10—"

"I already know that. Tell me how you helped them."

Agnes considered the following words carefully. She eyed the small table. He would start with her fingernails. She looked up at him. The man's green eyes bored into hers, and for the first time, she saw the true evil in the well-spoken man. She made a decision. "We organized extra medication."

"How? Did you steal it?" He leaned forward.

She shook her head. "We took a little extra from the Kanada warehouses. They were overflowing." She cast her eyes down. "It didn't hurt anybody. We were helping the women."

"And did it work?"

She looked up in surprise. "How do you mean?"

"Did the condition of the women improve? Did you help them?"

*Is he trying to trick me?* She couldn't read his face. "Yes. It helped them. The women who endured those experiments lived."

"Tell me about the escapes."

*What?* Agnes shook her head in confusion. "I know nothing about the escapes. I'm sorry."

"Hmm." The man drummed his fingers on the table and stood. He cracked his fingers, his eyes moving between Agnes and the instruments.

"Please! I swear! I know nothing about it." His hands hovered over the pliers and Agnes felt the blood drain from her face, her body convulsing against the chair. "I'll tell you everything you want to know about the medication and the experiments, please! I beg you, please don't do this!" Exhausted, she dropped her head in surrender, her trembling hands tingling from the lack of blood. She studied the dirty concrete floor at her feet and waited for the inevitable to happen. *I can't admit to something I didn't do.* From the corner of her eye she saw his feet moving toward her, almost in slow motion. She took a deep breath, trying to steady herself as he stood in front of her. She felt his hand on her chin, lifting her up. She opened her eyes and saw him standing there, his hands empty.

"Agnes, Agnes." He tutted, shaking his head as if she were a little girl. "I think you need some more time to remember everything you've done. It seems you're suffering from some memory loss." He snapped his fingers. "Guards!" Instantly, the door opened and the two men that had brought her here entered the room. "Take her back to her cell."

The straps were loosened, and Agnes felt life returning to her extremities. She tried to stand up, but her legs wouldn't respond to her brain's commands. The men lifted her and started dragging her out of the room. As they reached the door, the interrogator lifted a finger.

"Wait a second. Why don't you put her in one of the cells in the back instead? That should speed up her memories. There will be fewer distractions."

After Agnes was hauled back through the corridor, she barely perceived being tossed into a new cell. This one had no window, and as the guards shut and bolted the door, she was shrouded in complete darkness. She sank to her knees on the cold floor. Within seconds, sleep took her from the conscious world.

# CHAPTER FIFTY-SIX

When her cell door opened, the dim light from the hallway almost blinded Agnes. She shrank away in the corner, shielding her head with her arms. She couldn't remember how long she'd been down here. A week? Two weeks?

Every so many days someone would open the door and one of two things would happen. She would receive something barely edible, along with a bit of water. Those were the good days, and she could count them on one hand. More often, someone would drag her out of the cell and back to the man at the end of the hallway. He would spend hours—she thought—screaming at her, hurting her, telling her that Dr. Brewda had already confessed, and that she would do well to do the same. He never carried out his threat of pulling out her fingernails, though. She shuddered when she thought of what he *had* done, though. A cloth had been pulled over her face, and he'd poured water over it. Right there and then, she thought she would die, suffocated by the water they wouldn't give her when she was dying from thirst.

She peered through her fingers and saw two familiar figures enter. She knew all the guards of Block 11 by now. Agnes felt an odd sense of relief to recognize two of the more gentle ones.

"Get up, it's time."

Agnes reached for the wall and tried to get up. Her knees protested and she collapsed back on the hard concrete floor. One of the guards took her arm. She held on to him and took a couple awkward steps. When they stepped into the hallway, she realized they hadn't shackled her. *Maybe they forgot?* She wasn't going to remind them, and as they slowly walked on, her hands started to tremble. She had confessed to the medicine smuggling, but only because he threatened to kill Alina if she didn't. She stuck to her story that they only cared for the patients. They were headed in the direction of the interrogation room. There was nothing left to tell the man.

But now, as she faced more pain, Agnes knew she couldn't repeat the same information again. It wouldn't be enough. He would demand her confession. It was ironic: out of all the things she had done in the past years, aiding the resistance and sabotaging Dr. Wirths' experiments, she ended up in the torture chamber for something she had nothing to do with.

They reached the staircase and, to her surprise, the guards pushed her up the steps. She looked up, but the men kept their eyes fixed in front of them, ignoring Agnes but increasing the pressure on her arms as they dragged her up. Leaving the basement, it became a little brighter, and they soon reached the ground floor. People milled about on the far side of the hallway; guards and what looked like office workers—normality—but before she could process what happened, the guards took her in the opposite direction. They turned left, into an oddly placed bathroom—three sinks lined the wall. There was another door at the far end of the room, and one of the guards moved toward it.

"Wait," the second guard said. "The other woman should be here any minute. We'll take them together."

Agnes frowned. *The other woman?*

She didn't have to wait long before there were footsteps in the hallway. A few seconds later a woman with disheveled hair and torn clothes stumbled in, supported by two guards. Agnes shrieked when she raised her head, revealing a badly bruised face. Her left eye was swollen closed, the skin around it dark blue. The other eye showed a tired, lifeless expression until she recognized Agnes.

"You're here," she said in a croaking voice. Her good eye lit up, her cracked lips turning into a weak smile. She flinched and reached for her jaw as she did.

Agnes' hand shot to her mouth. "Alina, you're alive."

Their reunion was interrupted by the guard opening the door, and sunlight filled the room. Agnes and Alina both closed their eyes and shielded their faces from the overpowering light. *Am I in as frightening a state as her?* Agnes wished she could see herself in a mirror, suddenly aware Alina's shock in seeing her matched her own. She looked down at her torn clothes. She touched her face and quickly withdrew her hand as a sharp jolt of pain shot through her nose as she rubbed it.

"Enough of that, move along," the guard at the door said in a terse voice. "Let's get this over with."

Agnes waited for Alina to catch up with her, but her guard pushed her on and through the door. She stepped onto the sandy ground. It reflected the sunlight and she closed her eyes as she was blinded for a second time. The touch of warm sand beneath her bare feet felt good. Agnes slowly opened her eyes and realized where she was. In front of her was another building. Block 10. On either side, between the two buildings, was a wall that separated the area from the outside. The wall to her right had another, smaller wall forming a C-shaped backstop in front of it. It was riddled with bullet holes. Agnes' throat constricted as terror washed over her. She was in Block 11's yard, and she was being led to the wall of death.

Paralyzed by fear, Agnes was led toward the concrete slab. One of the guards turned her around, her back against the wall. Alina followed only a few meters behind her, and Agnes could see her friend also realized what was happening. Alina's face looked serene, as if she was at peace with what was happening. Agnes' eyes went to Alina's hands and she was horrified to see the tips of her fingers were bloody and misshapen. The torturer had carried out his threat.

A wave of nausea overwhelmed Agnes. Her guard managed to get out of the way just in time as she doubled over and retched in the sand. There was nothing but bile; she hadn't eaten or drunk anything for two days. She sat on her knees as the final bit of strength left her body. She breathed heavily as the sour taste in her mouth entered her nostrils, and she felt dizzy. Then two strong hands jerked her back upright and against the wall.

Alina now stood next to her, and took her hand. "Don't let them see you cry," she said softly. "We keep our heads held high."

Agnes swallowed hard, fighting to suppress desperate gulps as she stared vacantly. In the distance, the sky over Birkenau was black, darkened by the never-ending belch of the crematoria's chimneys. She wondered if Joel knew where she was, if he was thinking of her at this moment. She prayed he was still roaming around the camp, strengthening the resistance and preparing for the uprising. A tear rolled down her cheek. *I won't be there to see it.*

Alina squeezed her hand. "Thank you for everything, Agnes. You were my best friend in this place." Agnes turned to her and saw Alina had tears streaming down her face as well.

"And you were mine."

Two of the guards unbuckled their holsters, and the man holding Agnes tightened his grip.

She closed her eyes and waited. She thought of her parents, Yvette. They would soon be reunited. She saw Jacob's face, blurry and hard to make out, a memory from another life. She hoped he was still in Westerbork, defying the odds and staying alive long enough to witness the impending liberation. She breathed out and focused on the touch of Alina's fingers wrapped around hers. The yard was silent, and she tried to block out the sound of the men around her. Suddenly, a voice broke the silence.

"That's enough now. Take them back inside."

Agnes opened her eyes, stunned. The guards had holstered their pistols and stood at a distance. She looked at their impassive faces. Then, to their left, she saw a familiar face—their interrogator. He stood wearing his officer's uniform, his arms hanging loosely by his sides.

Agnes and Alina were escorted back inside the building, and the interrogator followed at a distance. They were marched past the stairway and to the other side of the building. *What's happening?* They went through the front door and stepped out onto the small street in front of the building. A truck stood waiting, its engine idling.

The interrogator stepped outside and lit a cigarette. As Agnes turned to him, he pointed at the truck. "Dr. Brewda, get in the truck, please."

Agnes and Alina exchanged a look, and Agnes moved to follow her.

"Not you, Agnes."

The man's voice was firm. Agnes' heart sank. She wanted to stay with Alina, and she wanted to get as far away as possible. Even Birkenau would do. Reluctantly, she stopped and watched her friend climb in. The driver revved the engine, and another SS guard climbed into the truck and sat next to Alina.

"Agnes," Alina said over the roar of the engine as the truck started to pull away. "I'm proud of you."

With tears in her eyes, Agnes watched the truck roll down the road. When it turned between two blocks and onto the main road, Agnes wondered if she'd ever see her friend again.

"Take her to her new post."

Agnes looked at him in amazement. *A new post?* She looked around for another vehicle. The guard stood next to her impatiently. "Come on, let's go. Or do you want to go back inside?" He took a few steps to the right, along the road where Alina had just disappeared down.

She followed him, and after a few steps looked back. The interrogator stood motionless, smoking his cigarette and following her with his eyes. The guard pulled on her arm. "I don't have all day."

They walked past Block 10, and Agnes wondered how the women inside were doing. They had walked for another fifteen minutes when the guard stopped in front of a large building on the other side of the camp. Agnes looked up in surprise. The administration block?

The guard opened the door and shoved her inside. "Hurry up. They're expecting you."

# CHAPTER FIFTY-SEVEN

Birkenau was shrouded in darkness; the only faint illumination came from the yard at crematorium 5 where Samson and another 50 men of the Sonderkommando stood waiting. SS guards carrying rifles had formed a corridor leading into the changing room, their eyes alert. It didn't take long for the rumble of the trucks in the distance to grow louder. A minute later, the gate to the yard opened, and seven trucks pulled in. The guards waited for the gate to close before opening the tailgates. Within minutes, some 300 men, women, and children disappeared into the changing room of crematorium 5.

Samson had followed them inside, and he watched as they undressed. These were the people from the Gypsy camp. In this separate camp in Birkenau they had been permitted to live in a somewhat normal fashion. They wore their own clothes, families were allowed to stay together, and they were allowed to keep most of their possessions. They had also been exempt from selections. Until now.

A few minutes later, another convoy entered, then another. There were now close to a thousand people in the changing room, and some of the guards stood near the doors of the changing room. A number of prisoners tried to talk to them, recognizing them from their time in the

Gypsy camp. The guards looked at them stoically, some telling them to hurry up and get undressed. The gypsies appeared baffled at first, then they understood what was happening.

"Why are you doing this to us? We are German citizens! We fought in the army!"

Some of the guards looked torn, as if they had suddenly grown a conscience about gassing people. The gypsies had never been classified as enemies of the Third Reich. Tonight, however, the remaining people living in the camp would find there was no place in the new world order for them anymore.

There was movement at the door, and Moll entered. His eyes quickly scanned the room and he barked orders at a number of the nearby guards. A few hesitated, and after only a moment he furiously repeated his demand. "Rifles out, shoot anyone that tries to run!" This got the attention of a number of prisoners standing near the door, and they cowered away from it. Fear quickly spread, and a deathly hush soon fell over the room. Moll looked pleased.

"Everybody who has already undressed, get into the shower room, now. This will give the other people in here some more space to undress in a civilized manner." He held his pistol loosely in his right hand.

The people closest to the door leading to the gas chamber moved inside, and the rest quickly followed. Within ten minutes, the changing room was empty, and one of the guards closed and sealed the door to the gas chamber. Moll nodded at a soldier standing by the door on the other side of the room, who ran up the steps and out of sight.

Samson took a step away from the door. Soon, the sounds of death filtered through. Fists banging desperately against the heavy steel door, cries of anguish, wails of mothers trying to protect their children. Twenty minutes later, everything on the other side of the room was quiet.

A guard stepped into the anteroom between the changing room and gas chamber. Samson and the rest of the men assigned to empty the gas chamber followed without needing to be prompted. Their ghoulish work started now. The guard was about to open the door to the gas chamber when Moll held up his hand.

"I want all the men of the Sonderkommando in here, right now," he said, urgency in his voice.

The other half of the men, who had started sorting through the clothing of the dead, filed into the room. Moll had moved to the door leading into the changing room, along with the guard. The door to the gas chamber remained shut. *This is odd.*

"There is an air raid warning, we need you to stay here until it passes." Then, without another word, he stepped outside, and the guard locked the door.

They stood in silence for a minute. Samson looked out of the barred windows. The lights in the yard were still on.

"They would've switched everything in the camp off if there really was an air raid warning," one of the men said. "Moll is lying."

There were murmurs of assent. "They're finally going to do it. They're going to kill us in here."

Samson looked around. Even though fear was rising to his throat, he knew they wouldn't be killed by gas. Not in this room. There was no way to get the gas canisters down here. But he knew that didn't mean Moll wouldn't find another way. It wouldn't be the first time a whole group of Sonderkommando was dispatched to the afterlife by machine guns. His eyes went to the door. Were they setting up their guns in the changing room at this very moment?

Every man had his theory on what was happening, and they all talked simultaneously. Their only hope was to stick together and rush the guards when they opened the door. They needed their leader. Samson looked around for Kaminski but didn't see him. That was odd; he recalled Kaminski saying he was assigned to lead the crew in the changing rooms earlier that evening. Samson desperately racked his brain for a way to unite the 50 men, and quickly. Moll would be back soon—

The sound of two gunshots came through the door leading to the changing room. Despite the door muffling the sound somewhat, everyone in the room had heard, and it instantly went quiet. The men who, only seconds ago, had the loudest voices looked terrified. They all stared at the door, frozen in fear. The sound of boots filtered through it, and the door was unlocked. Samson held his breath as the door swung open, half expecting to look into the barrel of a machine gun.

Instead, it was Moll. He looked calm as he told them to come back into the room. "Line up on the far side."

Samson stepped into the changing room and was relieved to find only the guards waiting for them. They looked alert but held their guns loosely by their sides. *Not like men about to execute us.*

When they were all lined up, Moll spoke, his voice booming through the empty room. "We received word of an impending assassination on *Oberscharführer* Muhsfeldt." He allowed the words to hang in the air for a moment. Samson kept his gaze firmly ahead of him, but from the corner of his eye he could see some of the men around him reacting in shock. *Don't give him anything.* "Thankfully, we were able to prevent this from happening at the very last minute. Unfortunately, Kapo Kaminski won't get a second chance." He pointed at the small pool of blood on the ground next to him.

Samson suddenly felt very cold. He blinked hard. *Kaminski dead? It can't be.* He kept his eyes on the blood on the floor while Moll droned on in the background.

"A more capable, trustworthy Kapo will join you soon, but for now —" He paused and the fog lifted from Samson's head as he looked at the SS officer. "I trust this is a warning to all of you with similar thoughts. We will find out, and there will be no mercy. Now, back to work! We have more gypsies on the way, and I want this done tonight!"

Shocked and numb from grief at the loss of his friend, Samson stepped into the gas chamber. Then, without thinking, he picked up the first corpse at his feet and dragged it toward the pits. There was an energy shift, the men around Samson in the same state of shock.

Samson stepped outside and lowered the body of the young man into the pit. There, two of the pit workers stood near a body covered with fir branches. They moved the branches to the side and Samson recognized the face of his friend. His left eye was shattered by a bullet, while his right eye looked up into the dark sky. Samson's heart never felt heavier as he looked at the lifeless body of the leader of the Sonderkommando. He mouthed a silent prayer and turned around just as Moll came out of the building.

As Samson walked back into the gas chamber, his grief turned into fury. They may have taken out Kaminski, but they wouldn't stop the uprising. He picked up the corpse of a girl no older than ten and looked at her. He vowed he would avenge his friend's death. "And yours," he whispered to the child as he closed her eyes.

# CHAPTER FIFTY-EIGHT

Agnes sat in a room larger than she was used to. Ten people worked in the hospital administration, all prisoners. They sat in their own room, and while the others chatted whenever they were confident there were no guards nearby, Agnes kept her distance. It was her third day working here, and she still wasn't sure why she had been spared whatever journey Alina had taken. She feared Alina had been shipped off to Birkenau's gas chambers. *But why am I still here?*

There was a stifled giggle from two of the younger clerks nearby. Agnes looked up, and the women smiled at her. "You know, you are allowed to talk. Just make sure the guards don't hear you."

Agnes nodded. "I'm trying to get the hang of this work."

"Just ask us if you need any help."

Agnes nodded and returned her focus to the files on her desk. Even though she longed to talk to the people around her, she wasn't sure who to trust. She was certain someone had betrayed Alina in Block 10, and she was wary of trusting people again.

"Agnes Markx?"

She looked up to find a middle-aged man next to her desk. Behind his glasses—a rarity in the camp—his eyes looked at her with interest. She nodded.

"Come with me, the *Lagerältester* wants to see you."

Agnes stood up and followed the man, a little surprised. *What does the chief of the hospital want from me?* She was led to a small office in the back of the building, where a man of slight stature sat behind a desk. He looked up and stood.

"Agnes, right?" He reached out his hand, and she cautiously shook it. "I'm Dr. Fejkiel, and I'm in charge of the hospital." He smiled and shook his head. "Well, technically the SS is in charge, of course, but they expect me to run it. Please, sit."

Agnes sat down and looked at Dr. Fejkiel. She'd seen his signatures on some of the orders coming into Block 10, but he'd appeared happy to give Alina free rein in how she ran the block.

"How are you settling in?" He leaned forward. There was kindness in his intelligent, alert eyes.

"I'm not sure, Dr. Fejkiel," Agnes started. "To be honest, I'm a little confused."

He smiled, unclasping his fingers and drumming them on the side of the desk. "I can imagine you are. I know you were in Block 11 before this."

Agnes tried to keep a straight face. "How?"

"Well, when I heard Alina and her assistant were taken from Block 10, I was interested to find out why." Agnes noted his use of Dr. Brewda's first name. "So I made some inquiries, and I found that you had been interned in that terrible place. Naturally, I was dismayed, but there was nothing I could do for you. Not at first, anyway." He paused for a moment and looked at Agnes. "But a few days ago, my contacts in the Gestapo office told me you would be transferred to Birkenau. You and Alina. This is where we intervened. I requested that both of you be reinstated to the hospital, but they wouldn't allow Alina back in. So she's in Birkenau now."

"Doing what?"

"She's helping in the hospital as a nurse. But, unfortunately, Dr. Wirths stripped her of her medical rights."

Agnes gasped. "She must be devastated."

"I didn't have a chance to talk to her, for obvious reasons, but from what I hear, she's just happy to be alive. But let's get back to you, Agnes.

You're still here in Auschwitz, in the administration." His eyes narrowed. "My sources tell me you and Alina were close."

"I was her assistant," Agnes said noncommittally.

"But you were also her friend. You were both involved in saving all those women in Block 10." Dr. Fejkiel smiled and leaned back in his chair. "We are on the same side, Agnes. I am also a prisoner and a Jew. So why do you think you're here?"

Agnes didn't know what to think of the man sitting across from her. His smile seemed genuine, he spoke passionately and was very well informed about what was going on in the camp. "I'm sorry, but this is all a bit much for me. What are you asking of me, exactly?"

"I want you to work with me like you did with Alina. I know you made extra efforts to keep the files of the patients clean. I want you to do the same here." His eyes shone brightly, and Agnes found herself nodding.

"Yes."

"And when you get a chance, take a look around the wards. Your medicine connection, along with a few others, is helping us keep people alive. Our staff is almost completely Jewish now; we've rid ourselves of many of the SS informers. Even the guards are different. We help them, Agnes. We give them tips on how to avoid being drafted to the front lines. That's why the hospital is such a better place now."

Agnes found herself getting enthusiastic. The doctor stood. "I'm not asking you to do anything out in the open. I understand you're nervous about being sent back to Block 11. But we need people like you in administration to make sure our patients are protected as well as they can be. Think about it, Agnes."

He nodded at her, and she took it as her dismissal. When she reached for the door handle, the doctor cleared his throat, and she turned back.

"One more thing. Is this accusation of helping prisoners escape and providing them with medical information about what was happening in Block 10 true? Did you keep a secret archive?"

Agnes met his eyes and held his gaze. She considered telling him the truth. "We were cleared of those accusations."

Dr. Fejkiel looked disappointed. "Well, that's a pity. It would've been mighty useful. Thank you, Agnes."

A few hours later, Agnes picked up her stack of files and placed them in the filing cabinet across the room. She said goodbye to the two other clerks and headed downstairs. As she left the building she turned onto the narrow gravel road and made her way to one of the hospital blocks.

Agnes was so caught up in her thoughts that she didn't immediately notice the man walking next to her. It wasn't until he spoke her name that she turned. Her knees almost buckled underneath her, but Agnes couldn't contain her excitement and relief. "Joel!" She threw her arms around him. She then pulled back and looked at him, his broad smile warming her. "I'm so relieved to see you!"

"Not as happy as I am to see you in one piece," Joel said as he looked her up and down. "Apart from those bruises, you seem to be doing all right?"

"I'm recovering. Working in the administration makes it easier. How did you know where to find me?"

He grinned. "I have my sources. Come, let's sit down." He guided her to a small bench in between two of the blocks. "I need to get back to Birkenau soon, but I had to see you. I was so worried, Agnes. When I heard you were taken to Block 11, I thought I'd never see you again." He took her hands. "How did you survive?"

"I don't want to talk about Block 11, Joel. I just want to hear from you." She looked around, making sure they were alone. "Did anybody else get arrested?"

"Nobody else was arrested, it was just you and Dr. Brewda. I saw her yesterday. She was worried about you, she said you were in a really bad state when she left you. I told her I was sure you were all right."

"Did you already know I was in administration by then?"

He shook his head. "I only found out this morning. I begged Bruno to give me an assignment near the hospital, but there was nothing there. So I spent my time working in the SS officers' quarters instead, and I thought I'd chance it on the way back. I'm glad that I did."

"How did you find out?"

"Find out what?"

"Where I was. The administration building."

"Oh, well, when I found Dr. Brewda in the hospital in Birkenau, I figured you would also be in the hospital somewhere. It wasn't in Birkenau, so I checked with our contact in Auschwitz. He confirmed you were here."

Agnes' head was spinning. She always assumed Dr. Brewda was the resistance's contact in Auschwitz. Now it turned out there were more? "Who's your contact?" She had a suspicion.

"You know I can't tell you that."

"Is it Dr. Fejkiel?"

He looked shocked for a moment, then regained his composure. "As a matter of fact, it is, yes. How did you know that? Wait, let me guess. You talked to him."

Agnes shook her head. It all made sense now. "That sneaky fox," she mumbled. "He was just testing me. He knew all along."

Joel laughed out loud. "Now I definitely know you've met him. What did he ask?"

"He asked me if everything Alina and I were accused of was true."

"What did you tell him?"

"I said we were cleared of all those accusations."

Joel nodded. "Smart, but he wasn't really asking, was he?"

"There was something else he asked about." She looked at Joel, whose eyes urged her on. "He asked about the copied files on those evil experiments they run in Block 10."

"What about them?"

"He wanted to know if we really had such an archive."

"And you did, didn't you?" Joel's eyes lit up eagerly.

Agnes nodded. "We still have the files hidden in the block."

"Agnes, there's something you need to know about the hospital administration." His face turned serious. "There's a reason Dr. Fejkiel asked you about those files."

"How so?"

"Ever since they cleaned the hospital of SS informers, the administration has been the most important chain in the resistance's communications with the outside world. Along with Raisko, all incoming and outgoing messages go through the people in the administration."

"And I'm one of them now," Agnes said.

"You are, and you aren't. It's clear Dr. Fejkiel wants to include you. But you know what you need to do."

She swallowed hard. "I need to get those documents from Block 10." Going back terrified her.

He nodded. "But you're not going to do this on your own. I'm coming with you."

# CHAPTER FIFTY-NINE

S amson lay in his bunk in the attic of crematorium 4. The ovens below hadn't been fired up yet, and all was quiet in the building. September was coming to a close and after the transports from Hungary had come to a halt a few weeks ago, the number of trains arriving at Birkenau's ramp had considerably slowed down. Moll had been transferred to lead the Gleiwitz camp northwest of Auschwitz. While it meant life for the Sonderkommando was less taxing, it also provided a new danger. With less work, there was no need for a large Sonderkommando. It was a blessing and a curse.

Samson looked at the other men. Some were asleep, while others were reading one of the tattered books shared around the Sonderkommando.

"Samson!" Feliks stood at the bottom of his bunk, a worried look on his face. "Did you hear about the roll call?"

Samson threw his legs over the side of his bunk and jumped down. "Who called it? Is it just for us?"

"The entire SK. We're supposed to be in the yard in half an hour. Not sure who called it. What do you think it means?"

"Could be anything, but if I had to guess they're going to change things around again. Since some of the crematoria aren't used anymore, it doesn't make sense to keep us spread out like this."

"Or maybe it makes a lot of sense, if they want to make sure we don't talk to each other too much. I spoke to one of the Russians in number two the other day, and he said the guards were acting strange."

"How so?"

Feliks frowned. "He overheard them talking about the Allied armies liberating Paris. They think they'll be sent to the front soon."

"They've already reached Paris?" Samson felt a flutter of hope. "Maybe Hitler will realize he won't be able to stop the forces coming from both sides, and surrender."

"That's what they're worried about. They don't think Hitler is going to give up. They're afraid he's going to fight 'til the end, taking the whole country down with him."

"As much as I'd like to see the country burn, I'm afraid we won't be there to see it."

Feliks nodded. "Exactly. I don't think they're going to wait around for American or Soviet soldiers to knock on the gates of Auschwitz."

"We'll be long dead by then."


The yard was surrounded by guards wielding rifles. The SS officers stood in front of the group were familiar to Samson. The most senior of the three was *Oberscharführer* Josef Hustek, whom he had known since working in Auschwitz's crematorium. Hustek was often assigned to assist in the selections at the ramp, and he did so with fervor. Wherever he showed up, death followed. He stood by idly as *Scharführer* Hubert Busch, also a veteran of ramp selection, addressed the assembled men. Excluding a handful of men sent on errands, the entire Sonderkommando, all 900 of them, were lined up.

"Gentlemen," he started, and Samson suppressed a frown. He glanced around and saw apprehension on the faces of the men around him. "As you know, we're not receiving as many transports as we used to. This is why we need to redistribute some of you."

They remained silent, only the shuffling of feet in the sand audible as the wind rustled through the yard. Everybody knew what it meant to be redistributed.

"Today, we'll need two hundred volunteers for one of the new camps. The food there will be better, as will be your accommodations." Busch smiled as he held up his right hand. "Please step forward if you'd like to volunteer."

Samson glanced to his left and right. Nobody moved. Tense faces looked straight ahead, avoiding the German's eyes as he paced in front of them. When it became clear nobody was going to volunteer, Busch conferred with Hustek and the other officer. They spoke in hushed tones for a few minutes, and Samson unsuccessfully tried to catch their words. It was useless, as they held their hands before their mouths and spoke in rapid German.

After a few minutes, the three men turned back.

"It's a pity none of you want to volunteer," Busch said as he stepped forward, pulled one of the younger men out of the lineup, and sent him to the other side of the yard, where two guards took his number. Then, the two other officers joined in and started picking out more men.

Feliks stood two rows ahead of Samson, and Samson held his breath when Hustek made his way down their column. He appeared to head straight for Feliks, and Samson momentarily closed his eyes. When he opened them again, he was relieved to see the man directly ahead of Feliks had been selected.

Within fifteen minutes, two hundred men had been isolated from the main group. Busch dismissed those who survived, and Samson caught up with Feliks as they left the yard.

"Those poor men," Feliks said as they turned the corner and headed for the relative safety of their bunks. "I hope they make it quick."

The next morning, they found out what had happened to their compatriots. Samson was told to report to crematorium 2, as there would be no work in number 4 that day. When he arrived, the Kapo sent him to the oven room.

Upon arrival, he was surprised to find the ovens were still hot, the embers smoldering. Some of the men of crematorium 2 were already working on getting the fires started. Samson approached them.

"Am I late? I thought the transport wasn't supposed to arrive until midmorning?"

The man looked at him for a moment and shook his head. "This isn't the transport. These are our brothers." He opened one of the oven doors and pointed inside. "Look, you can still see some of them. The SS didn't know what they were doing."

Samson was aghast at the sight of half-burned corpses in the oven. He turned back to the man. "What happened?"

"When we returned from the selection yesterday, we were told to stay in our quarters until further notice." He pointed up, where, just like in Samson's crematorium, the sleeping quarters were located. "Nothing happened for most of the day until we heard movement early in the evening. Some of us snuck down, and we saw the SS stoking the ovens. They were just dumping coke into the ovens until the flames burst through the doors. Then they started piling the corpses in. It was clear they had no idea what they were doing. When they finished, they added more coke, and most of them left. A few stayed behind but left somewhere in the middle of the night."

Samson shook his head. "How did you find out they were our men?"

"Our Kapo in the morning said the SS were burning civilians killed in air strikes, but when we opened the ovens, we recognized some of the faces of those corpses." The man looked downcast. "We're next, aren't we?"

"We don't have to be," Samson said, clenching his fists. "But we have to be ready when they have another selection."

# CHAPTER SIXTY

Agnes met Joel outside the administration building. Her heart fluttered as he stood waiting with his toolbox. A smile appeared on his face when he saw her.

"Did you get the papers?"

She patted her pocket, and they set off. "Dr. Fejkiel signed the order this morning. He said if anything happens, he's going to deny knowing anything about what we are really doing."

"And so he should, but we won't get caught."

She walked taller, growing in courage with Joel by her side. They turned onto the smaller side road leading to Block 10. She'd spent most of the night staring at the ceiling, kicking the covers off her body as she felt hot, then pulling them back as she shivered in the darkness. When dawn finally arrived, she felt relieved and terrified at the same time. What they were about to attempt appeared easy enough in theory. Agnes knew every nook and cranny of Block 10, and she would be in and out in minutes. The problem would be if someone asked questions. Or, heaven forbid, if she were to run into Dr. Wirths or Dr. Clauberg. They would instantly recognize her and know something was up. Even though Dr. Fejkiel's note explained she was there to pick up medication, it would be hard to explain why she was loitering in other areas.

Joel softly brushed her hand. "It will be fine, Agnes. I'll be with you every step of the way."

"Did Bruno give you any trouble?"

He raised an eyebrow. "What do you think? He told me he didn't want to know why I was needed at Block 10, but he got me a work order to inspect the X-ray machine."

"Isn't the chief physician of the block supposed to request that?"

"Yes, officially. But Bruno indicated he was concerned the X-ray machine hadn't been serviced for a long time. The administration agreed, and they provided him with the work order."

"That would be Dr. Fejkiel's administration?"

"Exactly."

Block 10 came into view, and Joel's expression changed. His face was serious as he spoke in measured words. "You should probably walk a few paces ahead of me. We don't want anyone to see us arrive together. You go in first, and I'll be right behind you. We can pretend you're escorting me to the X-ray machine if anyone sees us." He slowed his pace, allowing her to take the lead.

Block 10 was less than 100 meters away, and Agnes suddenly felt very conspicuous. Even though she'd spent most of her time in the camp there, the old army barracks had never felt like home. She'd hoped never to get anywhere near Block 10 again, yet here she was. She took a deep breath and steadied herself. *You can do this, Agnes. You've got the paperwork, you just need to get in and out real quick. And Joel will be there.* She resisted the urge to look back.

Her heart was in her throat for the last twenty meters. She kept her eyes focused on the door, hoping nobody would come out, or at least nobody who'd recognize her. As she mounted the steps, she glanced to her right and shivered. It had only been two months since she'd somehow walked out of the murder block, but the mere sight of Block 11 gripped her heart with fear. Without another thought, she opened the door to Block 10 and stepped into the long hallway.

The door closed, and the smell of cleaning product filled her nostrils, providing an odd sense of familiarity she hadn't realized she'd missed. Much to her relief, the hallway was deserted. She took a few steps forward and listened for sounds upstairs. She only heard soft footsteps and quiet chattering in the nearest wards. Nothing had changed since she had left, at least not on the surface.

The front door opened, and Joel entered. "All clear?" he whispered.

She nodded, and they headed down the hallway. Agnes held her breath as they neared the operating room. This would be the trickiest part of their mission. Even though Dr. Fejkiel had checked the schedule, and the room was supposed to be clear, it was always possible that one of the doctors decided now would be a good time to run an impromptu experiment. It was why Joel was here. He looked at her with conviction.

"I'll check if anyone is in there. If it's clear, I'll open the door."

"Yes. Be careful, Joel." She stepped to the side so that whoever was in there wouldn't see her when he went in.

Joel disappeared inside. Agnes stood still and kept her eyes anxiously on both ends of the hallway. The door to the operating room was in the middle of the hallway, and she was mostly worried about the closed door to what she assumed was now Dr. Wirths' office in the back.

After what felt like minutes, the door opened again, and Joel pulled her inside the dimly lit room. Agnes felt like she had stepped back in time. She looked at the gynecological table where she had seen so many women mutilated, and she felt a stab of sorrow in her heart. *So much pain and misery, and what for?*

"Agnes, the papers." Joel's voice was soft but firm. She looked at him, his eyes showing urgency, and she snapped back to the present.

"Of course." *I can't change the past, but I can do some future good.* Agnes rushed to the corner of the room and crouched down. She bit her tongue as she ran her fingers down the spaces between the tiles on the wall. The surface felt smooth, as if the tile work was recently done. *This can't be happening.* Her head throbbed as she frantically searched for an incision. *Come on, come on.*

"What's wrong?" Joel sounded concerned.

She didn't look up. "I can't find the right tile. It's supposed to be right here."

"Are you sure?"

"Yes! I hid them here myself!"

Joel knelt next to her, looking over her shoulder. She was about to tell him to back off, but then she felt something. She pulled on the jagged edge, softly at first, but when it shifted, she used more force. The tile gave way, and she carefully placed it on the floor. There was a small opening behind the tile, and she reached inside. Agnes had never been happier to feel the sharp crunch of paper between her fingers. "I've got them!"

Joel kissed her cheek as she held up the papers. In her elation, she pulled his face toward hers and kissed his lips. As he returned her kiss, Agnes knew if she didn't kiss him now, she might not get another chance. Who knew when they would be alone again? Or if they'd even make it out of this room?

Joel pulled back first. Agnes blinked for a moment, then saw the big grin on his face. "We should get out of here if we want to do this again," he said. "Is that everything?"

Agnes double-checked the cavity in the wall and nodded. Joel walked to the X-ray machine and gave it a casual glance.

"Checked." He made a check mark sign in the air, and they both smiled. Agnes was struggling with the tile. "Do you need a hand with that?" Joel asked. Just as he did, there were footsteps in the hallway. Joel lifted his finger to his mouth, and they both froze.

She held her breath and clasped her hands together as the footsteps reached the door. They slowed down, and much to Agnes' horror, the door opened. The light from the hallway streamed into the dimly lit operating room. A woman hurriedly entered, not noticing Agnes as she headed for the X-ray machine. Agnes immediately recognized her. It was Sylvia, Dr. Clauberg's assistant.

Sylvia cursed and turned toward the small desk in the corner. As she did, she noticed Agnes and let out a shriek. In the confined space, it sounded like a siren going off. Agnes held up her hands. "Sylvia, it's me. Agnes." She nodded at Joel. "And you know Joel, right? He does repairs."

Sylvia's eyes shot between them, then rested on the tile in Agnes' hand. She then spotted the hole in the wall.

Agnes' stomach sunk. Even though Sylvia claimed to have saved her once, she had never felt comfortable around her on her return. Sylvia had always been cold and distant, making Agnes feel almost like she harbored some grudge. She prayed the blond woman wouldn't sprint for the door and report them. There would be no explaining what she'd seen here.

Sylvia cocked her head and leaned closer to the cavity, still silent. She looked to Agnes, her eyes showing understanding. For a moment, Agnes felt they had a connection, after all. Then Sylvia turned around and went for the door. Agnes dropped her head, opened her mouth, and—

The Czech nurse didn't open the door. Instead, she leaned against it. "Are you going to replace that, or what?"

Stunned, Agnes didn't immediately respond. Joel crouched next to her and took the tile, fitting it back in seconds. He stood and pulled Agnes up. "Come on, let's go," he said softly.

They neared the door, but Sylvia held up her hand. "Wait here." She opened it and stepped into the hallway, quickly closing the door behind her. The thought that she would lock them in crossed Agnes' mind, and she looked at Joel. He looked nervous.

There were voices in the hallway. Agnes' heart dropped. Joel stood next to her with his eyes closed. She reached for his hand. The voices continued, and she made out Sylvia's. She thought of her returning with Dr. Wirths and SS guards. Memories of Block 11 flooded her brain. She would run for the electrified fence before letting them put her back in that dungeon. The voices trailed off, the silence in the hallway thundering as they waited for what felt like an eternity.

Then, the door opened. Sylvia motioned for them to come out. "Come, quickly. They're gone."

Agnes hesitated, but Joel stepped into the empty hallway, pulling her along. It took all of Agnes' willpower not to burst into a sprint for the exit. She realized Sylvia wasn't following them. She looked back and caught her disappearing into the operating room. Joel held onto her arm as he pulled her toward the door. He took a deep breath as he opened it. Agnes stepped into the crisp September air and realized Sylvia had saved her again. She had never been so wrong about someone.

# CHAPTER SIXTY-ONE

The atmosphere in the crematorium was mutinous. The Kapo stood hunched in front of the group of angry men. More than 100 prisoners crowded around the bunks in the attic. Fire spewed from their eyes as they all spoke simultaneously, hurling questions at the Kapo.

"Why me? I've always worked hard! That's a death sentence!"

Samson stood among the men, listening to the man at the front. He pitied him, for he couldn't win today. That morning, the SS had come to the Kapos of the crematoria, ordering them to draw up a list of 300 men to be transferred to clear rubble from bombing runs in a town no one had ever heard of. News of the list quickly spread, and by the evening, everybody knew the names of the doomed.

Samson had been in his bunk when his Kapo announced the names of the men selected from their crematorium. To Samson's horror, his name was called. At first, he thought he must have misunderstood. But when he checked the list, there was no mistaking his name and number. His people had selected him for death.

The Kapo waved his arms up and down to quiet the crowd. It only made them more angry. The Kapo's eyes were filled with panic, and

Samson couldn't stand by any longer. He was one of the more senior men in the room and wanted some answers.

He pushed forward, and as the men recognized him, they turned to him. "Samson, you'll tell him, right? They can't just send us to get butchered like this, can they? Kaminski wouldn't have done this to us!"

*No, he wouldn't have.* He reached the front and approached the Kapo. From up close, he could see the terror in the man's eyes.

"You need to tell us why we're on the list. You owe us that much," Samson said, his face hard. "You know you're sending us to our deaths."

The man scratched the back of his neck. His eyes shot between Samson and the increasingly unruly mob. He stepped closer and spoke in a shaky voice. "I don't have an explanation."

Samson's eyebrows shot up. "What do you mean?" Blood rushed to his head. "You'll need to do better than that."

"I can't." The man shook his head. "We picked people randomly."

Samson couldn't believe it. *Randomly?* He turned and looked at the men. They were indeed from all walks of life. He even spotted two doctors, who worked as stokers by day and treated the sick in the Sonderkommando by night. He shook his head. The Kapos hadn't planned this very well. He thought of his friend Kaminski. *He would have found a way.* Samson turned back to the Kapo. "That's not good enough. You need to tell them." His voice turned to ice. "Now. Or I will."

The man hesitated then dropped his head. Samson looked at him in disgust and faced the group. The men went silent. Samson felt their pain and desperation as he scanned their faces. He took a deep breath before speaking.

"We all know what this list means." Besides fear, there was something else in the men's eyes. Anger. "But we decide how we go down. Will we allow ourselves to be led to our deaths like lambs? On our knees?" He saw heads shaking. "Or will we finally rise up? If three hundred of the Sonderkommando are about to be killed, will the rest just watch? I think not!"

The atmosphere in the room changed. Men raised their fists, their faces showing defiance. "We will rise up together and make our stand!" A roar shook the room, and Samson joined in, pumping his fist. He looked at the men in the front, and his eye fell on one man who didn't partake in the battle cries. He stood and looked at Samson, studying him intently. While the others talked in excited tones, the man turned and quietly left the room. Even though Samson was cheered by the response, the man in the front had unnerved him. He suspected it wouldn't be the last time he saw him.

It was late afternoon when Samson saw the man again. Samson stood outside, taking in some fresh air. It was a chilly day, but he enjoyed the cold October air. It kept his mind sharp.

"That was an impressive speech earlier today." The man stood next to him, leaning against the side of the crematorium building. "For what it's worth, I agree with you."

"It didn't look like it. You seemed completely unaffected. I saw you leave."

The man shook his head. "You shouldn't judge a person's feelings merely on his exterior. I thought you would know that by now."

Samson looked at the man and racked his brain. He looked familiar, but he couldn't place him. The man was at least ten years his senior, although it was hard to tell: Auschwitz added years to people's faces. "What do you want?"

"After your speech, I realized you would have the support of most of the men on the list by the end of the day. And you do." He smiled. Samson's words had quickly spread through the Sonderkommando, and by the end of the day, almost all the men on the list had confirmed they would join the uprising. "So I thought it would be wise to inform the camp underground about your plans."

Samson was taken aback. "How? Who are you?"

"That's not important. The only thing you need to know is that I knew Kaminski. We were close, and I know he worked with several men in the Sonderkommando." Samson didn't respond. "We received word from the leadership half an hour ago."

"What did they say?" Samson felt his heart in his throat. The uprising would finally happen if the rest of the camp joined in. His fingertips tingled.

"They said no," the man replied, his eyes sympathetic. "They believe an uprising would have disastrous consequences for the rest of the camp's population." He spoke the words factually, suppressing any emotion he might feel. "I'm sorry, Samson."

Samson clenched his fists and looked at the man standing next to him. Whoever this man was, he had sought out Samson and contacted the leadership. He was on his side.

"What if we go at it alone?"

The man looked thoughtful. "We've considered that. But it won't be enough to free the whole camp. We need the rest of the underground."

It was the same old story. Samson was about to open his mouth and argue with the man, but he decided it wasn't worth his time. The underground leadership had once again let him down. *He wouldn't stand for this.* There was only one thing he could do.

The next morning, Samson stood in the yard. It was almost noon; the sun shone brightly and warmed his face as it stood high in the October sky. Scharführer Busch and a number of other officers stood in front of the group, and everybody knew why they were there. The guards looked more tense than usual, their eyes darting between the prisoners.

"Those whose number is called will move to the other side of the yard," Busch said without preamble. "If your number isn't called, you can return to your quarters."

Soon, around a hundred men stood on the other side of the yard. Samson's number hadn't been called yet. Busch barked a number. There was no response. He repeated himself, but again, no one moved. He double-checked his list, waited another few seconds, then frowned and made a note. When it happened again, doubt crept onto his face. When he reached the lower numbers, he looked up, then turned his attention back to his sheet of paper. Samson scanned the people in the yard: there were too few of them. Busch seemed to realize this as well, but before he could speak, a man from Samson's group stepped forward, moving toward the German determinedly.

The officer seemed surprised by the man's pace, for when he opened his mouth, the man had already reached him. Samson saw the guards reach for their weapons, but they were too late. Without a word, the man reached into the back of his pants and took out a hammer. Time in the yard seemed to slow down as the man brought it back, then swung it at the SS officer's left temple. The crack of the skull was audible, and Samson winced, but felt a tingle of excitement.

On the other side of the yard the group of selected prisoners sprang to life. They pelted the guards with stones they had hidden in their clothes. Pieces of wood appeared out of nowhere as they raced toward the guards.

At the front, Scharführer Busch collapsed onto the sandy ground, bleeding from his ears and nose, eyes rolled back in their sockets. The other officers had taken out their pistols, backing away from the mob, trying to make it to the safety of the gate. The prisoners no longer focused on them, as a number raced into the crematorium. Samson joined them, just in time to hear the rattle of machine guns exploding into life behind him.

Entering the building, the familiar scent of fire and smoke was in the air. But this time, it didn't come from the ovens. Looking up, he was pleased to see flames licking at the wooden roof of the building. The Sonderkommando had fitted rags soaked in oil and wood alcohol in various places in the crematorium. Some of those men hiding from the selection had stayed behind, waiting for the uprising to start. The fires were already blazing, and it wouldn't take long for the entire building to catch fire. *No matter what happens, at least they won't be killing any more people here.*

Samson raced to the oven room. He moved a large bucket used for storing coke. Behind it, he tugged at one of the bricks, and it quickly came loose. He removed the other bricks around it and reached inside the opening. He sighed in relief when he felt the soft fabric of a satchel. He opened it and pulled out a small pistol. It was a standard German army-issued Luger P08. He was impressed by its weight as he checked the magazine; eight bullets were neatly stacked, and he slid the clip back in place. Voices in different languages shouted from all directions. The gunfire in the yard died down, then returned with more intensity. Samson ran for the back door. His heart pounded as the roar of the flames overhead intensified. Smoke filled the rooms, and his eyes teared up as he ran on. There were shouts in German behind him, and he glanced over his shoulder. Through the smoke, he saw two figures wearing helmets in pursuit. He stopped, raised his pistol, and fired four shots in their direction. There were grunts of pain and at least one of them went down. He turned on his heel and ran, expecting a hail of bullets to strike him down at any moment. Instead, he couldn't have been more relieved to see the group waiting for him at the door. They had their weapons raised, but lowered them when they recognized him.

"What took you so long?" one of the men said.

Feliks stepped forward from the smoke. "I told them to wait another minute, I'm glad you're here!"

"Let's go! I've got a few Germans on my tail!" Samson said, pointing at the door.

The man closest to the door swung it open, and for a second, Samson half expected a squad of guards to be waiting on the other side. But judging from the gunshots coming from the yard, the guards were still focused on the initial uprising. Four men carrying insulated wire cutters sprinted for the fence. They started cutting feverishly while those carrying guns—three with *Błyskawica* submachine guns—spread out in a semicircle around them, keeping their eyes out for any guards. Samson kept his pistol trained on the back door of the crematorium, his finger hovering over the trigger. The roof was now completely ablaze—it was a beautiful sight.

A nearby siren howled into life. The uprising was now in full swing, and more soldiers would arrive soon. A soft clang at the fence. The men had cut through their first barrier and they crawled through the narrow opening. Samson stepped backward toward the fence, keeping his pistol trained on the door. Feliks waited by the opening.

"Samson, hurry up! We don't have much time."

Samson crouched down, getting ready to turn when the figure appeared from the smoke, like a ghost. Before the man realized what was happening, Samson squeezed off two shots. The men on the other side of the fence turned back, startled. A waft of smoke came from the Luger's barrel as the guard collapsed on the ground, dropping his rifle. He reached for his stomach, blood already gushing out. Samson considered applying a coup de grâce, but decided against it. *Let him suffer.* He turned and crawled through the opening.

They were now in no-man's-land, sprinting toward the outer fence. In front of him, the nearest guard tower loomed up. It was a hundred meters away, but guards with rifles were watching their every move. Beyond the fence, the trees to freedom. His lungs protested as he sprinted forward, following the men ahead of him. Those carrying rifles were in the front, ready to open fire on the guards.

They were a mere 30 meters from the guard tower when the first shots rang out. None of the men in their group were struck, and they ran on. Then, more shots rang out, and the head of the man in front of Samson exploded, sending his lifeless body crashing to the sand. Samson screamed in terror but jumped over the man to continue. *Just a little farther. You can make it.*

Bullets whistled by, and Samson clenched his jaw, putting all fear aside as he stomped on. Again, another man fell, this time struck in the gut. One of the others stopped and reached for him.

"No!" Samson shouted, out of breath. "Don't stop moving!"

It was too late. As the man turned to Samson, his neck exploded in a flash of blood. His head was almost jerked off his body as he smacked to the ground. The man with the gut wound shrieked in horror. Samson ran on, not looking back. *I'm sorry. I'm sorry.* The man's cries faded as Samson reached the guardhouse. There, the men with the rifles were firing up into the tower's wooden floor, sending splinters flying. Before long, cries of agony came from above as the guards had nowhere to hide. It was soon quiet. Two of the downed men had been carrying wire cutters, and the surviving two quickly set to work. They were now only a few cuts from freedom.

Samson looked back at the camp while Feliks climbed the guard tower, collecting the guns. Most of crematorium 4 was no longer visible, hidden in an inferno of flames and black smoke. The coke storage must've caught fire. A smile crept over his face. The sound of gunfire had died down somewhat, but trucks filled with soldiers were racing to the crematorium. On the other side, more gunfire came from where crematoria 2 and 3 were located. He hoped the Sonderkommando there managed to strike a similar victory, hopefully burning one, or both, of the wretched buildings down.

"We've got it! Let's go!" The men cut the final pieces of the fence away. The opening was just wide enough for Samson to crawl through. He was careful to avoid the remaining wires; the buzz of electricity confirmed any touch would still be lethal.

He was the last to make it to the other side, and for the first time in four years, he was a free man. The other men stood quietly for a few seconds in disbelief before Feliks spoke, "We better get moving. They'll find out we've made it out soon enough."

They sprinted for the woods. As they entered the cover of the trees, Samson looked back one last time at the hell that had been his home for more than two years. The last image he saw was crematorium 4's roof collapsing into itself in an explosion of sparks, ash and fire shooting up high into the sky.

# Chapter Sixty-Two

T he explosion made Joel stop in his tracks. He had been on his way to Kanada when the first gunshots could be heard. Even though it wasn't unusual to hear gunfire around the crematoria, the intermittent sound suggested a firefight, rather than the more routine executions. Joel had been in the camp long enough to hear the difference.

He'd sprinted to Kanada, where prisoners and guards had stopped to watch the events unfolding. They were equally shocked, and for once, the guards didn't seem to care about their prisoners not working hard enough. Scanning their faces, Joel saw fear, but not surprise. Considering their flagging morale, Joel suspected they had always known something could go wrong at any minute. The explosion a few seconds ago confirmed their fears, and Joel decided it was time to leave. He searched for Roza, but it was impossible to separate her from the many faces.

Joel left Kanada, heading for the main road between the men's and women's camps. Trucks stood parked in front of crematorium 3's gates, with more bundling down the road. The idle trucks were empty. The soldiers had already disembarked and were busy setting up machine guns. Their muzzles pointed menacingly in the direction of the gate. The wind carried the excited voices of the prisoners behind the fence. Even though there were no gunshots, it sounded like the men in crematorium 3 had caught wind of what was happening a little farther up the road.

Joel considered his next move. To get to the main camp, he needed to pass the nervous and trigger-happy soldiers. As he stood by the side of the road, the trucks passed crematorium 3 and headed in his direction. With a start he realized these were reinforcements for crematoria 4 and 5. They turned the corner and would reach him within seconds. He decided the safest way to handle this was to stand by the side of the road with his toolbox in front of him and his hands outstretched. *They might still shoot me, but at least it will be obvious I'm not trying to escape or attack them.*

Joel placed his toolbox on the dusty ground and held up his hands. The rumble of the trucks' engines increased and they soon drove by at high speed. Some of the soldiers in the back of the truck eyed him with mild interest. As he faced them, the guards looked tired and anxious. They had not expected any resistance in the camp, yet all of a sudden one of the crematoria was on fire and prisoners wielded guns. A Kübelwagen brought up the rear of the column, its driver and three passengers keeping their distance from the trucks. They screeched to a halt. The driver leaned out of his window while the other men looked on.

"What are you doing here? Where did you come from?" The man spoke quickly, and Joel spotted a few nervous tones in his words.

"I'm in the maintenance team." Joel pointed at his toolbox. "I was in Kanada but left when the shooting started in crematorium 4."

The driver looked at him with suspicion, but his passenger spoke next. "Fine, well, get back to your block now; the camp is going into lockdown. There will be roll calls soon. Make sure you don't miss yours."

"But my other job is in Auschwitz," Joel said. "They're expecting me in the hospital."

The man shook his head. "Not anymore, they're not. The gates are closed, and nobody is going in and out of Birkenau. Get back to your block." He signaled for the driver to continue, and the car sped off, chasing the trucks a few hundred meters ahead.

Joel stood for a moment. He had no way to warn the leadership, speak to Moshe. He was stuck in Birkenau, but for how long? At least Agnes would be safe. Relief washed over him.

He picked up his toolbox and followed the road toward crematorium 3. More trucks stopped and soldiers spilled out. They headed toward crematorium 2, across the road from crematorium 3. Both crematoria's entrances were now blocked.

Joel was only a hundred meters away when the ground near one of the machine guns exploded. Three soldiers' bodies were flung into the air in a blast of sand and dust. Nearby soldiers scrambled away as another explosion shook the ground on the other side. Joel froze as a number of SS men lay motionless on the ground, while others withered in the sand. They looked unsure what to do next when shots came from crematorium 3. The guards ducked to the ground or made for the safety of the trucks. A few more shots rang out behind the fence, but the soldiers had recovered and returned fire. The rattle of the automatic rifles bursting into life shook Joel's eardrums. He crashed to the ground and held his hands over his ears, digging his face into the sand. He didn't move until the gunfire stopped.

It was quiet for a moment, then he saw more projectiles hurled at the soldiers. Most landed harmlessly short of the line of soldiers, who had moved back after the first attack, but some rolled on to cause panic among the ranks. On the far side of the crematorium, Joel was stunned to see a couple dozen men wearing Sonderkommando uniforms making their way through an opening in the fence. The bombs had been a distraction as they sprinted for the outer fence. Joel was impressed by their grit. *If only Roza knew they were using her gunpowder. They were fighting back.* Apart from destroying one of the crematoria, the Sonderkommando couldn't have much of an impact; they would never win this battle. The underground leadership had steadfastly kept their distance from the proposed Sonderkommando uprising. *The crazy bastards had done it anyway.*

# CHAPTER SIXTY-THREE

They continued west, moving as fast as their tired legs would allow. At first, they had sprinted away from the camp, anxious to put as much distance between them and the mayhem as possible. But the tired, malnourished men soon found their bodies wouldn't allow them to keep running. The group of eight had slowed to a more manageable pace. Samson had looked over his shoulder for the first half hour, certain SS soldiers and barking dogs would be on their trail soon enough. But when all remained quiet, he'd felt more confident and instead focused on what was ahead.

They stopped at a stream to rest and quench their thirst. Samson was overwhelmed by the taste. Years of drinking the lukewarm, stale water in the camp had made him forget the sensation of cold, fresh water. The trees filtered the sunlight, and it gave Samson some feeling of safety. Feliks sat next to him, his face energized from the cold water.

"How are you, Samson? Looks like you're not having any trouble keeping up."

"I think we should be able to keep our pace like this. We're all in decent shape."

Feliks nodded. "I didn't think we were going to make it when they started shooting from the tower."

"We were fortunate. It could just as easily have been us back there." Samson thought of the fallen men. "But we need to keep moving."

"How many guards do you think were killed? I heard explosions and gunshots coming from the other side of the camp as well. Maybe the underground decided to join in, after all?"

Samson's mouth twitched. "I'm not sure they were ever serious about an actual uprising. There was always a lot of talk, but whenever I pushed Kaminski, the leadership was reluctant."

"Even after Roza's operation? All the bombs? The guns?"

"Even after all of that." Samson felt a stab of pain in his heart at the mention of her name. He'd spent most of the prior evening convincing the other men on the list to stand up and fight. Unsurprisingly, most of them had been keen; they'd seen what had happened to their comrades. Some said they knew where the bombs and guns were hidden, and they had hatched the plan to revolt whenever the SS showed up. The idea to escape had come from Feliks, who said they should make use of any confusion and make a run for it.

When Samson rose that morning, he'd spent most of the night thinking of what he would say to Roza. He wanted to tell her he would come back for her, that this was just the first step of breaking out and telling the world. The Allies and Soviets couldn't be too far away anymore. But when he headed for the gate, the guard told him he would not be going anywhere. No amount of cigarettes would change the guard's mind; he was to stay until that morning's selection.

"Hopefully, some of our brothers in the other crematoria will have managed to get out as well."

"And take down some of the SS soldiers on the way." There was excitement in Feliks' voice.

Someone a little farther ahead called for everybody to gather up. It was time to move again. Samson took one last gulp of water and rose. "We're lucky Mariusz knows the area."

They joined the group and stood in a semicircle around Mariusz. A strong man, he was sent to the Sonderkommando on arrival. Mariusz had connections with the resistance, which was why he was leading them now.

"The barn is another half hour from here," Mariusz said, his voice clear and confident. "The people who used to live on the farm were picked up a few months ago, so we should be able to stay there for the night. There shouldn't be anyone there, but let's be careful. We might be lucky and find some food."

Samson's mouth watered. He felt for the pistol in his waistband and followed Mariusz into the woods. They walked without speaking, only the occasional bird chirping disturbing the silence as the small group trotted through the mossy undergrowth. It was hard to fathom this serenity so close to the hell they had just escaped. Samson shivered as he thought of Roza.

They slowed as the trees made way for farmland. Mariusz pointed at a farm in the distance, some three hundred meters away. "The barn on the left is where we'll hide."

Samson looked around. They would need to cross the field to make it to the dirt road leading to the farm. The soil looked dry and uncultivated. It would be a tough trek, and even though the distance wasn't far, they would be exposed for at least five to ten minutes. Some of the men looked at each other, shuffling on their feet.

"If we want to have a chance at finding a hiding place before nightfall, we need to get ourselves into the barn. This place is very isolated, so we should be safe. We can discuss our next move when we're there, but now, we need to get moving." He took a step forward. "Follow me, and don't stop."

Without waiting for an answer, Mariusz ran into the field. The other men hesitated only for a moment, then stormed after him. The soil was hard and dry, nigh impossible to cross if it had rained. Despite that, Samson kept his eyes firmly on the ground before him. Halfway through the field, he paused and looked around. He half expected SS soldiers to burst from the trees or the road, but all remained quiet. Mariusz was well ahead of him, nearing the end of the field. Samson picked up his pace with renewed confidence. *We can do this.*

Samson was last to reach the road, and he caught up with the other men, who had broken into a jog, anxious to get to the safety of the barn. They approached the farmhouse, and again Samson felt his throat constricting. Mariusz held up his hand and directed them to the side, out of sight from the road approaching the farm. He raised his submachine gun and disappeared from sight as he circled the farmhouse.

About a minute later he appeared again. "The place is clear. Nobody has taken the farm since. We should stay in the barn, just to be safe, though." He pointed at the large structure behind the house. "Why don't you go ahead. I'll search for some food inside."

Samson and the others quickly walked to the barn. The smell of hay greeted them as they opened the door. Light filtered in through cracks in the wooden roof and walls. "It's just like Auschwitz," one of the men said with a chuckle.

"Yeah, but we're less likely to die in here," another said in response. They all laughed nervously as they spread out across the large space. There was plenty of hay to make their beds for the night. Samson took a deep breath as he sat down. For the first time since escaping, he didn't just feel hopeful. He took out the Luger and placed it on his lap as he sat facing the door. He felt safe.

That afternoon they feasted on a stew of potatoes, onions, and turnips. Mariusz had raided the house's large basement, and had even found some salt. Even though the food was basic, it was Samson's best meal in years.

Content, Samson sat in his little corner in the barn. While Mariusz was cooking, he had spent some time building a somewhat comfortable bed out of straw. He looked forward to putting his head down for the night.

Dusk was setting in when Mariusz spoke. "I'm sure you're all exhausted, so it would be a good time to take a rest. After that, we can discuss how we want to continue tomorrow. We'll all think clearer when we've had some sleep." The other men murmured their assent. Some had already closed their eyes and were stretched out on the hay. "But we'll need to remain vigilant. So I suggest two of us stay awake to keep an eye on anything happening outside. I'll take the first watch."

Feliks stepped forward. "I'll join you, Mariusz. I feel pretty fresh. I can stay awake for a few more hours."

Samson felt relieved. He was exhausted. "Wake me up when you need a rest," he said to Feliks.

His friend grinned. "Don't worry, I will. Get some sleep."

Samson fell back onto his makeshift bed, placed his pistol next to him, and closed his eyes. He didn't remember falling asleep.

Samson woke up in a daze. It felt like he had closed his eyes only moments ago. It took him a few seconds to recognize Feliks' face.

"Get up! They're here! We need you out there!"

Samson sat up, the urgency of the words jolting him into action. "Who? What's happening? Who's here?"

Before Feliks could answer, guns exploded into life outside. It seemed to come from multiple directions, and Samson and the men in the barn instinctively ducked. A shower of splinters erupted from the walls as bullets whistled overhead. Samson turned on his stomach and reached for his pistol as the gunfire stopped. He looked around and saw the other men in similar positions, crouching behind bales of hay. All but two were armed with pistols, but only Mariusz and Feliks had automatic weapons. *Where is Mariusz?* Samson spotted him next to the door, lying flat on his belly behind a metal trough. The door was completely shattered by the bullet salvo.

Mariusz waved his arms. "Take cover!" he said in a low voice.

Samson crawled for the cover of a high stack of hay, keeping his pistol trained on the door. Outside stood three trucks, their powerful headlights trained on the barn. It was hard to see what was happening behind the blinding lights, but he could hear the voices of the soldiers outside. They carefully moved about, staying within the cover of the trucks and their glow.

Nobody—inside or outside the barn—said or did anything for a moment. Despite his frayed nerves, Samson strained his ears. To his dismay, he heard heavy footsteps, those of boots, on all sides. *They're surrounding us.* Samson gripped his pistol tighter.

"They're not going to take us alive." Feliks sat next to him. His face was set in hard lines, his jaw clenched. "I'm not going to let them take me back to be tortured and murdered. We're going to die on our feet, Samson."

He looked at Feliks. From Kraków's scrapyard to the Sonderkommando of Auschwitz, they had come a long way together. It was a miracle they had survived for so long. Samson thought of his many chats with Kaminski, where he told his friend they needed to do something, to fight back. He thought of all those people he'd carried from the gas chambers to the ovens. What would they have done now, if they were in his position? *This is it. This is where I fight back.*

"We fight until the last man."

As Samson spoke the words, the barn seemed to explode. Bullets came from all sides, ripping through the wooden walls. Samson pressed his face into the ground and closed his eyes as the bullets zipped by. They made odd plopping noises as they buried themselves in the thick ramparts of hay. The barrage continued for a good five seconds, then it was quiet. Stunned, Samson opened his eyes and looked up. The walls were riddled with bullet holes. In some places entire planks had been blown out, leaving openings large enough for a man to crawl through. He could see some of the soldiers pointing their guns ahead outside. Samson's focus went to the door, which had been ripped from its hinges after the last salvo. He gasped. Behind the trough he saw the now lifeless, mangled body of Mariusz sprawled on the ground. He had been caught by a hail of bullets coming from the side and had been unable to get out of the way quickly enough.

Two other men had also been struck, their blood soaking into the hay. That left five of them. Five against a battalion of SS soldiers. Samson looked to Feliks, who seemed overwhelmed.

Before they had a chance to regroup, they heard a number of whooshing sounds, followed by bright explosions. Confused, Samson looked at the source of the sound. It took his brain a few seconds to comprehend what he was seeing. When he did, it was too late. The SS had launched Molotov cocktails at the barn from multiple sides. The dry wooden building caught fire immediately, and it was spreading to the hay.

Feliks was the first to react. "Out! Now! Or we'll burn alive!" He raised his *Błyskawica* submachine gun and climbed from the safety of the bales of hay. "Come on, Samson! We fight together!"

Samson felt all his fears dissolve as he looked at his friend with pride. Feliks was right. They had stood together for three years. Now, they would face their final fight together. He climbed over the hay, spotting the other men coming down on his left and right. Behind them, a beam screeched and crashed from the ceiling. The hay behind them instantly ignited. With the fire roaring around them, and the trucks lighting up the area in front of the barn, it was as clear as day.

Samson took a step forward and stood next to Feliks as the heat around them scorched their eyebrows. It reminded him of the crematoria, the intense heat, the never-ending smoke. Then, he saw them. The soldiers stood outside, in front of the headlamp beams. As the light of the raging fire intensified, he could make out some of the faces. They looked on with morbid fascination, their guns slightly raised as they peered into the inferno where five men stood facing them.

Samson gripped Feliks' shoulder tightly, and his friend looked at him. The flames reflected in his eyes, eyes filled with fear and anger. He nodded at Feliks, feeling the same emotions.

"We die on our feet."

He then let out an animal roar and started running toward the entrance. As he neared, his gun raised, finger on the trigger, he saw the faces of the soldiers change. For a few seconds, they seemed frozen, unsure what to do. To his side, he saw Feliks stomping forward, bursts of fire exploding from his gun's muzzle. One of the soldiers fell, clutching his stomach. Another was hit in the face, his head exploding like a watermelon.

Samson and Feliks neared the door. The rattling of Feliks' gun was music to his ears. Then, the soldiers sprang into action. Some dropped to their knees, others fell to their stomachs as they took aim. Samson pointed his gun at the nearest soldier and squeezed the trigger. The bullets landed harmlessly in the sand next to the man. He stopped for a moment, adjusted his aim, and squeezed again. This time, the bullets found their mark in the man's chest. He slumped forward. Samson felt elated. More gunfire sounded behind him as the other three men opened up on the soldiers.

Feliks was a few meters ahead of him. As he reached the door, he looked back for a second. There was a smile on his face as their eyes locked. Feliks stepped out of the barn and pulled the trigger, spraying bullets in all directions. Most of the soldiers had found cover by now, and Feliks only hit the headlights of one of the trucks. The area outside the barn went darker only for a second. Samson and the other men were running toward Feliks when the entire area lit up as dozens of guns sprang into life. Samson turned just in time to see Feliks go down in a hail of bullets.

Before he could respond, a blow with the force of a sledgehammer hit Samson in the shoulder. His body was jerked backward, and as he tried to grab his shoulder, another bullet in his groin forced him to the ground. He landed on his back with a thud. More bullets whizzed by, followed by distant screams. Samson tried to reach for his groin, but his body wasn't responding. He blinked and stared at the burning roof. He felt a warm sensation building on his thighs The gunfire died down, and he felt his head spinning, small stars blurring his vision.

He closed his eyes and started drifting away. He stood in Kraków with Roza, her smiling face looking up at him. He heard voices approaching in the distance, but they didn't matter. He opened the door to his childhood home for Roza, and they walked into the kitchen. It was warm, and the tangy smell of a *Bigos* stew cooking on the stove filled his nostrils. Roza said something he couldn't understand. Far away, the cocking of a gun. Roza repeated her words, and now he heard her.

"I love you, Samson."

He smiled, the warmth of her words flowing through his body as everything went dark.

# Chapter Sixty-Four

W hen Joel was unable to leave Birkenau, he went back to Bruno in the repair workshop. He was fortunate to be escorted back to Auschwitz the same evening. Repairs still needed to be done in the main camp, the guards said. He was told to bring his tools, which would be kept safe in the administration building. For the next three days, he worked only in Auschwitz, which was fine with him. He had caught up with Moshe and told him what he'd seen. He'd chuckled at the thought of the SS bringing him back to Auschwitz during a lockdown, inadvertently allowing him to inform the underground leadership on recent events.

The lockdown was lifted three days later. News of the destruction of crematorium 4 spread fast. As the SS fought the determined men of the Sonderkommando, the building had gone up in flames. For once, the prisoners of the camp rejoiced at the dark plumes overcasting the sky above Birkenau. Joel was keen to catch up with Roza; by now she might know more about what else had happened in the crematoria. Even though nobody had been allowed in or out of the camp, Joel was certain work inside the camp continued.

Bruno had expected him, and he had prepared work orders for both the women's camp and Kanada clothing commando for Joel. It was early in the morning, and Joel decided he was going to first try his luck at the clothing commando.

As he passed crematoria 2 and 3, he was surprised to find no evidence of the fighting of only a few days ago. The gates were closed, and smoke drifted from the chimneys. The only hint that anything had changed were the increased number of guards at the gate. They looked more alert, their MP40 submachine guns hanging loosely on their shoulders.

Kanada was a short walk from the crematoria and Joel was soon surrounded by people sorting luggage, shoes, and clothing. He passed a group of older women sorting underwear, expertly separating men's, women's, and children's garments.

There was a light brush on his arm and he flinched before recognizing Roza's dark brown eyes. "I had a feeling you might show up today," she said, her eyes scanning the people around them. "Come, follow me. I'll pretend I'm explaining what needs to be done."

Roza navigated her way between the people and baskets. As she talked, she pointed at specific baskets and people, and then at the lights. "It's important they keep functioning. We need those in the evening." She raised her voice as they passed two SS guards—oblivious to Joel and Roza as they chatted, both leaning on a pile of empty suitcases.

When they were out of earshot of the guards, Roza's tone changed. "The uprising didn't go as planned, did it?" Her tone was almost accusatory, and before Joel could answer, she continued, speaking rapidly. "The Sonderkommando were left out to dry when they attacked. Where was the rest of the resistance? I thought we were ready!" Her voice rose abruptly, and Joel involuntarily took a step back. This wasn't how he had expected the conversation to go.

"The Sonderkommando acted on their own. They were told to wait. They didn't. I'm sorry, Roza."

Roza shook her head. "Wait for what? From what I've heard, almost all of the men in the Sonderkommando were killed in the past few days."

"Some of them escaped, though. Have you heard anything from Samson?"

"No." Her voice weakened and she moved her gaze to the ground.

"I'm sure he would've found a way to contact me by now if he was still alive. He would've been part of the uprising, I'm certain. He knew time was running out."

"And he wouldn't have waited around for the SS to come and get him, would he?" Joel kept his voice low. "For what it's worth, I disagreed with the leadership. The Sonderkommando played a large part in the preparations for an uprising, and we knew they were in danger. If I were Samson, I would've done the same." Roza nodded and looked up. The sadness was heavy in her glistening eyes. Joel felt compelled to say something else. "I haven't heard from him, either. We need to believe he may have been part of the group that escaped. Not all of them have been found yet, from what I hear."

Roza nodded, then her expression changed. "There's something else you need to know, Joel. And no matter how I feel about the underground's leadership or their decisions, they need to know about this."

"What is it?"

"Last night, the SS came into the women's camp, into our barracks. I was almost asleep, it was that late, but they switched on the lights and arrested about a dozen women. I was terrified they would take me as they dragged them from their bunks. They knew exactly who they were looking for." She paused and Joel felt his throat constrict. When she looked up, her eyes were serious. "Four of the women were my friends. They worked in the Union factory."

Joel didn't immediately respond as he looked at Roza. The sound of people working and talking faded into the background. His mind was racing. How much did these women know? How would they behave under questioning? He looked at Roza. She was in grave danger.

"Joel, if they knew about my involvement, they would've taken me as well."

"But what about the girls? Do they know what you do with the gunpowder?"

"I never told them. I'm sure they have their suspicions." She took Joel's hand and gave it a little squeeze. "Although I'm sure they've put the past days' events and what they did together. But there's nothing tying them to the bombs of the Sonderkommando."

"Nothing but you."

A couple of guards approached. "What are you doing standing around?"

Roza pointed at the armband marking her as a forewoman, then at Joel's toolbox. "I'm briefing him on what needs to be improved with the lighting situations around here."

The guard frowned. "What's wrong with the lights?"

She pointed at some of the lights mounted on top of the buildings surrounding them. "They're not strong enough. We had a few accidents the other day, as well as people sorting clothing into the wrong baskets."

The guard looked unconvinced, but his partner seemed bored. "Come on, let them worry about lights. Let's get something to eat. I'm starving."

The guards walked off and Joel turned back to Roza. "You seem very calm."

"They're not going to talk. Trust me. And even if they do, the worst that can happen is they come for me, and only me."

Joel was stunned. "You know what will happen when they do, don't you?"

"Yes, but I knew the risks." Roza pulled back her shoulders and lifted her chin. "We destroyed one of the crematoria. And if some of the men in the Sonderkommando escaped, it's a sacrifice I'm willing to make."

"I don't know what to say, Roza. I'm not sure I would be as calm if I were in your position."

She smiled. "I trust my girls. They won't give me up."


A week later, Joel and Agnes sat outside the hospital administration building. Despite the cold weather, Agnes said she needed a short walk to clear her head.

"I'm indoors all the time, in a stuffy room with too many people, and too many dusty files." She stood and rubbed her hands together. "This is a good change, for a few minutes. Besides, I have you to warm me."

Joel stood and hugged her, grateful to Bruno for assigning him to

Auschwitz at least three days a week.

"From what I'm reading in some of the files, the number of experiments is going down," Agnes said. "But so is the number of women in the wards."

"Probably because they can't replace them as quickly as they used to anymore." Joel took her hand and led her off to the side of the building, away from the road.

"It feels like the end of the line, doesn't it?"

"It does. How do you feel about it?"

Agnes looked into the distance. "I don't know. I've spoken to Dr. Fejkiel about it several times, and we go back and forth between being elated when we hear about the liberation of cities and countries around us and thinking that we know too much to be allowed to live."

"You still think they'll execute everybody in the camp when the Allies or Soviets show up?" Even though he didn't voice them, Joel had the same concerns. The fervor with which the Sonderkommando had been thinned out when the transports dwindled had shocked him. He always had assignments waiting for him—nothing worse than being useless in Auschwitz-Birkenau.

Agnes shook her head. "Wouldn't you do the same? Dead witnesses don't talk."

"I don't know." He stopped and turned to her. "All I know is the underground leadership seems to be happy waiting everything out. They decided not to join in with the Sonderkommando's uprising, and they haven't shown any signs that they're looking to do anything now."

"And you think they're well informed?"

"About as best as one can be in here. You see the information coming in as well, don't you?"

"Not really. I only forward the incoming messages to Dr. Fejkiel, who then makes sure the right people know about them. But we have a lot of letters and small packages coming in these days."

"I think that's why the leadership is happy to wait it out. The news from the outside is giving them confidence."

"I hope you're right."

They finished their walk in silence. Agnes' position in the hospital had been a blessing and a curse. She probably wouldn't have survived up until now, but as hopes of liberation grew, her position became more dangerous. The SS wouldn't hesitate to kill everyone in the hospital if they had time to do so. *We better make sure they don't get the opportunity. Or we could hide.* He shook the thoughts from his mind as they returned to the building's front door.

"I better get back to work," Agnes said, quickly looking around to make sure they were alone. She pecked him on the cheek and reached for the door handle. "Be safe, Joel. See you soon."

She disappeared inside and Joel felt his cheek flushing. He picked up his toolbox. As the door closed, he vowed he would do anything to keep this woman safe.

After finishing his last job of the day, Joel handed in his toolbox and headed back to Auschwitz. He was surprised to see Moshe waiting outside their block in the cold. He upped his pace and approached his friend. Moshe looked excited, his eyes flashing as his head bobbed up and down.

"What's wrong?" Joel said, cocking his head.

"They're out, Joel."

"Who?"

"The girls from the factory. They were released this afternoon. We just found out about it."

Joel took a step back. This was unexpected. "How did they do that? Did they talk?"

"As far as we know they all kept their mouths shut and stuck to the same story. They denied knowing about the gunpowder smuggling and said they were horrified by the SK uprising."

"And the SS bought it?"

Moshe shrugged. "Apparently. You don't seem happy with the news. This means Roza is safe."

"Do you know where the girls were sent?"

"Back to their barracks in the women's camp."

He looked at his friend. *Maybe I should accept this as a win. Moshe seems happy enough about it.*

"The most important thing is they're out and alive. I'll celebrate that."

Moshe missed the lack of enthusiasm in Joel's voice as he slapped him on the back. "Great, come inside. We've organized a little bit of vodka. I'm sure it'll do you good."

Joel met Roza the next morning.

"The girls from the factory returned to the block early in the evening. I had to control myself not to run to them when I saw their faces. I was so relieved to see them alive," Roza said.

"I thought you were confident they wouldn't say anything?"

She frowned. "That doesn't mean I didn't fear for their safety. Not speaking and surviving aren't necessarily linked."

He held up his hands. "I'm sorry. You're right. I'm just a little nervous about everything."

"What do you mean?"

"When Moshe told me about their release last night, he celebrated it like a victory. You seem to feel the same way."

"I'm happy they're alive, Joel." The frown on her face deepened. "What are you saying?"

He ignored her question. "What work detail were they assigned to this morning?"

"The factory. They left early in the morning, like always."

He dropped his head, rubbing his temples. "That's what I feared." He looked up and met her eyes. "You need to tell them not to speak to anyone about what happened and how they were involved."

Realization dawned in Roza's eyes. "You think it's a trap?"

"All I know is that I don't believe the SS are giving up this easily. They didn't arrest them without reason."

"Maybe they believe they are innocent?"

"That's one theory. But if the SS think they're lying, sending them back to the factory is exactly what I would expect."

Roza thought for a moment, then nodded. "I'll talk to them tonight."

# Chapter Sixty-Five

J oel pulled up his collar as he approached the gate leading out of the women's camp. The guard was bundled up in the small guardhouse and looked annoyed when he spotted Joel. It was mid-December, and winter had truly arrived in Auschwitz. Even though there was no snow on the ground, dark clouds threatened overhead.

The guard grunted something and Joel held up his pass. After a halfhearted inspection, he was let through, and Joel quickly turned to Birkenau's main gatehouse. He had spent a good two hours fixing up some of the bunks, and plenty of women had approached him about the situation outside. He couldn't tell them anything more than what they themselves could hear. The Soviets were close, the rumble of artillery growing louder every day. The women were hopeful, although they worried about what the Germans would do.

A number of trains had left Auschwitz in the past few days, evacuating stronger prisoners to be reassigned to camps farther into Germany. This time, people believed they were being transferred instead of sent to their deaths. The gas chambers and crematoria operations had trickled almost to a standstill. The Sonderkommando only needed to burn the corpses of those dying of natural causes. In Auschwitz, of course, this could mean many things, but the demolition of crematoria 2 and 3 had already started last month, leaving only crematorium 5 operational. For Joel, it was a sign that the camp command was preparing for the inevitable surrender.

After half an hour, Joel reached the main camp. He entered the relative warmth of Block 26. Even though there was never enough fuel to keep the room at a comfortable temperature, it was still better than the icy cold outside. He had only just taken off his coat when Piotr appeared behind him. His friend looked at him anxiously. Joel felt a tingling sensation in his chest.

"What's wrong?"

"They brought in Roza."

Joel's stomach dropped. "Where?"

"Block 11."

Half an hour later, Joel sat in the corner of the block with Moshe and Piotr.

"How much does she know?" Moshe asked.

Joel glared at him. He didn't like his friend's accusatory tone. "What do you mean? You know what she knows. She's been one of the most important people in the resistance."

"Joel, calm down," Moshe said calmly. "I know you're upset, but we need to know how exposed we are."

"Are you kidding me? Calm down? Of everybody here, I'm probably the most exposed. I'm her contact, remember?" His neck burned as he pointed a finger at Moshe. "I spoke to her multiple times a week, I went into the women's camp, and I made sure the leadership knew what was going on." He took a deep breath as Moshe looked at him. "So I think I have a good reason to worry. It wouldn't surprise me if they came for me next. Don't tell me to calm down."

"I'm sorry." Moshe held up his hands. "I know you're worried about her. And yourself. And you have every right to be. But I need to let the leadership know what's happening, so we can make plans."

Joel looked up. "What plans? She's in Block 11. There's nothing we can do."

"That's not entirely true. We might be able to do something, but we need to make sure she hasn't been talking."

"Stop speaking in riddles, Moshe, and tell me what we can do. Can we help Roza?"

He shook his head. "Not yet. We need to be patient for a few days. We need to see what happens, and if they start arresting more people. Do you think she'll talk?"

"She won't," Joel said resolutely. "She would rather die than give up other people."

Moshe looked skeptical. "They can be very persuasive in there."

"She'll stay silent."

"Then there's nothing to worry about." Moshe looked around, then spoke softly. "I know one of the Kapos in Block 11. He works the night shift in the basement. We have to assume Roza is locked up there, probably being interrogated now." He paused as the words hung in the air. Joel felt sick thinking about the torture. "Let me reach out to him. If all remains quiet for the next two days, we can assume she hasn't broken."

"And then what?"

"We go see her."

Agnes handed him a small pouch. "These pills will give her the best chance to stay alive. There are vitamins, painkillers, and even some American antibiotics I found in the medicine storage. I don't know how that got here, but tell her to take those if she has an infection."

The pouch was heavier than Joel expected. "Thank you."

"She probably won't have enough water to wash the pills down, so she'll need to crush them and eat them as powder." Agnes made a face. "It will be difficult, because she'll be parched, but she has to take the vitamins every day. They're the yellow pills. Make sure she knows that."

*Yellow pills. Every day.* "I will. You know this is the second time you're about to save her life?"

Agnes shook her head. "I was there myself, remember? I only survived because, for some reason, that interrogator went easy on me. I can't imagine Roza having the same good fortune. Poor woman." Her forehead was wrinkled in worry. "Have you heard anything else since? Any arrests?"

"None. I hardly slept the night after. I was certain I would be next. If they found out about Roza, they must know she wasn't working alone."

"But they would only know if she gave up your name."

"And she didn't, or at least not yet."

"It's been three nights. She probably would have by now," Agnes said. "Trust me. They have ways to make people talk. When I was in there, most people cracked the first or second day. But now would be a good time to talk to her, strengthen her for what's next."

Joel nodded. "I suspect she will be in there for a while, especially if she stays quiet."

"You're not blaming yourself for this, are you?" Her eyes softened. "It was her choice."

"I know. I'm just worried."

Agnes put her hand on his arm. "That's only natural. But you're doing everything you can. Look at you. You're about to walk into the most dangerous building of the camp to help your friend. I'm proud of you, Joel. You're a good man." She kissed him and held him tight. "But you better get going. Moshe will be wondering what's holding you up."

Joel kept his arm around her a second longer before letting go. He steeled himself as he looked into Agnes' eyes. "I'll see you soon, my love."

"Be careful."


Moshe and Joel stood in Block 26's doorway. It was getting dark but still a few hours before the final roll call. Joel touched the pouch with the medication in his inner pocket. With his other arm, he held a small bottle of whiskey under his shirt.

"What's taking him so long? He should be here by now." Joel scanned the dirt road. "You said four o'clock, right?"

"He'll be here in a minute, don't worry," Moshe said without a trace of doubt. "Do you remember what you'll tell the guard?"

"Nothing. I'll let Yaacov do the talking, and I'll just hand him the bottle when we enter. You're sure he's reliable?"

Moshe nodded. "Yaacov? He's been a friend ever since I arrived in Auschwitz. He's helped me out many times." Joel debated asking Moshe about the extent of Yaacov's help but decided against it. Moshe probably wouldn't tell him.

A slender man appeared from around the corner on the far side of the little road. Despite walking with a limp, he maintained a quick pace as he shuffled toward them.

"That's him," Moshe said.

Yaacov Kozelchik wore a regular striped prison uniform, with the crucial addition of a Kapo armband on his right arm. He nodded at Moshe; then his eyes fixed on Joel. "Are you ready?"

Joel nodded, and Yaacov set off without another word. Joel looked at Moshe, who simply shrugged. "Good luck."

He caught up with Yaacov, who marched on, despite his bad leg. It didn't seem to bother him. After five minutes, Block 11 came into view.

"Remember, you are my friend, just visiting me for the first part of my shift. You brought some whiskey for the guard." Yaacov spoke without taking his eyes off the road. "Got that?"

"Sure." Joel felt slightly apprehensive. He had expected Yaacov to be nicer, more talkative perhaps. Then he realized the Kapo had probably survived for so long by keeping his mouth shut. He also appreciated the man was about to give him access to one of the most dangerous areas of the camp. Even if he didn't warm to Yaacov too much, he needed to trust Moshe's judgment. Despite that, he couldn't help asking, "Have you seen Roza in recent days?"

The Kapo didn't immediately respond as they passed Block 10. Joel looked up to see streaks of light filtering through the closed curtains on the second floor.

"I saw her last night. You best prepare yourself for the worst. She's been resisting the interrogators until now, and they don't care for that. The guards told me she refused to speak a single word. Brave woman, that." There was admiration in his voice. "Foolish one, too. If you don't give them anything, they'll kill you during interrogation or in the yard outside." He mimicked putting a gun to his head and pulling the trigger.

Joel ignored him, focusing instead on what he would say to Roza.

They reached the front door, and Yaacov repeated his earlier words. "Leave the talking to me." He opened the door into an empty hallway. Yaacov led him down the stairs into the basement. The air was cold and damp, and Joel shivered. He could feel the tension in the air, and it wasn't long until he heard the ragged breathing of prisoners struggling behind the doors of the tiny cells.

"Come, follow me." Yaacov led him to an open space in the middle of the hallway. A table and four chairs, with one sullen guard, greeted him. He looked up from his paper and frowned.

"What's this? You know you can't bring anyone down here," he said unconvincingly, not bothering to stand up.

"Ah, come on, Andreas. He's a friend of mine. He's even brought something nice." Yaacov gestured with his hands, and Joel took out the bottle of whiskey. The guard's demeanor instantly changed at the sight of the bottle. He leaned forward eagerly and took the bottle from Joel.

"This changes things," he said, inspecting the label. "A friend of Yaacov who brings whiskey is always welcome." He gestured at the chairs. "Come, sit, sit."

Joel sat down as the guard poured three small cups of whiskey. For show, Joel picked one up and raised it. He took a tiny sip as the guard downed his glass in one go. He quickly refilled his cup and took another large gulp.

Fifteen minutes later, the guard was slouched on the table, snoring loudly as Yaacov smiled. "Happens all the time. Come, let's go see Roza." He picked out a key chain.

"Wait." Joel remembered Agnes' words. "Can we bring her some water?"

Yaacov nodded and pointed at a small bucket behind Joel. "Fill it up there."

Joel filled the bucket and followed Yaacov into the hallway. His heart beat faster as the Kapo stopped at a nondescript cell door and turned the key. He opened the door and turned to Joel.

"Fifteen minutes, that's all you get. I'll lock the door if anyone comes down to check on anything. I'm usually alone here most of the night, but you never know. Keep your voice down."

Joel stepped into the cell, which went dark as soon as Yaacov closed the door. He stood motionless as he allowed his eyes to adjust to the darkness. Faint moonlight shone in through a small window. As Yaacov's footsteps faded, Joel heard soft, rhythmic breathing to his right. He squinted and saw the outline of a person curled up in a ball.

"Roza? It's me, Joel," he whispered as he crouched on his knees. He received only a faint whimper as a reply. "Roza, can you hear me?"

"Joel?" A croaked voice he hardly recognized spoke. "What are you doing here? Am I ... Am I dreaming?"

Joel's bit his lip, holding back tears as his heart ached for her. He pursed his lips and let out a breath he'd been holding in for days, relieved to hear her voice. "I've brought you some water." He formed his hands into a small bowl and scooped water. He held it near her mouth, and she drank eagerly.

"More, please." Her voice sounded somewhat closer to normal. She drank three more times from Joel's hands before she had had enough. "How did you get down here? I didn't say a word."

"I know you didn't, Roza. Stay calm." He put his hand on her forehead. Through the dried blood, he could feel her burning up. He gasped. Even though his eyes had adjusted to the darkness, there was still too little illumination for him to make out more than the shape of her face. "What have they done to you?"

Roza tried to sit up and stifled a groan as she did. She reached for the side of her chest and moaned in pain. "I don't know, Joel. I remember them tying me up on some sort of pole and hanging me upside down. I don't even know how long they kept me there. I must've passed out."

Joel shuddered. He'd heard of the infamous, much-feared torture method. He was amazed Roza was still alive. Most victims hadn't been able to tell the tale. It gave him hope for her survival. He took out the medicine pouch and placed it in Roza's hands.

"Are you able to hide this anywhere?" He scanned the room, but beyond the empty bunk she lay on, there were no other places to hide anything. He cursed inwardly.

"No, but I'll find a way," Roza said. "What is it?"

He repeated Agnes' instructions, hoping they registered with Roza. She took a handful of the pills and swallowed them. "I think in my situation, anything helps." *Hasn't lost her dark humor.*

They sat in silence for a minute, and then Roza spoke.

"I'm glad you came, Joel. It's good to know I have people that care for me."

"You have many friends."

"I want you to know one thing, Joel. And you need to tell whomever you think needs to hear this as well. I didn't give anyone up. Not a single name."

"I know, Roza. I know."

He could see her raise her hand in the darkness, barely suppressing a painful grunt. "No, you don't understand. I will never talk. The only name I've given them is Kaminski. But that's only because I know he's dead."

Joel looked down at her, moonlight reflecting in her dark brown eyes. Even though her body was shattered, the fury in her soul burned through her eyes.

"Joel, come closer." She stretched her neck toward him, and he moved his face closer to hers. Roza grabbed his face with her hands and brought his ear to her lips. He could feel her shallow, ragged breathing as she spoke. "You don't have to worry. I'll never betray you. They'll have to kill me first. And when they do, I'll be with my Samson again. It's okay. I've made peace with my fate."

A tear rolled down Joel's cheek as he turned to Roza. He closed his eyes, gently kissed her forehead, and carefully put his hands behind her head. He felt her relax as she exhaled and dropped her head into his chest. "I don't know anyone quite as brave as you, Roza."

She didn't respond, but he could feel her warm breath on his chest. After a few seconds, she leaned back against the wall and whispered, "And you are the best friend I've ever had, Joel."

# CHAPTER SIXTY-SIX

Three weeks had passed since Joel's first visit to Roza in Block 11. He had gone back twice since; when he came to visit her two days ago, the guard told him he was no longer allowed. Not even another bribe of whiskey and cigarettes helped.

The interrogations had stopped after two weeks, and now the SS appeared happy to leave her to fade away in her cell. The medication and vitamins Joel had smuggled in were keeping her alive.

"Maybe Yaacov can help? He still works there at night, doesn't he?" Agnes asked as they walked from the administration building to Block 10. Joel was scheduled to inspect some of the machinery and had picked up Agnes for a walk. A mild January breeze made it feel colder than it was, and they continued at a brisk pace.

"He said he doesn't have access to her cell anymore. I'm afraid they'll starve her to death, Agnes, and there won't be a thing we can do about it."

Agnes walked along in silence, a frown on her face. She looked thoughtful, then shook her head. "I'm afraid you're right. I don't know how we could if Yaacov can't even talk to her. There's one thing I do remember from my time down there, though."

Joel felt a glimmer of hope. "What is it?"

"It's not much, but it's something to hold onto," she said, immediately lowering his expectations. "If she truly stayed silent, there's a chance they might let her leave. I'm afraid there's one massive 'but,' though." She paused and looked at Joel. "She's probably not the only person they're interrogating. And if someone else spoke, Roza won't stand a chance. I think we need to be realistic."

A rumble in the distance made them stop and turn. It sounded like distant thunder.

"Sounds like it's closer yet again, isn't it?" Agnes said, a weak smile on her face.

"The Soviets might arrive in time for Roza to survive."

Agnes nodded but didn't say anything. Joel knew she was skeptical, and he couldn't blame her. She had spent almost a month in the same prison, and the fact that she walked alongside him today was nothing short of a miracle. Very few people entered Block 11 and lived to tell about it.

They arrived at Block 10 and hugged before Joel turned and walked up the steps in front of the building.

"Joel." He turned around to see her standing in the same spot. "It will all be over soon. And you're right; they might just make it in time for Roza to survive. We have to believe."

He smiled and nodded before entering the building. *We have to keep a little faith.*


At almost three, Joel left Block 10 and stepped into the crisp winter air. He headed toward the camp exit and reflected on his morning. Block 10 had always been different, even from the other hospital blocks. But today, everyone was even more on edge than usual. The once chatty nurses now hurried by without acknowledgment. He'd worked in the operating room independently, then fixed some of the lights in the upstairs wards. The one thing that caught his eye was the number of empty beds. Agnes was right: they were emptying the block, but why? And where did the women go? For the first time since Joel could remember, empty trains arrived at the Birkenau ramp and left full. But nobody wanted to be on the trains, especially with the hopeful thunder of Russian artillery closing in.

Joel left Auschwitz and made for Birkenau. The walk took him half an hour, and he was surprised by the traffic on the way. Germans' trucks and cars filled with supplies went back and forth. Two trucks approached, going in different directions, and he had to jump out of the way as they sped past him. Something had them spooked, and Joel cast his eyes east, to where Stalin's armies were surely pushing the Nazis back. He smiled and clenched his fists. *Just a few more days.*

He reached Birkenau and headed to the repair shop. He found Bruno in the back, sorting through tools. When he saw Joel come in, he rushed toward him, his eyes wide.

*Something's wrong.* "What is it?"

"It's the Union factory, Joel. Something's about to happen."

"What do you mean?"

"Ludwik was just there. He was there for some repairs this morning. When he returned, he told me the women were nervous."

"Nervous, how?"

"They were told they needed to return to the women's camp earlier than usual, well before dusk. They said there would be a special roll call this evening."

Joel checked the clock on the wall. It was a little before four. Outside, the sky was darkening. "They're probably back by now."

"Just about. But Joel, listen. There's something else you should know."

As Joel listened to the words that came out of Bruno's mouth next, he felt his knees buckle, then an explosion of anger. Even before Bruno could finish, he was out the door, sprinting toward the women's camp.

He arrived panting and sweating. The guard at the gate looked at him in surprise.

"A bit late to be carrying out repairs, isn't it?" His eyes went to Joel's empty hands. "Where are your tools?"

Joel realized he had no business at the women's camp. Without his toolbox and the correct papers, this area was off limits to him. He thought quickly; he had to get in. "I'm sorry, Tobias, I left my hammer in one of the barracks. Bruno was furious, he demanded I come back and get it, even this late. Would you mind? I'll be back before you know it."

The guard gave him a stern look. "You know I can't just let you in, especially at this time. All the women are back."

"It won't take a minute," Joel said with as much confidence as he could muster. Tobias wavered, and Joel pushed on. "I'll bring you two packs of cigarettes tomorrow. Bruno will kill me if I come back without the hammer."

The mention of cigarettes softened Tobias' stance and he opened the gate. "Ten minutes, or I'm coming to get you."

"I'll be back before you know it."

He suppressed the urge to run as he made his way to the roll call area. The paths between the barracks were deserted, and he stuck close to the sides. If he ran into another guard, he would again need to explain what he was doing here without his toolbox. Even though Tobias was responsible, they would assail him with questions.

He heard the murmur of voices before he saw the mass of women lined up in the open space. They were surrounded by guards who looked at ease. The women were chatting, urgency in their voices. Joel had spent countless hours in yards at roll call, and sensed something was different. As he moved closer, he saw why. His blood froze, and his heart went cold at the sight of a very familiar construction at the front of the group. A gallows.

The wooden structure was crude and clearly hastily erected. Two nooses dangled menacingly in the wind. Joel swallowed hard as he found a spot near one of the closest barracks. If anyone spotted him, he could pretend he was about to enter the barracks in search of his hammer.

Two men entered the yard and the women instantly went quiet. Joel didn't recognize either of them, but even from this distance he could see they were officers. It was unusual for officers to lead common roll calls.

They wasted no time as one of them spoke in a booming voice. "You're all here to witness justice carried out." He motioned to the side of the yard, where two guards appeared. They dragged a woman between them, and Joel squinted to make out her face. Her dark brown hair was all tangled up, and her face was battered. She was tall, despite her slouched posture. She walked with a limp as she struggled to keep up with the guards dragging her along. Joel didn't recognize her as she was lifted onto the gallows.

"This woman was involved in a vicious attack on the German Reich. She assisted in the killing of many brave SS men, but also in the unnecessary deaths of almost five hundred Sonderkommando."

Joel raised an eyebrow. This was one of Roza's women, surely. He looked more closely at her, then his eyes shifted to the other rope. He suddenly felt nauseous, and even before the SS officer lifted his hand again, he knew what would happen next.

Flanked by two guards, the woman entered the yard and held her head high. Even from a distance, defiance shone from her eyes. Judging by her clenched jaws, she struggled to walk the distance to the gallows. She walked past the rows of silent women and met their eyes. Joel's heart swelled with pride, but at the same time he felt an intense pressure on his chest as he fought to control his emotions. Roza mounted the gallows herself, with one of the guards holding on to her bound wrists to keep her from losing her balance. She ignored the officers as she focused on the other woman and smiled.

Joel stood paralyzed by the barracks, his eyed fixed on Roza. He wanted to run to her, take out the guards and lift her from the gallows. But he would be shot before he made it halfway through the yard.

"And this woman organized the whole rebellion of the Sonderkommando. She is not only responsible for the deaths of our guards, but also for the killing of your own people. She willingly deceived you and your colleagues in the factory for her own purposes."

Roza stood motionless. Her eyes remained fixed on the crowd. Joel could see her mouth twitch into a smile every few seconds. Her hands were tied behind her back, but he knew they were clenched into fists. He was so proud of her.

"And that is why they will die a traitor's death here today. We will not stand for rebellions in this camp." The officer took a step away from Roza and the other woman, then nodded at the guards standing beside the two women. The men moved behind the women; it would all be over soon. Joel forced himself to keep his eyes on Roza, and as she scanned the crowd, their eyes met. Even though she was far away, he saw the recognition on her face. There was only a hint of surprise as she held his gaze. Then, she smiled and nodded. Joel returned the smile as he felt his eyes burning. He swallowed hard and clenched his teeth, determined to match her bravery.

The guards moved back, ready to kick the stools from underneath the women's feet.

"*Chazak V'amatz!*" Roza bellowed the words, the muscles in her neck bulging as the words thundered through the silent yard. "Be strong and courageous!"

The other woman repeated the words, and together they started singing. "*As long as in the heart within, the Jewish soul yearns.*" Their strained voices stunned the guards, who froze in place. "*And toward the eastern edges, onward, an eye gazes toward Zion.*"

Joel mouthed the words, a lump forming in the back of his throat. His fingertips tingled as the wind carried the women's voices across the yard.

"*Our hope is not yet lost, the hope that is two thousand years old, to be a free nation in our land, the Land of Zion, Jerusalem.*"

It was quiet for a few seconds, only the rustle of the wind disturbing the silence. Roza looked up and met Joel's eyes one more time. She smiled, then her head was violently jerked backward as she dropped a few inches, the noose tightening around her neck. Her eyes at first registered surprise, and then, serenity washed over her face. Joel held her gaze until the very end. Only then did he allow his tears to flow freely. As he looked at her broken body dangling from the rope, he comforted himself with the one thing that mattered. Roza would no longer suffer. She was on her way to Samson.

# CHAPTER SIXTY-SEVEN

It had been nearly two weeks since Roza's death. Yet, despite the sounds of the Soviet artillery growing louder, camp life carried on almost as usual. Work details set out to the mines and quarries, the experiments continued in Block 10, and the chimney of crematorium 5 continued to bellow smoke into the frosty January air.

There were some subtle changes. Joel had seen the Birkenau ramp packed with people in the past two weeks. They carried their meager belongings and set off, destination unknown. All the men, and some women, were taken west, away from the approaching Red Army. The SS were in a hurry to empty the camp.

Today, however, was very different. When Joel and the rest of the men in Block 26 awoke and prepared for roll call, they were told to stay in their block. Roll call would be later, at noon.

Piotr leaned against his bunk. "What do you make of that, Joel?"

"It either means we're getting on a train today, or we're all going to die." Joel was surprised at the speed at which he'd drawn this conclusion. Piotr looked at him in shock, and he quickly added, "I don't know, Piotr, could be anything, right? Let's wait for roll call."

Moshe appeared next to Piotr. He was usually well informed, but he was at a loss. "Latest news from the front is that the Soviet progress has slowed down, but they should be within twenty kilometers of here. They could be here any day now."

"Do you think that's what the roll call is about?"

Moshe shrugged. "No reason to the SS logic, is there?"

Joel lay back in his bunk and picked up a book. He tried reading, but the letters moved around the page too much. His mind wouldn't let him focus and his thoughts drifted. He was certain they were about to be put on a train. He was torn: on the one hand he had dreamed of the day he would leave Auschwitz for so long, and he couldn't wait to leave. On the other hand, he also knew every day he stayed, the chances of a liberation by the Soviets became more of a reality. *Will they bring us somewhere else where they still have working gas chambers?*

"Are you coming?" Piotr looked at him. "It's time."

"Already?" It wasn't noon yet.

His friend nodded. "Didn't you hear them call us just now?"

Joel climbed down from the bunk and followed the rest of the men outside. There, a procession marched from the other blocks toward the yard. Even though they did this every morning, today felt different. Despite everything that had happened to them, the men dragging their weary bodies to roll call had a spring in their step, a look of optimism on their faces.

Joel lined up with his block while the last prisoners streamed in and found their places. He looked at the guards. They were spread out around the yard as always, a number looking down from their towers. Their faces were nervous about something. The ground shook a little, immediately followed by a deep rumble in the distance. Smiles appeared on the faces of the prisoners, quickly hidden before the guards noticed. But the guards didn't seem to care. They looked on apathetically, their faces devoid of emotion as their guns hung harmlessly on their shoulder straps.

An officer appeared. His posture was immaculate, in sharp contrast to the guards. He confidently marched to the center and stood looking at the group. His gaze was intense and made Joel remember where he was. *You're not free yet.*

The officer raised his hand, and all murmurs died away. He nodded, content with the discipline. "Prisoners of Auschwitz, the day has come.

We're leaving the camp tonight. Pack your things and dress warmly, it will be a long walk. Everybody will report back here at six sharp. Anyone refusing to leave will be shot." He looked around once more, then marched off, back to where he came from.

The silence in the yard was deafening as the men looked at each other. Joel turned to Piotr.

"We're finally leaving this hell," his friend said.

*Yes, but what fresh horrors await us?*

Joel rushed down the narrow thoroughfare, where people hustled to find warm clothing for the journey. Whoever had anything of value left bribed guards to take them to Birkenau to plunder Kanada for warm clothing. Joel knew there would be absolute mayhem in Birkenau as people fought over the best garments. The guards had abandoned any pretense of order and scooped up the bribes. The men in the watchtowers looked over the activities like hawks, rifles pointing down.

Joel arrived at the administration building and stopped in his tracks. Small fires burned around it, and guards and prisoners rushed in and out of the building. They carried piles of index cards, files, and paper. Everything was dumped on one of the fires before they dashed back inside. Joel looked on in fascination. Even the senior SS administrators had joined in.

He easily blended into the chaos and entered. He found Agnes near her desk, boxing up files from the cabinets that lined the wall. As soon as she spotted him, her face spread into a wide smile.

"Joel! I'm so glad you're here. I was worried I wouldn't find you."

"I came here immediately after the announcement." He stood next to her and took her hand. "We need to make sure we stay together tonight. Do you have enough warm clothes? It will be a long walk, wherever they take us. We need to look out for—"

"I'm not going, Joel."

He looked at her, open mouthed. "What do you mean? Of course you are."

"I can't abandon the people in the hospital. They won't survive without nurses."

Joel felt dizzy as he struggled to comprehend Agnes' words. "But what about the SS? They'll kill everyone once the Soviets show up."

Agnes looked at him curiously as she leaned against the filing cabinet. "When I arrived here, I vowed to care for these people." The windows shook as another shell landed in the distance. Her green eyes shone with determination as she moved closer to Joel. He opened his arms, and she stepped into his embrace. He felt an ache in his chest as he considered leaving Agnes behind in a few hours.

"If you're not leaving, I'm not leaving."

Agnes moved her head back, surprise on her face. She opened her mouth, but he held up his hand. "You're the reason I'm still alive, Agnes. You've been the one thing that's kept me fighting when there were days when it would've been easier to give up. I can't imagine living without you. Remember what we promised each other?"

"We will leave this place together." Tears formed in her eyes.

Joel nodded, his voice unsteady as he choked back his tears. "You are right. These people won't survive without help. You can't abandon them. And I won't abandon you."

Agnes smiled through her tears and put her hands on his cheeks. "Joel, you can't imagine how happy I am to hear you say that. I felt sick thinking about losing you tonight."

He smiled and kissed her. For now, he decided to live in the moment. When they broke their kiss, he looked at her. There was something mischievous in the way she looked at him. He frowned.

"We'll need to find you a nurse's uniform."


Moshe and Piotr looked at him in shock.

"You're staying? That's madness." Moshe pulled his jacket tighter. "You'll be locked in. When the Soviets arrive, the guards will kill everyone in the hospital."

Joel gave him a stern look. "I'll take my chances. I don't think the guards are going to be sticking around."

"How can you be so sure?" Piotr shook his head.

"I'm not. But I can't leave Agnes. Even if what you say happens, and they kill the last people in the camp, I want to be with Agnes when that happens. I can't abandon her."

"You've really made up your mind." Moshe smiled.

"I have."

"I just want you to know one thing. The underground is planning to escape during the march. The partisans will follow wherever the Germans take us, assist us, and bring us to shelter. Are you sure you don't want to try to escape with us? You could join the fight."

Joel considered Moshe's words. It was ironic to hear the camp resistance would finally spring into action once they were outside the fence. For years, Joel had worked toward an uprising. He'd assisted in escapes; he'd smuggled paperwork out and guns into the camp. Nothing had ever come from it, but now, on the eve of the camp exodus, the brave leaders of the underground were going to do something. Joel shook his head and met Moshe's eyes. "No, thank you. My decision is final. I'll stay here."

There was acceptance on Moshe's face. "All right then, Joel. Whatever happens next, I hope it works out for you." He held out his hand, and Joel shook it before pulling his friend in for a hug.

"Make the escape count, Moshe. We worked too hard for this to have it go to waste."

They broke their embrace, and Moshe slapped him on the shoulder. "Damn right we did, Joel. They'll be disappointed you're not coming with us, but I'll let them know you had someone more important to take care of." Moshe gave him a final nod, and then walked to his bunk, checking the bag carrying all his worldly belongings.

Joel turned to Piotr, who eyed him with an odd expression. "She must be something special."

"She is, Piotr. I need her by my side, and she needs me. I know we're going to make it out alive. And so will you." He lowered his voice as he moved closer to his best friend. "Be careful. The leadership has been a lot of talk. Look after yourself; if it doesn't feel right, don't go for it."

"I know. I'm a little skeptical about it myself," Piotr said evenly.

"I'm not going to follow them blindly. I saw what happened to the Sonderkommando."

"Good." Joel felt a wave of relief wash over him. Piotr would be fine. He wouldn't throw his life away. "When all this is over and we return to Ciechanów, you'll see what a wonderful woman Agnes is."

A sad smile appeared on Piotr's face. "Ciechanów? I'm not sure I'm going back. And you might feel different about that as well."

Joel was taken aback by his friend's words. He always assumed he would return to find the home he'd grown up in waiting for him. Piotr was right. Home might not be home anymore.

"You better make your way to the hospital before anyone finds out you're missing." Piotr held out his hand, and Joel clasped it firmly. Then Piotr pulled him in, and they embraced. He closed his eyes and thought of all the memories they had growing up together, and he clenched his teeth. When they broke their embrace, Joel winced at the idea of letting his friend go.

"Take care, my friend. Until we meet again." Joel turned and left Block 26 for the last time. He didn't look back.


It was past midnight when Joel and Agnes stood near the window on the second floor of Block 10. The last prisoners made their way toward the exit on the other side of the camp. Snow had started falling, and the prisoners trudged through the few inches that covered the cold ground.

From their vantage point, they had seen the disorganized roll call. Prisoners lined up haphazardly, guards shouting commands at them. Nobody checked any papers, and it soon became apparent the guards just wanted to get the group moving. When they did, Joel was relieved. Nobody would come looking for him. And even if they did, he had been registered as one of the nurses, for what that was worth.

"Where do you think they're going?" Agnes asked as the last people turned the corner, the falling snow erasing their tracks.

"I've been thinking about that all evening, but I have no idea. If I were in charge, I would take them back to Germany."

"Why didn't they just send trains here?"

"They're probably in too much of a rush to get out. The front line is moving quickly. I could hear gunfire when I walked here this evening. It can't be much longer."

They stepped away from the window and slowly walked through the silent hallway. The doors to the wards were open, and most of the patients were asleep, a few reading books.

"What did they say when they heard about the evacuation?" Joel had wanted to ask her since that morning, but they had been too busy to talk.

"Most were worried about how they would make the trek. I told them they would stay here. Some people said they wanted to try anyway, but I managed to talk most of them out of it."

"But not all?" Joel was surprised.

Agnes looked troubled. "Some insisted. In the end, Alina and I decided we couldn't stop them if they could walk out of the hospital themselves."

"You can't blame them; I hope they make it." They reached the stairs and continued down. "How's Alina?"

"Happy to be back here, most of all." Agnes smiled. "She returned just in time not to join the march. I think she would've been devastated if she couldn't be with the patients until the end."

"She's so dedicated, just like you." Finally, they reached the bottom of the stairs. "So, what do we do now?"

Agnes smiled. "It's been a long day. How about we turn in? I'll show you your new quarters." She motioned to the other side of the hallway.

Joel took her hand. "I'm glad we're here together. Whatever happens next, we'll have each other."

Agnes' eyes glittered. "Me too, Joel. Wherever life takes us next, I'm happy it will be with you by my side."


Ten days later, Joel was handing out water in one of the wards. The patients took it gratefully, and he smiled. In his short time at the hospital, he'd experienced only a fraction of what Agnes had done, but every time he took one of the patients for a walk, helped them eat, or simply chatted with them, he felt a purpose he'd not experienced before.

"It's a bit quiet today, isn't it, Joel?" a woman of around forty said as she took the cup from him, her eyes on the window.

"It does seem different, Ella." There had been heavy gunfire near the camp in the past few days. Yesterday, Joel thought an artillery shell had hit one of the buildings, for the ground and windows shook as a nearby explosion rocked the camp. He later heard it had been the SS blowing up crematoria 2 and 3. *Trying to erase the evidence of their murderous deeds.*

Today's silence was odd, and Joel wondered what caused it. Had the Red Army halted their assault? He left the ward and walked to the window in the hallway overlooking the camp. There were no people on the small streets between the buildings. It was freezing outside, with everyone staying within the relative safety and comfort of the buildings. Despite that, Joel needed some fresh air.

He made his way down and ran into Agnes in the hallway. "Want to take a walk outside? I'm feeling a bit boxed in."

"Sure, I'll grab us some coats." She disappeared into the nurses' room and returned with two woolen coats.

They stepped outside, and Joel enjoyed the cold biting into his face. His breath made small clouds in front of him as they wandered along the deserted street. They headed in the direction of the administration building.

"Say, where are the guards?" Joel said as he looked around. "I haven't seen one all morning."

Agnes looked up in surprise. "Now that you mention it. Me neither. Although that's not saying too much. I've hardly seen them in the hospital these past days."

"Hmm." Joel frowned as they passed the gallows and approached the camp's main gate. The SS quarters were next to the gate, and he imagined most of the guards would be there. When they approached the closed gate, he stopped in his tracks. "Agnes."

"Yes?" She turned to him, then followed his gaze.

"There are no guards at the gate."

"That can't be." Her voice was trembling. "They're probably taking a break."

"At the main gate? Hardly." Joel stomped toward the closed gate and peered into the guardhouse. It was empty. The lights in the adjoining SS barracks were off, and it was eerily silent. He looked at Agnes in disbelief. "They've abandoned us."

Agnes opened her mouth when they heard voices in the distance. She moved closer to him, and Joel felt her hand slip into his. They stood facing the gate as the voices grew louder. Agnes squeezed his hand. Joel felt his heart beating in his ears as he held his breath. He tried to make out the words of the voices but couldn't.

The soldiers seemed to appear out of nowhere. There were at least 50 of them, and they smoked cigarettes and chatted carelessly, smiles on their faces. Their heavy gray overcoats were unfamiliar to him. Joel's throat went dry.

The soldiers approached quickly. Their demeanor changed when the men in the front spotted Joel and Agnes. Their faces turned serious as they hurried to the gate. The other soldiers followed suit, the almost boisterous atmosphere quickly dissolving. The group stood on the other side of the gate, curiously studying Joel and Agnes. For a few seconds, nothing happened. Then, one of the men stepped forward. Like the other soldiers, he wore a gray cap with flaps covering his ears. A red line ran prominently across the forehead of the cap. His short message was in heavily accented German, but they were the words Joel had prayed for but for years thought he wouldn't live to hear.

"It's over."

# Author's Notes

I never intended to write this book. When I finished Beyond the Tracks, I thought the story was done. But then I started receiving messages from readers. They all wanted to know one thing: What happened to Agnes?

It was obvious, wasn't it? She and Yvette died upon arrival at Auschwitz, like most people transported from Westerbork.

Or didn't she? It's interesting how a side character can make such an impression on readers. At the time, I was writing Warsaw Fury, my second novel. It wasn't until I finished my third book, Orphans of War, that I picked up Agnes' story. And I'm glad I did. Agnes turned out to be one of my favorite characters.

Any story about the Holocaust is intimidating for a writer. But with Agnes, I knew her story needed to be set in Auschwitz-Birkenau. And as a nurse, there was only one place she could end up. Reading the first-hand accounts of people who'd lived through the horrors of Block 10, I knew this was where Agnes needed to be. Almost everything she experienced in this block happened. The medical experiments were run by Dr. Clauberg and Dr. Schumann, under the leadership of chief physician Dr. Wirths.

Dr. Samuel, Dr. Brewda, and Dr. Fejkiel played their parts in the hospital. Because the latter two survived, testified, and documented their experiences, I'm confident I've portrayed them to the best of my ability. For Dr. Samuel, I've relied on testimonies from the women he performed the experiments on. A number of them went on to have children after the war. They credit Dr. Samuel for this "miracle."

The Czech nurse Sylvia also existed and is mentioned in the same testimonies. I've given her a rather prominent role to show the complicated moral dilemmas faced by the prisoners forced to assist in the Nazis' atrocious deeds.

The prisoners that suffered from the stigma of "willing collaborators" more than any other were, without a doubt, the men of the Sonderkommando. Reading the autobiographies of a number of the men forced to work in the crematoria, I decided Samson needed to be one of the main characters in this book. Through his interactions with other prisoners, both inside and outside the crematoria, and depictions of how the Sonderkommando was talked about, I believe I've created a realistic portrayal of life in the crematoria.

It was also essential to show the different approaches of those in charge. Several of Samson's Kapos were real people. The sadistic and brutal Vacek and Mietek existed, and I included them to show other prisoners could be just as deadly as the SS guards—if not more so. Their survival often depended on their willingness to inflict pain and misery on fellow prisoners.

But Kapos like Kaminski showed there was another way. In numerous eyewitness accounts, his ability to display competent leadership in the eyes of the SS is often used to explain his exceptional longevity in the camp. I firmly believe that the Sonderkommando revolt would not have been possible without his involvement in the preparations. My representation of Kaminski is based on these eyewitness accounts, and I admit that it's likely a romanticized version of the man. But he deserves it.

You won't be surprised to learn Roza Robota of Ciechanów was a real person. When I learned of her part in the Revolt, I was surprised to find so little written about her. It wasn't easy to piece her history together, relying on many different sources describing her involvement in broad terms, but unfortunately, with little detail. I've taken the liberty to fill in the details of her day-to-day life in the camp while showing her heroic efforts in preparing for the Sonderkommando Revolt. This includes her relationship with Samson; there was no mention of a romantic relationship in any of the sources I've used. Nevertheless, I'd like to hold on to the hope that there was at least something good in her short life.

Samson Tarski is a fictional character based on the memoirs of a number of Auschwitz survivors. Among other sources, I primarily used the accounts of Filip Müller (Eyewitness Auschwitz) and Dr. Miklós Nyiszli (Auschwitz: A Doctor's Eyewitness Account) to gain an insight into life in the Sonderkommando. Reading these autobiographies has been some of the most difficult reading of my life.

I based Joel Kozak on memoirs by Noah Zabludowicz and Moshe Kolko. Noah Zabludowicz was an electrician from Ciechanów who became an essential messenger for the resistance in Auschwitz. Moshe Kolko was one of Noah's friends from home. Both men survived the war, with Zabludowicz testifying in the trial against Final Solution architect Adolf Eichmann in his 1961 trial in Jerusalem, Israel.

Finally, Agnes Markx is entirely fictional. Many of her encounters, however, aren't. She was crucial in telling the story of Block 10, and the defiance of the prisoner doctors and nurses as they attempted to preserve some humanity and dignity in the block of terrors.

If you enjoyed reading the book, I'd appreciate a review. Even if it's just a few words, they help tremendously in the exposure of my work. And if you'd like to be among the first to hear about new books, make sure you sign up for my newsletter on my website, michaelreit.com. I often share preview chapters of upcoming work there.

All my very best,
Michael

# About the Author

Michael Reit writes page-turning historical fiction. His books focus on lesser-known events and people in World War II Europe.

Born in the Netherlands, he now lives in beautiful Vienna, Austria, with his partner Esther and daughter Bibi.

Connect with Michael via his website:
www.michaelreit.com

Or via Facebook:

facebook.com/MichaelReitAuthor

# ALSO BY MICHAEL REIT

Made in United States
North Haven, CT
12 September 2023

41471597R00253